KT-441-204

SOLOMON CREED

Book One

SIMON TOYNE

HARPER

Harper
An imprint of HarperCollins*Publishers*
1 London Bridge Street
London SE1 9GF

www.harpercollins.co.uk

This paperback edition 2016
1

Copyright © Simon Toyne 2015

Simon Toyne asserts the moral right to
be identified as the author of this work

A catalogue record for this book
is available from the British Library

ISBN: 978 0 00 755138 5

This novel is entirely a work of fiction.
The names, characters and incidents portrayed in it are
the work of the author's imagination. Any resemblance to
actual persons, living or dead, events or localities is
entirely coincidental.

Printed and bound in Great Britain by
Clays Ltd, St Ives plc

All rights reserved. No part of this publication may be
reproduced, stored in a retrieval system, or transmitted,
in any form or by any means, electronic, mechanical,
photocopying, recording or otherwise, without the prior
permission of the publishers.

MIX
Paper from
responsible sources
FSC™ C007454

FSC™ is a non-profit international organization established to promote
the responsible management of the world's forests. Products carrying the
FSC label are independently certified to assure consumers that they come
from forests that are managed to meet the social, economic and
ecological needs of present and future generations,
and other controlled sources.

Find out more about HarperCollins and the environment at
www.harpercollins.co.uk/green

Epworth Mechanics' Institute Library
Tuesday 10a.m – 12 Noon
Thursday 1.30p.m – 4p.m
Friday 7.30p.m – 9.30p.m

12 . 4 . 18

Si
tr
S.
o
2
b
p
b

S
o

s

**Please return books as soon as you have finished with
them so that others may read them**

Also by Simon Toyne

Sanctus
The Key
The Tower

For Betsy
(No Bean No!!)

I

'... *all I know
is that I know nothing.*'

Socrates

1

In the beginning is the road – and me walking along it.

I have no memory of who I am, or where I have come from, or how I came to be here. There is only the road
and the desert stretching away to a burnt sky in every direction
and there is me.

Anxiety bubbles within me and my legs scissor, pushing me forward through hot air as if they know something I don't. I feel like telling them to slow down, but even in my confused state I know you don't talk to your legs, not unless you're crazy, and I don't think I'm crazy – I don't think so.

I stare down the shimmering ribbon of tarmac, rising and falling over the undulating land, its straight edges made wavy by intense desert heat. It makes the road seem insubstantial and the way ahead uncertain and my anxiety burns bright because of it. I feel there's something important to do here, and that I am here to do it, but I cannot remember what.

I try to breathe slowly, dredging a recollection from some deep place that this is meant to be calming, and catch different scents in the dry desert air – the coal-tar sap of a broken creosote bush branch, the sweet sugar rot of fallen saguaro fruit, the arid perfume of agave pollen – each thing so clear to me, so absolutely itself and correct and known. And from the solid seed of each named thing more information grows – Latin names, medicinal properties, common names, whether each is edible or poisonous. The same happens when I glance to my left or right, each glimpsed thing sparking new names and fresh torrents of facts until my head hums with it all. I know the world entirely it seems and yet I know nothing of myself. I don't know where I am. I don't know why I'm here. I don't even know my own name.

The wind gusts at my back, pushing me forward and bringing a new smell that makes my anxiety flare into fear. It is smoke, oily and acrid, and a half-formed memory slides in with it that there is something awful lying on the road behind me, something I need to get away from.

I break into a run, staring forward, not daring to glance behind. The blacktop feels hard and hot against the soles of my feet. I look down to discover that I'm not wearing shoes. My feet flash as they pound the road, my skin pure white in the bright sunshine. I hold my hand up and it's the same, so white I have to narrow my eyes against the glare of it. I can feel my skin starting to redden in the fierce sun and know that I need to get out of this desert, away from this sun and the thing on the road behind me. I fix on a rise in the road, feeling if I can reach it then I will be safe, that the way ahead will be clearer.

The wind blows hard, bringing the smell of smoke again and smothering all other scents like a poisonous blanket. Sweat starts to soak my shirt and the dark grey material of my jacket. I should take it off, cool myself down a little, but the thicker material is giving me protection from the burning sun so I turn the collar up instead and keep on running. One step then another – forward and away, forward and away

– asking myself questions between each step – *Who am I? Where am I? Why am I here?* – repeating each one until something starts to take shape in the blankness of my empty mind. An answer. A name.

'James Coronado.' I say it aloud in a gasp of breath before it is lost again and pain sears into my left shoulder.

My voice comes as a surprise to me, soft and strange and unfamiliar, but the name does not. I recognize it and say it again – *James Coronado, James Coronado* – over and over, hoping the name might be mine and might drag more about who I am from my silent memory. But the more I say it, the more distant it becomes until I'm certain the name is not mine. It feels apart from me though still connected in some way, as if I have made a promise to this man, one that I am bound to keep.

I reach the crest of the road and a new section of desert comes into view. In the distance I see a road sign, and beyond that, a town, spreading like a dark stain across the lower slopes of a range of red mountains.

I raise my hand to shield my eyes so I might read the name on the sign, but it is too far away and heat blurs the words. There is movement on the road, way off at the edge of town.

Vehicles.

Heading this way. Red and blue lights flashing on their roofs.

The wail of sirens mingles with the roar of the smoke-filled wind and I feel trapped between the two. I look to my right and consider leaving the road and heading out into the desert. A new smell reaches me, drifting from somewhere out in the wilderness, something that seems more familiar to me than all the other things. It is the smell of something dead and rotting, lying somewhere out of sight, sunbaked and fetid and caramel-sweet, like a premonition of what will befall me if I stray from the road.

Sirens in front of me, death either side, and behind me, what?

I have to know.

I turn to gaze upon what I have been running from and the whole world is on fire.

An aircraft lies broken and blazing in the centre of the road, its wings sticking up from the ground like the folded wings of some huge burning beast. A wide circle of flame surrounds it, spreading rapidly as flames leap from plant to plant and lick up the sides of giant saguaro, their burning arms raised in surrender, their flesh splitting and hissing as the water inside boils and explodes in puffs of steam.

It is magnificent. Majestic. Terrifying.

The sirens grow louder and the flames roar. One of the wings starts to fall, trailing flame as it topples and filling the air with the tortured sound of twisting metal. It lands with a *whump*, and a wave of fire rolls up into the air, curling like a tentacle that seems to reach down the road for me, reaching out, wanting me back.

I stagger backwards, turn on my heels.

And I run.

2

Mayor Ernest Cassidy looked up from the dry grave and out across the crowded heads of the mourners. He had felt the rumble as much as heard it, like thunder rolling in from the desert. Others must have felt it too. A few of the heads bowed in prayer turned to glance back at the desert stretching away below them.

The cemetery was high up, scooped into the side of the Chinchuca Mountains that encircled the town like a horseshoe. A hot wind blew up from the valley, ruffling the black clothes of the mourners and blowing grit against the windscoured boards marking the older graves that recorded the town's violent birth with quiet and brutal economy:

Teamster. Killed by Apaches. 1881
China Mae Ling. Suicide. 1880
Susan Goater. Murdered. 1884
Boy. Age 11 months. Died of Neglect. 1882

A new name was being added to this roll call of death today and almost the whole town was present to see it, their businesses closed for the morning so they could attend the first funeral to take place in this historic cemetery for over sixty years. It was the least they could do in the circumstances – the very least. The future of their town was being secured this day, as surely as it had been at the ragged end of the nineteenth century when the murdered, the hanged, the scalped and the damned had first been planted here.

The crowd settled as the memory of the thunder faded and Mayor Cassidy, wearing his preacher hat today, dropped a handful of dust down into the dry grave. It pattered down on the lid of the simple, old-fashioned pine box at the bottom – a nice touch, considering – then continued with the solemn service.

'For dust thou art,' he said in a low and respectful voice he kept specially for situations like this, 'and unto dust shalt thou return. Amen.'

There was a murmur of 'Amens' then a wind-shushed minute of silence. He stole a glance at the widow, standing very close to the edge of her husband's grave like a suicide at the edge of a cliff. Her hair and eyes shone in the sunlight, a deeper black than any of the clothes flapping in the wind around her. She appeared so beautiful in her grief – beautiful and young. She had loved her husband deeply, he knew that, and there was a particular tragedy in the knowledge of it. But her youth meant she had time enough ahead of her to move on from this, and that leavened it some. She would leave the town and start again somewhere else. And there were no children; there was a mercy in that too, no physical ties to bind her, no face that carried traces of his and would remind her of her lost love whenever she caught it in a certain light. Sometimes the absence of children was a blessing. Sometimes.

Movement rippled through the crowd and he glanced up to see a police chief's hat being jammed back on to a close-cropped salt-and-pepper head moving quickly away towards the exit. Mayor Cassidy looked beyond him to the desert, and saw why.

A column of black smoke was rising up on the main road out of town. It wasn't thunder he had heard or rain that was coming, it was more trouble.

3

Chief Morgan pulled away from the cemetery as fast as he could without sending a cloud of grit over the other mourners hurrying to their cars behind him.

He had heard the rumble too and had known straight away it wasn't thunder. The sound had transported him back to a time when he had worn a different uniform and watched flashes of artillery fire in the night as shells pounded a foreign city in a different desert. It was the sound of something big hitting the ground and his mouth felt dry because of it.

He picked up speed as he headed downhill and pushed the comms button on the steering wheel to activate the radio. 'This is Morgan. I'm heading north on Eldridge en route to a possible fire about three miles out of town, anyone else call it in?'

There was a bump and a squeal of rubber as his truck bottomed out and joined the main road, then the voice of Rollins the duty dispatcher crackled back. 'Copy that, Chief, we got a call from Ellie over at the Tucker ranch, said she heard an explosion to the southwest. We got five units responding: two fire trucks, a highway patrol unit, an ambulance from County and another heading from the King. Six units, including you.'

Morgan glanced in his rear-view mirror, saw flashing lights behind him on the road. He stared ahead to where the column of smoke was growing much faster than his speed could account for. 'We're going to need more,' he said.

'What is it, Chief?'

Morgan studied the wall of smoke. 'Well, I ain't there yet but the smoke is rising fast and high, so there's gotta be some heat in the fire, burning fuel probably. There was the explosion too.'

'Yeah, I heard it.'

'You heard it in the office?'

'Yessir. Felt it too.'

Rollins was a mile or so further away than he had been. Some explosion. 'Can you see it yet?' Morgan listened to dead air and pictured Rollins leaning back in his chair to catch a view out of the narrow window of the dispatch room.

'Yeah, I got it.'

'Well, it's coming your way so you better get busy. Call the airfield, get the tanker in the air. We need to step on this thing before it gets out of hand.'

'I'm on it, Chief.'

Morgan clicked off the comms and leaned forward. The top of the smokestack was several hundred feet high and still rising. He was closer now, close enough that he could see something burning at the centre of the fire each time he crested a rise in the road. He was so fixated on it, wanting to see it and confirm what he already knew it must be, that he didn't notice the figure running down the middle of the road until he was almost upon him.

His reaction was all instinct and panic. He threw the wheel hard right and braced himself for a thump that didn't come, then jerked the wheel left again. The rear wheels caught the soft dirt of the verge and he started to slide. He stamped on the brakes to stop the wheels then back on the gas to give him some traction. He was in a full sideways skid now, wheels spinning and throwing grit into the air. He hit the brakes again and clung to the wheel, steering into the slide until he slammed into a bush or something that stopped the truck dead and made him bang his head against the window.

He sat perfectly still for a moment, hands on the wheel, heart pounding in his chest, so loud he could hear it above the roar of the burning desert and the patter of grit on the windshield. The first fire truck roared past, throwing more grit over him and a crackle of static flooded the car. 'Chief? You there, Chief?'

He took a breath, pressed the comms button. 'Yeah, Rollins, I'm here.'

'How's it lookin'?'

The second fire truck thundered by and he followed its path towards the wall of flame, the burning plane twisted at its centre. 'Like the end of the world,' he murmured.

He glanced back to the road and was half-surprised to see the running man still there, rising from the ground where he had thrown himself. He looked strange, extraordinary, his hair as white as his skin.

Morgan had heard all the stories about how this road was built on the old wagon trail and was supposed to be haunted. People had seen plenty of things out here, especially at night when the cold hit the ground like a hammer, releasing wisps of vapour that drifted through the headlights and imaginations of people who had heard the same stories he had. He'd had reports of everything from ghost horses to wagons floating a foot above the ground. But he had never seen anything himself until now.

'Chief? You still there, Chief?'

Morgan snapped to attention, his eyes fixed on the stranger. 'Yeah, I'm here. What's the word on those tankers?'

'You got the unit from the airfield on its way and two more possibles inbound from Tucson. They're dragging their asses a little, but I'm working on it. If they get the go-ahead they should be with you in twenty.'

Morgan nodded but said nothing. In twenty minutes the fire would have doubled in size, tripled even. More sirens wailed closer, everything the town had to send but not nearly enough.

'Call everyone you can,' he said. 'We're going to need road-blocks on all routes in and out of town. I don't want anybody riding out into this mess, and we're going to need to set fire-breaks too. Anyone with a truck and a shovel they can swing needs to report for duty at the city-limit billboard if they want this town to still be here by sundown.'

He disconnected and fumbled in his pocket for his phone. He found a contact and opened a new message. His fingers shook as he typed: 'Clear out now. Funeral finished early. Find anything?'

He sent the message and looked back at the stranger. He was gazing up at the fire with an odd expression on his face. Morgan held up his phone, snapped a photo and studied it. The man seemed to glow in the midst of all the grit. It reminded him of the pictures he'd seen in the books and on the websites devoted to the town's ghosts. Only those all seemed fake to him. There was nothing fake about this. He was there, large as life, staring back at the crashed plane with pale grey eyes the colour of stone. Staring into the fire.

The phone beeped in his hand. A reply: 'Nothing. Leaving now.'

Goddammit. Nothing was going right today. Not a damned thing.

He grabbed his hat and opened the door to the roar of fire and the heat of the desert just as the pale man turned and started to run.

———

4

I stare into the heart of the fire and feel as if it's staring back at me. But that can't be right. I know that. The air swirls and wails and roars around me like the world is in pain.

The first fire truck stops at the edge of the blaze and people run out, pulling hose from its belly like they are drawing innards from some beast in sacrifice to a burning god. They seem so tiny and the fire so big. The wind stirs the flames and the fire roars forward, up the road, towards the men, towards me. Fear flares inside me and I turn to run and almost collide with a woman wearing a dark blue uniform, walking up the road behind me.

'Are you OK, sir?' she says, her eyes soft with concern. I want to hold her and have her hold me but my fear of the fire is too great and so is my desire to get away from it. I duck past her and keep on running, straight into a man wearing the same uniform. He grabs my arm and I try to pull free but I cannot. He is too strong and this surprises me, as if I am not used to being weak.

'I need to get away,' I say in my soft, unfamiliar voice, and glance back over my shoulder at the flames being blown closer by the wind.

'You're safe now, sir,' he says with a professional calm that only makes me more anxious. How can he know I am safe, how can he possibly know?

I look back and past him towards the town and the sign, but there is a parked ambulance blocking my view and this makes me anxious too.

'I need to get away from it,' I say, pulling my arm away, trying to make him understand. 'I think the fire is here because of me.'

He nods as if he understands, but I see his other hand reaching out to grab me and I seize it and pull hard, sweeping his feet from beneath him with my leg at the same time and twisting away so he falls to the ground. The movement is as natural as breathing and as smooth as a well-practised dance step. My muscles still have memory it seems. I look down into his shocked face. 'Sorry, Lawrence,' I say, using the name on his badge, then I turn to run – back to the town and away from the fire. I manage one step before his hand grabs my leg, his strong fingers closing round my ankle like a manacle.

I stumble, regain my balance, turn back and raise my foot. I don't want to kick him but I will, I will kick him right in his face if that's what it takes to make him let go. The thought of the solid heel of my foot crashing into his nose, splitting his skin and spilling blood, brings a sensation like warm air rushing through me. It's a nice feeling, and it disturbs me as much as my earlier familiarity with the smell of death. I try to focus on something else, try to smother my instinct and stop my foot from lashing out, and in this pause something big and solid hits me hard, ripping my leg from the man's grip.

I hit the ground and a flash of white explodes inside my skull as my head bangs against the road. Rage erupts in me. I fight to wriggle free from whoever tackled me. Hot breath blows on my cheek and I smell sour coffee and the beginnings of tooth decay. I twist my head round and see the face of the policeman who nearly ran me down. 'Take it easy,' he says, pinning me down with his weight, 'they're only trying to help you here.'

But they're not. If they wanted to help, they'd let me go.

In a detached part of my mind I know that I could use my teeth to tear at his cheek or his nose, attack him with such ferocity he would want to be free of me more than I do from him. I am simultaneously fascinated, appalled and excited by this notion, this realization that I have the power to free myself but that something is holding me back, something inside me.

More hands grab me and press me hard to the ground. I feel a sting in my arm like a large insect has bitten me. The female medic is crouching beside me now, her attention fixed on the syringe sticking into my arm.

'Unfair fight,' I try to say, but am already slurring by the time I get to the last word.

The world starts turning to liquid and I feel myself going limp. A hand cradles my head and gently lowers it to the ground. I try to fight it, willing my eyes to stay open. I can see the distant town, framed by the road and sky. I want to tell them all to hurry, that the fire is coming and they need to get away, but my mouth no longer works. My vision starts to tunnel, black around the edges, a diminishing circle of light in the centre, as if I am falling backwards down a deep well. I can see the sign now past the edge of the ambulance, the words on it visible too. I read them in the clarifying air, the last thing I see before my eyes close and the world goes dark:

WELCOME TO THE CITY OF

REDEMPTION

5

Mulcahy leaned against the Jeep and stared out at the jagged lines of wings beyond the chain-link fence. From where he stood he could see a Vietnam-era B-52 with upwards of thirty mission decals on its fuselage, a World War II bomber of some sort, a heavy transporter plane that resembled a whale, and a squadron of sharp-nosed, lethal-looking jet fighters with various paint jobs from various countries, including a MiG with a Soviet star on the side and two smaller ones beneath the cockpit windows denoting combat kills.

Beyond the parade of military planes a runway arrowed away into the heart of the *caldera*, snakes of heat twisting in the air above it. There were some buzzards to the north, circling above something dead or dying in the desert; other than that there was nothing, not even a cloud, though he had heard thunder a while back. A spot of rain would be nice. God knows they needed it.

He checked his watch.

Late.

Sweat was starting to prick and tickle in his hair and on his back beneath his shirt as the trapped heat of the day got hold of him. The silver Grand Cherokee he was leaning against had black tinted windows, cool leather seats and a kick-ass air-conditioner circulating chilled air at a steady sixty-five degrees. He could hear the unit whirring under the idling engine. Even so, he preferred to stand outside in the desert heat than remain in the car with the two morons he was having to baby-sit, listening to their inane conversation.

– *Hey, man, how many Nazis you think that bird wasted?*
– *How many gook babies you think that one burned up?*

They'd somehow made the assumption that Mulcahy was ex-military, which, in their fidgety, drug-fried minds, also made him an expert on every war ever fought and the machines used to fight them. He'd told them, several times, that he had not served in any branch of the armed forces and therefore knew as much about war planes as they did, but they kept on with their endless questions and fantasy body counts.

He checked his watch again.

Once the package was delivered to the meeting point he could drive away, take a long, cold shower and wash away the day. A window buzzed open next to him, and super-cooled air leaked out from inside.

'Where's the plane at, man?' It was Javier, the shorter, more irritating of the two men, and a distant relative of Papa Tío, the big boss on the Mexican side.

'It's not here,' Mulcahy replied.

'No shit, tell me something I don't know.'

'Hard to know where to start.'

'What?'

Mulcahy took a step away from the Jeep and stretched until he felt the vertebrae pop in his spine. 'Don't worry,' he said. 'If anything was wrong I'd get a message.'

Javier thought for a moment then nodded. He had inherited some of the boss man's swagger but none of the brains so far as Mulcahy could tell. He had also caught the family looks, which was unfortunate, and the combination of his squat stature, oily, pock-marked skin and fleshy, petulant lips made him appear more like a toad in jeans and a T-shirt than a man.

'Shut the window, man, it's like a motherfuckin' oven out there.' That was Carlos, idiot number two, not blood, as far as he knew, but clearly in good enough standing with the cartel to be allowed to come along for the ride.

'I'm talking,' Javier snarled. 'I be closing the window when I'm good and ready.'

Mulcahy turned back and stared up at the empty sky.

'What kind of plane we looking for? Is it one of these big-assed nuke bombers? Man, that would be some cool ride.'

Mulcahy considered not replying, but this was the one piece of information about aircraft he did know because it had been included in the brief. Besides, the longer he talked to Javier, the longer the window would remain open, leaking cold air out and hot air in.

'It's a Beechcraft,' he said.

'What's that?'

'An old airplane, I guess.'

'What, like a private jet?'

'Propellers, I think.'

Javier pursed his boxing-glove lips and nodded. 'Still, sounds pretty cool. When I had to run, I sneaked across the river on some lame-assed boat in the middle of the night.'

'You got here though, didn't you?'

'I guess.'

'Well, that's the main thing.' Mulcahy leaned forward. A dark smudge had appeared in the sky above one of the larger spill piles on the far side of the airfield. 'Doesn't matter how you got here, just so long as you did.'

The smudge darkened and became a column of black smoke rising fast and thick in the sky. He heard the faint sound of distant sirens. Then Mulcahy's phone started to buzz in his pocket.

6

Movement rocked him awake.

His eyes flickered open and he stared up at a low white ceiling, a drip bag hanging over him, a clear tube coiled round it like a translucent snake, moving gently in time with the ambulance.

'Hey, welcome back.' The female medic appeared over him and shone a bright light into his left eye. He felt a stab of pain and tried lifting his hand to shield his eyes but his arm wouldn't move. He looked down and his head swam with a chemical wooziness. Thick blue nylon straps were wrapped round his arms and body, securing him tightly to the gurney.

'For your protection while we're on the move,' she said, like it was no big deal. He knew the real reason. They'd had to sedate him to get him in the ambulance and the bindings were to make sure they wouldn't need to do it again.

He hated being bound like this. It pricked at some deep emotional memory, as if he'd known confinement and never wanted to know it again. He focused on the feeling, trying to remember where it came from, but his mind remained stubbornly blank.

The movement of the ambulance was making him feel sick

and so was the cocktail of smells trapped inside it – iodine, sodium bicarbonate, naloxone hydrochloride, all mixed in with sweat and smoke and sickly synthetic coconut air-freshener drifting in from the driver's cab. He wanted to feel the ground beneath his feet again and the wind on his face. He wanted to be free to focus and think and remember what it was he had come here to do. The pain in his arm flared again at the thought and the bar rattled when he tried to reach for it.

'Could you loosen the straps?' He forced his voice to stay low and calm. 'Just enough so I can move my arm.'

The medic chewed her lip and fiddled with a thin necklace round her neck with 'Gloria' written on it in gold letters. 'OK,' she said. 'But you try anything and I'll knock you straight out again, understand?' She held up the penlight. 'And you've got to let me do my job.'

He nodded. She paused a little longer to let him know who was in charge, then reached down and tugged at a strap by the side of the gurney. The nylon band holding his hands came loose and he lifted his arm to rub at his shoulder.

'Sorry about that,' Gloria said, leaning in and flashing the light in his eye again. 'Quickest way to calm you down before you injured someone.' The light hurt but this time he put up with it.

'What's your name, sir?' She switched the light to his other eye.

She was so close he could feel her breath on his skin and it made him want to reach out and touch her to see what she felt like and make gentle rather than violent contact with someone. 'I don't remember,' he said. 'I don't remember anything.'

'How about Solomon?' a new voice answered for him, a

man's voice, high-pitched but with a touch of gravel in it. 'Solomon Creed, that ring any bells?'

Gloria leaned down to write some notes on a clipboard and he saw the cop who had nearly run him down perched on the gurney behind her.

'Solomon,' he repeated, and it felt comfortable, like boots he had walked long miles wearing. 'Solomon Creed.' He stared at the cop, hoping he might know more than his name. 'Do you know me?'

The cop shook his head and held up a small book. 'Found this in your pocket, personally inscribed to a Solomon Creed, so I assume that's you. Name's in your jacket too.' He nodded at the folded grey jacket lying on the gurney next to him. 'Stitched right on the label in gold thread and written in French.' He said *French* like he was spitting out something bitter.

Solomon studied the book. There was a stern, sepia-tinted photograph of a man on the cover and old-fashioned block type that spelled out the title:

RICHES AND REDEMPTION
THE MAKING OF A TOWN

A Memoir
by the Reverend Jack 'King' Cassidy
Founder and first citizen

He wanted to snatch the book away from the cop and see what else it contained. He didn't recognize it. No memory of it at all. No memory of anything, but it had to be important. Frustrating. Maddening. And why had the cop been through his pockets? The thought of it made his hands clench into fists.

'So, Mr Creed,' the cop continued, 'any idea why you were running away from that burning plane?'

'I can't remember,' Solomon said. A badge on the cop's shirt identified him as Chief Garth B. Morgan, hinting at Welsh ancestry and explaining why his skin was pink and freckled and clearly unsuited to this climate – like his own.

What the hell was he doing here?

'You think maybe you were a passenger?' Morgan asked.

'No.'

Morgan frowned. 'How can you be sure if you can't remember?'

Solomon looked out of the rear window at the burning plane and a fresh torrent of information cascaded through his head and crystallized into an explanation. 'Because of the way the wings are folded.'

Morgan followed Solomon's gaze. One wing still stood at the centre of the blaze, folded up towards the sky. 'What about it?'

'They show that the aircraft flew straight into the ground. Any passengers would have been thrown downwards, not outwards – and with lethal force. A crash like that would also have caused the fuel tanks to rupture and the fuel to ignite. Aviation fuel in an open-air burn reaches between five hundred and seven hundred degrees Fahrenheit, hot enough to burn flesh from bone in seconds. So, taking that into account, I could not possibly have been on that plane and still be talking to you now.'

Morgan twitched like his nose had been flicked. 'So where *did* you come from, if not the plane?'

'All I can remember is the road and the fire,' Solomon said, rubbing at his shoulder where the pain had now settled into a steady ache.

'Let me take a look at that,' Gloria said, stepping closer and blocking his view of Morgan.

Solomon started undoing his buttons, watching his fingers moving, the skin as white as his shirt.

'Back there you said something about the fire being here because of you,' Morgan said. 'Any idea what you meant by that?'

Solomon remembered the feeling of total fear and panic and his overpowering desire to get away from it. 'It's a feeling more than a memory,' he said. 'Like the fire is connected to me. I can't explain it.' He unbuttoned his cuffs, slipped his arms out of his shirt and became aware of a shift in the atmosphere.

Gloria leaned in, staring hard at Solomon's shoulder. Morgan was staring too. Solomon followed their gaze and saw the angry red origin of his recurring pain.

'What is that?' Gloria whispered.

Solomon had no answer for that either.

7

'Crashed? What do you mean crashed?'

The Cherokee was kicking up dust, Mulcahy at the wheel, eyeing the smoke rising fast to the west as they drove away from the airfield. 'Planes crash,' he said. 'You know that, right? They're kind of famous for it.'

Javier was staring out at the smoke, the obscene cushions of his lips hanging wet and open as he tried to get his head round what was happening. Carlos was in the back, hunkered down and saying nothing. His eyes were wide open and unfocused and Mulcahy knew why. Papa Tío had a reputation for making examples of people who messed things up. If the package had been lost in the crash, this package in particular, then the shit was going to hit the fan like it had been fired from a cannon. No one would be safe, not Carlos, not him, probably not even cousin Lips in the passenger seat.

'Don't panic,' he said, trying to convince himself as much as anyone. 'All we know is that a plane has crashed. We don't know if it's *our* plane or how bad it is.'

'Looks pretty fuckin' bad from where I'm sitting!' Javier said, staring at the rapidly widening column of smoke.

Mulcahy's fingers ached from gripping the wheel too tight and he forced himself to let go a little and ease off the gas.

'Let's wait and see what shakes out,' he said, forcing calm into his voice. 'For now, we follow the plan. The plane didn't show, so we relocate to the safe house to regroup, report, and await further instructions.'

Mulcahy's instinct was to run, put a bullet in his passengers, dump them in the desert and take off to give himself a good head start. He knew it didn't matter that the plane crash wasn't his fault – Papa Tío would most likely kill everyone involved anyway to send one of his famous messages. So if he killed Javier and Carlos right now then disappeared, Papa Tío would definitely think he was behind the crash, and he would never stop looking for him. Not ever. And despite his less than honourable résumé, Mulcahy didn't especially like killing people, and he didn't like being on the run either. He had a nice enough life, a nice enough house and a couple of women with kids and ex-husbands who weren't looking for anything more than he could offer, and who didn't seem to care what he did or ask how he had come by all the scars on his body. It wasn't much in the grand scheme of things, and it was only now, when faced with the prospect of walking away from it all, that he realized how badly he wanted to keep it.

'We stick to the plan,' he said. 'Anyone unhappy with that can get out of the car.'

'And who put you in charge, *pendejo*?'

'Tío did, OK? Tío called me up himself and asked me to collect this package as a personal favour to him. He also asked me to bring you two along, and like the dickhead that I am, I said "fine". If you want to take over so all this becomes your responsibility then be my guest, otherwise shut your fat mouth and let me think.'

Javier slumped back in his seat like a teenager who'd been grounded.

Mulcahy could see flames to the west now. A twisting wall of fire curling up from the ground and spreading fast. He could see emergency vehicles, too, which meant at least the cops would be well occupied.

'Plane!' Javier shouted, pointing back to where they had just come from.

Mulcahy felt a flutter of hope take flight in his chest. Maybe it was all going to be OK after all. Maybe they could turn the truck around, pick up the package as arranged and have a damn good laugh about it all over some cold beers later. Maybe he would get to keep his nicely squared away, uncomplicated life after all. He took his foot off the gas and twisted in his seat, taking his eyes off the empty road for a few seconds to see what Javier had seen. He saw the bright yellow plane banking in the sky above the airfield and spun round again, stamping down hard on the gas to claw back the speed he had lost.

'The fuck you doing?' Javier said, looking at him like he was crazy.

'That's not the plane we're waiting for,' Mulcahy said, feeling the full weight of the situation settling back on him. 'And it's taking off, not landing. It's a tanker of some sort, probably MAFFS.'

'MAFFS? The fuck is MAFFS?'

'They've been talking about them on the news ever since this dry spell set in. Stands for Modular Airborne Fire Fighting System. It's what they use to fight wildfires.'

The chop of propellers shredded the air as the plane flew directly overhead, the sound thudding in Mulcahy's chest.

Javier slumped back in his seat, a teenager again, shaking his head and sucking his teeth. 'MAFFS,' he said, like it was the worst curse word he had ever heard. 'Tole you, you was some kind of a military motherfucker.'

8

Solomon's skin glowed under the lights, the mark on his shoulder standing out vividly against it. It was red and raised and about the length and thickness of a human finger, with thinner lines across the top and bottom making it resemble a capital 'I'.

'Looks like a cattle brand,' Morgan said, leaning forward. 'Or maybe …' He left the thought hanging and pulled his phone from his pocket.

Gloria gently probed the skin around the raised welt with gloved fingers. 'Do you remember how you got this?'

Solomon recalled the intense burning pain he had experienced when the name James Coronado had first appeared in his mind, like hot metal being pressed to his flesh, only he had been wearing his shirt and jacket when it had happened and it had felt like it had come from inside him. 'No,' he said, not wishing to share this information with Morgan.

Gloria dabbed the reddened area with an alcohol wipe.

'You visited our town before, Mr Creed?' Morgan asked.

Solomon shook his head. 'I don't think so.'

'You sure about that?'

'No.' He glanced over at Morgan. 'Why?'

'Because of that cross you're wearing round your neck for one thing. Any idea how you came by it?'

Solomon looked down and noticed the cross for the first time, a misshapen thing hanging round his neck from a length of leather. He took it in his hand and felt the weight of it. 'I don't recognize it,' he said, turning it slowly, hoping his scrutiny might shake a memory loose. It was roughly made from old horseshoe nails welded together and twisted at the bottom so the points stuck out at the base. There was a balance and symmetry to it, as though whoever made it had been trying to disguise the precision of its manufacture by constructing it from scrap metal and leaving the finish rough. 'Why does this make you think I've been here before?'

'Because it's a replica of the cross standing on the altar of our church. You're also walking around with a copy of the town's history in your pocket that appears to have been given to you by someone local.'

Someone local. Someone who might know him and tell him who he was.

'May I see it?' Solomon asked.

Morgan studied him like a poker player trying to figure out what kind of hand he was holding, and Solomon felt anger simmering up inside him at his powerlessness. His body started to tense, as if it wanted to spring forward and grab the book from Morgan's hand. But he knew he was too far away and the nylon bindings were still strapped tight across his legs; he would never be fast enough, and even if he was Gloria would react and stick him again with whatever she had knocked him out with the first time – propofol most likely, considering how quickly he had recovered from it –

… Propofol … how did he know this stuff?

How did all this information come to him so easily and yet he could remember nothing of himself?

I have an 'I' burnt into my skin and yet I have no idea who 'I' am.

He breathed, deep and slow.

Answers. That was what he craved, more even than an outlet for his anger. Answers would soothe his rage and bring some order to the chaos swirling inside him. Answers he was sure must be contained in the book Morgan held in his hand.

Morgan glanced down at it, deciding whether to hand it over or not. He chose not to. He held it up instead and turned it round for Solomon to see. It was opened at a dedication page, something designed to encourage people to gift the book.

A GIFT OF AMERICAN HISTORY

– it said –

TO – *Solomon Creed*
FROM – *James Coronado*

Pain flared in his arm when he read the name and again he felt what he had experienced back on the road, a feeling of duty towards this man he couldn't remember but who apparently knew him well enough to have given him this book.

'You have any idea how you might know Jim?' Morgan asked.

Jim not *James* – Morgan knew him, he was here. 'I think I'm here because of him,' Solomon replied, and felt a new emotion start to take shape inside him.

The fire was here because of him
But he was here because of James Coronado.

Morgan tipped his head to one side. 'How so?'

31

Solomon stared out of the rear window at the distant fire. A yellow plane was flying low across the blue sky. It reached the eastern edge of the fire and a cloud of vivid red vapour spewed from its tail, streaking across the black smoke and sinking to the ground. It sputtered out before it had covered half of the fire line. Not enough. Not nearly enough. The fire was still coming, towards him, towards the town, towards everyone in it. A threat. A huge, burning threat. Destructive. Purifying. Just like he was. And there was his answer.

'I think I'm here to save him,' he said, turning back to Morgan, certain that this was right. 'I'm here to save James Coronado.'

A shadow flitted across Morgan's face and he stared at Solomon with an expression that could not mean anything good. 'James Coronado is dead,' he said flatly, and looked up and out through the side window towards the mountains rising behind the town. 'We buried him this morning.'

II

*'What lies behind and
what lies before are tiny matters
compared to what lies within.'*
Ralph Waldo Emerson

Extract from

RICHES AND REDEMPTION

THE MAKING OF A TOWN

⚜

The published memoir of

the Reverend Jack 'King' Cassidy,

Founder and first citizen of the city of Redemption, Az.

⚜

(b. DECEMBER 25, 1841, d. DECEMBER 24, 1927)

IT IS, I SUPPOSE, a curse that befalls anyone who finds a great treasure that they must spend the remainder of their life recounting the details of how they came by it. I therefore hope, by setting it down here, that people might leave me alone, for I am tired of talking about it. I had a life of a different colour before riches painted it gold, and if I could return to that drab and unremarkable life I would. But you cannot undo what is done, and a bell once rung cannot be un-rung.

The story of how I found my fortune and used it to build a church and the town I called Redemption is a brutal and tragic one, yet there is divinity in it also. For God steered my enterprise, as he does all things, and led me to my treasure. Not with a map or compass, but with a Bible and a cross.

The Bible came to me first. It was delivered into my possession by the hand of a dying priest, a Father Damon

O'Brien, who had fled his native country under a cloud of persecution. I made his acquaintance in Bannack, Montana, where he had been drawn, as had I, by the promise of gold, only to discover that it had all but run out. He was already close to death when our paths crossed. I was down on luck and short on money and I took the bed next to his at a discount as no one else would have it, too fearful were they of the mad priest's ravings and his violent terror of shadows that he could see but no one else could. He believed they were after stealing his Bible away, which he later told me in confidence would lead the bearer to a treasure that must finance the construction of a great church and town in the western desert.

The foundation is here – he would say, clutching the large, battered book to his chest like it was his own child. *Here is the seed that must be planted, for He is the true way and the light.*

The owner of the flophouse was too superstitious to turn the priest out on to the street, so he slipped me some extra coin to take care of the old man, keep him in drink and, most importantly, keep him quiet. Being close to destitute, I took the money and mopped the priest's sweats and brought him bread and coffee and whiskey and listened to him mutter about the visions he had seen and the riches that would flow from the ground and the great church he would build and how the Bible would act as his compass to lead him there.

And when his time came, he told me with wide staring eyes that he could hear the dark angel's wings beating close by his bed, and he pressed that Bible into my hands and made me swear solemnly upon it that I would continue his mission and carry the book onward.

Carry His word into the wasteland, he said. *Carry His word and also carry Him. For He will protect you and lead you to riches beyond your imagining.*

He also told me he had money hidden in a bag sewn into the lining of his coat, a little gold to seal the deal and help me on my way. I took his money and swore I would do as he asked and he signed the Bible over to me like he was signing his own death warrant, then fell into a sleep from which he never woke.

To my eternal shame those promises I made to the dying priest were founded more on baser thoughts of the riches he spoke of than the higher ones of founding a church. For I believed he had lost his mind long before he let go of his life and all I heard in the clink of his gold was the sound of release from my own poverty.

I used it to fund my passage west and I read that Bible, from Genesis to Revelation, in railroad diner cars, then mail coaches and finally in the back of covered wagons all the way to the very edge of civilization in the southernmost parts of the Arizona territories. I expected it might contain a map or some written direction telling where to search for the fortune the priest had promised, but all I found was further evidence of his cracked mind, passages of scripture marked by his hand and other scrawlings that hinted at desert and fire and treasure, but gave no specific indication as to where any such riches might be found.

During my lengthy travels and study of the book, and to keep it safe from thieving hands, I used it as my pillow when I slept. Soon the priest's visions started leaking into my dreams. I saw the church in the desert, shining white like he had described, and the Bible lying open inside the doorway and a pale figure of Christ on a burned cross, hanging above the altar.

The church I had to somehow build.

9

– Mrs Coronado?

Holly Coronado stared down at her husband's coffin, a couple of handfuls of dry sand and stones scattered across the pine lid.

– There's a fire blowing this way, Mrs Coronado, and I been called away to help.

When the stones had first fallen on to the boards the sound of the larger pebbles had seemed hollow to her. They had made her think, for a flickering moment, that maybe the coffin was actually empty and all this some kind of elaborate historical re-enactment they had forgotten to tell her about.

– I'm supposed to stick around until after everyone's gone.

The coffin had not been her idea. Neither had the venue.

– I'm supposed to fill in the grave, Mrs Coronado. Only they need me back in town … because of the fire.

She had only gone along with everything because she was numb from grief, or shock, or both, and knew that Jim would have loved the idea of being buried up here next to all the grim-faced pioneers and salty outlaws no one outside Redemption had ever heard of.

– I'm going to have to come back and finish up later, OK?

Jim had loved this town, all its history and legends. All the earnest foundations upon which it had been built.

– *Maybe you should come back with me, Mrs Coronado. I can drop you back home, if you like.*

He had told her about the strange little town in the desert the very first time she'd met him at that freshman mixer at the University of Chicago Law School. She remembered the light that had come into his eyes when he talked about where he was from. She was from a nondescript suburb of St Louis so a town in the desert in the shadow of red mountains seemed romantic and exciting to her – and so had he.

– *Mrs Coronado? You OK, Mrs Coronado?*

She turned and studied the earnest, sinewy young man in dusty green overalls. He held a battered starter cap in his hands and was wringing the life out of it in a mixture of awkwardness and respect, his short, honey-coloured hair flopping forward over skin the same colour.

'What's your name?' she asked.

'Billy. Billy Walker.'

'Do you have a shovel, Billy?'

A line creased his forehead below the mark his cap had made. 'Excuse me?'

'A shovel, do you have one?'

He shook his head as it dawned on him where this was headed. 'You don't need to … I mean, I'll come straight back and finish up here after.'

'When? When will you come back?'

He looked away down the valley to where a moving wall of smoke was creeping across a large chunk of the desert. 'Soon as the fire's under control, I guess.'

'What if you're dead?' The crease deepened in his forehead. 'What if the whole town burns up and you along with it – who will come back and bury my husband then? You suppose I should just leave him here for the animals?'

'No, ma'am. Guess not.'

'People make all sorts of plans, Billy. All sorts of promises that don't get kept. I planned on being married to the man in that box until we were old and grey. But I also promised I would get up out of bed this morning and comb my hair and fix my face and come up here to give my husband a decent burial. So that's what I'm fixing to do. And a shovel would sure help me keep that particular promise.'

Billy stared down at the twisted cap in his hands, opened his mouth to say something then closed it again, turned around and loped away down the hill to where his truck was parked in the shade of the large cottonwood in the centre of the graveyard. Tools bristled from a barrel in the back and a solid, ugly bulldog sat behind the wheel, ears pricked forward. It was watching the smoke rising up from the valley. It didn't even move when Billy jumped on to the flat bed and set the springs rocking, just kept its eyes on the distant fire, its tongue lolling wetly from its mouth.

The smoke filled almost a third of the sky now and continued to spread like a black veil being slowly drawn across the day. Vehicles and people were starting to congregate by the billboard at the edge of town, black dots against the orange roadside dust. A few weeks ago Jim would have been right at the centre of it, organizing the effort, leading the charge to save the town, risking his life, if that's what it took. And in the end, that's exactly what it had taken.

Holly heard boots hurry up the hill then stop a few feet short of where she was standing. 'I could drop you back home,' he said, talking to his feet rather than to her. 'I'll come back before sundown to finish up here, I promise.'

'Give me the shovel, Billy.'

He held the shovel up and examined the blade. It looked new, the polished-steel surface catching the sun as he turned it.

'If you don't give me the damn thing, I'll bury my husband with my bare hands.'

He shook his head like he was disappointed or maybe just defeated. 'Don't feel right,' he said. Then he flipped the shovel over and jabbed it into the dirt like a spear. 'Just leave it round here someplace,' he said, turning away and hurrying down the hill. 'I'll fetch it later.'

Holly waited until the noise of his engine faded, allowing the softer sounds of nature and the empty cemetery to creep back in. She stood for a long while, listening to the cord slapping against the flagpole by the entrance, the Arizona state flag fluttering at half-mast, the wind humming in the power lines that looped away down the hill. She wondered how many widows had stood here like her and listened to these same lonely sounds.

'Well, here we are, Jimbo,' she whispered to the wind. 'Alone at last.'

The last time they'd been up here together was for a campaign photo-op about two or three months previously. They had not been alone back then; there had been a handful of other people – press, photographers. She had stood here by his side, framed by the grave markers with the town spread out below them while he outlined his plans for its future, not realizing he wouldn't be around to see it.

She walked over to a mound of dirt set to one side of the grave. She grabbed the edge of the stone-coloured sheet of canvas covering it and started dragging it off, stumbling as her heels sank into the ground and her tailored dress restricted the movement of her legs. She had bought it for his investiture, a little black number designed to be classy but not too showy to draw attention away from her handsome husband, the real star of the show. It was the only black dress she owned.

She stumbled again and nearly fell, the tight dress making it hard to keep balance.

'SHIT!' she shouted into the silence. 'SHIT FUCKING SHIT.'

She kicked her shoes off, sending her heels sailing away through the air. One skittered to rest against the sword cluster of an agave plant, the other bounced off a painted board that marked the final resting place of one *J.J. James, died of sweats, 1882.*

She grabbed the hem of her dress either side of the seam and wrenched it apart with a loud rip. She was never going to wear it again; no amount of dressing it up with a new scarf or belt was ever going to accessorize away this memory. She gave it another yank and it tore all the way up to her thigh. She planted her bare feet wide apart and felt the heat of the earth beneath them. It felt good to be free of the constricting dress and the heels. She felt more like herself. She grabbed the shovel and stabbed the blade into the pile of dirt, the muscles in her arms and shoulders straining against the weight of it as she heaved back and tipped it in the hole.

Dry earth *whumped* down on the wooden lid of her husband's coffin.

Wood. Fifth anniversary is wood. Jim had told her that.

They had spent their first anniversary here in this town, a break from study so he could show her the place where he hoped to be sheriff one day. He had introduced her to everyone, taken her dancing at the band hall where everyone knew him, taken her riding in the desert, where they'd made love on a blanket by a fire beneath the stars like there was nothing else but him and her and they were the only two people on earth. She had bought him a tin star from one of the souvenir shops and given it to him as a present, a toy sheriff's badge until he got a real one.

First anniversary is paper – he had told her with a smile – *tin is what you give on the tenth*.

She had always loved it that he knew stuff like that, silly romantic stuff that was all the more sweet and surprising coming from the mouth of such a big guy's guy like he was – like he *had* been.

He never got to pin the real badge on, and the gift of wood she ended up getting him for their fifth anniversary was a pine box lying at the bottom of a six-foot hole.

She wiped her cheek with the back of her hand and it came away wet.

Goddammit. She had promised herself she was not going to cry. At least there was no one around to see it. She didn't want to give them the satisfaction. She didn't want to give them a damned thing, not after they had taken so much already.

She remembered the last time she had seen Jim alive, sitting behind his desk in his office at home, looking as if he had been crying.

I need to fix this – was all he would tell her. *The town needs fixing*.

Then he had stuffed some papers in his case and driven off into the evening. But it had been Mayor Cassidy who had driven back, knocking on her door at three in the morning to deliver the news personally, his words full of meaning but empty at the same time.

Tragic accident … So sorry for your loss … Anything the town can do … Anything at all …

She hauled another shovel-load into the grave, then another, numbing herself against her sorrow and anger through the real physical pain of burying her husband. And with every shovelful of earth she whispered a prayer, but not for her dead love. The prayer she offered up, as tears smeared her face and the smell of smoke drifted up from the desert below, was that the wildfire was actually a judgment, sent by some higher power to sweep right through the town and burn the whole damned place to the ground.

Anything the town can do – Cassidy had said, his hat in his hands and his eyes cast down. *Anything at all.*

They could all die and burn in hell.

That was what they could do for her.

10

'How did he die?' Solomon kept his voice calm but he felt like howling and breaking something. His frustration was like a physical thing, a storm raging inside him, a stone weighing him down. Being confined in the tin can of the ambulance wasn't helping.

'Car wreck,' Morgan said, his eyes still looking up and out of the side window towards the slopes of the mountains. 'He was driving late at night, fell asleep at the wheel or maybe swerved to avoid something and ended up in a ravine. Bashed his head and cracked his skull. He was dead by the time we found him.'

Dead by the time I found him too …

Solomon stared past Morgan and out of the window. The town was starting to rise from the desert in scraps of broken fence and crooked shacks with rusted tin roofs or no roofs at all. None of it seemed familiar. 'Where are all the people?'

'Oh, those are the old miners' houses,' Morgan said. 'They keep it like this for atmosphere, I guess, a curtain-raiser for the tourists before they get to Main Street. Most people live around the centre nowadays.'

A large sign whipped past – old-style lettering telling travellers they were now entering 'The Historic Old Town of Redemption' – and the place came suddenly to life. Pastel houses were lined up in neat rows behind white-painted picket fences along well-paved roads. A Wells Fargo wagon stood beneath the shade of a cottonwood tree, the horses tethered by their reins to a wooden rail running along a trough filled with water from an old-fashioned pump. They were twitching their heads, spooked by the smoke blowing their way and anxious to run from it. Solomon knew how they felt. He wanted to run too, away from the fire, away from this town and this strange feeling of responsibility to a man who was already dead.

'Did James Coronado have family?' he asked.

'Holly,' Gloria said, fixing a dressing over the burn mark on his arm. 'His wife.'

'Holly Coronado,' Solomon repeated. 'Maybe I should talk to her.'

Morgan shook his head. 'I don't think that's a good idea.'

'Why not?'

'She just buried her husband. She'll want to be left alone, I should imagine.'

'She might know who I am.'

Morgan shifted in his seat like it had suddenly become uncomfortable. 'She should be left alone, time like this.'

Solomon cocked his head to one side. 'It's an odd custom, don't you think, to abandon people when they are at their loneliest? If her husband knew me, then she might know me too. And she might be glad to see an old friend.'

'I can run a check on your name, if you want,' Morgan said, fishing his phone from his pocket, 'see if anything comes up.'

Solomon wondered why Morgan seemed reluctant to let him talk to this woman. It made him want to talk to her even more. He watched as he dialled a number then fixed him with a level stare as he waited for someone to answer.

'Hey, Rollins, it's Morgan. Run a name for me, would ya – Solomon Creed.' He glanced down at the book, used the inscription to spell out the name, then looked back up. 'He's about six feet tall, mid-to-late twenties, Caucasian – and by that I mean white: white skin, white hair.' He nodded. 'Yeah, like an al-bino.' He split the word up and stretched it out, in the same way that he might say *neee-gro*. 'No, I'll wait. Run it through NCIC, see if you get anything.'

Solomon felt the ball of anxiety expand in his stomach a little. The NCIC was the National Crime Information Centre. Morgan was checking to see if he had a criminal record or was wanted on any outstanding warrants. And the fact that Solomon knew what NCIC stood for suggested to him that he might.

He looked down at himself, his white skin glowing under the bright lights, no pigment, no marks at all except for the 'I' branded on his arm, now hidden beneath a dressing. A blank page of a man. He crossed his arms in front of himself, feeling vulnerable and exposed with his shirt off.

The ambulance turned off the main road and a huge white building filled the ambulance with reflected light. Solomon narrowed his eyes and peered through the rear windows at the church, far too large for such a small town, its copper-clad spire needling its way up into the desert sky. He felt it tug at him, as if he recognized it, though he couldn't say for sure. Morgan had said the cross he wore round his neck was a replica of the one on the altar, and he felt a strong urge to slip out of the straps that held his legs and break out of the ambulance so he could run to it and see for himself.

'Yeah, I'm here.' Morgan nodded and listened. 'OK,

thanks.' He hung up. 'Well, Mr Creed,' he said, tucking the book back into the folded jacket pocket. 'You'll be pleased to learn that you are not in the criminal database.'

He sounded vaguely disappointed and Solomon was too, a little. At least if he had been in it he would have more of an idea who he was.

The ambulance slowed, turned off the road and pulled up in front of a large stone building. Gloria handed Solomon his shirt and moved with practised speed, pushing past Morgan to the rear doors to throw them open in an explosion of sunlight and heat. She turned back and released the lock holding the gurney in place and the other medic appeared beside her, ready to pull Solomon out of the ambulance.

'I can walk,' Solomon said, slipping his arms into the shirt.

'You can't,' Gloria said. 'It's hospital policy. Sit back.'

The driver tugged hard and the gurney slid out of the ambulance with Solomon still lying on it. The steel legs rattled as they unfolded and the sunlight made him screw his eyes shut. 'I'm not hurt,' he said, squinting up at copper letters spelling out KING COMMUNITY HOSPITAL across the facade of the building.

'Sir, you are injured and you have amnesia.'

'How was my PERL test?' Solomon said, covering his eyes with his arm.

'It was … How did— do you have medical training?'

'Possibly. My pupils are both equal and reactive to light?' They were certainly reacting to the light now.

'Yes.'

'Then I don't need to go to the hospital.' He reached forward to undo the straps holding his legs in place, swung his legs free and down to the ground. The moment his bare feet touched the ground he felt calmer.

The driver moved forward and Solomon pulled the gurney between them and stepped out of reach. He wanted to run and get away from these people but he couldn't. Not yet. Morgan climbed down from the ambulance, the jacket dangling from his hand, the book sticking out from the pocket. 'Why don't you just go with these people and let them run their tests,' he said. 'Better safe than sorry.'

Safe. Interesting word. Safe from whom. Safe from what?

'My jacket,' Solomon said, holding his hand out.

Morgan held it up. 'You want this? Go with these people and you can—'

Solomon darted forward, shoving the gurney at Morgan in a loud clatter that made him flinch. He instinctively reached out and the jacket swung close enough for Solomon to snatch it. He had moved clear again before Morgan even realized what was happening.

'I don't need to go to the hospital,' Solomon repeated, slipping his arms into the jacket and backing away from the gurney, and the people, and whatever they wanted to do to him. 'I need to go to church.'

11

Mayor Cassidy closed the door of his study, shrugged off his jacket and let it fall to the floor. He stood in the downdraught of the ceiling-fan, pulling his string tie loose and undoing the top button of his shirt. His collar was soaked with sweat.

The funeral had turned into a disaster, his big unifying gesture undone at a stroke by the whiff of wildfire. Everyone had drifted away before the ceremony had ended; a few at first, then a stampede as soon as the sounds of sirens had reached them and they'd seen how fast the smoke was rising and which way it was headed. They all had homes and businesses to worry about, so he couldn't blame them, but it wasn't exactly the gesture of community support he had hoped for. There was also the little matter of what might have started the fire, and he didn't even want to think about that.

His phone buzzed in his pocket and his heart clenched in his chest like a hand had taken hold of it and begun to squeeze. He looked down at the crumpled jacket, the black material shivering where the phone vibrated inside it like some large insect had crawled in there and was now trying to get out. There was a small hole in the fabric and the sight of it made him burn with anger. Damn moths, the house was plagued with them. There had been a Cassidy living in this house ever since Jack Cassidy had built it and now it was all being eaten away, pulled apart fibre by fibre, everything unravelling. He felt embarrassed knowing that he had stood in front of the assembled town with a hole in his jacket – their shabby, moth-eaten mayor.

The phone stopped buzzing and silence surged back into his study. It could have been anybody calling. There was a wildfire burning on the edge of town, all kinds of people would be trying to get hold of him, wanting him to lead, wanting him to reassure them, wanting – something. Everyone wanted something, but there was no one there for him. Not any more.

He glanced over at the photograph on his desk of Stella in the garden standing under one of the jacaranda trees, Stella with the sun glowing in her long hair, taken about a year before the cancer wore her away to nothing and took her hair along with everything else. He still missed her, six years after he had stood over her grave, and never more than in these last few months when he had badly needed someone to talk to and share the burden of all he'd had to bear, someone to tell him that it was OK to do a bad thing for a good enough reason, and that God would understand.

The phone buzzed again at his feet, like the last effort of a dying insect, then fell silent again.

He tipped his head back and let the cool air wash over him. He felt done in. Defeated. He wanted to lie down on the floor next to his crumpled jacket and go to sleep, close his eyes on his crumbling, moth-eaten world and slide away into blissful oblivion. He half-wished he were a drinking man so he could grab a bottle and disappear into it. But he was a Cassidy and his name was written across half the buildings in town. And Cassidys did not drink, nor did they lie down on floors and close their eyes to their responsibilities. And this *was* his responsibility, all of it – the town, the people, the widow he'd left standing alone by her husband's grave, the fire out in the desert – everything. He was trapped here, bound by blood, and by the name he carried, and by the generations of bones lying buried in the ground.

He looked up at the portrait hanging above the great stone fireplace, Jack Cassidy's eyes staring sternly back at him across a hundred years of history as if to say, *I didn't build this town from nothing only for you to run away and let it die.*

'I've got this,' Cassidy whispered to his ancestor. 'I'm not going anywhere.'

The desk phone rang, sharp and sudden, its old brass bell cutting right through the silence. It echoed off the oak panelling and leather-bound books lining the walls. Cassidy plucked his jacket from the floor, slipped his arms into the sleeves and stepped out from beneath the cool flow of air. It made him feel more official, wearing the jacket, and he felt he would need authority for whatever conversation he was about to have. He took a deep breath as if he was about to dive into one of the cold-water lakes up in the mountains and snatched the phone from its cradle.

'Cassidy.' His voice sounded as though it was coming from a long way off.

'It's Morgan.'

Cassidy collapsed into his chair with relief at the police chief's voice. 'How bad is it?'

'Bad. It's the plane.'

Cassidy closed his eyes. Nodded. The moment he'd seen the smoke rising he'd feared this. 'Listen,' he said, naturally easing into command. 'I'll call our associate, tell him what happened here. We'll work something out, some sort of compensation. Accidents happen. Planes crash. I'm sure he'll understand. I'm sure he'll …'

'No,' Morgan said. 'He won't. Money won't work here.'

Cassidy blinked. Not used to being contradicted. 'He's a businessman. Things go wrong in business all the time and when that happens there has to be some form of restitution. That's all I'm talking about here. Restitution.'

'You don't understand,' Morgan said. 'Nothing can make up for what happened here. There is no amount of money that can fix this, trust me. We need to come up with another plan. I'm not going to talk about this on the phone. I need to head back out to the fire, but I'll swing by your office first. Don't move and don't call anyone, OK – not until we've talked.'

12

Mulcahy eased off the highway on to the up ramp of the Best Western.

They were driving through Globe, a mining town that had seen better days and was clinging on in hope that it might see them again.

Javier kissed his teeth with his oversized lips and shook his head at the grey concrete-and-brick motel complex. 'This it? This the best you could manage?'

Mulcahy drove slowly round the one-way system then swung into a parking bay outside a room he had checked into the previous night under an assumed name. He had avoided all the independents and franchises because he didn't want some over-attentive owner manager giving him that extra bit of service you didn't get from the chains. He didn't want good service and he didn't want the personal touch, he wanted the impersonal touch and some bored desk clerk on minimum wage who would hand over the room key without glancing up from their phone when he checked in.

He cut the engine and took the keys out of the ignition. 'Give me five minutes, then follow me inside.'

'Five minutes? The fuck we got to wait five minutes for?'

'Because a white guy entering a room on his own, no one

notices. A white guy and two Mexicans, everyone notices because it looks like a drug deal is going down and somebody might call the cops.' He opened his door and felt the dry heat of the day flood in. 'So give me the five minutes, OK?'

He got out and slammed the door before Javier had a chance to say anything then walked over to a solid grey door with 22 on it. With the engine and air switched off it would become stifling in the car fast. He'd give them maybe three minutes before they followed him in. Three minutes was all he needed.

He unlocked the door and opened it on to a dim, depressing room with two lumpy beds and an old style wooden-clad TV. There was a kitchenette in back leading to a bathroom – the standard layout of pretty much every motel he'd ever stayed in.

He pulled his phone from his pocket, checked the WiFi connection then opened a Skype application, selected 'Home' in the contacts and raised it to his ear.

A coffin of an A/C unit rattled noisily beneath the window, moving the grey sheer curtain above it and filling the room with cool air and the smell of mildew. Outside Mulcahy could see the Cherokee with the outline of Javier in the front seat. A dark blue Buick Verano was parked next to it, covered with a fine desert dust that spoke of the miles it had travelled to end up in this nowhere hub of a place. Salesman's car.

The phone connected and Mulcahy's own voice told him he wasn't home. 'Hey, Pop, if you're there, pick up.'

He listened. Waited. Nothing. He hung up, found a new contact and dialled.

His old man had driven a Buick when he'd worked the roads, hawking office supplies then pharmaceuticals all over the Midwest. Mulcahy must have been only, what, ten or eleven at the time? Mom had been long gone, so it can't have been much earlier. His pop would get him to wash and wax the car every Sunday afternoon in exchange for five bucks that had to last him through the week. He would drive him to school in the shiny car on a Monday morning then take off, heading for different states and places that sounded exotic to an eleven-year-old kid who didn't know any better: Oklahoma City; Des Moines; Shakopee; Omaha; Kansas City. His old man would always come back late on a Friday, pick him up from his aunt's or, later on when it was clear Mom wasn't coming back, some girlfriend or other, and the Buick would always be covered in dust, exactly like the Verano parked outside.

The phone connected, his dad's voice this time. 'Leave a message. I'll call you.'

'Pop, it's me. Listen, if you're not at the house then stay away. Don't go back there for a while, OK? Call me when you get this. Everything's fine, just … call me.'

He hung up. Everything was not fine. This was not how it was supposed to go. Someone had changed the script and now his father was missing. He checked the time. Tío would be wondering why he hadn't called. Most likely he already knew. He should have told his father to go on a trip, get him out of the way, in case something like this happened, only Tío's men would have been watching and they would have grabbed him anyway. About a year back one of Tío's lieutenants had been turned by the Federales. He'd promised to give them a large shipment and several key players in Tío's organization in exchange for immunity and a new life. The day before the shipment, the lieutenant had sent all his family away somewhere – and Tío had been watching. The Federales found the lieutenant and his whole family a week later, lined up and headless in a ditch along the border. The message was clear: *I am watching. You will be loyal or you will be dead, and so will anyone you hold dear.* So Mulcahy had left his father where he was. And now the plane had crashed and he couldn't get hold of him and everything was fucked and he had to un-fuck it and fast.

Sunlight flashed on the passenger window of the Cherokee as Javier threw it open and escaped from the oven of its interior. He looked furious. Carlos got out too, head down, eyes jumping. They shambled towards the door, doing the most piss-poor impersonation of two people trying not to look suspicious Mulcahy had ever seen. He selected a new contact from the Skype menu and raised the phone back to his ear just as a heavy knock thudded on the other side of it.

'It's open,' he called out and Javier burst in.

'The fuck's up with that, leaving us out in the car like a pair of motherfuckin' dogs?'

The phone clicked as it connected. 'Tío,' he said, as calmly as he could manage but loud enough for Javier to hear. 'It's Mulcahy.'

Javier stopped dead in the doorway, so suddenly that Carlos bumped into him from behind.

'There was a problem at the pick-up.' Mulcahy was looking at Javier but talking into the phone. 'The plane never showed. We didn't collect the package. We don't have your son.'

13

Solomon walked quickly, keeping to the shadows of the boardwalk and out of the sun, feeling the warm, worn timbers beneath the soles of his bare feet. He didn't look back at the hospital. He would hear if anyone was following him.

He took deep breaths to try to calm himself, and smelled the town all around him, paint and dust and tarpaper and decay. He felt calmer now he was out of the confines of the ambulance with its sickening movement.

Why did he dislike confinement and crave freedom so strongly?

Maybe he had been incarcerated, even though he hadn't shown up on the NCIC. Perhaps he had been imprisoned another way.

Ahead of him the church glowed, as if lit from within, and towered over the surrounding buildings: a town hall; a museum; and a grand house partly visible behind a screen of jacaranda trees, its roof clad in copper like the church and similarly aged, suggesting it had been built at the same time. The rest of the buildings making up the street and lining the boardwalk were all variations on the same theme, souvenir shops selling the same things: flakes of gold and copper floating in snow globes; treasure maps with 'Lost Cassidy Riches' written on them in old-style block letters; T-shirts

with the name of the town printed in a similar style; and Jack
Cassidy's memoir stacked high in every window.

Solomon pulled his own copy from his pocket and flicked
through the pages, hungry to see what else was written inside,
hoping something might spark a new memory. Apart from
the dedication the only other thing he found was a single
passage at the end of the book that had been underlined:

> I had always suspected the book contained a clue
> that would lead me to riches, but by the time I
> found it and understood its meaning it was too
> late for me and so I resolve to take the secret of it
> to my grave.

More secrets, but none that interested him. He turned
back to the dedication and studied the handwriting, neat
and smooth and written with a wide-nibbed pen. It appeared
formal and old, but he didn't recognize it. Maybe there were
clues in the printed words. He flicked to the first page and
started to read:

> It is, I suppose, a curse that befalls anyone who
> finds a great treasure that they must spend the
> remainder of their life recounting the details of
> how they came by it ...

He carried on reading, sucking in Jack Cassidy's story as
fast as he could turn the pages, his head filling with all the
images and horrors Jack Cassidy had encountered on his
odyssey through the desert. The memoir was ninety pages
long and he had finished it by the time he was halfway to
the church. He turned to the photo on the cover again and

wondered why James Coronado might have given this book to him. Perhaps he hadn't. Perhaps he wasn't even Solomon Creed. Except he felt that he was. The name fit and so did the jacket. That had his name in it too.

He slipped the book in his jacket and read the label stitched inside his pocket: *Ce costume a été fait au trésor pour M. Solomon Creed* – This suit was made to treasure for Mr Solomon Creed.

This *suit* …

So where was the rest of it? Why did he only have the jacket? Where were his shoes? And how in Jesus's name could he read French? How could he read English so fast, for that matter?

'*Je suis Solomon Creed*,' he said, and the language felt comfortable in his mouth, his accent smooth and slightly thick and syrupy – southern French, not northern Parisian.

Southern French! How did he even know that? How could he speak French and know the origin of his accent and yet have no memory of learning it or speaking it before or of ever being in France? How much of himself had he lost?

Some smaller writing was stitched on the edge of the label: *Fabriqué 13, Rue Obscure, Cordes-sur-Ciel, Tarn*.

The Tarn. Southwestern France. Cathar country. Formed in 1790 after the French Revolution. Capital Albi. Birthplace of Toulouse-Lautrec. Fine medieval cathedral there, larger even than the church he was now walking towards. Built of brick not stone.

He hit himself on the side of the head to silence the noise.

'Shut up,' he said aloud, realizing how mad he would appear to anyone watching. He looked around. No one was. Maybe he was genuinely mad, some delusional freak with an equally freakish mind: all this information tumbling through it like white noise and none of it any use.

'I am a crazy man.' He stated it, as if admission might be the first step towards cure. He said it again, then repeated it in French, Russian, German, Spanish, Arabic. He hit himself on the head again, harder this time, desperate to make it all stop or coalesce into something useful. He needed to tune out the noise and focus only on the concrete things that might help him remember who he was, the things that bound him to his forgotten past – the suit, the book, the cross around his neck. Physical things. Undeniable.

He reached the end of the boardwalk, stepped out of the shadows and into the stinging heat of the sun. The church was even more impressive up close, its spire forcing his eyes up to heaven, the way ecclesiastical architecture was designed to do.

Know your place, it seemed to murmur. *Know that you are insignificant and God is almighty.*

There was a large sign planted in the ground beside a pathway leading up to the church with CHURCH OF LOST COMMANDMENTS written across it in copper-coloured letters, a reference to something he'd read in Jack Cassidy's memoir.

He continued past the sign and down the pathway towards the church. There was a fountain over to one side with a split boulder at the centre and marks on it showing where water had once flowed over the stones. He recognized this from the memoir too – water coming from a split stone, a miracle out in the desert commemorated here by a fountain that was no longer running.

He drew closer to the door and saw words cut into the stone above it, the first of the lost commandments the church had been named for:

I

THOU SHALT HAVE
NO OTHER GODS BEFORE ME

It reminded him of the 'No Guns' sign he'd seen outside the old saloon on the outskirts of town; no firearms allowed there, no other belief systems allowed here. His eyes lingered on the carved numeral, the same mark he carried on his arm. Maybe it was not an 'I' but a number. Or maybe it was nothing at all and the church would hold no answers for him.

'Let's see, shall we?' he whispered, then passed into the cool, shadowy relief of the entrance and through the door into one of the oddest churches he had ever set foot in.

14

Cassidy sat behind the oak expanse of his desk, mouth slack, eyes staring up at Morgan. When the doctors had told him Stella's cancer had not responded to treatment and she had only weeks to live, it had felt exactly like this, as if the oxygen had been sucked out of the room and what was left was difficult to breathe.

'Ramon,' he said, repeating the name Morgan had just given him.

Morgan nodded. 'Ramon Alvarado. Tío's son.'

'But – what was he ... I mean, why was he on the plane?'

Morgan shrugged. 'Some trouble south of the border. He needed a fast ride out of Mexico. I didn't ask for the details.'

Cassidy stared out of the tall window of his study and down the avenue of jacaranda trees that framed the church beyond the wall. Above the roof he could see smoke rising out in the desert. That's what had been filling his mind until Morgan had told him what had caused the fire. Now it seemed the very least of his worries.

'But why didn't you tell me?'

'I didn't think you needed to know.'

'You didn't think I ... but this has ... Tío's son!! Don't you think you should have run it by me?'

'It was a last-minute thing. I got a call. I made a decision.'

'You made a decision?'

'I didn't have a choice, all right? When someone like Tío calls and asks for a favour, he's not really asking. What would you have done different? Said, "Sorry to hear your son's in trouble, but we're not going to help you"? Don't start blaming me for this. I didn't make the damn plane crash.'

Cassidy rose from his chair and started pacing. 'We need to do everything we can to speed up the crash investigation,' he said. 'Get proof that it was an accident.'

'What if it wasn't?'

Cassidy glared at him like he had suggested the earth was flat. 'Of course it was an accident.'

Morgan took his phone from his pocket and stepped into the room. 'When I went out to the crash site I nearly ran this guy down.' He held the phone out.

Cassidy took his reading glasses from the desk and the photo on the screen came into focus as he put them on. It had been taken from inside Morgan's car, the air outside filled with grit that softened the image, though the figure of the man standing at the centre was clear. He seemed to shine in the sunlight, his face gazing up at something the photograph did not show. 'Who's that?'

'Says he can't remember, but the label in his jacket says he's called Solomon Creed.' He swiped the screen and the picture changed. 'He also got this on his arm.'

Cassidy looked at the livid red mark upon the man's skin then at Morgan for an explanation.

'Looks like a kill tag to me,' Morgan obliged. 'Cartel hit men get them to show they've clipped someone important. Usually they're tattoos, but sometimes they cut themselves or brand themselves, like this.'

Cassidy looked back down at the photo as he realized what Morgan was suggesting. 'You think this guy might have …'

'Shot the plane down? Maybe. Say he knocked it out with some missile, got caught in the blast, banged his head and now can't remember who he is. Or maybe he knows exactly who he is and just isn't saying. The cartels use some pretty unusual characters as gunmen south of the border – gives the *norteños* something to sing about. So I don't think the notion of an albino being used as a hit man is beyond the realm of possibility. They're superstitious about albinos down there anyways. Hell, they're superstitious about everything. They think the white skin shows they got divine power, like they've been touched by God or something. Anyway, it doesn't really matter. What does matter is that he *might* have done it. He was there, he was running away from the crash, he even said the fire was there because of him, and he's got this mark on his arm. It's all circumstantial, but we don't need it to hold up in a court of law, we only need Tío to buy it. Someone is going to have to pay for his son's death – and I don't mean offer him cash, say "sorry" and hope everything's going to go away. Blood will have to pay for blood here, so that's what we have to give him. We give him this guy. We give him Solomon Creed.'

Cassidy swiped the screen and stared hard at the picture of the pale man standing on the desert road. Then he shook his head and handed the phone back. 'I think I should talk to Tío first, try for a diplomatic solution before we start … throwing human sacrifices at him. We don't even know who this guy is. Have you run an ID check?'

'He's not on the NCIC.'

'That only proves he's not a criminal. What about the missing persons channels – DMV, Social Security?'

'What's the point?'

'The point is we're talking about a man's life here.'

'No. The point is we're talking about several people's lives, including yours and mine. We're talking about the survival of this town. I don't want to know who this guy is. I don't need to know. But I'll tell you something else: he had a copy of Jack Cassidy's memoir in his pocket, personally inscribed to him from Jim Coronado.'

Cassidy felt the blood drain from him. 'You think he knew Jim?'

'He says he can't remember, but when I asked him about the book he said he felt like he was here because of Jim. He said he thought he was here to save him.'

'Jesus. He said that?'

Morgan nodded. 'Asked me how he died and whether he could talk to Holly. So, whichever way you chop it up, this guy is a potential problem for us. Or maybe he's not. Maybe he's actually a solution. The way I figure it, Tío's going to find out about him sooner or later, which means he's a dead man whatever we do or don't do. So if we give him up, we win ourselves some loyalty points and hopefully cut ourselves some slack. And we no longer have to worry about what his connection to Jim may have been and whether that might turn into another problem for us.'

Cassidy felt sick about what they were discussing. He gazed back up at the stern portrait of his ancestor. He had always felt like the Reverend Jack was looking down on him, judging him and how he was running the town he had built. He had faced some tough challenges over the last few years, real tough challenges, but nothing like this. This was like Armageddon, apocalyptic – world ending.

Outside, the wail of a siren rose and he glanced up to see a cruiser come to an abrupt halt on the driveway, its spinning lights painting the panelling red and blue.

'There's my ride,' Morgan said, heading to the door.

'Where is this guy?' Cassidy asked. 'You taken him in for questioning?'

'No. I thought it best to keep him off the record, in case he has to – disappear. Last I saw, he was heading to the church.'

Cassidy stared out of the window at the white stone of the church beyond the wall. 'Let me go talk to him first.'

'Now why would you want to go and do that?'

'Because if I'm going to sacrifice a man's life to save my town, the least I can do is have the courtesy of looking him in the eye first. And I still think we should establish whether the crash was an accident or not.'

Morgan shook his head and took in the room. 'Must be nice, living in your oak-panelled world where everyone plays by rules and any disputes can be resolved with a handshake. Let me tell you how things work out in the real world. Talking to this guy is going to achieve absolutely nothing. If anything, it's going to complicate things. You don't strike up a friendship with a man you're about to execute. And it won't matter a damn to Tío whether the crash was an accident or not. His son died and someone is going to have to pay for it. Someone – or something. Ever hear of a place called El Rey?'

'Rings a bell.'

'It's a little town up in the Durango Mountains. The local banditos took it over and it became a sort of Shangri-La for criminals fleeing south across the border. Anyone who made it there with enough money to pay for protection could stay as long as they liked, knowing no law would ever touch them. El Rey is also Tío's hometown. Or it was. It's not there any more.'

'What happened?'

'Tío happened. I don't know the exact details, but when Tío was a kid there was some kind of family tragedy involving his father and brother. Could be they fell foul of the bosses or something but whatever happened, Tío never forgot it. When he rose to power years later, he got his revenge. El Rey was the headquarters of the old bosses, so it made sense for him to take it over. But he didn't. What he did was massacre every living soul in the town and burn the place to the ground. It was symbolic, I guess: out with the old and in with the new. But it was also revenge, pure and simple; an old-fashioned blood vendetta. Tío did the killing himself, the way I heard it. Showed the world what would happen if anyone dared to hurt him or his family.' He pointed out of the window at the smoke rising beyond the church. 'And his son just died, flying into our airfield. So you think about that when you talk to this guy. I'll be at the control line if you need me.' Then he opened the door and was gone.

15

Solomon stood inside the door of the church letting his eyes adjust to the gloom after the fierce sunlight outside. Huge stained-glass windows poured light into the dark interior, splashing colour on what appeared at first glance to be a collection of old junk.

To the left of the door a full-sized covered wagon stood behind a model of a horse and a mannequin dressed in nineteenth-century clothes. A fully functioning Long Tom sluice box stood opposite with water trickling through it, making a sound like the roof was leaking. A collection of gold pans was arranged around it, beneath a sign saying '*Tools of the treasure hunter's trade*'. There were pickaxes too and fake sticks of dynamite and ore crushers and softly lit cabinets containing examples of copper ore and gold flake and silver seams in quartz. Another cabinet contained personal effects – reading glasses, pens, gloves – all carefully labelled and arranged, and there was a scale model of the town on a table showing what Redemption had looked like a hundred years ago. And right in the centre of the strange diorama a lectern stood, angled towards the door so that anyone entering the building was forced to gaze upon the battered Bible resting upon it.

Solomon walked forward, feeling the cold flagstones beneath

his feet. He could see the remnant of a lost page sticking out from the binding, its edge rough as if it had been violently torn from the book. The missing page was from Exodus, chapters twenty through twenty-one, where Moses brought God's ten holy laws down from the mountain on tablets of stone.

'The Church of Lost Commandments,' Solomon muttered, then continued onward into the heart of the church, breathing in the smells of the place: dust, polish, candle wax, copper, mould.

The commandments were everywhere: carved into the stonework and the wooden backs of the pews, inscribed into the floor in copper letters, even depicted in the stained glass of the windows. It was as if whoever had lost the page from the Bible had built the church in some grand attempt to make up for it. The altar lay directly ahead of him, the large copper cross standing on a stone plinth. As he drew closer he studied it, his eager eyes tracing the twisted lines and spars identical to the cross he wore around his neck, hoping for some jolt of recognition. But if he had ever been here before or stood and gazed upon this cross and this altar he couldn't remember it and he felt frustration flood into the place where his hope had been.

The church seemed gloomier here, as if the walls around the altar were made of darker material, and as he drew closer he saw the reason for it. The stonework, bright white in the rest of the building, was covered in dark frescoes. They depicted a desert landscape at night, populated with nightmarish creatures: hunched men and skeletal women; children with black and hollow eyes, their clothes ragged and tattered. Some rode starved horses with ribs sticking out from sunken hides, their eyes as hollow as their riders.

Beneath the ground, emerging from a vast, burning underworld, were demons with sharp, eager teeth and leathery wings that stirred the dust, and taloned hands that reached up through cracks in the dry land to grab at the wretched people above them. A few of the demons had snagged an arm or a leg and were gleefully dragging some poor soul down into the fire while their terrified eyes gazed up at the distant glow of a painted heaven. And there was something else, something moving in the shadows – a figure, pale and ghostly – walking out of the painted landscape towards him. It was his reflection, captured in a large mirror that had been positioned so that anyone looking at the fresco became part of what they observed. Either side of the mirror were two painted figures – an angel and a demon – gazing out of the picture, their eyes focused on whoever might stand and gaze into it.

Solomon moved closer until his reflection filled the frame. He studied his face. It was the first time he had seen himself properly and it was like looking at a picture of someone else. Nothing about his features was familiar, not his pale grey eyes nor his long, fine nose nor the scoops of his cheeks beneath razored cheekbones. He did not recognize the person staring back at him.

'Who are you?' he asked, and a loud bang echoed through the church as if in answer. Footsteps approached from behind a curtained area in the vestry and he turned just as the curtain swept open and he found himself facing a modern version of Jack Cassidy. They held each other's gaze for a moment, Cassidy's face a mixture of curiosity and suspicion as he looked him up and down, his eyes lingering on his shoeless feet. 'You must be Mr Creed,' he said, walking forward, hand extended. Solomon shook it and his mind lit up as he caught the hint of a chemical coming off him.

Napthalene – used in pyrotechnics, also a household fumigant against pests.

72

He saw a small frayed hole in the pocket of his jacket –
Mayor Cassidy smelled of mothballs. It was a dark suit, a
funeral suit. 'You just buried James Coronado,' Solomon said,
and pain flared in his arm again at the mention of his name.

Cassidy nodded. 'A tragedy. How did *you* know him?'

Solomon turned back to the painted landscape. 'I'm trying
to remember.'

There was something here, he felt sure of it, some reason
the cross around his neck had brought him to this place
where its larger twin sat.

'Impressive, isn't it?' Cassidy said, stepping over to the wall
and flicking a switch. Light faded up, illuminating the fresco
in all its dark and terrible detail.

There were many more figures populating the landscape than Solomon had first thought, their black arms and
shrunken bodies almost indistinguishable from the land, as
if they were made from the earth and still bound to it. The
ones with faces had been painted in such realistic detail that
Solomon wondered if each had been based on a real person,
and what those people had thought when they had seen themselves immortalized as the damned in this macabre landscape.
They seethed over the desert, their faces ghostly, their eyes
staring up at the too distant heaven. Solomon looked up too
and saw something he had missed when the fresco had been
sunk in shadow, something written in the sky, black letters on
an almost black background.

Each of us runs from the flames of damnation
Only those who face the fire yet still uphold God's holy laws
Only those who would save others above themselves
Only these can hope to escape the inferno and be lifted unto heaven

The brand on his arm flared in pain again as he read the words, bringing back the feeling he'd first felt back on the road, that he was here for a reason, that there was something particular he had to do.

Only those who would save others ... can hope to escape the inferno ...

'I'm here to save him,' he muttered, his hand rubbing at the burning spot on his arm.

'Who?'

'James Coronado.'

Cassidy blinked. 'You're ... but we just buried him.'

Solomon smiled. 'I didn't say it was going to be easy.'

A noise outside made them both turn, a siren howling past, heading somewhere in a hurry. Solomon could smell smoke leaking in through the open door.

The fire.

... Only those who face the fire ...

The whole town would be heading to the city limits now, preparing to defend their town from the oncoming threat. Most of them would have known James Coronado. Maybe his widow would be there too.

'Are you OK?' Cassidy asked, stepping closer. 'You seem a little shaken. Maybe you should head to the hospital, get yourself checked over.'

Solomon looked back at his reflection, trapped between the angel and the demon, their painted eyes looking at him as if asking: 'Which of us are you?'

Let's find out, Solomon thought, and the pain in his arm flared again.

He shook his head. 'I don't need the hospital,' he said. 'I need to go back to the fire.'

III

*'Thou shalt have no other
gods before me.'*

Exodus 20:3

RICHES AND REDEMPTION
THE MAKING OF A TOWN

⁂

The published memoir
of the Reverend Jack 'King' Cassidy

I ARRIVED AT FORT TUCSON with the priest's gold all but spent. To raise more funds – and to my eternal shame – I tried to sell the Bible to an itinerant preacher name of Banks who balked at the size of the book, saying if God had meant him to have such a thing He would have sent it in smaller form. He told me instead of a Jesuit mission south of Tucson where a fine old example of scripture might find a permanent home on some sturdy lectern where no poor soul nor mule would have to carry it more.

I blamed encroaching poverty on my decision to try and part with the Bible, but in truth I could feel the hold it had on me and I was frightened by it. The visions of the white church and the pale Christ on the cross haunted my waking hours now and I feared I might be losing my mind, as the priest had lost his. But setting it down now, it seems clear to me how all of this was God's design – the priest travelling from Ireland and finding himself in the bed next to mine, the Bible being signed over to me, the gold funding its journey west, and my chance conversation with the preacher who sent me on the path that would lead me to the Jesuit mission and the pale Christ on his burned cross.

We saw the smoke rising in the morning sky a couple of hours after sunrise on the second day. I had joined a cavalry supply train heading south to Fort Huachuca via the trading post where the Jesuit mission was based. We smelled them long before we saw them, poor murdered souls roughly delivered to God at arrow point or at the keen edge of a savage's knife. The trading post was an inferno, roof timbers sticking up from burning buildings like smoking ribs and a large burning cross standing by a pile of smouldering timbers that had been the Jesuit mission. At first I thought the cross and crucified figure of Christ upon it too large for such a humble chapel. It was only as we drew closer that I saw the truth. The burning man was real.

He blazed like a grotesque torch, all signs of identity razed from him, his head thrown back in agony and fire pouring from his open mouth as if his screams were made of flame.

Captain Smith, the officer in charge, ordered someone to throw a rope round him and drag the cross to the ground and away from sight, but no rope could ever drag the image of that burning man from my memory. I uttered a prayer, commending his immortal soul to God where it would be forever at peace and free from whatever demons had made their evil sport here. And when I finished I heard a murmur of 'Amens' around me and realized that my prodigal companions, normally so cavalier and contemptuous of God when in the warm embrace of a bottle or by the light of a campfire, were drawn straight back to His goodness and love when faced with this bleak and terrible example of its opposite.

We set to work smothering the smouldering church with shovels of dirt and I wondered how an all powerful and merciful God could allow such monstrous sport to be visited upon His faithful servants and lay waste to His own house of worship. I could see no purpose in it and wondered if, in the battle between God and the Devil, it was the Devil who had already won. It was only then, in the deepest depths of my doubt, that Christ Himself appeared to me, rising from the ashes of His father's ruined church to show me the way and the truth.

I saw His face first, shining white against the grey-black ashes. He was staring straight at me with an expression of such agony and anguish that I stumbled back in shock and my boot trod heavy on the charcoaled remains of a roof spar, which levered the thing up further and I saw it entire. It was the Christ crucified, carved from pure white marble and fixed to a cross of hard wood that had been burned by the fire but not destroyed.

I guessed from its position in the ruined church that it must have hung above the altar and I imagined how the Christ must have stared down in lament as flames consumed His father's house. It was a miracle the cross had survived, a miracle that I had found it, and I recalled the words of the raving priest as he had pressed the Bible into my hands and transferred his mission to me.

– You must carry His word into the wasteland. Carry His word and also carry Him. For He will protect you and lead you to riches beyond your imagining.

And here He was.

I walked into the smoking ruin of the church and

took the pale Christ in my arms – His cross now mine, my
burden now His. I could feel the trapped heat of the fire
radiating out of the solid wood and it felt like the warmth
of His love flowing into me and I realized then why God
had allowed the savages to slaughter good Christian folk
and burn His house to the ground.

It had all been for me.

He was showing me, in such a way as a simple soul
like mine could understand, that the church I had to build
must be stronger than this. If it was to stand against such
evil as thrived here in this blasted wilderness, it had to be
like the pale Christ who had been untouched by the fiery
instruments of evil that had destroyed all else.

The church I was to build had to be made of stone.

16

'He said we should stay right here?'

'That's what the man said.' Mulcahy was standing by the window of the motel, cell phone in hand, staring out through the grey sheer curtains at the parking lot beyond.

Behind him, Javier paced, stamping dust and the smell of mildew from the carpet. 'He didn't say nuthin' else?'

'He said plenty, but the main thing he said was that we should stay put and wait for him to call back.'

Javier shook his head and continued to pace. He'd already visited the john several times in the twenty or so minutes they'd been in the room and Mulcahy had only heard him flush once, suggesting either that he had terrible hygiene or he was doing something in there other than pissing. The slime-shine in his eyes gave Mulcahy a pretty good idea what.

'You think Papa knows where we're at?' Javier said, twitching and flicking his fingers as if they had gum on them.

'Probably.'

'Probably? The fuck does "probably" mean? Either he know or he don't.'

The only illumination in the room was coming from the TV. It was tuned to a local news station with the volume turned low. Carlos sat silently on the edge of one of the beds, his eyes fixed on the flickering screen as if he'd been hypnotized by it. He'd been like that ever since they'd walked in the door and heard what Papa Tío had to say. Mulcahy had seen that look a few times before: once in a jail cell outside of Chicago when he was still in uniform and Illinois still had the death penalty, and a couple of times since when he'd been the cause of it. It was the look someone got when they'd resigned themselves to whatever was coming their way, like a rabbit when the headlights were speeding towards it and there was no time to get out of the way.

'You got a cell phone, either of you?' Mulcahy asked.

'Yeah, I got a phone.' Javier said it like he'd just asked him if he had a dick or not. He held up a BlackBerry in a gold-and-crystal encrusted case, the blank screen angled towards Mulcahy. 'I switched it off though, motherfucker. I ain't stupid.'

'Good for you. Who pays the bill?'

'The fuck's that got to do with anything?'

'Because if Tío pays the bill then he'll be able to track it whether it's switched off or not. Does he pay the bill?'

Javier didn't answer, which was answer enough.

Mulcahy nodded. 'Then he knows where we're at.' He turned back and looked outside, squinting against the brightness. Beyond the reception building he could see the traffic out on the highway.

He checked his own phone, making sure the Skype app was still running. Tío had said he was going to call some people then call him back, but that wasn't why he was checking. His pop still hadn't called.

'How come your phone's still switched on, *pendejo*?'

Mulcahy stared out at the day, felt the heat of the outside burning through the window and the cool air from the ancient air-con unit blowing feebly against his legs.

'I asked you a question, motherfucker.'

He took a deep breath and let it out slowly. If he had to kill Javier in the next few minutes – which was entirely possible – it would definitely be the highlight of an otherwise shitty day. 'Papa Tío doesn't pay my bill,' he said. 'He doesn't pay my bill, so he doesn't know the number or the network, and I called him on Skype so it would take him at least a few hours to trace the call and I don't plan on being here in two hours' time. But the main reason I've still got it switched on is because he said he was going to call me back – on Skype – so if I switched my phone off he wouldn't be able to. And if he couldn't get hold of me he might get all suspicious and send a bunch of guys round to find out why I'd turned my phone off. And he'd know exactly where to find me because you're too cheap to pay your own bill. That answer your question … motherfucker?'

'Shit, man. Oh shit, shit.' Carlos was rising to his feet and pointing at the TV.

A shaky aerial shot of a big fire in the desert filled the screen. It wobbled unsteadily behind a caption saying: **BREAKING NEWS** – plane crash starts large wildfire outside Redemption, Az.

'Where's the remote?' Javier had stopped pacing, his eyes fixed to the screen now. 'Where's the fuckin' remote at?' Carlos held it up. 'Turn it up, man.' Javier jabbed his finger at the screen.

Carlos pointed the remote at the TV, nudged up the volume and the room filled with the sombre tones of someone reporting on something serious. Mulcahy stared at the twisted wreckage of the plane, fuel and desert burning all around it, catching snatches of what the reporter was saying:

… believed to have been a vintage airliner … en route to the aircraft museum outside Redemption …

This was not how it was supposed to happen. The plane crash was not in the script. It was most likely an accident, it was an old plane, old planes crashed more than new ones he imagined. Except Papa Tío didn't believe in accidents. He didn't believe in coincidences or apologies either. If something went wrong then there was always a reason and there was always someone who had to pay.

And Tío hadn't called back yet.

And neither had his pop.

He turned to study the traffic out on the road, a slow-flowing river of metal and glass, and felt envious of the safe little lives each car contained. He wanted to join them and slide away from here, but that wasn't going to happen. He knew that as soon as he saw the truck ease off the road and up the ramp towards the motel. It was a Jeep Grand Cherokee, just like his. Black-tinted windows, just like his. It slowed to a stop at the top of the ramp by the reception building, but the two men inside showed no interest in going in. They were checking the parked cars, looking for someone.

Looking for him.

17

Cassidy drove, Solomon sat in the passenger seat, his window wound right down so he could feel the wind on his face. It was an old car, leather seats, chrome trim, lots of space.

Lincoln Continental Mark V, Solomon's mind informed him.

It was nicer than being in the ambulance, the leather seats and padded doors made the experience less synthetic, but he still didn't like it.

'Would you mind closing the window, the air-conditioning doesn't work so well with it open.'

Solomon pressed the button to raise the window. He was thinking about the church and the altar cross and the words written on the wall, all of it revolving around the remembered image of his reflected self, the stranger in the mirror, the big mystery at the centre of it all. The church was peculiar. Maybe that was why he felt an affinity to it. For a start it was way too big for a town this size, like it had been built as a declaration of something grand or maybe to compensate for something. The interior was odd too, the fresco more reminiscent of a medieval European basilica than a church from the Old West. And then there was the strange collection of memorabilia cluttering up the entrance like an afterthought.

'Why have a mining exhibition in a church?' he wondered

out loud, his toes gripping the carpet as his sense of confinement started to gnaw at him.

'Tourists,' Cassidy replied, like he was cursing. 'About a year back we moved some of the exhibits from the museum into the church to try and get more people through the door, on account of people being far more interested in treasure than God these days, and ain't that a sorry state of affairs?'

Solomon nodded and gripped the edge of his seat, trying to relax away his growing nausea.

'A lot of folks thought it was inappropriate, said it's not what the church is for. They cash the subsidy cheques the trusts give out, but they don't want to think about where that money comes from. One of the joys of being mayor: all the grief and none of the credit. Like being a parent, I guess.'

'You don't have children?'

'Never was blessed. Are you OK? You seem kind of uncomfortable.'

'I'm fine,' Solomon said. 'Just don't like being confined.'

Cassidy looked across at him like he was afraid he might throw up in his nice antique car. 'Leave the window open if it makes you happy.'

'Thanks.' Solomon opened it all the way down again and relished the wind on his face. It carried the smell of smoke with it now and he could see it ahead of them, a curtain of darkness spreading right across the sky with tiny figures and vehicles spread out in front of it. 'Only those who face the fire,' he murmured, 'can hope to escape the inferno.'

'You know who wrote that?' Cassidy asked.

Solomon dredged his mind and was surprised to discover that he didn't. And in the perverse nature of his teeming brain he regarded any knowledge that didn't come easy to him as significant. 'No,' he said. 'No, I don't.'

'It was Jack Cassidy. He designed the whole church then painted the frescoes too. He was what you might call a renaissance man. Could turn his hand to anything: miner, businessman, architect, painter, author – you name it, he tried it. And most likely mastered it too. Not bad for a man who started life as a locksmith.'

'Quite a troubled man too, I think. A man with his fair share of demons.'

'Well, he … maybe so, but … what makes you say that?'

'The figures in the fresco. The black words he wrote on a dark, dark sky. The fact he painted hell so vast and vivid and heaven so small and distant.'

'He was complicated, I would say. A serious man. You should read his memoir.'

Solomon pulled his copy from his pocket and turned it over in his hand. 'I have.' He opened it to the dedication page, felt the familiar stab of pain in his arm when he read James Coronado's name. 'What about James Coronado, was he a troubled man?'

'Jim? No, I wouldn't say so. I would call him pretty straightforward.'

'Was he in some sort of trouble?'

'No.'

'You sure?'

'He was very well liked.'

'That's not what I asked. What about his death – is there any question hanging over that?'

'No,' Cassidy snapped, a little too quickly, then took a hold of himself. 'Listen, I don't know what ideas you have about how you might save him, but he's gone. Jim Coronado is dead. It was an accident, is all. A terrible, terrible accident. He was driving at night, he crashed his car. That's all there is. There ain't no point in raking up the mud searching for something that ain't there. You're only going to hurt people who been hurt bad enough already.'

He said it as though he was pushing a door closed and Solomon left it shut. The mayor clearly didn't want to talk about it and Solomon didn't think he'd get anything out of him anyway. The person he really wanted to talk to was James Coronado's widow. Maybe she would be at the city limits along with everybody else, lining up to try and save the town from the fire.

They rounded a corner and started dropping down towards the edge of town. Beyond it the whole world was on fire. The smoke was so high it blotted out the sun, and the flames at the base twisted and leaped in the air as the bright line of fire slithered closer. The fire crews were positioned half a mile out of town and about the same from the fire, working in lines, their forms smudged almost to nothing by the dust they were stirring up with rake and shovel as they cleared the ground of anything that might burn in an attempt to stop the flames from advancing. To the left of the road a tractor was creeping like a clockwork toy, plough-ing up the ground behind it. It was making its slow way towards a concrete storm drain that cut across the ground in a straight line all the way to the slopes of the mountains. To the right a grader was struggling over uneven terrain it wasn't built for towards the anaemic piles of crushed stone that rose sterile and ugly around a tall skinny tower with a lifting wheel at the top. Between the mineworks and the storm drain the flanks were pretty well protected, but there was nothing in the centre but a mile or so of clear ground and dry vegetation. Two vehicles and maybe a hundred men against an army of flame.

'You should tell everyone to clear out,' Solomon said.

'Be a waste of breath,' Cassidy replied. 'The folks here are kind of stubborn that way. Most of 'em would rather burn than abandon their town.'

'Then they may well get their wish.'

They pulled off the road and came to a halt next to a line of parked cars and trucks. Cassidy cut the engine and Solomon was already out of the door, desperate to feel the ground beneath his feet again. The wind gusted a greeting, roaring out of the desert and bringing the smell of the fire with it.

'Now I appreciate you volunteering to help here, Mr Creed, I really do,' Cassidy said, climbing out the driver's side and fixing his Stetson on his head. 'But if you want to help us fight this fire, then you're going to need something on your feet.' He pointed to a pick-up parked over by an ambulance that had lots of activity buzzing round it. 'See that man in the green shirt? His name's Billy Walker. Tell him I sent you over and ask if he's got a pair of work boots he can loan you, then report to one of the fire crews. Sorry to cut and leave, but I've got a town to try to save and people look to me to lead.' He walked away, heading over to where Chief Morgan was standing by a tow truck, his own stricken truck perched drunkenly on the back.

Shouts drifted out of the desert. Out on the control line someone was pointing up at the sky where the yellow tanker was levelling out and getting ready for another run. It settled into position and the sky behind it turned red, as though the wings had sliced through the flesh of it and made it bleed. A bright scarlet cloud spread and fell on to a section of desert, then the vapour trail sputtered out. The red line had covered a little less than a quarter of the leading edge of the fire on one side of the road and the air around Solomon was already starting to thicken with ash and embers falling softly around him like black snow. He held out his hand and caught one, rubbing it to nothing with his fingers. It was warm, most of the heat blown out of it by the wind, but the ashes falling closer to the control line would be fresh from the fire, maybe even still glowing as they settled on the dry grass. Soon there would be spot fires breaking out all over the control zone. It would only need one to take hold and the fire would have breached the thin line they were drawing in the sand. They were in the wrong position, wasting time and energy with what they were doing. At this rate the whole town was going to burn, along with everything in it. Then where would he be? What answers might he sift from the embers?

The wind roared again, twisting the distant flames into columns of orange and red, and Solomon felt as if the fire was sniffing him out, searching for him. He headed over to the ambulance and into the welcome shade of the billboard.

The man in the green shirt was helping set up a make-shift field hospital around the ambulance. Men and women in green scrubs and white rubber clogs were weaving in and out of each other, checking lists, carrying boxes of supplies, filling movable stands stacked with suture packs and dressings. Solomon recognized Gloria. She was unpacking boxes of gel dressings and FAST-1 infusion kits.

'Billy Walker,' Solomon said, and the man in the green shirt turned round. 'Mayor Cassidy sent me over to see you.'

The man looked him up and down, his eyes lingering on Solomon's bare feet. 'Lemme guess – pair of boots, right?'

'Actually no, I was hoping you might have a hat.' Walker shook his head then loped off towards his truck.

The wind surged again, so hard it rocked the billboard and drove the smell of smoke into Solomon's face like a threat.

There was something else there too, something ominous and familiar.

Gloria appeared at his side. 'You feeling OK now, Mr Creed?'

'I'm fine,' he said, sniffing the air again. 'How ready are you here?'

She looked around at all the activity. 'About as ready as we'll ever be, I guess.'

'Good. You're about to get busy, I think.' The sound of a distant siren whooped out in the desert and the radio in the ambulance crackled to life.

'Incoming,' a voice said with an urgency that made everyone else go silent. 'The grader got caught in a fire surge. The driver's hurt bad. We're bringing him to you now.'

18

Mulcahy's eyes never left the Jeep.

The angle of the sun and the tinted windows turned the two men inside into dark shapes. It was impossible to see if anyone was in back. There could be two or three more guys in there, but he doubted it. One maybe: two to do the job, one to stay in the car, ready to roll when it was done. He had a pretty good idea what the job was too. He guessed they were on the phone right now, talking to whoever had sent them. He had a pretty good idea about that too.

They were staring over in his direction, towards the parked Jeep. He wondered if they could see the movement of the curtain and thought about shutting the air-con off. If he did Javier would pick up on it and he didn't want him to know what was unfolding outside. He'd freak out most likely, start shooting and they'd end up in a siege situation which no one would walk away from.

The passenger door of the Jeep opened and a short, solid Mexican man slid out. He had a Mike Tyson style tattoo curling round his left eye and rolled his neck like a boxer preparing to spar as he sauntered over to the reception building, no doubt to ask the clerk about the Jeep parked over by G-block. Mulcahy imagined him walking up to the desk now and flashing some fake ID – FBI or Border Patrol. The clerk was probably illegal anyway and likely to freeze in the face of anything official. He would do whatever the guy asked, tell him whatever he wanted, even give him a master key. Except that wasn't what happened.

Tyson reappeared, walking fast, tucking something into his jacket and Mulcahy knew he had been wrong. All wrong. There had been no fake ID because there had been no need for one. He hadn't heard a gunshot but over this distance and with the TV noise he might have missed it. More likely they were carrying suppressed weapons. Assassination pieces.

Tyson climbed back into the Jeep and leaned over to talk to the driver. Then the Jeep started to move.

'Anyone want ice?' he said, moving towards the door, forcing himself not to hurry. 'I'm going to get a bucket and stick it on this shitty unit. Might cool us all down a little. Who knows how long we're going to be stuck here, right?' He placed the car keys down on the counter by the door and made sure Javier saw him do it.

Javier stared at them. 'Yeah, ice,' he said, like it was his idea. He sounded guarded, all the strut ground out of him by the flow of bad news from the TV, his face rippling with drug-tweaked tics and suspicion. He knew that being third cousin – or whatever the hell he was – was going to cut him zero slack in their current situation. Tío's relatives might get a leg up in the organization, but if they messed up they paid the same price as anyone. 'Don't be long,' he said, like he was in charge.

'Be right back,' Mulcahy said, looking out through the window in the door. He watched the Jeep make a right past the reception building and disappear from sight, then he opened the door in a burst of heat and sunlight, stepped outside and closed it quickly behind him.

He forced himself to saunter past the window because he knew Javier would be watching, his amphetamine-sharpened paranoia ready to catch the slightest whiff of haste. It would take ten seconds for the Jeep to clear the east side of the complex and swing back into view; he knew because he'd spent a whole afternoon on a previous stay timing cars, watching the sedans peel off the highway and work their tired way round the one-way system. But if the guys in the Jeep had left a body back at reception they'd be in more of a hurry to get this done and get out.

Call it five seconds.

The moment he cleared the window he took off, running smoothly and keeping low, past the ice-machine in the shadow of the stairwell, feeling in his pocket for a second set of keys.

Four seconds.

The lights flashed on a two-year-old white Chevy Cruze sedan parked near the end of the block, the backup vehicle he had intended to drive away in – the one he *still* intended to drive away in. It was America's third most popular car, painted in its favourite colour – utterly unremarkable, totally unmemorable, perfect. He glanced back toward C-block, at the spot where the Jeep would reappear. Still no sign.

Three seconds.

He reached the Chevy and moved along the passenger side, squeezing alongside a Pontiac that had parked too tight against it.

Two.

He grabbed the handle, opened the door and squeezed through the narrow gap and into the car.

One.

He fell into the seat and pulled the door shut, reached

down to the side, found the adjustment lever and tugged hard.

Zero.

He leaned back, throwing the seat almost flat and dropping from view just as the black shadow of the Cherokee appeared round the edge of the far building.

He lay there, taking deep breaths. Calming himself. Sweating. The Chevy had been parked out front for most of the day, soaking up the heat until the inside felt like a pizza oven.

The throaty rumble of the Cherokee's V8 engine drew closer. He could hear it through the thump of his heartbeat and the low whisper of the cars out on the highway. He tried to think himself into the minds of the two men, assuming it was only two. Tyson had already killed the desk clerk, so they were not about stealth and finesse, they were about speed and surprise, which meant they would most likely storm the room. Javier and Carlos would be dead before they even knew what was going down, but the crew would know they were looking for three men so would think he was in the bathroom. One of them would move fast through the smoke-filled room towards it, past the still figures of Carlos and Javier, leading with his gun, maybe firing to keep him pinned down while the other guy – or guys – covered. And that was when he would move. That was his best chance of getting out of this alive.

The Cherokee's wide wheels swept into a space seven or eight spots short of where he was lying. The engine cut out and there was the muffled clunk of doors opening then the double thud of them closing again at almost the same time.

Two doors. Two men. Maybe one still in the Jeep.

Mulcahy glanced down at the glove box. His Beretta was

stashed inside, along with loaded magazines and a sound suppressor. He dearly wanted to feel the comforting weight of it in his hand but he didn't dare reach for it in case the car moved and someone saw it.

He pictured them outside, walking toward the grey door of room 22. They would be reaching into their jackets, pulling their hands out high to clear the long barrels of their silenced weapons. The lead man would take the key, stolen from the front desk, and fit it in the lock. The other would stay high, checking behind before taking a step away from the wall to get a better angle. He would level his gun at the door, give a nod – then …

There was a loud bang as the room door flew open, then a shout cut short by the staccato taps of rounds hitting thin walls and furniture and everything else in the room.

Mulcahy reached forward, keeping his head below the window. He yanked open the glove box, grabbed the sunglasses case and the duster the gun was wrapped in, then popped his door open and rolled back out onto the narrow strip of hot tarmac between the Chevy and the Pontiac.

The popping of suppressed gunfire stopped and he heard the sound of the TV drift out through the open door. He tipped the gun and a spare magazine from the duster into his hand, stuffed the clip in his back pocket then took the suppressor out of the sunglasses case and fixed it to the barrel of the gun.

The men would be checking the room now, making sure the two men were down. Then they would start searching for the third.

He checked the suppressor was secure, flipped the safety off with his thumb and started making his way round the back of the Chevy, keeping low, heading towards the Jeep the

Mexicans had arrived in. The blackened glass made it hard to see inside but there was no one in the driver's seat and the engine wasn't running. Two then. You always left the driver behind in a three-man team. He reached the dusty Buick, peered round the edge of it.

The driver was standing inside the open door to the room. He had his back to him, the material of his jacket stretched tight across his shoulders suggesting he was holding a pistol in a double grip. Mulcahy moved forward, keeping low, aiming centre mass, the best percentage shot given the distance and added inaccuracy of a silenced weapon. He couldn't see into the room but he imagined Tyson would be at the bathroom door now, ready to kick it in and spray rounds into the room. He kept on moving, increasing his odds of a clean shot with every step. Then he heard a voice from inside, a voice he recognized.

'He went that way.' Carlos pushed past the driver and pointed along the block where Mulcahy had headed. 'Said he was gettin' ice.'

He had a gun in his hand, an un-silenced Glock. It *was* a three-man team after all.

Mulcahy re-sighted on Carlos's chest just as his eyes swung round and spotted him. The Glock rose fast but not fast enough. Mulcahy squeezed off two rounds and Carlos twitched twice and spiralled to the ground.

The driver spun round, swinging the long barrel of his pistol to where the shots had come from. Mulcahy hit him with two shots in the chest that knocked him backwards into the room, leaving him half in and half out of the door.

Mulcahy was already moving forward, firing as he went, spreading his shots left, right, level and low, hoping to clip Tyson with at least one of them, or keep him pinned down until he was in the room. He passed through the doorway, stepping over the driver and opened his eyes wide to adjust for the dark interior.

Javier was lying dead in the far corner, a smear of blood on the wall behind him. No sign of Tyson. Mulcahy dropped down to the side, behind the bed, making use of its limited cover. He kept his gun and eyes on the bathroom door.

The TV cast a flickering light into the dark of the room and the modulated tones of the news report filled the silence. Mulcahy listened through it for breathing, or the snick of a gun being reloaded. He thought about shooting out the TV so he could hear better but he had already used ten rounds and his Beretta only held eleven. He needed to reload but Tyson might know that and be waiting in the bathroom, listening out for the *snick* of a magazine release, ready to capitalize on the few seconds Mulcahy would be unarmed.

He glanced at the two men sprawled in the doorway: Carlos on his back, his eyes open and staring up at the water-stained ceiling; the driver lying across him, legs sticking out the door where anyone could see them. He needed to get him inside and out of sight but couldn't risk it until Tyson was dealt with. He reached for the spare magazine and switched his attention back to the far end of the room.

There was no blood around the bathroom door or on the white tiles of the kitchenette, and if he'd clipped him there should be. He would expect to hear something too, the laboured breathing of someone fighting pain and going into shock. There was always the chance he had killed him outright and the impact had spun him into the bathroom, but he didn't believe in luck and he knew better than to rely on it. He'd seen too many people lying dead with looks of surprise on their faces.

He held the spare magazine up in front of him and sighted on a spot by the bathroom door, four feet up and a foot away from the wall. He took a deep breath to steady his breathing, blew it out slowly then moved his thumb across to the magazine release button and pressed it.

The magazine slid cleanly out with a distinctive *snicking* sound, a blur of movement appeared in his sights and Mulcahy fired his last bullet. He dropped down, rolled on to his side, jammed the fresh magazine into the empty slot then flicked the safety off and peered through the gap between the base of the bed and the floor. Through the twisted condom wrappers and dust bunnies he could make out a dark shape over by the bathroom door, dragging itself across the floor towards a gun lying on the tiles a few feet away.

Mulcahy sprang up, swinging the Beretta round as he cleared the top of the mattress. He fired two rounds. The first caught Tyson between his shoulders in a puff of white padding and pink mist. The second hit him in the back of the head and sent a small section of his skull spinning across the tile to the far wall. Mulcahy waited until it stopped spinning then moved to the centre of the room. He grabbed the remote from the bed and muted the sound on the TV so he could hear sirens or anything else heading his way. He tossed his gun on the bed and hauled Carlos inside first, dumping him next to Javier before grabbing the arms of the driver. He was heavier than Carlos and he had to tug hard to get him moving. Something cracked in the man's chest and a yelp of pain squeaked out of him.

Mulcahy dropped the man's arms like they were snakes, grabbed his Beretta from the bed and pointed it down at the driver. Blood was leaking out of a chest wound that was gently rising and falling. He was breathing.

The driver was still alive.

19

The ambulance screamed to a halt in the shade of the billboard and medics and doctors swarmed around it. Everyone else stood back, grimly fascinated by what would emerge from inside and frightened at the same time.

Solomon knew what was coming. The strangely familiar smell of charred flesh had already told him. It warned him exactly how bad it was going to be too. The siren cut out and was replaced by a howl that came from inside the ambulance.

'Here –' Billy Walker appeared at his side and handed Solomon a starter cap, his attention fixed on the ambulance. 'Best I could do. Got you some boots too.'

'Thank you.' Solomon took them and inspected the cap. It had a red flower logo and the name of a weedkiller on it. He pulled it over his head, folding the peak round with his hands until he was looking at the ambulance through an arc of shadow.

'You should use this too –' Walker handed him a tube of heavy-duty sunscreen squeezed almost empty.

The howl doubled in volume with the opening doors and there was a clatter of tubular steel as a man, or what remained of one, was pulled from the ambulance. He lay twisted and charred on starched white sheets, his whole body shaking, his hands baked to talons by furnace heat and clawing at the smoke-filled air above him while the inhuman noise howled from the seared ruin of his throat.

'Jesus,' Walker said, his voice flat with horror. 'I think that's Bobby Gallagher. He was driving the grader.' The medics wheeled the gurney to a covered area and doctors clustered round him. 'You reckon they can save him?'

Solomon squeezed sunblock from the tube and rubbed some on to his neck and the back of his hands, disliking the greasy feel of it but disliking the growing itch of sunburn even more. 'Not a chance,' he said.

Bobby Gallagher stared up at the ring of faces crowding over him. Worried eyes stared down.

A doctor leaned in, his face filling his vision. His mouth was moving but he couldn't hear what he was saying. Too much noise. Someone screaming close by. Someone in pain. At least he didn't feel nuthin'. That was good, wasn't it? Surely that was a good thing.

A penlight snapped on, shining in his eye and making the world turn bright and milky, like everyone was wrapped in white smoke ... smoke ...

The fire ...

He had seen the flames curling towards him, the desert writhing in heat like the surface of the sun. The fire running alongside him, chased by the wind, leaping from shrub to shrub like a living thing. Never seen fire race so fast, faster than that old grader, that was for sure, but not as fast as that Dodge he'd had his eye on, the silver-grey one with the smoked windows and the V8 under the hood. That would have evened the race out some. Would have bought it too, taken the hit on the finance and all, if he hadn't been saving for something else. He wanted to see old man Tucker's face at summer's end when he cashed in all the extra shift hours he was pulling and slipped that big ole ring on to Ellie's finger. Eighteen-carat yellow-gold band with a one-carat, heart-cut diamond right in the centre: three and a half grand cold, every cent he had in the world and all of it for Ellie – fuck old man Tucker, the way he treated him, like he wasn't good enough to even speak his daughter's name.

The penlight snapped off and the doctor leaned in, his mouth moving again, everything slow like he was underwater. Still couldn't hear a damn thing, what with that howling. He'd heard something like it before and the memory of it needled into making him shake with more than cold.

When he was eight his daddy had taken him hunting. They'd tracked a big old mule deer out into the desert for almost three hours and when they caught up with it his daddy had handed him the rifle. It was that old Remington, the one that hung above the fire with the walnut stock worn smooth at the neck by the bristled cheeks of his daddy and his daddy before that: beautiful rifle, but heavy, and tight on the trigger.

Maybe it had been the weight of it or the excitement of being handed something he'd only ever seen in a man's hand before, but when he beaded up on that big old bull his heart had pounded so hard he felt sure the deer must be able to hear it even with him two hundred yards away. It had lifted its head and sniffed the air, its haunches tightening as it readied to run. He snatched the shot just as it moved, missed the heart and punched a hole right through its belly. Gut shot or not, that thing took off, blood pumping out all over the desert, innards flyin' out behind it like streamers. His daddy said nothing, just grabbed that rifle back and took off after it, carrying it as easy in his hand as it had sat so heavy in his.

The blood trail was wet and bright against the dry orange earth. And the deer howled as it ran, a great bellowing noise, like fury and pain mixed together. Ever after, when he sat on the hard wooden pews in the cool dark of the church and heard the reverend deliver his 'hell and damnation' sermons he would remember that noise. It was like he imagined hell must sound, the echoing tormented howl of a soul trapped deep underground – the same thing he was hearing now.

The doctor leaned in again, swimming down through the milky air. He still couldn't catch what he was saying. He tried to tell him he couldn't hear above the howling, managed to snatch a ragged breath and the noise stopped. He made to speak and it started up again even louder than before, so loud he could feel it deep within his chest. Then he realized where the sound was coming from, and began to cry.

They had caught up with the deer not so far up the track from where he'd shot it, down on its front knees like it was praying. He wanted to shoot it and put it out of its pain, but his daddy had the gun and he daren't ask him for it. They stood a ways back, watching it trying to get up and run, eyes rolling in its skull, and that awful sound coming out of it. He had turned to look away but his daddy put his hand on the top of his head and twisted it back round again.

You need to watch this, he'd said. *You need to watch this and remember. This is what happens when you don't do a thing right. This is what happens when you fuck somethin' up.*

The jolt of him cussing like that, his best-suit-on-a-Sunday daddy who he'd never even heard say 'damn' before that day had been more shocking than the sight of the dying deer or the noise it made while it was about it.

I'm sorry, Daddy, he whispered now, and the faces moved closer as the howl took the rough form of his words.

I think he's calling for his daddy, the doctor said.

Bobby, we're doing everything we can for you, OK? Just hang in there.

He had been trying to steer away from the fire but the damn grader could only run over the flat land and the contours had kept him too close. He'd seen a place to turn ahead of him and he'd kept his eyes focused on it, too focused to notice the wall of flame sweeping in from his left. He could have jumped and run but he didn't. He knew they needed the grader to draw the fire line and help save the town. Might be old man Tucker would show him some respect if he came out of this a hero.

The heat had closed round him like a fist, the skin on his knuckles bubbling where they curled around the wheel. He'd kept his eyes ahead of him and his foot on the gas, holding his breath like he was deep underwater and kicking for the surface. He'd known that if he breathed in, the flames would get inside him and he would drown in that fire, so he had held on, thoughts of Ellie and diamond rings running through his head until he reached the turn and steered the grader away and out of the fire. He didn't remember much else.

He looked up into the doctor's face now and realized that the fact he could feel no pain was actually a very bad thing. He didn't care for himself. It was Ellie he felt bad for. Maybe old man Tucker was right, maybe she was better off without him. He had spent his life running away from that sound, the sound of failure and pain, and now it was coming out of him.

I'm sorry, he said, *I messed up. I messed it all up.*

Then the pale man stepped into view.

20

Mulcahy moved to the door, keeping as far from the wounded driver as he could. He checked outside, scanning the parking lot and all the curtained windows to see if any were twitching.

Nothing.

He closed the door. Pulled the heavy drapes across the window then turned his attention back to the man on the floor.

The driver was lying on his back, lit by the glow from the TV, the flickering-fire images making it appear he was smouldering. He moaned softly, a slow creaking sound that came from somewhere deep inside him. His hands clutched at his chest wound, working at the sodden material of his shirt and squeezing foamy blood between his fingers. A second wound oozed in his gut, soaking his shirt further, the blood looking black in the darkness of the room.

Mulcahy crouched down, keeping his gun pointed at the man's head. 'Hey,' he said, 'can you hear me?' The man's eyes opened a little. 'What's your name?'

The driver's lips pulled back in a grimace. 'Luis,' he said through bloodied teeth.

'Hi, Luis, I'm Mike. Listen, I'm not going to dick you around and tell you everything's going to be fine, because it's not. You've been hit in the chest and the stomach and you're bleeding out fast. The good news is the blood loss won't kill you, but that's only because the stomach acids leaking into your body cavity or the blood filling your lungs will get you first. But if you get medical help in the next ten minutes or so I reckon you have a pretty good chance of surviving.' He took his phone from his pocket and held it where Luis could see it. 'You want me to call an ambulance, Luis?'

Luis shivered like he was cold, though the room was hot from the door standing open so long. He managed another nod.

'Good.' Mulcahy leaned down. 'Then tell me who sent you.'

Luis closed his eyes tight and a groan wheezed from his throat. He took a breath and the wound made a slurping sound as it sucked air. 'Fuck you,' he said, then pain clamped his mouth shut again.

Mulcahy nodded slowly. 'Look at you. Big strong guy, sucking up the pain, keeping it together in the face of death. It's impressive, really. Impressive but pointless. Because if you don't talk to me you'll die right here in this room and I'll put the word out that you talked anyway. So you can either talk and live a little longer, maybe a lot longer, or you can hang tough, stay silent and die right here for nothing.'

Luis stared out through the wet slits of his eyelids, weighing up what Mulcahy had said. Mulcahy knew from the many situations he'd been in before that they had reached a tipping point, the moment when a subject would decide to talk or clam up for good. Sometimes the best thing to do was shut up and let the subject slide into talking; other people needed a little help, one last nudge to push them over on to the side of cooperation. The trick was knowing what sort of person you were dealing with. Luis was clearly the strong silent type, a man of few words, probably the sort who was happy to stay silent while others did the talking. So that's exactly what Mulcahy did.

'Tell you what,' he said, speaking low and intimate. 'I'll say a name and you nod if it's the right one, OK? That way if you get out of this alive and anyone asks, you can tell them you never talked and you won't be lying.' Luis's eyes were starting to glaze. In a minute or two he wouldn't be able to say anything at all. 'Was it Tío? Did Papa Tío send you?'

Luis didn't move. He just kept staring through the slits of his eyes.

'You hear what I said: did Papa Tío send you?'

Luis took a sucking breath, closed his eyes against the pain, then shook his head, a slow movement that made him screw his eyes tight with the effort.

Mulcahy sat back on his heels and glanced over at Carlos lying nearby, a surprised expression on his dead face. Ever since Carlos had appeared in the doorway with a gun in his hand he had suspected Papa Tío was not behind this. Tío would never trust a stranger over a blood relative for something like this.

He turned back to Luis to try a new name on him but saw it was already too late. The man's eyes had rolled back into his head, his mouth opening and closing but the wound in his chest no longer sucking. He was drowning or suffocating, trying to breathe but getting nothing. He breathed out one last rattling breath and his mouth went slack. Mulcahy pressed two fingers into his neck and felt nothing.

He lifted Luis's left arm and pulled the sleeve of his jacket back as far as it would go. His left forearm was almost entirely covered by a large, colourful tattoo of Santa Muerte

– the saint of death – her grinning skeletal face framed by the hood of a long robe, her bony hands holding a globe and a scythe. This told him nothing; plenty of Mexican gang members had tattoos of Santa Muerte – but his right arm told a different story.

The wrist was encircled by a barbed-wire design, showing Luis had served jail time, and above it was a carefully inked column of Roman numerals – one to four – next to the outline of a gun with the barrel pointing down towards the hand. It showed that Luis was a shooter, a dedicated hit man for the cartels, and the numerals showed how many high-level hits he had carried out. There were notches on the barrel too: fifteen marks scratched into the skin with a needle and ink showing lesser kills, soldiers and civilians taken out in the usual course of business and recorded in a casual way that reflected their lesser importance. They reminded Mulcahy of the mission decals he'd seen on the planes earlier – same principle, different war. Only one gang used Roman numerals to record their high-level kills, a nod to the Catholic faith they professed to defend and honour: the Latin Saints – Papa Tío's main rivals.

Mulcahy took his phone from his pocket to take a photo and saw he had one message – Pop: Missed Call. He breathed a little easier when he read it. Once he was clear of this mess he'd call him back, but first he had to clean up.

He took a picture of Luis's forearm then checked to make sure it was in focus. The first three numerals were solid black but the fourth was only an outline, ready to be inked once the hit had been carried out. There was only one person who would warrant the high status of a numeral and it wasn't him or Javier.

It all made sense now – Carlos being the insider instead of Javier. Carlos wasn't the hit man, he was a plant, a human homing beacon with his phone transmitting their location to the real kill crew. That's why he had been so edgy. He had known what was coming. He was probably only doing it to pay off some debt, betraying one set of killers to appease another and trading one shitty situation for a slightly less shitty one. Mulcahy knew all about that kind of deal. He slid his phone back into his pocket and rose to his feet.

He worked quickly by the flickering glow of the TV, pulled the duster from his back pocket and wiped down all the places he'd touched since entering the room. He took a few more pictures then grabbed Javier's gold- and jewel-encrusted phone and a plastic laundry sack from the closet and started collecting the guns.

Luis and Tyson had both been carrying FN Five-sevens, known as *Mata policiers* or cop killers because of their ability to penetrate body-armour. They had two spare magazines each in their jacket pockets and almost a thousand dollars in cash. He found the keys to the other Jeep in Luis's pocket and took those too. Javier had a knife tucked inside his boot. Mulcahy dropped it into the sack with the rest of the weapons, twisted it closed then pulled his phone from his pocket, found the missed call message and selected 'recall'.

He stood by the door a moment, scanning the room and checking it over for anything he might have overlooked. His eyes settled on the TV screen where the desert still burned. A reporter was talking about the plane crash that had caused it. The strap beneath him said they were getting reports of a possible survivor. Mulcahy took an involuntary step forward, not quite believing what he was reading, then the phone clicked and someone picked up.

'Hello,' a voice said. It was not his father.

21

Solomon looked down at the burned man on the stretcher.

The medics were still trauma focused: elevating the blackened horror of his legs, taking his temperature with a non-contact digital thermometer, covering him with sterile sheets to prevent heat-loss and hypothermia, talking to him the whole time, telling him he was doing OK, telling him to hang in there, that they were going to airlift him to some specialist unit in Maricopa. They were too preoccupied to notice Solomon standing there, a stranger in their midst. But the burned man saw him. He stared directly up through milky eyes that might once have been pale blue.

The vitreous liquid in the human eye is protein, Solomon's mind told him. *When you heat it up it goes white like a boiled egg.*

He surveyed the wreckage of the man, his blackened body curling into a foetal position, the result of muscle contraction caused by intense heat. The medics were cutting away what was left of his clothes before the cooked flesh beneath swelled too much and turned them into tourniquets.

Solomon held the man's eyes and smiled. The smell of him was overpowering, an almost sweet, burnt barbecue smell of human flesh, so reminiscent of pork that in some cannibalistic tribes, humans were referred to as *long pigs*. He reached out and gently took one of the blackened stumps of the man's hands, his own perfect white skin making the ruined claw seem all the more tragic in contrast.

'Hey!' the voice came sharp and angry. 'Step away right now! Do not touch the patient.'

Solomon gripped the man's hand more firmly, knowing it would cause him no pain. He could feel the splits in the baked skin and see distal phalanx bones poking out through the charred, dead flesh of his finger ends. Such acute damage would have destroyed all the nerve endings so he would never feel pain or indeed anything in this hand ever again. But he held it anyway in such a way that the burned man could see it, even if he couldn't feel it.

'You need to step aside, sir.'

'What you're doing is a waste of time,' Solomon said, his eyes never leaving the burned man's face.

'I'll be the judge of whether I'm wasting my time or not.'

'I wasn't talking about your time,' Solomon said, 'I was talking about his.'

Morgan stepped up behind him and laid a heavy hand on Solomon's arm. 'You need to let go and step away from here, let the doctors get on with their jobs.'

'You know the rule of nines, I assume?' Solomon asked the doctor.

'Excuse me?'

'The rule of nines – you assign a factor of nine to different areas of the body to quickly assess the severity of burn trauma.'

'I know what the rule of nines is.'

'And have you applied it to this patient?'

'Mr Creed,' Chief Morgan said. 'I ain't gonna ask you again.'

'Wait,' the doctor said, regarding the man on the stretcher afresh. His arrival had been so fast that he had clicked into autopilot, falling back on his core training, checking the patient's airway, his breathing, making sure his legs were elevated and he was getting fluids. There wasn't much else he could do; they weren't set up for serious burns trauma. He was only doing what he could to stabilize him before sending him on to the specialist unit. He turned to Chief Morgan. 'It's OK,' he said. 'We're OK here.'

Morgan looked like he had just been slapped, but removed his hand from Solomon's shoulder and stepped away.

'How do you know the rule of nines?' the doctor asked, turning to Solomon.

'I don't know,' Solomon said, all his concentration fixed on the eyes of the man whose ruined hand he held.

The man looked down at him, his eyes dove grey, his skin and hair white as clouds. He looked so extraordinary that Bobby wondered if he was imagining him. But the doctor spoke and the man answered with a soft voice that sounded like it was coming from a long way off then smiled down at him and took his hand, and leaned down until his face was all Bobby could see.

You are close, he said with that soft, calm voice. *You know what I mean by that?*

Bobby tried to nod but his neck was too stiff. Stiff as wood.

The man tilted his head to the side, like he'd spotted something curious in him.

Are you afraid?

Bobby turned the question over in his mind like he was checking the blade of his knife. He did feel a little afraid, but not out-and-out scared like he had been at different times in his life, like when his mom told him she had cancer and was going to die and there wasn't a thing anyone could do about it. The thing he felt most was regret. He regretted he would never see Ellie again, or be there to help guide her through life. He regretted he would not be there to hold her and tell her it was OK when she heard the news of what had happened to him, stupid as that sounded.

It was too fast.

The pale man leaned in closer, turning his head to catch the whisper of his words.

What was too fast?

Something in the fire. Something alive. Tell her I'm sorry. Tell her it's all right. Tell her she'll be all right. Tell her …

Tell me her name, the man said. *I'll tell her she was in your thoughts and that hers was the last name you spoke.*

The voice was like warm water being poured over his head.

Ellie Tucker, he said, and a shiver ran through him that made the gurney shake. He wanted to close his eyes but he didn't want to stop staring at the man either. There was something compelling about him, like staring into deep water. He didn't feel afraid any more and he didn't feel sad either. He felt like he was weightless and this man was the only thing stopping him from floating up into the sky.

I'm sorry, Ellie, he said again. Then he closed his eyes – and let go.

IV

UNKNOWN SOLDIER:
'General, all Arizona needs is some good people and more water.'

GENERAL SHERMAN:
'Son, that's all hell needs.'

Apocryphal

Extract from

**RICHES AND REDEMPTION
THE MAKING OF A TOWN**

✢

*The published memoir
of the Reverend Jack 'King' Cassidy*

WE ARRIVED AT FORT HUACHUCA less than a day after departing the ruins of the burned church, such was our haste to quit that place and arrive at the other. Here I spent three days and the last of the dead priest's coin gathering what provisions I needed for my onward expedition into the vast southern desert where I believed great riches awaited me.

I purchased dry food and as many extra canteens as my pack mule could carry, and a map showing the known and charted terrain to the south of the fort. The map had waterholes marked upon it and Sergeant Lyons, the quartermaster there, spoke all hugger-mugger as he removed it from a niche beneath the table that served as his shop counter, touching the side of his nose all the while and looking about him as if he feared discovery. The chart was army property, he said, and therefore not rightly his to sell to civilians. I parted with my last ten dollars to secure it and considered it a bargain, for water is worth more than gold to a man in the desert in want of it and I knew I would need to fill my canteens with more than prayer.

I waited for the next full moon, intending to slip away in the night and avoid the heat of the day and any eyes that might be watching the fort. I spent my time re-reading the marked passages in the Bible and staring south at the vast empty land beyond the stockade walls, though what I was searching for I knew not. The only directions I had, if you would call them such, was a small drawing in the priest's hand on the back page of the Bible – a picture of crossed sabres with an arrow pointing south and a verse from Deuteronomy beside it:

"He found him in a desert land, and in the waste howling wildernesse: He ledde him about."

I took the sabres to mean the fort, the crossed swords being the symbol of the cavalry. The rest I supposed to be a test of my faith, or maybe of my sanity.

I set out shortly after midnight on the first day of the new-minted month – All Fool's Day, a fitting day upon which to begin my fool's errand. The night was as frozen as the day had been molten and I had my blankets wrapped about me for extra warmth. My pack animal was laden with all my other supplies save for the cross and the Bible. These I carried myself, for they were my compass and my guide and, I believed, my protection against whatever evil awaited me.

A group of prospectors watched me leave. They were squatted on the ground close by the sentry hut, huddled around a fire they had built to keep away the cold and the darkness and to light the patch of ground where their dice rolled. They had been drinking, passing the whiskey round and gambling away fortunes they had yet to find.

Their faces seemed grotesque in the flickering firelight, like cathedral gargoyles come to life, and the sight of them, huddled over their orange fire, sent a chill through me to rival the one nature had already sent.

'There goes Jesus,' a man shouted as I waited for the guard to open the main gate, pointing at the plaster figure on the cross I carried slung across my back where most men would bear a shotgun or a rifle. I recognized the voice as belonging to a Scotch man named Garvie, one of the group I had travelled in with, a man who liked a crowd when in drink and his own company when not. He was holding court royally now. 'Ye'll not find God oot there, Preacher man,' he said, which shook a rattle of laughter out of the others. 'All ye'll find are demons and hell and damnation.'

I walked out with the sound of laughter at my back, feeling the weight of the cross pressing down on me and clutching my Bible to my chest, shaking with far, far more than the desert's chill.

It was on the second week of my trek, with water supplies starting to run low, that I began to follow the map Sergeant Lyons had sold me. The directions were vague, distances measured in days' rides rather than miles, but there were certain features that corresponded to the terrain around me and I followed a low ridge to the east that ran due south like a long, brittle spine pushing up beneath the dry skin of the land. The map showed two high peaks rising above it and a river running betwixt them down to a stand of trees with a cross marked beside them showing where a well was to be found. I could see the twin peaks shimmering in the far distance and made my steady way towards them.

After several hours of travel I came across a dry river-bed with cart tracks running along the centre of it. I followed their course with my eyes and saw that they wound their way up the rising ground east towards the peaks, the same place I was headed. The tracks appeared fresh, the sharp edges of the ruts not yet blunted by the grit-filled wind that scoured the land. They were deep too, even though the ground was baked and hard compacted, suggesting the wagon was exceptionally heavy laden. I figured it must have passed this way no more than a day ahead of me, possibly less, and my heart lifted at the prospect of meeting another human soul out there in that lifeless wilderness. I steered my mule between the twin wheel ruts, glad of the small degree of order created by this narrow, man-made path in the middle of nature's chaos and started to follow the cart.

It was by this measure that I realized the wagon had started to sway in transit, gently at first then to an increasingly marked degree as it continued on its way. The riverbed was wide and flat and easy to cut a straight path along and yet the tracks suggested the wagon was following some unknown course of its own, as if, during its journey, it had been forced to negotiate obstacles that I could not see or were no longer there.

After an hour or so of following the increasingly erratic path of the wagon I spied a curious object ahead of me, lying between the wavering wagon tracks. It was a wire birdcage, finely made and painted white, the like of which you would find in the parlour of a genteel hotel or on the end of the bar at one of the more exotic city saloons. It was lying on its side, dented by the fall, the cage door open with no sign of a bird inside save for some downy feathers sticking to the wire hinge of the open door.

It was an odd thing for a prospector to own and so I concluded he must not be travelling alone. I fancied the birdcage must belong to his wife and he had indulged her desire to bring it with her as some small comfort and reminder of the home they had left behind. I supposed the jostling of the cart had shaken the birdcage loose and it must have fallen unheeded. I leaned down as I passed by, the mule being close enough to the ground for me to scoop it up without stopping. I had a mind to return it to its owner once I caught up with the wagon, and imagined the happiness its restoration would bring to someone who had valued it enough to bring it this far into the wilderness.

But such happiness was not to be. For the dented cage was not the only thing I found on the track.

22

'Hello?' the voice said again in accented English.

Mulcahy gripped the phone and heard something crack inside it. 'Let me speak with my father.'

There was a pause, followed by handling noise as the phone was passed over. He could smell the metallic tang of blood in the air, mingling with the mildew and the dust. He was sweating hard now, the phone damp and slippery in his hand.

'The hell's goin' on here, Mikey?' His pop's voice was full of piss and vinegar but he could hear the fear in it. He also sounded echoey, so he was probably on speakerphone and the crew who had him were listening in – a crew like the one lying dead all around him with kill tags on their arms.

'Just take it easy, Pop, OK?' he said, his eyes fixed on the news. 'I got it covered.'

'Don't seem that way from where I'm standing.'

'Let me talk to the main guy for a second.'

'You in some kind of trouble here, Michael?'

Mulcahy closed his eyes and shook his head. It was typical of his father to assume that he must have messed up in some way and all this was his fault. He had done the same thing back when he had first fallen into bed with the cartels to stop them chopping his father into small pieces, somehow managing to twist it round so it felt like just another example of his failings as a cop, a person and a son. 'No, Pop,' he said. 'I'm good. Some people getting the wrong idea is all. Hand the phone back over. I'll take care of it.'

More handling noise, then the man who wasn't his father came back on the line. It didn't sound echoey any more.

'He doesn't get hurt,' Mulcahy said.

'Oh really?' There was a pause then he heard a yelp in the background and his phone cracked again as he squeezed it hard. 'You don't get to give no orders,' the Mexican said. 'You understand?'

Mulcahy's mind sped through his options like a racing driver approaching a corner too fast. The Saints wouldn't have known where to find his father, which meant these must be Tío's men, an insurance move to make sure he stayed loyal.

'OK,' he said. 'I don't give orders. But I know who does, so here's what I'm going to do. I'm gonna call Tío right now, I'm gonna call him and straighten this out, then I'll get him to call you back, all right? So just hang tight and give me ten minutes.'

He hung up before the man could say anything or hit his father again to show him who was in charge. He already knew who was in charge and didn't need some cold-eyed psychopath beating on his dad to prove it. He also figured they'd only hurt Pop if he was listening, so the quicker he got off the phone the better for everyone.

Ten minutes.

He peered through a crack in the curtains, squinting against the daylight to check there was no one outside, then wiped his prints from the door and went out, clutching the laundry sack full of weapons.

The day was still burning but it felt cooler after the stifling room. He headed over to the Jeep the Mexicans had arrived in, unlocking it with the key he'd taken from the dead driver. He opened the passenger door and checked the glove box. There were two more loaded magazines inside and a box of shells. He added them to his sack. The rest of the car was clean and professional: no personal items, no empty drink cans or food wrappers, nothing that could harbour DNA traces or fingerprints in the event they needed to dump the Jeep and run. It looked and smelled like it had been recently collected from an airport rental lot, which it probably had. The constant vacuuming and cleaning a rental went through was a pretty effective way of getting someone else to cover your tracks, and the residual soup of accumulated forensic matter acted like a smokescreen, hiding anything left behind by even the most careful of criminals.

He moved to the rear of the vehicle, listening out for sirens. He had a hunch about the trunk and when he popped it he saw he'd been right. It contained a car battery booster pack and a large square bag made from heavy-duty green plastic. Inside the bag was a set of electric jump cables, two plastic dust sheets, some padded leather garden gloves, rolls of Duck Tape, some pliers, and a bag of cable ties. To the casual observer it would look like someone had been getting supplies for a weekend of home improvement projects. To Mulcahy it looked like a torture kit. Papa Tío's son was clearly supposed to suffer before Luis finally got to ink in the numeral on his arm.

He took everything out, locked the Jeep, then walked away, carrying the bags and the battery booster pack in case he might need them.

He pulled the keys to his own Jeep from his pocket,

opened the trunk and dumped everything inside except the laundry sack. He wanted the guns close, so he stashed them in the passenger footwell, out of sight but easy to reach, then moved round to the driver's side and got in.

The Chevy Cruze was supposed to be his clean getaway ride, but there was no chance of that. He didn't know what he might have to do in the next few hours in order to turn his situation around and a black-windowed tank of a car with a big engine and four-wheel drive would be a lot more useful than an old Chevy with shot suspension.

The engine growled to life and he cranked the air up to maximum, eased out of the parking space, away from the buildings and down the exit ramp. He'd used maybe a third of his ten minutes, but waited until he'd slipped into the flow of evening traffic on the highway before dialling a number from memory using Javier's phone.

Someone answered and he gave a code word then listened to handling noise and the background sounds of some café. The cartels were deeply paranoid about wiretaps and call-tracing and had come up with a simple but effective solution. The man he had called sat in cafés all day reading the paper, drinking coffee and redirecting incoming calls through an internet-based phone system like Skype. Calls came in, the caller gave a code corresponding to whoever they wanted to talk to and the middleman would call that person on a second phone then sixty-nine the phones so the earpiece of the in-coming phone was pressed against the mouth-piece of the outgoing one. It meant the bosses could talk directly to anyone in their organization without being traced. The best the DEA could do was trace calls to the middleman, who wouldn't know anything other than a few phone numbers and codes.

The handling noise stopped and he heard a phone ringing through the background hum of the café. He took long breaths, pulling the cold air into him as though he was about to dive into deep, deep water.

Then Papa Tío answered.

23

They wrapped Bobby Gallagher's corpse in a hospital sheet shroud and carried him over to a pick-up truck to be driven back to the morgue. They couldn't spare an ambulance, not now the fire had overrun the control line and everyone was in full retreat. The energy in the field hospital was different too; it had settled and hardened, like everything did under pressure. No one spoke, everyone carried on preparing for casualties, knowing now exactly what those casualties would look, smell and sound like.

Solomon studied the fire from the shade of the billboard, his mind ticking with information – wind-speed calculations, open burn rates of desert wildfires, what fire did to human flesh. He listened to the roar of the flames, and the gusting wind and the birds, shrieking raptors and carrion birds drawn by the promise of death. He followed their shrieks until he spotted them, high above the town, wheeling in the thermals that rose up the red-sided mountains, then blown forward by stronger winds whipping across the mountaintop. They were blowing in the opposite direction to the one pushing the fire towards town. Different weather fronts.

'I wanted to say thank you.' The doctor who had treated the dying man was standing in front of him, a badge pinned to his breast pocket identifying him as *Dr M. Palmer*. 'I panicked, I guess,' he continued. 'I wasn't thinking. You were right to do what you did. Bobby died in peace instead of clinging to false hope. It was a very kind thing you did for him.'

Kind …

Had he held the dying man's hand out of kindness? He didn't think so. He had done it because he had known no one else would and that it was the right thing to do. He had known this with the same certainty he knew what things were just by looking at them, and that he was here to save someone.

'James Coronado,' he murmured.

The doctor frowned. 'Excuse me?'

'He was brought to the hospital, I assume, after his accident?'

'He was DOA, so would have gone straight to the morgue. They only come to the ER if they're still breathing.'

'But his notes will be on record at the hospital?'

'Yes.'

'Do you think I might see them?'

Palmer shook his head. 'The only people allowed to see that would be next-of-kin.'

Holly Coronado. All roads led to the widow. 'Thank you, Dr Palmer,' Solomon said.

He shrugged. 'You're welcome.' He looked past him to where the refugees from the desert were now gathering around a pick-up truck. Some were still wearing their old-style funeral clothes, making them seem like they'd stepped out of the town's past, drawn by the prospect of witnessing its end.

Mayor Cassidy climbed up on to the back of the truck and held his hands up for silence. 'Friends. Listen to me now.' All eyes turned to him. 'We have all witnessed a tragedy here, a terrible tragedy, and there will be a proper time to dwell on that. But that time is not now. Bobby Gallagher gave his life helping defend his town from the threat of this fire and the threat still remains and continues to grow. So the best way we can honour our friend is to make sure he did not lay down his life in vain. Now we got more fire tankers, big ones, in the air and on their way here – am I right, Chief?'

Morgan climbed up next to him. 'Yessir. Two C-130s heading up out of Tucson.'

A picture of a solid plane with a snub nose appeared in Solomon's mind – broad fuselage, four sturdy propeller engines slung below a wide straight wing.

'We also got the local unit back at the airfield, readyin' up for another run. Between those and what we all can do here on the ground, we can beat this thing.'

C-130 payload is 2,700 gallons. It could lay a fire line sixty feet wide and a quarter mile long.

Solomon stared back out at the desert, estimating the size of the fire using the burning grader for scale. The grader was thirty feet long, which meant the fire was …

Too big. Much too big.

'Now you all need to regroup and get back out there fast. Take some water then grab your tools and head back out …'

The distant shrieks of the high-flying birds snagged Solomon's attention again. He looked up and zoned Morgan out, listening to their cries as they were blown forward by the high winds. He caught a scent now too, drifting down from higher up, something buried so deep it was hardly there at all, but was enough to pin a hope on.

He looked back at Morgan finishing his speech.

'… We'll set back-burns to clear the ground about a half a

mile out of town. The tankers will draw most of the line for us, but until then it's up to us to hold it.'

'That's no good,' Solomon called out, before he realized he had spoken.

All eyes turned to him. 'What's that?' Morgan said.

'Half a mile is too far.' Solomon moved towards the truck. 'Too much desert to cover.' He held his hand up and swept it through the grey ash falling all around them. 'This is going to start falling hot soon, so any control line with dry desert behind it is going to start catching alight. You'll have spot fires springing up all over and not nearly enough people to cover them.' He reached the truck and leapt nimbly up to join Morgan and Cassidy. 'The fire will jump your line and keep on coming. Your best chance is to try and hold it at the narrowest point.

Morgan's face went pink. 'You an expert on firefighting too, Mr Creed?'

'No, but I know history.' He turned to the crowd. 'Over two thousand years ago three hundred Spartan warriors held back a quarter of a million Persian warriors by forcing them into a narrow pass between the mountains and the sea.' He pointed left out into the desert. 'The desert is narrowest right here in the bottleneck between the storm drain and the spill piles from the mine. This is where we can hold the fire.'

A murmur rose from the crowd, then the crackle of radio chatter silenced them again.

This is Charlie three-one-four-niner, inbound from Tucson, do you read, over?

Morgan tilted his head to his lapel mic. 'This is Chief Morgan, I read you. Glad to have you with us, over.'

Roger that. I'm hailing you on an open frequency with Charlie eight-six-five-zero, also inbound from Tucson. We

*have a visual on the smokestack and will be starting our run
in less than a minute. Tell us what you need.*

In the distance the twin specks of the planes appeared in
the sky. 'How long will it take them to refill and fly back
here?' Solomon said.

The air was thick with ash now, billowing in the gusting
wind like clouds of insects.

'Forty minutes,' Cassidy said. 'Maybe less.'

'This fire will be at the church doors in forty minutes. You
should get the tankers to lay the line right here. It's your best
chance. Your only chance.'

Solomon felt all eyes upon him and saw fear and uncertainty in them. They were desperate to be led but unsure
who to follow, and this indecision made the rage rise in him
again. Part of him wanted to leave them to it, just walk away
and up into the mountains where he could sit and watch the
town burn, as surely it would if they followed Morgan's plan.
The fire was mighty and these people were nothing.

But …

If the town burned he would have failed. He knew that
too. And if the town was gone, any chance of discovering
what had happened to James Coronado would be gone with
it. And where would that leave him? Would the fire keep
coming? Would the world burn wherever he walked until
eventually the flames caught up with him?

'What about the buildings?' Cassidy said. 'The hot ash
will drift on to those too.'

A murmur spread through the crowd and heads nodded in
agreement.

*Sheep. All sheep. Agreeing with whatever the last person said.
They deserved to be slaughtered.*

Solomon's arm flared in pain, a reminder of his mission

here. He could hear the chop of the propellers getting louder above the roar of the fire. Another minute and they would be here. Less.

He turned to the crowd. 'If a glowing ember falls on a patch of dry grass or a roof shingle, which is more likely to catch fire?'

The faces stared up at him, some of the heads nodding in agreement with him now as they realized what he was getting at.

'If we douse the buildings and spread out with buckets of water and rakes, we can deal with any fires that start. There aren't enough of you to do the same out in the desert and the fires will catch faster. Too much area to cover, not enough bodies on the ground. You need to make your stand here. Make your stand, or start running. Your choice.' He turned back to Morgan and lowered his voice so only he and Cassidy could hear: 'Make it fast.'

The first plane roared overhead, the deep bass rumble of its engines pounding in Solomon's chest.

This is Charlie three-one-four-niner. I see a partial control line southeast of the road and a breach to the northwest. We can lay a line along the fire's edge, if that's what you need, keep it back for ya. Give the word and we'll set up for a run, over.

Morgan didn't move. He stared at Solomon, blinded by his fury at being told what to do in front of his people by this stranger.

'Give me the radio,' Cassidy said, grabbing it from Morgan's belt. 'This is Ernest Cassidy, town mayor. We want you to lay a line right on the edge of town, understand. All along the old mining shacks. Give us a minute to pull back then paint the town red, over.' He thrust the radio back to

Morgan. 'Someone's got to take charge of this mess.' He stuck a smile on his face and turned back to the crowd. 'You heard me. Everybody needs to fall back and we'll split into teams to make sure we got the whole area behind the line covered. OK, let's move it.'

The crowd splintered like a dropped plate, glad to be doing something again, glad to be following a leader.

'It's a fine thing,' Morgan said quietly; 'the man who brought this fire now telling us how to put it out.'

Solomon smiled. 'I didn't say we could put it out, I only said we could hold it back. The fire is a force of nature, an act of God.'

'So what do we do – pray for a miracle and hope for the best?'

Solomon looked up at the birds again and breathed in. The smell was clearer now and getting stronger as the higher winds blew it ever closer. It was the coal-tar smell of wet creosote bush. His force of nature. His act of God.

The smell of rain in the desert.

24

Holly Coronado felt the ground tremble beneath her feet. She looked up from the half-filled grave to the dirt pile and saw dry rivulets of dust trickling down the sides. There was a noise too, a low rumbling that juddered through the air and trembled somewhere deep inside her. For a moment she wondered if it was coming from her, some physical manifestation of her anger. She had read a book once about a persecuted young girl with a strange and terrible power, who had snapped one day, killed her tormentors and burned a whole town to the ground.

She had always been a sucker for horror stories, enjoying the thrill of being scared whilst wrapped in the comfort and safety of her own life. Now she doubted she would ever read one again. No imagined horror could possibly compare to what her life had become. And if this was an earthquake, then let it come. Let it tear up the ground and level the town and crack open the earth to spill the dead from their graves so they could witness the end of the cursed place they had helped build.

The sound grew, huge and raw like her anger, then something rose from the valley with a noise like the sky ripping open. The propeller-wash from the tanker struck her hard, nearly knocking her from her feet and she closed her eyes and turned away from the grit-filled air and felt something wet and warm patter down from the sky. She glanced down and saw red spots on her arms as if blood had fallen from the clear blue sky.

Blood was what had tipped the girl in the story over the edge, raining down on her at the high-school prom. Holly wondered if she was imagining all this – the plane, the blood, the trembling ground – her brain throwing up phantoms born from thirst and tiredness and drenched in all the dark emotions that came with grief.

She stuck the shovel back in the ground and leaned heavily on it, imagining what she must look like, standing by the grave, her black dress torn and flapping in the hot breeze, her skin streaked with sweat and dirt and dotted with spots of what appeared to be blood. She looked like an insane person, that's what, like a black-lined etching from the pages of a Victorian gothic novel – the grieving wife with a broken mind, a Miss Havisham figure dressed in black instead of wedding white. Was that the future that awaited her – the tragic bride in a house where all the clocks had stopped?

She rubbed at one of the spots on her arm and felt the wetness of it as it smeared red across her skin. She had not imagined it; blood had dripped from the sky. She had not imagined any of it. It was all real. She was stuck in the middle of her own horror story. She knew that people in horror stories generally hung around long after they should have fled. Not her. Once she had buried Jim and fulfilled her promise to him, she would leave this place and never come back.

The ground started to tremble again and the air began to shake, but this time she knew it was not some terrible energy born of her pain that she could unleash on the town. The only thing her pain would turn into was anger, then tears and ultimately back to pain again. And the only way out of this cycle was to break it.

She picked up the shovel and drove it into the earth, continuing her act of remembrance for her dead husband, savouring the pain in her arms and shoulders as she slowly buried him beneath the dry Arizona ground.

A second plane roared overhead, rending the sky with its noise and dripping more drops of red on to the tattered widow labouring by the grave, and the dry rocky ground, and the white-painted grave markers that spoke of all the other cycles of pain that had ended here by gunshot, and hanging, and suicide.

25

'You seen the news?' Papa Tío's voice was oddly calm, which made Mulcahy feel the exact opposite.

'Yeah, I saw it. It said someone survived the crash.'

'That's what they're saying.'

'Listen, if it's Ramon, I can get him out, but I'll need to move fast. I'm less than half an hour away and—'

'It's not Ramon.'

'It's … are you sure?'

'A local source sent me a picture. The guy who walked away from the crash is a six-foot albino. That sound like Ramon to you?'

Mulcahy gripped the steering wheel hard, releasing some of his energy, his mind casting round for a new angle to try.

'You got any kids?' Tío asked, like they were just two guys in a bar, shooting the breeze over a beer.

'No. No I don't.'

'Course you don't. If you did I would have some of my men babysitting them right now – just like your father. You two close?'

'Close enough that I would like to sort this situation out.'

'That's good. It's good that you care about your father. Shows you got values. If you don't have family values then what have you got? You should have yourself some kids, you feel that way; man's not a man until he becomes a father. You know I had two daughters, as well as Ramon?'

Mulcahy knew. Everybody knew. He knew what had happened to them too.

'Beautiful girls,' Tío said, a smile lighting up his voice. 'Smart too, smarter than Ramon, that's for sure – smarter than me even. They wanted to help run the business, but I told them no one's going to take me seriously if I put women in charge – just the way it is.' He chuckled. 'They got real pissed about that, wouldn't talk to me for weeks, stopped telling me where they were going, slipped their guards so they couldn't tell me neither. That's when they got kidnapped. Someone called me up, said my daughters would be returned untouched and unharmed if I backed away from certain areas I had been expanding my business into. I'd recently taken over Lázaro Cárdenas – you know how much cargo that port ships each year?'

Mulcahy's fingers drummed on the steering wheel, releasing his nervous energy as the clock continued to tick. 'A lot.'

'Thirty-six million tons last year: cars, clothes, toys, building materials – all kinds of things. Thirty-six million tons of opportunity to someone like me. I told them no one tells me how to do business. I vowed that I would find the people responsible and anyone they had ever loved and I would nail them to a wall and eat the hearts of their children in front of them. I didn't plead for my daughters' lives. I knew they were already dead. If I had caved, it would show I was weak and they would have killed them anyway to prove they didn't fear me no more. But they do still fear me. Everybody fears me. So my daughters did help me in the business after all. They helped show everyone how strong I was. I never loved anyone like I loved those two girls.'

138

Mulcahy heard the anger in Tío's voice and sensed the glimmer of an opportunity in it. 'You ever find out who killed them?'

'It was the Saints. The Latin Saints did it.'

'The Saints killed Ramon too,' Mulcahy said. 'They sent a killing crew to my rendezvous point.' He picked up his phone, found the photos he had taken in the motel and attached them to a secure e-mail address he had for Tío. 'Carlos was a rat. He sold out your son to the Saints. But I don't figure him for some kind of mastermind. Someone else must have given the order and I can find out who. I can do that for you, Tío. I can get you a name.'

'How do you know it was the Saints?'

'I've sent you some pictures. See for yourself.'

There was a long, long pause as the message left his phone and wormed its way through some complicated, encrypted network. Mulcahy's fingers drummed on the steering wheel in time with his heartbeat. Before circumstance had led him down a different path he had been a trained police interviewer, skilled in the art of drawing people out and building trust. He was trying to do it now with Tío, drip-feeding him information to get him to engage and make him realize he was worth more to him alive than dead. So far, Tío wasn't biting.

'You got them?' Mulcahy asked.

'Yeah, I got them.' He heard the contained fury in Tío's voice and it made him feel hopeful.

'The survivor,' Tío said at last, 'my source says he's got a tag too. A Roman numeral burned on to his arm.'

'I can get to him,' Mulcahy said, pouncing on this fresh information. 'Right now we have chaos on our side, but it won't last. I can use that confusion, swing through, flash some

ID, take him right out of their hands. Hell, they'll be glad for one less thing to worry about, what with the fire and all. I can take this guy and find out everything he knows. You know I can do that, better than anyone.'

Tío went quiet again. Mulcahy checked the clock on the dashboard. His ten minutes were almost up. He imagined his father, sitting with his captors, probably trying to strike up a conversation with them, get them to play a hand of cards while they waited, calming himself by behaving as if everything was normal. He was a pretty charming guy, a guy's guy; Mulcahy had learned a lot from his father, like how to win a hand with weak cards or even no cards at all. Like now.

'The people who killed your daughters,' he said, playing the only card he had, 'did you ever get a name?'

'I got a whole list of names. My men get a bonus for every Saint they deliver to me alive. I got a special place I go to work on them, my own place of worship and remembrance. I got pictures of my daughters hanging on the walls and I do to those pigs exactly what they did to them. First I rape them with a metal bar, then I break a few bones, then I start with the questions – who killed my daughters? Who gave the order? Tell me and I'll end your pain. But torture and pain breaks men's minds, makes them tell you anything you want to hear.'

'Not if you do it right.'

'You telling me my business?'

'No. I think you're a very loving father and your emotions are getting in the way. I bet they tell you all kinds of other things too, vile things that make you so mad you hurt them more, am I right?' Tío said nothing. 'They're using your rage against you. They know you're going to kill them, so they've got nothing to lose and nothing to gain by telling you what you want to hear. You need a middleman, someone they can place trust in. The survival instinct is strong and you can use it to get at the truth.'

'And would that middleman be you?'

'It could be.' Mulcahy thought about his next step. He had no more cards so there was no point in pretending he did. 'Listen, Tío, I know it's unlikely I'll see my way through to the end of this, I know that. I'm one of the few people who knew about the flight and I can see how that looks. There's also a bunch of bodies in a motel room, and I walked away. I know how that looks too. But I didn't sell out your son. I can't make you believe that, but it's the truth. Maybe the plane crash was an accident, maybe it wasn't. But I bet I'm not the only person still breathing who knew about it.'

'I got things under control.'

'I'm sure you do, I don't doubt it. But will any of those people give you the name you want, the name of whoever was really behind all this? I can. If you give me the chance, I can get that name for you. Tell me who else knew about the flight and I'll find out what they know. I'll get this survivor too. You know I can do this better than anyone. I'll do whatever it takes and then I'm yours to do what you want with. Like I said, I don't expect to get through this. All I ask is that you let my father go.'

There was a long pause and Mulcahy let it stretch. There was nothing more he could say, nothing else he could offer.

'It's a credit to you,' Tío said at length, 'this thing you do for your father. You think Ramon would have done the same for me?'

Mulcahy considered the question. Ramon was a well-known, grade-A scumbag who lived in the protective shadow of a father he hated. 'I'm sure he would have done exactly the same,' he said, figuring right now was not the time for honesty.

'It's nice you think that. Shows you're a good son who respects his father. Truth is, Ramon would not have crossed the road to piss on me if I was on fire. You know what that piece of shit son of mine did that forced me to stick him on that plane in the first place? He raped a general's daughter. A two-star *generale* who also happens to be in charge of the border divisions. You think that's good for business? He couldn't just keep to the coked-up *putas* with the big asses and the plastic titties. No, he had to go and fuck everything up, leaving me to clean up his mess again. And how do you think a thing like this makes me look when it's my own son that's done it? Makes me seem weak, like I can't even control my own blood.'

He went silent again and Mulcahy let the silence stretch as he stared ahead at the slow-moving river of evening traffic, ordinary people heading home to their ordinary uncomplicated lives. He could see a sign up ahead – right to Tucson, left to Redemption. He still didn't know which turn he would take. His ten minutes were up. If he ended up turning right to Tucson, time would be up for his father too.

'Step out of line here or fuck it up and your father dies hard, understand? And when I catch up with you I'll show you that room I told you about with my daughters' pictures on the wall.'

'Thank you,' Mulcahy said, more breath than words.

'Go get this guy, this survivor. Squeeze him hard to find out what he knows. Make him suffer. And I want you to go to the crash site too. If my son is dead, I want to see a body.'

Mulcahy frowned. Getting access to the crash site would be risky. 'What about your local guys? Couldn't they …'

'I don't trust them. Some of them knew about the plane. I don't want them to even know you're there. I might need you to talk to them too. And use this phone to keep me informed. It's safe.' Then the phone clicked and Tío was gone.

Mulcahy blew out a long stream of air. He swapped Javier's phone for his own and tapped to call his father back, his hand trembling as the adrenaline in his system started to curdle.

The same voice answered. 'That weren't no ten minutes, motherfucker.'

'Go tell it to your boss, that's who kept me talking. Put my dad on, would you?'

There was a pause then his father came on the line.

'What the hell's going on?' He sounded more rattled than before. 'You coming over here to straighten things out or what?'

Mulcahy thought about the deal he had just done with Tío and how unlikely it was that he would ever see his father again. He swallowed hard against a tightness in his throat. 'I'm coming, Pop,' he said, 'but I got to square a couple of things away first. You hang in there and remember not to take all their money if they get the cards out, it'll only piss them off and they sound like vindictive types.'

'They don't look like they got much to take,' his father replied, his voice low.

Mulcahy smiled. Even with a gun to his head his old man still had the instincts of a born hustler.

'I'll see you soon, Pop,' he lied. He hung up before his voice betrayed him, then indicated and turned left towards the town of Redemption.

26

Morgan stood at the edge of town inspecting the red line the tankers had painted, the ash falling thickly around him now. He turned to the crowd and held up a loud-hailer so everyone could hear. 'OK, everyone, we have a line to hold here. The tankers will be back soon as they can, but we need to do our part and split you up into pairs.'

Solomon sat at the back of the pick-up, studying the women in the crowd, wondering if one of them was James Coronado's widow.

'Once you're in a pair,' Morgan continued, 'come see me and you will be assigned an area.' He held up a tourist map that had been roughly gridded up with a Sharpie. 'Soon as you have your area, go there and make it safe. Knock on doors to check no one's inside, then commandeer as many containers as you can, fill them with water and soak everything that's flammable, shift any woodpiles and anything else that looks like a bonfire waiting to happen, and keep your eyes open for the first sign of smoke in your area. If you see smoke, call out and put it out before it becomes anything worse. Shovel dirt, use a garden hose, roll on it if you have to, but do not let a fire take hold in your area, you understand?'

There were nods and murmurs. Everyone was subdued now the tankers had gone and the fire was roaring closer, pushed by winds that seemed angered by the town's attempts to defend itself.

'The fire trucks are spraying down the area immediately behind the control line and will act as frontline defence. Most of the fires are going to start here anyhow, so we'll cover those. Your job is to watch our backs. We need you to stop any small fires from becoming big ones. If we can hold the fire here, it will have nowhere else to go and will eventually burn itself out or the tankers will come back and put it out. We just gotta hold on here. Y'all think you can do that?'

A small chorus of 'Yeahs' rumbled up from the crowd.

'Come on,' Cassidy said, stepping forward with his campaign smile. 'Don't let me be the mayor who let the whole dang town burn down. Can we beat this thing?'

'YEAH!' the crowd hollered back.

'All right.' Cassidy turned to Solomon. 'You got anything you want to add, Mr Creed?'

Solomon stood up, regarded the assembled faces and leaned into the loud-hailer. 'You're all going to die,' he said, and watched every expression shift from hope to fear. 'But when and where you die is up to you. The tankers won't save you; this will all be over by the time they make it back. Only you can save you. So stay alive – and pray for rain.'

He stepped back and smiled at Morgan, who raised the loud-hailer to his mouth, looking at Solomon like he couldn't make head nor tail of him. 'Well, I guess prayer never hurt at that,' he said. 'All right then, get yourself into pairs and get busy.'

The crowd quickly split and formed a line in their new

pairs in front of the truck. Morgan pointed to sections of the map, marking each one off once it was assigned.

'I don't think that was a particularly smart trick to pull, Mr Creed, frightening everybody like that.'

'Fear is powerful fuel,' Solomon replied, studying the faces of the women as they filed past.

'So is hope.'

'Yes, but they're already frightened, look at them. Might as well use what we have. James Coronado's widow, she wouldn't be here, would she?'

'No, she would not.'

'Pity.' The wind blew again, a deep roar carrying more ash that stung Solomon's face. He tilted his head back and sniffed the air. He had lost the scent of the rain, the smell of smoke far too strong now. 'If we make it through the next hour, I would like to talk to her, if I may.'

'*If* we make it? *If* – don't be talking that way. Of course we'll make it.'

'I *hope* you're right.' He glanced over at the two fire trucks, their hoses sending arcs of water across the buildings closest to the control line. 'I *fear* you may not be. How much water do they hold?'

Cassidy followed his gaze to the trucks. 'About three thousand gallons apiece.'

Solomon nodded. 'I don't see a hydrant system on the streets.'

'That's because we don't have one.'

'So what happens when the fire trucks run out of water?'

'What happ—' Cassidy leaned in, his face flushing red. 'If we run out of water then we'll run hose from the houses and do what we can with that. Hell, we'll start a bucket chain, if that's what it takes.'

Solomon shook his head. 'You don't have the manpower. But at least you're getting angry now. That's good. Anger is almost as powerful as fear.'

Cassidy made to say something but never got the chance. 'FIRE! WE GOT A FIRE HERE!' someone hollered.

Smoke was pouring through a gap between two houses a block back from the control line and a little way off the main road. The crowd in front of the truck broke up and started running towards it. Solomon shook his head. The first whiff of smoke and everything fell apart. The town was doomed.

'Go to your area,' Morgan hollered through the loud-hailer. 'Go to your area. Let the trucks deal with this one.' His amplified words cut through the roar of the main fire and the hiss of the fire hoses. 'We start running after every fire and we will lose this town.'

One of the fire trucks disengaged and sped down the street towards the smoking house, turning its hose towards the fire. Everyone else hurried to their section, running now, frightened of the fire, the memory of Bobby Gallagher still fresh in their minds.

Fear.

Solomon could feel it crackling in the dry air. He could smell it, mingling with the sweat and the stench of smoke. Fear was good. Fear could make people do almost anything. Maybe the town wasn't doomed after all.

Another blast of wind brought heat and embers flying out of the desert. The billboard was starting to steam now, the water-soaked images of old-style cowboys looking like they were sweating for real. The fire was coming fast but the heat was coming faster, a solid pressure wave so dry it made the air uncomfortable to breathe. Solomon remembered the coach horses, restless and desperate to run but tethered by

147

their reins. He felt like that too – wanting to run but bound here by a promise he did not understand. He felt like the fire was a part of it, part of his story.

Only those who face the fire … can hope to escape the inferno.

He took a step forward, his feet cracking the red-stained crust of the earth, and stared into the heart of the fire. He could feel the heat of it like a solid thing and he was breathing fast, drawing the hot air inside himself, feeling like he was part of the fire already. The flames roiled and twisted like something about to strike and Solomon braced himself as the wind gusted and roared in his ears. He felt it buffet his body and rock him on his feet. But the fire did not surge forward. Instead it pulled back, rearing up and away like a horse from a snake.

The wind had changed. The gust had come not from the desert but from behind him. It had come from the mountains.

'You smell that?' The shout came from behind him and he turned and saw one of the medics turn towards the town. 'You smell it?'

Others stopped work and turned their noses to the air, breathing in the coal-tar smell of the creosote bush being carried to them on the wind, a smell desert folk learned to identify before they learned their ABCs.

'Look –' someone else shouted and pointed up at the high mountains. A raft of grey cloud had appeared over the ridge and was sliding fast across the sky. 'Rain. There's rain coming. Lord be praised, there's rain on its way.'

Solomon turned back to the fire and stared up at the great arch of smoke like the vaulted roof of a burning cathedral. A loop of fire lashed out like a tentacle, whipping across the air above Solomon's head.

'Go,' he said.

And the first drops of rain began to fall.

The fire hissed and the rain hissed back, falling fast and washing the heat and ash from the air.

Cheers rang out behind him. Cheers, and prayers of thanks, and sobs of relief.

The flames began to shrink away and melt into steam, and rain ran down Solomon's face like tears, soaking his clothes, cooling his skin. A surge of people surrounded him, some still holding the tools they no longer needed. Arms snaked round his shoulders, a woman kissed him. They were all talking and laughing and treating him as if he had personally summoned the rain in order to save their town. Someone offered him shoes, another asked if he needed a place to stay while he was in town. But there was only one thing he wanted. He turned to Cassidy.

'I'd like to visit Holly Coronado,' he said.

V

*'The unexamined life
is not worth living.'*

Socrates

THE NEXT THING I found on that dry riverbed was a wooden box, its surface darkened by wax and wear and splintered open at one corner where it had struck the hard ground. It lay between the wheel ruts, just as the cage had done, with white cotton sheets and clothes spilling out from it and on to the dirt. There were petticoats and aprons, some boy's britches and a pair of men's trousers all scattered and dusty on the ground, the Sunday best of a small family. There was a twist of cloth too, knotted at the corners to make the arms and legs of a child's doll. I scooped this up, imagining the distress of the child that had lost it, but the box looked to be too heavy to carry so I left it in the track along with its spilled contents. As I passed it I saw sunlight glint off a rectangle of brass on the lid and read the name etched upon it – ELDRIDGE.

It was evident the box must have fallen with some force for it to split open like this and yet the noise of the splintering wood had clearly not caused the wagon to stop. The wheels had carried on rolling, meandering away along the wide riverbed, following their strange course without break or pause, and I found something deeply unsettling in the way this well-cared-for box with its precious contents had been so casually abandoned.

I picked up my pace, disregarding all previous resolve to take things slowly and preserve both energy and water. I had been anxious for human company but now I feared some misfortune or disease or delirium had befallen the party to cause such aimless transit and the steady abandonment of their belongings.

I had seen things like this before on my travels, items that had seemed so essential at the beginning of a trek steadily losing value as the days and weeks wore on until they became nothing more than a worthless burden. I had once seen an upright piano, standing alone in the middle of a prairie with the stool in front of it slightly askew as if the pianist had stopped playing then vanished into the air. I wondered now whether the birdcage I had retrieved had not been lost at all but jettisoned, along with the linen box, to lighten the load on the heavy-laden wagon. Nevertheless I kept hold of the cage and the linen doll and uttered a silent prayer that the wagon party's arrival at the well might revive them, and the subsequent appearance of a stranger returning something lost might cheer them still further. I clung on to these hopes and pressed on. Then I saw the third thing, and knew that no amount of water or rest or the retrieval of lost valuables was ever going to restore that poor family to whatever former joy they may have known.

She must have been about three years old. Her tiny body curled up the way babies do when sleeping. She wore clothes that would have been too big for her even before starvation had withered her away to almost nothing. She was lying on her side, her auburn hair spilling from beneath a salt-stained cotton bonnet and spreading out in a puddle of dark copper. Her eyes were shut, as if she were merely sleeping, but the dark line of flies clustered around her lashes as they scavenged the salt of her dried tears showed it was a slumber from which she would never wake.

She had been dead a while, I could smell the rot coming off her as my mule drew closer, and she lay so rigid and flat upon the uneven ground that I could see she had the death stiffness already, that peculiar hardening of the flesh that takes place in a body a few hours dead. I imagined the girl curled up on the floor of the covered wagon, perhaps the smallest of a family all lying in the wagon alongside her in exhaustion. This would explain the unusually deep wheel marks in the dirt. Folks generally walk alongside their wagons during the heat of the day to spare the horse – but not if they are dying.

Maybe the poor girl had been shaken loose by the jostling of the cart as her body started to stiffen. Or someone had pushed her out to rid the wagon of her growing smell and lighten the burden some, though the poor starved thing could not have weighed much more than a sack of coffee. I like to think it was the former, though I know what survival and being close to death will make a person do. I would soon come to the edge of that dread abyss myself.

I kicked my mule onward, whispering a promise to the dead child that I would return as soon as I might and properly commend her soul to God and bury her deep enough in the ground so that scavengers would not nose her and dig her up for a meal. And though it pained me to abandon her that way, I knew my Christian duty lay with the living, if any of the wagon party lived still, and I doubted but they were too far ahead of me.

My mule was labouring now, sweat foaming around the saddle straps, but I had no water to spare and precious little for myself so I pushed on, knowing that somewhere ahead of me, where the ground began to rise up to the twin mountain peaks, I would find fresh water and here my mule could rest and drink, and so could I.

I saw the trees first, a small thicket of mesquite, the crowns rising darkly beyond the bleached banks of the dead river, then, as I spurred the mule on in prospect of shade, I saw the wagon. It had come to rest in the first fringe of shadow, the dusty canvas of its cover standing out against the dark background of the trees. I took the wagon's rest as a good sign, imagining the party's horse must have halted the moment it came upon water.

I entered the shadows and felt the instant relief of it. The temperature beneath the trees was many degrees cooler than out in the crucible of the riverbed and it took my sun-scorched eyes a few moments to adjust to the gloom. I blinked away my sun-blindness as my mule trudged closer and saw the horse, not halted at a waterhole but lying on its side, its foam-flecked hide stretched tight across ribs that were sharp-edged and still. It looked like it had been dead for days, but I knew this could not be so. I smelled death though, and saw the flies in thick clouds, seething about the horse and cart. I reached the wagon and peered through the rear flap.

Flies were everywhere, thickening the air and crawling over every surface, so many that I wondered how they had hatched so quickly. There were three people inside, a mother and two children stretched out one next t'other between sacks of dry goods. They were folded into each other as if in some deep slumber, the woman on the left, one arm raised as a pillow for her head, the other draped over a boy of around twelve. He in turn had his arm round a girl of five or six and it was the sight of her that nearly undid me. Her arm too was extended, the arc of it preserved by the death stiffness over a small empty space on the bare boards of the wagon floor. This was where the tiny child I had found on the track must have lain until death and the movement of the wagon had edged her away from her family. There was something unutterably beautiful and unspeakably sad about this and I offered a prayer for them all, which I did silently, not daring to open my mouth on account of the flies and a fear that if I tasted that foul air I would never again rid myself of its flavour.

I said an Amen then manoeuvred past the wagon where I expected to find the last of the party, the man of the family, fallen by the horse he had led here. But I did not find him.

Instead, I found blood.

157

27

Holly Coronado felt like she was floating and looking down at herself, putting one foot in front of the other, her black dress torn, her feet and hands blistered and bleeding. She had buried Jim and fulfilled the promise she had made to him. Now all she wanted was to be home and curl up in the bed they had shared: fall into a numbed sleep, wrapped in the fading scent of him that still clung to the sheets. She never wanted to face the pain of another day.

The rain made it heavy going, soaking her clothes and weighing her down and making it hard to see too far ahead. She had been thinking a lot lately about the time when she and Jim had first got together, looking back at the start of their relationship from the bleak vantage point of its end, torturing herself with thoughts of whether Jim would still be alive if they had done things differently. But the truth was that, for Jim, all roads led here. The town had a peculiar hold on him, always had done from way before she even met him, and now it would never let him go.

The first time she told him she loved him he had gone quiet and sat her down, looking so serious and sad she'd thought he was going to tell her he was already married or something. Instead he had told her about this place, the town, and how it was like a family to him. He'd told her how it had cared for him when he was a baby, clothed him, fed him, educated him, impressed good Christian moral values on him, nursed him whenever he fell sick, even provided a scholarship for him to go to college.

He'd also told her that the town, his family, was in trouble: that it was struggling to survive and he felt he could help. That was why he was studying trust law; not so he could get a fancy job in a big city law firm and get rich, but so he could help the town get back on its feet. He said he'd made a promise to himself that when he graduated he would return there and run for public office and spend his life in the service of the town, and that, though he loved her more than he had ever thought it possible to love another person, if she didn't want that, if she wanted to go off and be a big city lawyer, then he would understand and she should not waste any more time on him.

He had cried when he'd told her all this, a big bear of a guy holding her hands and talking with the kind of pain only love can bring, so selfless and loyal and noble. How could any girl turn away from a guy like that? Not her, that was for sure.

So when they both graduated, him top of his class and with several big firms dangling six-figure salaries in front of him, he had kept his promise and turned them all down and come back here to try to save the town that had raised him. And now he was dead and she felt like a piece of her had been torn out and replaced with a jagged block of ice. His future was gone and so was hers. She couldn't see a way through it. To top it all, she was broke too.

Broke and broken.

Fancy educations were expensive. Jim had got a scholarship from the town, but it hadn't covered much. They had both graduated with student debts and gone even deeper while Jim ran for sheriff. When he got elected they thought the tide was about to turn, but he hadn't taken office before he died. No salary. No widow's pension. The house was rented and she couldn't afford to keep it – not that she wanted to. But she had nowhere else to go. Her parents were dead. She had no brothers or sisters. She had nothing. Jim had been her everything. She'd felt like a better person when she was with him. Even the colours had seemed brighter. Now the world was grey and black and ugly.

The rain was torrential now, hammering the ground and throwing up mist that washed the heat from the air and the dust of the grave from her hands and clothes. Rivers gurgled down gutters and into storm drains that fed into the main run-off channel running out of town towards where the flames had been replaced by clouds of steam. So much for the town burning to the ground.

She had to leave here, get away from all the ugliness and pain. She had been thinking about that a lot too. How she might do it. How she *would* do it.

She'd prepared everything the night before. Jim had always been a troubled sleeper and she had hunted through the house for his various stashes of sleeping tablets. Jim had his own mini closet in the bathroom where he kept his 'man stuff' and going through it had felt like a small betrayal, like she was trespassing on something private. He was everywhere inside: in the old Gillette razor he had used since college, in the few strands of hair trapped in his hair brush, in the half-empty bottle of cologne. She had sprayed it in the air then walked through it as if she was stepping through the ghost of him.

She found three bottles of Ambien in total and emptied

them out on to the granite counter-tops in the kitchen. A search online had proved mostly unhelpful, her question 'How many sleeping pills will prove fatal?' directing her to sleep forums and links to suicide helplines. The closest she had got to real information was a post from a nurse who said an adult would need to take at least fifty. She had sixty-three and figured, with her slight frame, that it should be enough, but she crushed them inside a freezer bag to make sure she didn't lose any, the jagged edges of the breaking pills piercing the plastic and leaving small traces of white powder on the granite. She had also noted the warnings on the label not to take the pills with alcohol and had taken a bottle of Glenfiddich single malt from the cabinet and placed it by her bed. She planned to dissolve the powder in a large Scotch, drink it straight down, then lie back and drift away on a pleasant whiskey haze. All she had to do was get home.

She forced herself on through the hammering rain, one foot in front of the other until her house appeared in the mist up ahead. She reached her driveway and almost staggered up it, forcing her legs to walk the last few feet home. Her car was tucked right up at the top of the drive to make room for Jim's and she felt the absence of him come crashing down when she thought of how his car would never be parked there again. It made her feel sick, really sick, and she grabbed at the wooden rail, leaning heavily on it for support until the nausea passed. Then she hauled herself up the steps and on to her wide, covered porch. There was a couch to the right of the door and she was so wrung out and bone-deep exhausted she felt like lying down on it and resting a minute. If her dress hadn't been so wet she might have done just that, but she felt wretched and chilled and there were no blankets to warm her and, besides, she had a job to do. So she carried

on, heaving the screen door open and twisting the handle
of the front door her urban girl heart still got a kick out of
never having to lock.

She pushed it open, stepped into the sanctuary of her
home – and stopped dead when she saw what was inside.

28

The rain drummed on the roof of the cruiser as they pulled away from the billboard and headed back into town and Holly Coronado's house. Morgan was driving – he had insisted, though Solomon would have been happier to walk, even with the rain. He kept the window wide open as a compromise, the rain blowing in through it as they drove along. They headed up Main Street, past the rain-glossed storefronts and all the closed stores.

'I guess it's going to put a big dent in your tourist income, this fire,' Solomon said.

Morgan nodded. 'Guess so.'

'Must be a worry, town this size.'

'Money's always a worry, but we do OK.'

'How?'

Morgan sighed, as though talking was a burden. 'Are you genuinely interested or just passing the time?'

'I'm interested.'

'OK, so we got the airfield, that brings in more than tourist dollars, what with the storage fees we get from the military and salvage money too. We also got a number of long-standing civic trusts in place that keep things running and the bills paid. We're all right, don't you worry about that.'

'I'm not worried. I don't live here.'

They turned off Main Street and started heading towards the spill piles. Beyond it Solomon could see the airfield, lines and lines of parked aircraft sitting wing to wing, their engines and windows wrapped in some kind of white protective covering to keep the dust out. There were hundreds of them, thousands; military, commercial, old, new, their various shapes prompting names and information to riffle through his mind as well as a question. 'The plane that crashed, what kind was it?'

'It was a Beechcraft, AT-7. You know planes, Mr Creed?'

He pictured a compact, single-winged plane with two big engine cowls and a wide twin-finned tail. 'Advanced Training version of the Model 18,' Solomon said. 'Used to train navigators in World War Two.'

Morgan smiled and shook his head. 'For a man with no memory you sure seem to know a lot of stuff.' He pulled his phone from his pocket. 'This model was a real beaut. Re-conditioned Pratt and Whitneys, brand-new hydraulic systems and electrics, the whole nine yards. Here –' he showed him a picture – 'ain't she something?'

Solomon studied the screen. It matched the image his mind had already conjured, but there was one crucial difference. The plane that crashed had *shone*. Apart from its serial number the fuselage had been stripped of all paint or markings and polished until the aluminium shone like chrome, or …

'… Mirror.'

'What's that?'

'It looks like it's made of mirror.'

'They call it brightwork: no paint just a real high polish on the aluminium then a clear lacquer to seal it. Cuts down on drag. Damn shame we lost it. Was looking forward to flying it myself.'

Solomon thought back to the mirror in the church and the momentary illusion he had experienced that his reflection was not his own, that the mirror was in fact a doorway with someone else standing on the other side of it. He looked at the picture of the plane, taken on a desert runway, so highly polished it reflected the land and sky.

'Maybe that's how I got here.'

'You think you *were* on that plane now?'

'No, I meant ...' He shook his head, his thoughts incomplete and tricky to explain. He changed the subject. 'You a pilot, Chief Morgan?'

'Me? Oh yeah. I guess if you live by the sea, everyone's a sailor, right? Here everyone's a pilot. I was in the Air Reserve, 944th Fighter Wing. Ground crew. Some of the F-16s I maintained are now parked out there in the Boneyard – that's what we call the storage part of the airfield. We get a lot of old planes coming through here. Some for repair, some for storage. Climate here is dry as it gets, means metal don't corrode much, and the desert is caliche – you know what that is?'

'Calcium carbonate. Like a naturally occurring cement.'

'Exactly. Means the planes can sit right out there on the ground without the need to build concrete parking areas. We got whole squadrons of B-52s been standing out there twenty years with not so much as a crack in the ground. Damn shame. Birds like that should be in the air, not sitting around gathering dust.'

'How come they're here?'

'Timing, I guess. The main copper seam ran out at about the same time the Second World War was ending. The military needed somewhere to store all the war surplus and the town needed to find new jobs. It was Bill Cassidy's idea to expand the airfield, Ernie's – the present mayor's – grandfather.'

'Jack Cassidy's son?'

'Grandson.'

'Quite a dynasty.'

'That's for sure.'

'And it's all coming to an end.'

Morgan turned slightly in his seat. 'How do you mean?'

'Mayor Cassidy has no children.'

'Oh. Right.'

Morgan went quiet and Solomon stared out at the town slipping by: souvenir stores, an empty parking lot, a livery yard with blood-red barns and a sign promising 'Desert trekking' and 'Stagecoach Rides up to the Historic Cemetery'. There was a corral spread out back from the road, horses huddled inside it against the weather. Then the mine slipped into view, the spill piles rising up in gravelled mountains behind a high fence topped with razor wire. The rain ran in fresh rivulets down the sides of them, thrumming on the roofs of empty-looking buildings and forming puddles around a closed gate with a sign saying **DANGER. KEEP OUT. WORKING MINE.**

'You said the mine gave out at the end of the Second World War?'

Morgan glanced over at the sign. 'It did. We opened her up again 'bout five years back. New methods of extraction.'

'All the buildings look deserted.'

'Most of them are. The new operation is much less labour intensive.'

He turned off the road and accelerated away from the mine and into a maze of neat residential streets. The further they rose up the hill and away from the mine, the nicer the houses became, their gardens wide and deep and opening

166

out on to the desert beyond. American flags flew on poles in front of most of them, some Arizona state flags too – thirteen rays of red and yellow radiating from a copper star with a band of blue beneath. Solomon watched them flapping wetly in the rain, his mind automatically decoding the symbolism:

Blue the colour of liberty.

Copper for the state's main industry.

Thirteen original colonies of the United States.

Red and yellow for the Spanish flag carried here by conquistadors like Francisco Vasquez de Coronado, namesake of the woman he was about to meet.

'This is us,' Morgan said, turning into a drive and pulling to a stop behind a small car. 'Now remember this lady just lost her husband.'

Solomon gazed up at the perfect-looking house – white picket fence, rocker on the stoop, grey-painted weatherboards. 'I only want to see if she knows me,' he said, then stepped out of the car and into the rain, glad to be outside and feel the ground beneath his bare feet again.

Morgan turned off the engine and followed him out, fixing his hat to protect him from the rain. 'Let me go first,' he said, hurrying over to the covered porch. 'She might not be in, or she might not want to—' He turned at the sound of the screen door banging open and stopped when he saw the woman step through it, dress torn, eyes blazing, shotgun in her hands pointing straight at him.

29

'Mrs Coronado,' Morgan said, slowly raising both hands in a gesture that was part instinct and part surrender. 'You need to put the gun down.' He took a careful step towards her, his eyes fixed on hers, ignoring the gun.

'No,' she said, her voice low and hard. 'You need to leave. Take one more step and I'll shoot you for trespassing.'

Morgan stopped.

Solomon could feel the anger radiating out of her, could see it shining in her like a dark light. She was all blackness and dark focus, the gun like an extension of her fury. She was beautiful. Magnificent.

'Is this why you wanted the funeral up in the old cemetery?' she said, her words like rocks. 'Invite the whole town, make a big show, get everyone out of the way, get *me* out of the way so you could break in to my …'

'You're upset,' Morgan said, raising his hands higher. 'But this ain't going to solve nothing. This is only going to make things worse.'

'Worse! Nothing could possibly make this worse.'

'Mrs Coronado. Holly.' Morgan took another step. 'Let's all calm down here. You're not going to shoot me. That's not going to happen, so why don't you just—'

The explosion punched a hole in the rain and knocked Morgan clean off his feet.

He fell backwards and hit the ground hard, yelping in shock and pain. He kicked at the wet earth, instinctively trying to flee, his bloodied hands reaching for his side-arm.

'That was rock salt,' Holly said, racking another shell into the chamber and taking a step forward. 'The next one is double-ought buckshot. If you touch that gun I will shoot you. If you do not leave right now I will shoot you.'

Morgan scrambled to his feet and stumbled across the wet grass towards the cruiser. Solomon watched, his brain singing with it all. She had shot him without hesitation and there had to be a reason for that, a powerful reason. Morgan crawled into the car, keeping low, and Solomon felt the dark light shine on him now. 'You're trespassing too,' Holly said, and he turned to face the black hole of the shotgun barrel.

Behind him the cruiser roared into life and the passenger door popped open. 'Get in,' Morgan hollered.

Solomon glanced at him through the open door, bloodied and smeared with mud, the front of his shirt peppered with white powder and small holes where the salt crystals had penetrated. He stepped forward, pushed the door shut and turned back to Holly. 'I'm not with him,' he said.

Holly took a step forward. 'You came with him, you can leave with him. And you're still trespassing.'

Solomon looked down at the ground, his bare feet white against the wet grass, then started walking backwards, down the drive to the road.

'What are you doing?' Morgan shouted, putting the cruiser in gear and rolling backwards, keeping pace with Solomon's retreat.

'I only want to talk,' Solomon answered, loud enough that Holly could hear. 'I have something your husband may have given me but I can't remember why. I was hoping you might help me.' He stopped walking when he reached the road and was no longer trespassing. Behind him the cruiser jerked to a halt and the passenger door popped open again. 'Get in the car,' Morgan hissed. 'She's not going to talk to you. She's not rational. She just shot me, for Chrissakes.'

Solomon studied Holly through the curtain of rain. Despite her steel he could sense a brittleness in her. She was shaking slightly, maybe because of the wet and the cold, or because the gun was heavy, or because her anger was so fierce it was difficult for her to contain. He knew that feeling. Maybe that was why he felt drawn to her.

'Go,' he said to Morgan. 'She's not going to talk until you've gone.'

Morgan hesitated for a moment then put the car in drive. 'Well, don't come running to me if she winds up blowing your head off.'

The engine growled and the car squealed away, tyres slipping on the wet road, leaving Solomon standing in the rain.

The shotgun barrel followed the car until it was out of sight then drooped suddenly, as if it had become too heavy to hold, and Holly staggered forward and grabbed at the hand-rail. Solomon was already running. He could see she was going to fall. If she tipped down the steps she could smash her head or break her neck. He reached the porch and leaped up the steps, catching her as she started to crumple.

'You're OK,' he said, gathering her into his arms. 'I've got you.' He could smell the graveyard on her, the wet dust trapped in her clothes, the metallic tang of blood on her hands and feet. He carried her over to the door, pulled the screen door open with his foot and carried her inside. Then he saw what had put the fury in her.

30

Morgan turned the corner back on to Main a little too fast and the steering wheel slipped in his hands. He was trying to dial and steer and not get blood over everything all at the same time and doing a lousy job of it. The phone started ringing and he switched to hands-free and dropped the phone in his lap. It rang three times before Mayor Cassidy answered.

'She shot me.'

'What?'

'Holly Coronado, she shot me.'

There was a pause and the background sounds of the control line filled the car – laughter, celebration. 'Are you OK?'

'Well, I've been better. It was rock salt – stings like hell, but I'll live. Listen, Creed is still there.'

'What? You said you were going to stay close, hear what he had to say.'

'What was I supposed to do? I had a shotgun pointed at my head. He wanted to stay, I had to let him.'

'But what if we get a call from Tío's men? What if they want to know where he is?'

'We know where he is. You heard anything?'

'No.'

'Me neither. I'm going to call them when I get to the office, but first I'm going to call dispatch, get them to send a unit round to bring Holly in to the station.'

'You think? Shouldn't we let it go?'

'She shot me in front of a witness, if I don't do anything about it, how's that going to look? She needs to be cautioned at least. You can't go around unloading shotgun shells into police officers with no consequences. Besides, this might work out for us. If we remove her from the house, it leaves Solomon there on his own.'

There was a pause and Morgan could almost hear the sound of the other shoe dropping. 'You think we should tell them where he is?'

'We need to give them something, show them that we're cooperating. The fact that we haven't heard anything is bad. So I'm going to call them up, tell them where he is and get my guys to clear the way for them. Then we'll see what happens.'

He hung up to avoid further conversation and examined his hands. When he was a kid he'd come off his bike riding down the spill piles and the sharp stones and gravel had taken the skin off his palms. That's what they looked like now. He twisted the rear-view mirror round and checked his face. A few cuts, nothing major, though he could easily have been blinded if she'd aimed higher. Goddamn that woman. He fumed all the way to the King Community Hospital, thinking about Holly and Solomon and all the things that were making this about the worst day he could ever remember.

Not long, he told himself. *Hold your nerve and stick to the plan and it will all fall into place and this will all become a memory.*

He pulled to a halt in the ambulance bay and reached over to the passenger seat for his phone. There was something lying in the footwell. He bent down to pick it up and discovered it was the cap Solomon had been wearing. He held it by the peak and turned it slowly, smiling when he spotted the single white hair trapped in the mesh at the back of the cap, almost glowing against the deep red material of the band.

'Hello, Mr Creed,' he said. Then he turned the cap over and folded it in on itself to seal the hair inside. 'Let's see if we can't find out who you really are.'

31

Mayor Cassidy stood beneath the black dome of his umbrella and surveyed the carnival the control line had become, everyone laughing, staring out at the scorched desert and shaking their heads in disbelief that they had, somehow, managed to face down the fire. The rain thundered down but hardly anyone took shelter from it. It was the rain that had saved them. Cassidy smiled too, but he knew this wasn't the end of it. New danger was coming to their town and it would take more than rain to send it away. He checked his phone. Still nothing.

'Mayor Cassidy?'

The voice made him turn and something clenched inside him when he saw the athletic-looking stranger in the dark suit walking towards him under a plain black umbrella. 'I'm with the National Transport Safety Bureau,' he said, and produced a wallet with a Federal ID inside. 'I was on the road to Tucson when I heard about the crash so I thought I'd head straight here. The main unit are on their way, but they asked me to secure the site. Mind if I head out and take a peek?'

Cassidy peered out at the steaming road. 'You think it's safe?'

'Safe enough. The thing of it is, this rain is both an asset and a liability. It put the fire out but now it's washing away evidence. By the time the forensics teams get here, some of it might be gone. So it would sure be a help if I could get started. Sooner we find out what happened here, the sooner we can get this road opened up for you again.'

Cassidy looked out at the desert, the misting rain and steam drifting across the road like ghosts. 'All right,' he said, 'I'll go with you, Mr …?'

'Davidson,' Mulcahy said, and held out his hand.

'Davidson,' Mayor Cassidy repeated, shaking his hand and looking him square in the eye like his daddy had taught him. 'Welcome to Redemption, Agent Davidson.'

32

The interior of Holly Coronado's house was open-plan and tasteful and looked like the home of a young professional couple. Except someone had totally trashed it. Every drawer had been opened and the contents dumped on the floor. The couch was lying on its back, its lining slashed open and its springs exposed. Solomon levered it upright with his foot and set Holly down on it. She was blinking, her eyes struggling to focus. 'I'm fine,' she said. 'I just came over a little—'

'Where's the kitchen?'

She studied him curiously, as if she had only now noticed him. 'You look so pale.'

'So do you. The kitchen?'

She gestured at a doorway and Solomon headed over to it, passing a TV unit that had been pulled away from the wall and emptied, its contents strewn across the pale oak floorboards.

The kitchen was a similar story: drawers pulled out, some cupboard doors hanging open, but not all. There was a line beyond which the neat order remained undisturbed, which suggested to Solomon that the intruder had either found what they were searching for or they had been disturbed, warned maybe that the funeral had ended and Holly was heading back.

It would be odd to hide something that was so clearly valuable in the kitchen, so his money was on them being disturbed. Which meant they had not found whatever it was they were looking for.

He grabbed a glass from the drainer and filled it from a filter jug while he breathed in the smell of the room – detergent, polish and an outdoor smell, engine grease and dry hay, that seemed to float above the other household scents like an oily film. He breathed deeper and caught something else too, the chalky trace of something that hinted at the true depth of the widow's despair. He looked down at the granite worktops and saw the source of it: traces of white powder. He dabbed it with the tip of his finger, tasted it and his mind identified it for him.

Zolpidem – muscle relaxant – anticonvulsant – most commonly used as a sleeping pill.

He shut off the water and headed back into the living room.

'Sip this,' he said, handing Holly the glass. He placed his hand on her forehead. She was warm but not dangerously so. 'Have you taken anything?'

She stiffened. 'No.'

'You sure?'

'Yes, I'm … who are you?'

'That I was hoping *you* might tell *me*.' He pulled the copy of Jack Cassidy's memoir from his pocket and held it out. 'I think your husband may have given me this.' He opened the book to the dedication and handed it to her.

'Solomon Creed,' she said, and shook her head. 'I never heard Jim mention your name. Why do you only *think* he gave it to you?'

'Because I can't remember anything – not my name, not

where I'm from, nothing. All I have is this book and a strong feeling that I'm here because of your husband. I think that I'm here to …'

'What?'

'To save him.'

Pain clouded her face and she handed the book back. 'Then you're too late. My husband is dead. He can't help you, and neither can I.'

Solomon took the book and thought about the white powder he had found in the kitchen. 'Maybe I'm here to help you too?'

'I don't need your help. I need to be left alone. Thank you for your concern, but I think you need to leave now.'

Solomon didn't move. 'I can't do that.'

'You're in my house. If I ask you to go then you should go.'

He continued to look at her, taking her in, her fragile beauty, her pain, her wide pupils, dilated with shock or perhaps something else.

'If you don't go right now, I'll call the police.'

Solomon shook his head. 'No you won't. The police were just here. You shot the police in the face. Why did you do that, I wonder?'

'What do you want?'

'I told you. I want to find out who I am.'

'But I don't know who you are.'

'Maybe your husband did. Why would he send me this book if I wasn't connected to him in some way? And why would I feel so strongly that I'm here because of him? I think something is wrong here. I think your husband was in trouble and you know what it is, and that I am tied up in it somehow.'

Holly stared up at him, her black eyes solid with mistrust. 'Why do you think Jim was in trouble?'

Solomon nodded at the trashed room. 'Because of this. Because you shot a police officer in the face. Because I get the feeling that no one wants to talk about what happened to your husband.'

A flicker of interest. 'Who doesn't?'

'The mayor, Morgan. I think the only reason he agreed to bring me here was because he wanted to stick around while we talked and see what you had to say, or make sure you said nothing because he was here. But he's not here now. So what is it he didn't want you to tell me?'

Holly opened her mouth as if she was about to say something, then stopped herself. 'I just buried my husband,' she said. 'I can't help you right now. I'm sorry, I need to take care of myself. So, please, leave me alone.'

Solomon nodded. Took in the mess. Breathed in the smells of the house, the engine grease and hay, and the chalky note floating beneath it all. 'All right,' he said. 'If you want me to go, I'll go. But you should know that sleeping tablets are a notoriously unreliable method of self-destruction.'

She blinked and her hand rose up and across her chest, the gesture of someone who felt exposed, which told him he had guessed correctly.

'I can only imagine the pain you're feeling now, losing someone so close and so young, so if you want to end that pain who am I to stop you? But if you're really serious you should run in place before swallowing the pills, get your heart pumping a little – it'll make the drugs work faster. And don't dilute them too much. It weakens the effect.'

Holly studied him for a long time, her face unreadable, her mind trying to work out what Solomon was up to. 'Who are you?' she said at last.

'I genuinely have no idea. And trust me, I don't want to be

here, bothering you like this, but I don't know what else to do. I have and am nothing more than what you see in front of you. This is the sum total of me. I'm lost and trying to find myself. And I'm asking you if you will help me?'

'You came here with Morgan,' she said.

'I didn't leave with him though, did I?'

'Doesn't prove anything. You could still be with them, brought here to show me sympathy and talk about wanting to help Jim to get me to trust you and find out what I know.'

'You think if they wanted to do that they'd bring someone who looked like me?'

She studied him, her eyes lingering on his bare feet for a moment before fixing back on his face. The rain thrummed above them, filling the silence like a drumroll anticipating her answer. She held out her hand. 'Show me the book.'

Solomon handed her the memoir and watched her read the dedication page again then frown and nod her head as if she had made her mind up. Then she stood and smoothed her dress down.

'Come with me,' she said. 'There's something you should probably see.'

33

Cassidy watched the charcoaled world slip past his window and despaired. It was going to cost a fortune to fix all this, let alone the amount of lost revenue that would come from having major roadworks on the main highway into town.

'Looks like ground zero up ahead,' the NTSB agent said.

What was his name again? Not like him to forget a name. Shows how distracted he was. His daddy had taught him the value of remembering a man's name when he was still a boy. 'They'll know yours,' he'd said. 'Everyone knows a Cassidy in this town, so it's up to you to even the score and put people at their ease. You shake their hand like you've been waiting all your life to meet that person and you repeat their name twice while staring them straight in the eye. Nothing wins respect more than remembering someone's name. You forget someone's name, you might as well spit in their face.'

And he'd forgotten the agent's name.

They cruised to a bumpy halt twenty or so yards short of what was left of the plane. The fire had burned away everything but the metal, the road surrounding it looked like a puddle of boiling tar had been dumped on the ground and left to set.

'I'm going to take a look,' the agent said. 'Stay in the car if you want.'

'I'd like to see what nearly destroyed my town, if you don't mind.' – *What might still destroy it.*

'Suit yourself,' the agent said – Davidson, that was his name. 'Just stay back from the wreckage and don't touch anything.'

Mulcahy could have done without the mayor tagging along but he couldn't do much about it. He opened the trunk and sheltered from the rain under the tailgate as he gathered what he needed from his own kit bag – a pair of nitrile gloves, some evidence bags, a Maglite. He had learned that the best way to remove something from a crime scene wasn't to sneak in and try to smuggle it out, it was to walk up as if you belonged there, put it straight in an evidence bag and carry it away. It helped to get there fast while the local cops were still in charge and the situation was still fluid. Like now.

'OK, let's go take a peek,' he said, closing the trunk and opening his umbrella with a sound that always reminded him of a silenced weapon being fired. The mayor joined him beneath the umbrella and they moved forward together, picking their way across the melted road.

Mulcahy could feel trapped heat radiating up through the soles of his shoes. 'Some fire here, huh?' he said, trying to relax the mayor and soften him up a little so he might talk. 'Looks like the road boiled.'

The mayor nodded. 'You must see things like this all the time,' he said.

'Nope,' Mulcahy said truthfully. 'Planes don't generally crash on roads.'

'What about runways?'

'Runways are not roads. They're much tougher – usually paved concrete or a concrete asphalt mix – so they tend to hold up better in a fire,' Mulcahy said, reciting some, quite possibly bullshit, Wikifacts Siri had read out to him on the drive over. 'Most planes crash at sea. Actually, most planes don't crash at all, it's still the safest form of transport. And even when they do crash, it's not always fatal. You had someone walk away from this one, didn't you?'

'Yes. Well, he walked away from the crash site, but he says he wasn't on the plane.'

'We'll need to talk to him, get an official statement.' He stopped and turned to the mayor. 'I'm sorry, but I'm going to have to ask you to stop here, sir.'

'Of course.'

'I need to take the umbrella with me.'

'That's OK, you do what you gotta do.'

Mulcahy turned and moved on alone, picking his way carefully through the rising forest of jagged aircraft parts and steam towards the large mess of twisted metal in the centre of a crater. He pulled out an evidence bag and the Maglite from his pocket and squatted down at the edge of it.

The rain thrummed on his umbrella and made pinging sounds as it struck metal inside the twisted structure. He shone the Maglite through the blackened ribs into the dark centre, picking up details of what lay inside. The asphalt had melted here and various heat-damaged objects were embedded in it. He swept the torch beam over them, recognizing very little of what he was seeing but searching for something very specific.

Once, back when he was still working homicide, he'd been called to a warehouse fire set to hide evidence of a triple murder. He'd seen plenty of death in his career but the blackened pile of bones he had gazed upon in that warehouse had made a deeper impression on him than anything. There were the remains of three people lying on that warehouse floor, three people who had woken up that morning, kissed their wives and kids or whatever and ended the day as nothing more than a pile of blackened bones. There's not much of a human body that won't burn if the temperature is high. Hell, even bone will crumble to nothing if it's hot enough, and this fire must have been like a furnace.

He was starting to wonder whether all of this was a waste of time and he should get back to the mayor and start pumping him for more information about the survivor. Then he saw something among the wreckage.

It was sticking up from the melted road and lying in a spot where the rain ran off the tangle of metal in a steady stream. It was a human bone, a femur, largest bone in the whole body. He changed his position, moving round to where he imagined the front of the aircraft might have been, probing the twisted metal with his torchlight. Beneath one of the thicker metal bands he spotted the jagged edges of a couple of shattered ribs. He traced backwards and the torchlight picked out a blackened jawbone embedded in the surface of the road, then a little way up from the jawbone he found what he was looking for.

The skull was lying on its side, mostly crushed by a large metal strut with rain running over it, making the white bone easier to see. A small rectangle of metal was fixed to it with surgical screws, about an inch or so above what was left of the right eye socket.

'There you are,' Mulcahy murmured, putting the flashlight in his mouth. He shone the beam at the skull and took several photos on his phone.

'You found something?' the mayor shouted, his voice cutting through the thrumming rain.

Mulcahy pulled the flashlight from his mouth. 'Human remains,' he called back.

He stood and slipped the phone in his pocket to protect it from the rain, then turned away and headed back to the car. The real Feds would be here soon. He needed to stay out of their way if he wanted to remain useful and keep his father alive.

'I've seen enough,' he said, walking straight past Mayor Cassidy towards the car. 'The crash scene investigators can take it from here.'

He got in the car, fired up the engine and started backing away before the mayor even had a chance to buckle his seat belt. 'I'll drop you at the control line,' he said, turning around and driving as quickly over the ruined road as he dared. 'If you could keep this road clear until the main unit arrive. I'll call in what I've seen to get them up to speed. They'll do everything they can to get the road open as soon as possible.'

The mayor nodded. He seemed distracted and Mulcahy could guess why.

They drove in silence and Mulcahy dropped him at the billboard where people were still celebrating. The mayor peered out anxiously at the crowd, checking for faces he didn't recognize.

I'm here already, Mulcahy thought. *You're looking in the wrong direction.*

'Thanks for your help,' he said, eager for the mayor to get out.

'You're welcome,' Cassidy replied, still scanning faces. 'If there's anything else you need …'

'Actually, there is,' Mulcahy said, pulling his phone from his pocket and opening up the map application. The Jeep had built-in satnav, but he never put information into a car he might have to dump. 'The survivor you were talking about. If you could tell me where I might find him, I sure would like to talk to him about what happened here.'

34

Holly led Solomon through the quiet house, the only sound the rain on the roof above them.

'This is Jim's study,' she said and pushed open a door into a room that looked like a tornado had ripped through it. Every drawer had been pulled out, every filing cabinet opened and emptied. Financial documents carpeted the floor, along with leather-bound legal books that had once lined the walls, their covers lying open like the wings of dead birds. A computer monitor sat in the middle of a desk that had been swept clear, the screen lighting up the devastation in the room.

Solomon stepped inside and breathed in, catching the musky scent of the room, leather and wood. The smell of engine grease and hay was here too, lifted from the skin of the man who had trashed it by the heat of his efforts.

'You say you want to find out who you are.' Holly moved over to the far wall. 'Well, so did Jim.'

The wall was entirely covered with file cards, scraps of paper, maps, photographs. There seemed to be two distinct columns of information: on the left was a large map of the local area covered with old photographs and photocopied pages from an old journal written in old-style copperplate that reminded Solomon of the dedication in his copy of Jack

Cassidy's memoir; on the right a column of dates ran from floor to ceiling – 1850 at the bottom to the present at the top – with names written on separate cards next to various dates in between. A copy of the page of an old Bible had been pinned at the top between both columns. It was from Proverbs. A section had been underlined: 'A good name is rather to be chosen than great riches, and loving favour rather than silver and golde.'

'This is Jim's family tree,' Holly said, pointing to the right-hand side of the wall. 'As far as he'd managed to trace it. He'd been contacting all kinds of people recently in connection with it. Perhaps you were one of them.'

Solomon stepped closer, blood humming in his ears at the thought that the wall might contain a clue as to who he was. Some names had photographs next to them, the more recent ones mostly, but there were also a few steely tintypes capturing the firm jaws and faraway stares of folk long dead. Solomon's eyes picked hungrily at it all, sucking in the details, but his name was not there, and his face did not stare out at him from the jumble of images.

He turned to the maps and documents filling the left-hand side of the wall. 'What's this?'

'Research for a book Jim was writing about the lost Cassidy fortune – you know what that is?'

Solomon recalled all the books and treasure maps he'd seen in the souvenir shops that referenced it. He had also read something in Jack Cassidy's memoir that had hinted at it. '"*I have become famous in my lifetime*",' he quoted from memory, '"*for finding a great fortune out in the desert, but in truth there is another treasure far greater than the first, that I discovered late in my life after a great amount of study*".'

'You've read his memoir.'

'Yes.'

'So have lots of people. Ever since it was first published people have been coming here looking for it. They still get busloads of folks turning up to search for the lost fortune.'

Solomon studied the maps, the documents, the photocopies of Bible pages with notes scrawled on them. 'Was your husband searching for it too?'

Holly shrugged. 'Maybe. I don't know if he actually believed in it. He liked the idea of it, he was a romantic that way, but he kind of abandoned writing the book once he got a lead on his real family.'

Solomon turned back to the column of dates and names. 'How long had he been working on his family tree?'

'Not long. Only since he got elected, a month maybe. As sheriff elect he got access to the town's confidential records so he could familiarise himself with the finances and all the charitable trusts he was going to be managing. But it also gave him access to other parts of the archives, including the admission papers to The Cassidy.'

'The Cassidy – what's that?'

'The orphanage. It closed about ten years ago when money started getting tight. Jim grew up there. He was an orphan.'

The word was like a bright lamp shedding new light on everything: the white picket fence outside, the white gables, the rocker on the porch – it was all a projection, a child's idea of a perfect family home, imagined and then created by someone who had never had one. It also explained James Coronado's obsessive need to find out where he was from and who he was. Solomon understood that well enough.

'One of the things Jim campaigned on was re-opening The Cassidy,' Holly continued, 'putting the heart back into the community, he called it, returning the town to what

Jack Cassidy had always intended it to be, a place of charity and Christian goodness. Jack Cassidy originally set it up as a home for abandoned women and children, but over the years it became an orphanage. It was Jim's home for the first seventeen years of his life, the closest thing he ever had to a family. But the admission files opened a door to his real family.' She took a photocopied form from the wall and handed it to Solomon. It detailed the admission of the infant James Coronado. There was a girlish, looping signature at the bottom of the page in the section for next of kin: 'Carol Nielsen' then, in brackets, 'mother'.

'Jim managed to track her down to a trailer park north of Nogales. She'd been living there for years with some guy. He was still there, but she had died of cancer a few years back. He had a bunch of her stuff and was more than happy to get rid of it.' She looked up at a bookcase that had been swept clean, then down to the pile of things on the floor below it. She crouched and retrieved a clear plastic bag from the pile and handed it to Solomon. 'He found this among her things.'

The seal at the top of the bag had been opened then folded back over again, presumably when it had been found not to contain whatever the intruder had been searching for. Inside was a small black book. He opened the bag and a smell of old cigarettes billowed out like a foul genie escaping a bottle. He pulled the book out and turned it over in his hand. It was old and worn and bound in thin leather that might have been pale blue when it was new but had gone a mottled, greasy bluish-grey from years of being handled by unclean hands. The spine had started to crack and the gold lettering mostly worn away, leaving only the outline of the words 'HOLY BIBLE' stamped into the leather.

He opened the cover and saw tiny writing inside recording

a family's history stretching back to the middle of the eighteenth century. It was the same list of names pinned to the wall in front of him, only with one significant difference. In the Bible the family tree ended at Carol Nielsen's name. She had not recorded the birth of her son.

'Look at her birth date and then Jim's,' Holly said. 'She was sixteen when she had him. We thought maybe she'd fallen pregnant and either the father didn't want to know or wasn't around, so she brought him to The Cassidy and left him with nothing but a name she'd borrowed from her oldest relative.' She pointed at the first name written in the greasy Bible – *James Coronado (b. 1857 – d. ?)*.

'She was so young and she must have been so scared. I can't imagine how awful it must be to walk up to a building with your baby in your arms and walk away again without him.'

In these words, Solomon caught a fresh glimpse of how enormous Holly's loss had been. When James Coronado died she had lost more than her husband, she had lost her own future as well, the years they would have spent together, the family they'd planned on having. He looked up at the top of the wall where a card with five blank spaces marked on it was pinned next to James and Holly's names.

'That was kind of a joke,' Holly said, following his gaze. 'Jim always said he wanted enough kids to form a junior soccer team.'

'How about you, how many did you want?'

She looked at the empty card and her eyes misted. 'One would have been fine.'

Solomon felt her sadness deepen and wondered whether he should move away from this tender subject. He glanced down at a small square of paper he had spotted when he had first stepped in the room, half-buried in a pile of papers by the desk. Maybe it was nothing to do with him, but he felt, somehow, that it might be.

'So what happened?' he asked.

'What do you mean?'

Solomon stepped over to the desk, picked up the square of paper and handed it to her. 'What happened to your baby?'

Holly caught her breath when she saw what it was. She took it and crumpled slowly down into the chair by the desk. 'I didn't know he'd kept this,' she said, her finger tracing the lines of the barely formed nose and chin picked out on the ultrasound scan. 'This is the twelve-week scan. We lost him a week later.'

'Him?'

A single tear dripped down her cheek. 'Jim Junior, we called him, though I don't think he would've ended up being called that. We thought we had plenty of time to come up with another name.' She wiped her cheek with the back of her hand. 'Turns out we didn't.'

'How did your husband take the loss?'

She let out a long sigh. 'Like a man, and by that I mean he was strong and stoic and supportive but kept his own feelings hidden. He did that a lot, it seems, more than I knew.' She turned in the seat and moved the mouse across the screen. 'I found this the other day.' She clicked on an icon with 'ForJJ' written beneath it and a screen popped open showing a still of a man sitting in the chair Holly now sat in.

'Hi,' the man said as the clip started playing and Solomon felt the skin on the back of his neck tighten when he realized who it must be. 'I just found out you were coming and felt like I wanted to talk to you, so here I am. I never had a dad when I was growing up so I don't really know how this works. I always wished I'd had one, so I could talk to him, ask him about stuff. So that's what I want to say to you, little man, that I was thinking about you and wanted to talk to you before you were even born. So remember that, if you ever feel like you can't tell me anything. Because you always can. I'll always be here for you. You'll always have me and your mom. And I can't wait to meet you. Take care, little man.'

The picture froze and Solomon studied the face of James Coronado, the man he had come in search of, the man he was here to save. He looked up at the wall behind the screen and the same face stared out of a series of framed photographs showing a group of five boys standing by a campfire and in front of what appeared to be a house with no walls and a woven, wooden roof.

Ramada – the word floated up in Solomon's mind – *Hohokam Indian word for a shelter.*

The landscape beyond the ramada was prehistoric, unchanged since before the Hohokam or anybody else had stood there. An escarpment rose behind them on the horizon, a deep V-shaped niche cut into it by an ancient river.

Solomon studied the boys' faces, frozen in time by flash-bulbs that had charted their childhood in yearly increments. Each year they grew a little more until the last picture showed men in their twenties, some fatter, some with hair that was starting to thin, but still recognizably the same boys who had posed for that first photograph. James Coronado stood at the centre, a little taller than the rest and with a gravity to him that seemed to pull the others in. If this group of boys had a leader, it was him.

Solomon studied his face, willing it to be familiar. But he didn't recognize him. James Coronado, the man who had recorded this message for the son he would never see, the man he was here to save, was a stranger to him.

35

Mulcahy eased the Jeep to a stop several houses short of the address the mayor had given him. He cut the engine and scanned the street through the rain. It was small-town Americana perfection with decent-sized plots and double-car drives with garages at the top. Only one car was parked in the drive of Holly Coronado's house, but he could see a light in a lower window showing someone was there.

He picked up his phone and studied the archived webpage of a local newspaper. The article had a picture of the other car that was usually parked here, all twisted up at the bottom of a ravine like an empty beer can. The headline above it read:

SHERIFF ELECT DEAD IN TRAGIC ACCIDENT

He scrolled down the article and found another picture, a photograph of the dead man and his wife standing in an old graveyard and smiling for the cameras. She was pretty. They were a handsome couple. They looked like they had it all worked out and everything going for them. Just goes to show.

He looked up again and studied the street. A single porch light was glowing weakly in the shade of a wide verandah a few houses down from the widow's home but he could not sense any life behind the windows of the house. Probably just a sensor that had tripped automatically in the flat grey light beneath the storm clouds. Most of the townsfolk were still down at the control line. He figured they would stay there a while, even with this rain. It wasn't every day you saved your town from destruction. If he lived here, he would want to stay there too, savouring every happy, noisy, back-slapping moment before he had to return to his nice house on a safe street like this where lights came on automatically to keep the darkness at bay.

This was the kind of street he had once imagined living in, before his life had veered off in a different and darker direction. For a long time, when the life he had left behind was still fresh in his mind, he had replayed certain events over and over like an armchair quarterback trying to win a lost game, thinking about how things might have turned out if he had made other choices, or been a better man, or a stronger man, or a smarter one. It was only over time he gradually realized that he had never had any choice in the first place. Nobody did really. The truth of it was that if someone with power wanted to reach into your life and tear the heart out of it, there was nothing much you could do about it. Just like now.

He attached the photograph he had taken at the crash site to a new message, pressed send and watched it go. It would get bounced around a few times before it got to Tío. Then things would get interesting. People would die because of what had happened here. Some of them would deserve it, but not all. He clicked on another message and studied the blurry photographs Tío had sent of the man with white skin and hair, and a mark on his arm that may or may not have been a kill tag – the man who was in the house he was looking at now.

He opened the glove box, took out his Beretta and the sunglasses case with the suppressor inside. He replaced the partially spent magazine with a full one, checked his gun then screwed the suppressor to the muzzle. Tío had said he wanted the man alive, but Mulcahy wasn't going to take any chances. He laid the gun down on the seat and looked back up at the house. The storm was easing now, the drumming of the rain on the roof of his car getting softer.

He would have liked it if his pop had lived somewhere nice like this instead of the ratty three-room apartment over the laundromat. Then again, Pop didn't seem to mind where he lived. He had never been particularly good at holding on to money either. Easy come, easy go, that was the closest they got to a family motto. He remembered when he was eleven and Pop would return from his week-long trips to those exotic-sounding places, his car covered in road dust. It was only later in life, when Mulcahy had been to these places himself, that he figured out why Pop had sometimes returned happy and bearing gifts and other times quiet and broke.

He ran through the names in his mind again, a roll call recalled from his youth: Oklahoma City; Des Moines; Shakopee; Omaha; Kansas City. He went through it a second time, adding other names: Remington Park in Oklahoma City; Prairie Meadows in Des Moines; Canterbury Downs in Shakopee; Ak-Sar-Ben in Omaha; Woodlands in Kansas City. Racetracks. Every place had a racetrack.

He reached down and pulled the laundry sack out from beneath the seat, the sharp edges of magazine clips and gunsights stretching the plastic and poking through in some places. He picked out Carlos's Glock and a spare magazine then stashed the bag back in the footwell. He tested the Glock's action and swapped out the magazine for a full one.

He would need a backup weapon in case the guy was cartel like Tío suspected. The Glock was reliable and had no safety, which made it a good choice for a backup piece – you didn't want to be fiddling round with safety options in the middle of a firefight. It was also generic and untraceable. Carlos had done him the service of filing off the serial number. He laid it on the seat next to the Beretta and checked the street again.

If he had managed to buy a house like this for Pop, chances are he would only have re-mortgaged it on the sly for some up-front cash and lost it all at the track or in some back-room poker game. Just the way it was, no point in getting bent out of shape about it. If you started having issues with the bad things in people and trying to change them, you were in danger of losing sight of what was good about them too. And for all his faults, he wouldn't change Pop for anything. If it hadn't been for him he might not even have made it out of childhood.

He picked up the Glock, slipped it into his shoulder holster then took the silenced Beretta in hand. He owed him everything, could never repay him for what he had done, but right now, in the next hour or so, he was going to have to do whatever it took to try.

36

Holly watched Solomon moving around the study, his head turning slowly, taking everything in. He seemed unreal in some ways, his white skin and hair making him seem like a beautiful, classical, marble statue that had been brought to life and dressed in ordinary clothes. He had an extraordinary stillness about him and she found it calming, like staring at the surface of a deep lake.

During her recent internet trawls she had come across several accounts of potential suicides who had been saved by what one had described as a 'familiar stranger', someone who had appeared and seemed to know them and understand their pain. Some described these strangers as angels, others as the spirits of loved ones – fathers, mothers, grandparents – who had come to stop them crossing over to the other side. When she had read these stories she had put it down to some kind of extreme mental and emotional state creating sub-conscious projections of the survival instinct. Perhaps that's what he was. Except in all the reported cases the stranger had dissuaded the witness from suicide whereas Solomon had given her specific instructions on how she might do it more effectively. Then again, that was exactly the slightly perverse, counter-intuitive way her subconscious would work, tell her to do something, knowing she was most likely to do the exact opposite.

He turned and looked at her, his pale, grey eyes so piercing she imagined he could read her thoughts. 'What do you think they wanted?' he asked.

'A file, something like that – I don't know for sure. I think Jim found out something about the town, something they didn't want getting out.'

'Who's "*they*"?'

'The town elders. The sheriffs. They run this place. Redemption is more like a corporation than a town, with members of a board instead of public officials. There's the mayor, who is the chief executive, then there are two sheriffs who answer to him, one for commerce and one for philanthropy. Jim had been elected sheriff in charge of philanthropy.'

'Seems a grand title for such a small town.'

'This whole place has delusions of grandeur. Have you seen the church? It's like they shipped a cathedral over from Europe and dropped it in the middle of the desert. Can you imagine what it must have looked like when most people here were still living in tents or one-room cabins? Redemption was built on Christ as much as copper, Mr Creed, never forget that. And you can't win a fight against someone who thinks they have God on their side.'

'I thought God was supposed to be on everyone's side.'

'Not in this town. Here, if your name is Cassidy then you are God. Morgan and the other sheriffs, they're disciples. Except Jim wasn't. He was never part of their club. I think to them he was always going to be an orphan boy from The Cassidy who made good. But they needed him because of the trusts.'

Solomon nodded. 'Morgan mentioned those. What are they?'

'They're the lifeblood of this town and also why the Cassidy family is so powerful here. Jack Cassidy set them up when he founded the town. They act like a localized welfare system, a large charity fund, run by his family, that supports the community. As long as a Cassidy lives here they're protected and so is the town. But no more Cassidys, no more trusts.'

'And Mayor Cassidy has no children.'

'Exactly. As soon as he dies the trusts will revert to the church. When Jack Cassidy set them up this wasn't a problem because the church was part of the town. But now it's not, now it's part of the Episcopal Diocese of Arizona. So when Cassidy dies the trusts will no longer be owned or administered by the town alone, they will be managed by the church, which means the funds could go anywhere in the state – and probably will. And most people here rely on subsidies from the trusts to keep going.'

'What about the mine? Morgan said it was still producing.'

'If it is, it can't be much. They had to close down production about fifteen years ago because of groundwater contamination. Bunch of people got sick from the chemicals they were using. Cost the town a fortune to clean it all up and pay damages. If it wasn't for the trusts this whole place would have gone under. The trusts are where the money is, not the mine, not the airfield and not the tourists. Jim's job was to try to find ways of securing them for the town. It was his area of expertise. That's why they needed him.' She spotted a card on the floor, picked it up and gave it to Solomon:

Mayor Ernest Cassidy
and the Sheriffs of Redemption
request the presence of
Mr James Coronado
at a formal dinner at the Cassidy residence
to celebrate his election as sheriff

'Jim got it the day after the election, an invite to sit at the big table. I teased him about it, saying he'd probably have to go through some kind of hazing ceremony where they'd paint him copper and get him to recite the Lord's Prayer while they smacked him on the ass with Bibles or something. He laughed, acted like it was no big deal, but I knew it was, the orphan kid being invited to dine at the Cassidy residence.

'Anyway, the day of the big dinner came and he had been studying hard for it like it was the bar exam or something. He'd been going through the old town budgets, reading through all the trust paperwork going back years. The finances were in a worse state than he thought, I know that much.

'I remember kissing him goodbye and telling him not to worry, that he should enjoy the moment and that they should be glad to have him in their corner. He had his best suit on. He looked so handsome. And he was happy, nervous but happy. And I was so proud of him because he'd done exactly what he'd set out to do, and all he had in front of him was hard work, and he had never been afraid of that.

'I suppose in some ways it was the last time I saw him properly, the last time I saw the Jim that I knew. I went to bed that night hoping they were being kind to him and that he was having a good time. The bed seemed too big without him. I wasn't used to him not being there – I'm still not used to it. Anyway, I woke up just after dawn. The sun was coming up and the birds were getting noisy and the bed was still empty. I sat up and, I don't know why but I could feel that Jim was in the house – you know sometimes when you can feel someone's presence, even if you can't hear them?'

Solomon nodded. He knew.

'I called his name but he didn't reply, so I got up and went to find him. I found him here, sitting in this chair. He had a bottle of whiskey open and a glass that was half full. I could smell the alcohol before I even stepped into the room. There was something about the smell of it and the fact that Jim hadn't answered when I had called that made me feel uneasy, like something terrible had happened, like someone had died and he didn't want to face me and have to tell me the news.

'He was pretty drunk, which made me think he must have been home a while, because Mayor Cassidy is not a drinking man. He must have downed about half the bottle, sitting in the dark on his own.

'I asked him what had happened, thinking it must be something terrible to have made him drink like that, but he wouldn't tell me. He just kept shaking his head and staring at the bottle. I was scared. I had never seen him like that before.

'I made him get up and walked him to the bedroom and put him to bed, thinking he would sleep it off and talk to me about it later. But he never did. Whatever had happened at that dinner, whatever they had talked about, whatever he found out, killed something inside him. I think it broke his heart.

'After that night I hardly saw him. He slept it off, got up, showered and changed then drove into town. He came back later with a trunk full of archive boxes filled with files and went straight to his study. The only thing he said to me was that there was something he needed to fix but he couldn't tell me what it was because he needed to protect me from it. That was the word he used – "protect" – like he'd found something poisonous and was trying to keep it from me for my own safety.

'So I left him alone. He was unreachable anyway, so I kept away, figuring he would work through whatever it was then come back to me. But he never did. Three days later he was dead.'

'What about the others who were at the dinner, have you spoken to them?'

'After Jim died the mayor called and offered condolences. I asked him about the dinner but he wouldn't talk about it, kept saying that I was upset and it was all a tragic accident.'

'But you don't think it was – an accident.'

'No. Something happened. I don't know if they killed Jim to silence him or whether whatever he found drove him off that road, but either way I blame them for it.'

'Have you talked to the other sheriffs?'

'The only other one is Pete Tucker, sheriff for commerce. He's a big landowner around here, has a majority stake in the airfield because a lot of it is built on his ranch. I haven't spoken to him.'

'What about the coroner's report, have you seen a copy?'

'No.'

'It would be useful to see exactly what killed him, whether it was a car crash or something else. Though if your husband was trying to save the town, it doesn't make sense for them to—'

A loud knock echoed through the house, three raps on the front door.

'Stay here,' Holly said. 'I'll go see who it is.'

She left the study and walked down the quiet halls of her house, thinking about the pale stranger in her husband's study and wondering if he was really there at all. She felt slightly panicked at the thought that she might return and find him gone, his mission to distract her complete. She didn't want him to go. Talking to him was comforting. She moved through the disordered mess of her living room and opened the front door. She saw the gun first. Then she saw the man who was holding it.

37

Morgan pushed through the door into his office and closed it behind him, muffling the sound of ringing phones in the outer office. There was no one there to answer them, everyone out in the field dealing with the aftermath of the fire.

He dropped a plastic hospital sack on his desk, made his way over to a battered locker in the corner and took out a fresh shirt. The locker had been in his life longer than most of the people he knew, a souvenir from high school he'd saved from the bulldozer when it closed its doors for the last time eight years earlier.

He shrugged out of his ruined shirt, his eyes fixed on the initials he had scratched into the locker door when he was eleven. There was something instinctive about making your mark on things. Some people scratched their names on lockers, others, like the Cassidys, on the side of buildings, but the impulse was the same; it showed that you had been there, it showed that you had existed.

He dropped the ruined shirt in the trash can by his desk and studied the red spots on his chest where the salt crystals had hit him but not broken the skin.

Goddamn woman. He knew she was upset but, Jesus! Did

she have to go unloading shotguns on people? As if he didn't have enough to deal with.

He slipped his arms into the new shirt, his hands stinging inside fresh dressings as he fastened his buttons, then he settled behind his desk in the same oak-and-leather chair that had been intimately familiar with the behinds of every single one of the town's police chiefs. He tapped a password into his computer and opened up the National DMV database. Now the fire was out, his mind had fixed on what would happen next. A firestorm of a different kind was heading their way and he needed to tread very carefully if he was going to survive it. He liked to be prepared and have all the information to hand and there was one variable he was increasingly unhappy about.

'OK, Mr Creed,' he said under his breath, typing Solomon's name into the search field. 'Let's find out who you really are.'

He hit return and got three matches, all African Americans aged between fifty-five and seventy. Whoever Solomon Creed was, he wasn't on this database, which meant he didn't have an American driving licence. He opened a new window and set up searches on all the other national and inter-national identity databases he had access to – Social Security, passport agencies, Interpol – then he sat back in his chair and stared at the wall opposite while he waited for the searches to run.

Sixteen faces stared back at him, portraits of every one of his predecessors stretching right back to a silver nitrate print of Nathanial Priddy, first police chief of the town of Redemption. He was a flinty-looking character, stiff-necked, impressive whiskers and the flat eyes of a killer – which is exactly what he was. Even with God on their side and the Rev. Jack preaching love and understanding from the pulpit,

Nathan Priddy had been a necessary evil at the birthing of this town. He was buried up the hill in the old cemetery, along with several people he had personally put there.

Simpler times. Direct solutions. No comebacks.

Morgan traced the line of faces representing over one hundred and thirty years of law enforcement. You could see how things had softened over the years just by looking at them. They started with bony, humourless faces captured in stark black and white, their profiles strong, their eyes gazing past the camera as if something far more important was happening just out of frame. Then, with each new photograph, the poses softened and the lean bones of harder times slowly disappeared beneath the padding of prosperity and easier lives. Smiles started to creep in, then colour too. Any fool could keep the town running while a river of money flowed through it. But when it dried up and the earth started to crack, it took someone with real strength of character to stop it all from falling apart. Someone like Nathan Priddy. Someone like him.

His computer chirped, telling him it had finished its search. He glanced at the screen – eighty-two matches – opened the first and started working through them.

He was convinced Solomon must be working for someone; he was too accomplished to be just some guy who had happened along – the way he had taken over at the fire line, the fact that he seemed to know more than the doctors, even the manner in which he had dumped Lawrence Hayes on the ground when he'd first appeared on the road. Lawrence had been all-state wrestling champion before becoming a medic and Solomon had tossed him on the ground like he was leaving a dollar tip for a diner waitress. And there was that burn on his arm, and the copy of Jack Cassidy's memoir in his pocket with Jim Coronado's name on it – far too many question marks to be hanging over a stranger's head with things standing the way they were. But Morgan was also cautious. He was treading a fine line and couldn't afford to put a foot wrong. He needed to know who Solomon Creed was before he threw him to the wolves, or decided which wolves to throw him to.

It took him less than ten minutes to go through all eighty-two results and he drew a blank on every one of them. The Solomon Creed he had dropped off at Holly Coronado's house did not appear to officially exist, which told a story in itself. People couldn't not exist these days, it was almost impossible. So either he was some off-the-grid undercover operative – or he was using a false name.

Morgan picked up the plastic sack he had brought from the hospital and took an evidence bag from his desk drawer. He carefully removed the starter cap from inside the sack, holding it by the peak and turning it slowly until he found the single strand of white hair trapped in the seam of the headband. He held it over the opened evidence bag and squeezed his finger and thumb to nip the hair between the plastic then pulled the cap away to leave the single strand of hair inside. He sealed it and held it up to the light. The hair glowed. At one end he could see the bud of a root where it had been pulled from Solomon's scalp, carrying a nice little plug of DNA-rich cells with it.

He filled in the paperwork for the DNA sweep, clipped the evidence bag to the requisition form and dropped the whole lot in his out-tray, ready to hand it to the Feds when they took over the crash investigation. The presence of the NTSB would add some weight to things and speed up the paperwork. He would intercept the results before anyone else saw them and make them disappear, pass them up a different food-chain, the one he was helping put in place.

He opened the top drawer of his desk and reached to the back where he had taped a phone to the underside of the desktop. It was a cheap contract-free throwaway with internet capability so he didn't need to go through one of the networks to make a call. He switched it on and looked up at the wall of faces again while he waited for it to power up. He doubted any of them would have had the guts to do what he was about to do, except maybe Nathan Priddy, who'd put five people in the ground to protect the town. That was all he was doing really – making sacrifices for a greater good.

The phone finished its start-up routine and he dialled a number from memory.

'*¿Si?*' someone answered after three rings and Morgan caught the sound of a busy street or café behind the voice.

'*Soledad,*' Morgan replied, giving the code word.

He heard handling noise as the middleman fumbled with another phone and called a different number. Then Morgan heard the sound of a phone ringing through the burble of conversation and clink of coffee cups.

'*¿Si!*' someone new answered.

'The fire's out,' he said, his hand stinging as it curled round the small phone. He didn't need to identify himself. The phone had been given to him when he had brokered the deal beneath a star-spattered sky on a desert track running parallel with the Mexican border. They would know who was using it.

'You all set your end?' The voice was flat and cold.

'Almost. There's a guy here, an albino, showed up by the crash. Calls himself Solomon Creed. He anything to do with you?'

'Never heard of him. He a problem?'

Morgan shook his head. 'Not any more.' He looked up at Nathan Priddy, killer of five men, and wondered if he'd beat that number by the time this thing was over. 'What now?' he asked.

'Now we wait,' the voice on the line said. 'The trap is all set. We just got to see if we catch anything.' Then the phone clicked and went dead.

38

'Mrs Coronado,' the man pointing the gun sounded embarrassed. 'I'm sorry to have to do this but you're going to have to surrender your firearm and come with me.'

There were two of them, uniformed cops wearing flak jackets, side-arms drawn. Holly recognized the lead cop but couldn't recall his name. His jacket was hiding his badge. He was Bobby or Billy, something like that. All the men in town seemed to have names that ended with an 'ee' sound. Even those who didn't twisted them round until they did, like Mayor Ernest Cassidy insisting everybody call him 'Ernie'.

'You need to surrender your firearm and come with us,' the cop repeated.

Donny! That was his name.

'We need to talk to you about what happened here.'

Donny McGee – two 'ee's for the price of one. Fairly new guy. One of Morgan's men. The thought made her lips thin.

'I can give you a statement,' she said. 'There was an intruder on my property. I asked him to leave and warned him that I would shoot if he did not. He did not, so I shot him – with rock salt. Then he left. The gun is legal and licensed to my husband at this address. That's my statement.' She started to close the door but Donny stepped forward, planting his boot over the threshold to keep it open. 'I'm sorry, Mrs Coronado. I still got to take you in.' His voice dropped a little as if the whole street might be listening and he didn't want them to hear. 'You didn't shoot just anyone and we can't let a thing like that slide, don't matter what you been through.'

'You mean the fact that I only finished burying my husband a couple hours ago?'

Donny lowered his gun a little. 'Like I said, I am real sorry about this, but it's for your own good as much as anything. You shouldn't be left on your own with a loaded firearm, not at a time like this.'

'She's not on her own.' The voice made Donny look up.

Holly turned and felt a rush of relief to see Solomon standing in the hallway. If he was a figment of her imagination he sure was a persistent one. She turned back to Donny. 'Can you see him?'

He looked confused. 'Sure!'

'Then you can see I'm not on my own, so thank you for your concern.' She attempted to close the door again but Donny's boot still blocked it. He lowered his gun and slipped it into its holster. The cop behind him held his position. Holly was pretty sure he was called Tom, which inevitably meant he was known as Tommy.

'Listen, Mrs Coronado,' Donny said in his best *let's be reasonable* voice. 'I'm sorry we had to come knocking on your door like this, but you unloaded a shotgun into Chief Morgan's chest. We were dispatched here to bring you in and make sure you're OK. That's the full extent of it, for now. But if you don't come voluntarily then we're going to bring you in anyway, which means we will have to arrest you. I don't want to do that, but if you make me I will. I'm sorry.'

'You keep saying "sorry",' she said, listening to the water gurgling in the gutter. 'If you truly are then stop doing the thing you're having to apologize for and leave me alone.'

'Can't do that,' Donny said as if the words caused him pain. 'I hate having to do this, but I do think it's for your own good. Where's the shotgun?'

Holly stared past him at the rain. It was easing now and the day beginning to lighten as the sun broke through the clouds. Raindrops fell through shafts of sunlight and shone like diamonds against the wet road and the dark houses opposite. There was probably a rainbow somewhere but she couldn't see it from where she was standing.

'Mrs Coronado.' She looked back into the earnest face of the cop. 'The shotgun?'

She let out a sigh then opened the door and pointed at the floor. 'Over there by the couch. Safety's on.'

Donny moved past her, nodding politely as he entered the house like he was just Sunday visiting. He pulled a large evidence bag from his pocket and shook it out as he walked over to the shotgun. 'What happened here?' he said, looking around at the disordered room.

'Isn't that what *you* should be finding out?' Solomon said.

The second cop moved forward to cover the room like this smart suburban home might actually be a meth lab and he expected armed resistance to manifest at any moment.

Donny turned the evidence bag inside out and used it to pick the gun up from the floor without touching it. 'You notice anything missing?'

'I don't know,' Holly replied. 'I haven't had chance to check. Maybe you should ask Chief Morgan about it – he didn't seem too surprised when I told him there'd been a break-in.'

Donny stood up and turned the bag the right way again, sealing the shotgun inside. 'We can get someone out if you want to report it.'

'You're already here,' Solomon said. 'Why don't you take a look?'

'We were only told to bring Mrs Coronado in and grab this.' He held up the bag with the shotgun in it.

'*Who* told you? Morgan?'

Donny looked over at Solomon but didn't say anything.

'Did he tell you to bring me in too?'

'Just Mrs Coronado and the gun.'

'What if she doesn't want to come?'

'Then we'll have to arrest her.'

'It's fine,' Holly said, stepping forward and giving in to the flow of things like someone tired of swimming against a strong current. 'I'll come with you, but can I change out of this first?' She held up the tattered ends of her dress.

'Sure,' Donny said.

Holly left the room with Solomon and the cops staring each other out. She stripped her dress off the moment she stepped into her bedroom and threw it in the tub in the en-suite so it wouldn't drip everywhere. It left muddy smears on the side and made her want to shower, but she figured the cops might take exception if she made them wait so instead she splashed water on her face then opened her closet, dug out a pair of grey jeans and a blue work shirt and pulled them on. She felt a knot tighten in her stomach when she spotted the bag of crushed sleeping pills next to the bottle of Scotch. She wondered, if things had happened differently – if she hadn't come home to find the place ransacked, if Morgan hadn't turned up and got her mad, if Solomon hadn't refused to leave – whether she would be lying on this bed now, a half-drunk, cloudy glass of Scotch on the night stand next to her. She shuddered at the thought and hurried over to hide the pills like a guilty secret she didn't want anyone else to know.

Solomon stood in the living room waiting for Holly to return. He was watching the two cops who were looking around the room, down at the floor, outside at the street, anywhere but directly at him. No one spoke.

'Don't you need a statement from me?' he asked.

'No,' Donny replied, still not meeting his eye.

'Why not? I'm a witness to what happened.'

'We were only told to bring Mrs Coronado in.'

'I'm here,' Holly said, reappearing in the living room and handing Solomon a pair of work boots. 'Jim was a size eleven, you look to be about the same, you can't go walking around barefoot, people will think you're strange.'

Solomon took the boots. 'I am strange,' he said.

'There's some thick socks in there too, in case they're too big. You might as well have them. They're good boots. They should be worn.'

Solomon took them and frowned. 'Does this mean you want me to go?'

'No, not at all.' She seemed flustered. 'Stay, please. Have another look through Jim's research, see if there's anything there that sparks a memory. I want to help you if I can.' She turned to the two cops, 'I won't be long, will I?'

Donny shrugged. 'Guess not.'

'Good,' she moved to the door. 'Then let's go get this over with.'

39

Solomon watched them drive away and listened to the silence flood back into the house. The rain had almost stopped now, the thrum of it falling on the roof replaced by gurgles and drips as it ran off the sun-baked land.

He breathed deeply and caught the gun-oil and boot-polish smell of the cops mingling with the faint, citrus scents of Holly and the house and the greasy hay overlay of the intruder.

There had been something odd about the cops and their unwillingness to engage with him. He would have understood if it had been regular small-town unfriendliness, but that would usually manifest itself as suspicion and some kind of territorial power display. They had demonstrated neither of those things. Instead they had practically ignored him, and he wondered at this as he sat on the couch, brushed away the loose dirt and dust from his feet and pulled the socks then the boots over his feet. He stood up and walked around. They were solidly built but the leather was supple and well broken in by the man who owned them. A phrase floated into Solomon's mind, one that had been coined by Cherokee Indians then stolen by the colonial invaders along with everything else:

Don't judge a man until you have walked a mile in his shoes.

He liked wearing James Coronado's boots. It felt right somehow. He liked the sound they made, the hard-leather soles staccato across the oak floorboards, as he walked to the back of the house. There was a door that hadn't been open before and he paused by it. Holly had left her bedroom door open in her hurry to leave and the citrusy smell of her flowed out from it, mingling with soap and the chalky odour of the crushed sleeping pills. He stepped across the threshold and followed his nose to the closet, opened the door and picked up the bag of white powder, enough to put an adult to sleep permanently. He thought about the sequence of events that had brought him here and how his insistence on coming to talk to Holly had probably saved her life. He glanced into the bathroom and saw her wet funeral gown in the bath, wet and ragged like a shed skin. He thought of her now, in the back of the car with the two cops who hadn't met his eye. Then he frowned, turned and headed out of the room.

Mulcahy watched the cruiser drive away then looked back at the house.

The street was still quiet, no new cars or activity. The rain was easing so he imagined people would stay down at the city limits even longer. Even so, he needed to be quick. Now he'd sent Tío the photograph of the blackened skull he would need to show him something else to prove his value and make sure the anger Tío would feel at the evidence of his son's death would not be turned on him or his pop.

He checked the Beretta one last time then slid the long, silenced barrel inside his jacket, then opened the car door and stepped out into the street.

40

Solomon returned to the study and went straight to the map pinned on the wall. His heart was beating hard, though from anxiety or excitement he couldn't quite tell.

His eyes moved across the drawn contours of the land, north to where the airfield was marked and beyond. A straight line cut across the desert showing where the storm drain marked the boundary of the airfield. Beyond it haphazard tracks cut across flat land and converged about a mile or so outside of town at a cluster of buildings with 'Tucker Ranch' written next to them. He recalled the dying words of the burned man.

Tell her I'm sorry, he had said. *Tell Ellie Tucker I'm sorry.*

He stared at the map, committing it to memory, then moved to the desk and picked up the formal invite to the sheriffs' dinner. Tucker had been at the dinner too so he would know what had been said there. Most likely he wouldn't share that information, but Solomon wanted to look him in the eye when he asked him the question. Besides, he had a promise to keep to a dead man. His eyes shifted to the monitor where James Coronado was still frozen. Two dead men.

He hit the space bar to set the message playing and listened again to the voice of the man he was here to save, a dead father talking to his dead son.

Mulcahy moved quickly across the street and up the slope of the drive. He softened his footfalls as he mounted the wooden steps of the porch and stopped by the door. He checked the street once more, pulled the Beretta from inside his jacket then pulled the screen open. The main door was unlocked, like he'd expected it to be. He had seen Holly leaving with the two cops and she hadn't paused to lock it. Why would she when there was someone still inside?

He pushed the door open and heard a man's voice coming from somewhere in back of the house. He moved inside, closing the door quietly behind him, then across the floor and past the couch, checking around as he went, zeroing in on the voice.

He passed an open bedroom door, checked it was clear and carried on down the hallway towards the voice.

He already knew what would happen here, had planned it all while sitting in the car. He would put the guy down then plant the Glock on him, fire it at the wall before he left so it would look like he'd come second in a gunfight. He would tell Tío the stranger had been working for the Saints, because that's what he wanted him to believe. It didn't matter whether he was or not, he was collateral, that was all, a pawn about to be played in a bigger game.

He reached the door, the voice loud now, loud enough to cover any noise he might have made though he knew he had made none. He took a breath. Swung the long barrel of the gun into the room and followed it in, eyes wide, following where it pointed, almost enough pressure on the trigger to fire but not quite. Instinct would add the rest as soon as he saw someone appear at the end of his barrel.

Except no one did.

He swept the gun around fast, checking all four corners of the room, but there was no one here and nowhere anyone could hide.

He moved round the desk so he could see the screen. A man was looking out and talking to the empty room. The clip reached the end and it jumped back to the start again.

Hi. I just found out you were coming and felt like I wanted to talk to you …

Mulcahy tapped the barrel of his gun on the space bar to stop it.

He listened in the silence that followed for movement, or the creak of a floorboard, or breathing, or – anything. All he heard was the trickle of water outside. There was no one here. The house was empty.

Solomon watched the man tap the keyboard with the long barrel of his gun and listen. He was in the garden, crouched low behind some clumps of deer grass that formed a natural screen. The garden was deep, running all the way back to the desert, no fences to hem him in. He could see the house but no one looking out would see him.

He wondered who this man was, stalking him with a weapon designed to kill quietly, and why the police were clearly helping him. The sight of him with the long lethal gun in his hand stirred a burning anger inside him, boiling and dangerous and ready to explode. He wanted to steal back in the house, pluck the gun from the man's hand, shoot him in the knees and ask him who had sent him while he writhed on the ground. He could picture it clearly in his head, hear the pops of the bullets and the howl of his agony. It would be so nice to give into it, but he knew he could not. He tensed every muscle and remained perfectly still, then relaxed them one by one, blowing out a steady stream of air like he was letting off steam.

It had been the cops' refusal to take him in for questioning that had made his instincts bristle, that and the sight of Holly's funeral dress. She had accused Morgan of using the funeral to get her out of the way, which made him think they were doing it again, only this time they were getting her out of the way so someone could get to him. The man standing in James Coronado's study proved he'd been right.

He watched the man move over to the window and stare out into the garden. It looked like he was staring straight at him but knew he couldn't be because Solomon's skin and hair were almost the same colour as the sun-bleached grass and he was staying perfectly still. He wondered who this man was and why he had come to kill him. He turned away from the window and disappeared from view. Solomon imagined him searching the house, looking for him or whatever James Coronado had found and most probably died for. He was now certain that he had been killed and that his part in James Coronado's salvation was to find out why.

After a while he heard a car engine start up on the far side of the house then drive away, its tyres hissing across the wet road. He waited a few minutes longer. Watching. Thinking. Then he stood and turned his back on the house James Coronado had called home and walked straight out into the desert.

VI

'*There is only one good – knowledge;*
and only one evil – ignorance.'

Socrates

IV

Extract from

**RICHES AND REDEMPTION
THE MAKING OF A TOWN**

⁑

*The published memoir
of the Reverend Jack 'King' Cassidy*

THE BLOOD WAS FRESH.

It stained the sandy bottom of a shallow pit clawed through the layer of dry mesquite straw and into the dry, rocky earth beneath. There was another hole close by. Another further along, all with the lighter dirt thrown out around them like a dog had passed through searching for a buried bone.

I slipped from my saddle, aware that my mule was labouring after its long ride and badly in need of both rest and water. I tethered it to the low branch of a mesquite bush, unhitched the pack saddle and let it fall to the ground, relieving the poor exhausted beast of its burden, then continued on foot, searching for the man I knew must be here.

The bosky ground crackled dryly beneath my boots as I followed the trail of shallow holes, some barely more than a few inches deep. Blood darkened the dirt around them and the grooves of finger marks showed the painful desperation of their construction.

I found him a few hundred feet from his wagon, face

down in the dirt, his body inert except for his ruined right hand which clawed at the ground, as if it were the only part of him still living. His left hand clutched a square of folded paper stained red by his torn flesh.

I dropped to the ground by his side, my breath puffing the dry dust as I called him 'Eldridge', the name I had seen etched on the side of the discarded linen chest. I hoped that the familiarity of it and the sound of a human voice might drag him up from whatever desolate place he had sunk to. But so far gone was he in his grief and exhaustion that he did not seem to hear or acknowledge me.

I reached for my canteen and carefully dripped a few drops of my remaining water on to his neck and the shock of it made his hand scratch at the land more fervently and a single word croak from his dry throat – 'water'. I poured a little more on the side of his face near his mouth, holding my hand beneath to catch the drops then placing my damp palm on his forehead. His skin was burning from fever and whispered words tumbled from his mouth. He kept saying the Devil was following them, had been close behind them for days and they needed to get to water for the only thing the Devil was afeared of was water.

I tried to reassure him by saying that the only thing following him had been me, but this sent him flinching away, crawling over the dirt to the gnarled trunk of a mesquite bush which he clung to, staring out at me with wild eyes. I believe in his fevered delirium he thought that, if I had been following, then it must be I who was the Devil.

I held up my canteen and poured a little water over my face, catching the drips with my tongue to show him I had no fear of it and I told him I would search for the water we both knew to be here someplace and fetch him to it once it was found.

I left him with my canteen in the shade of the tree and followed the terrain down to its lowest point, hoping to find a strand of green that might indicate where water could be found. I knew Eldridge would join his family in death if he did not have water soon, though perhaps that would be a kind relief. I found a hollow that might once have been a pool where cool water eddied and was now filled with dry mesquite straw. I kicked through it, hoping to discover mould in the mulch or any other small sign of moisture but the bottom layer was as dry as the top. I carried on scuffing my way across the lower contours of the land in this fashion, kicking through the straw and rolling rocks aside, making sure I examined every inch in search of the slightest evidence of moisture.

It was hot work and even in the shade of the trees I could feel the wooziness of heat fatigue starting to fall heavy upon me after my hard ride in pursuit of the wagon. I had been incautious, emboldened by the prospect of human company and of soon finding water. Now I was aware that if I found none it would not only be Eldridge who breathed his last breath in the shade of these trees. I figured there had to be water here somewhere or the trees would not grow, though I had searched everywhere and found nothing. Then I realized with a cold feeling of dread that there was still one place I had not yet searched.

I headed back, past Eldridge and past the spot where I had left my mule tethered to where the covered wagon stood ghostly and still in the shade of the trees.

I pulled my neckerchief up and over my nose to try and filter out some of the death stench, but it seemed to make little difference. I tried breathing through my mouth but found I could taste the stink and the thought of what flavoured the air made me breathe through my nose again. The land beyond the wagon fell away into a shallow gully thick with bushes and here I headed, hoping that the smell might lessen. If anything it was worse. It was as if the foul stench had pooled into this lower depression to form some kind of rank and malodorous puddle. I could hardly breathe, the smell was so solid, and when I pushed through the thicket and down into the gully I saw at once why the smell of death was so strong here.

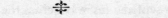

41

Hector Rodriguez Alvarado – 'El Diablo' behind his back, 'Papa Tío' to his face – sat in the centre of a semi-circular desk that resembled a huge bagel with a bite taken out of it. It was lined with flat-screen monitors, seven in total – one for each deadly sin, someone had once said. Right now they were displaying a stock chart, an Arizona news station and an article on the Forbes website detailing how Hector 'Papa Tío' Alvarado had made it on to that year's list of billionaires again. The rest of the screens were filled with photographs blown up and arranged like exhibits at a gallery, blue tattoo lines on dead flesh, numerals, outlines of guns, a pale man with a red burn on his arm, and a blackened skull in the rain, the metal plate shining in the shadows. He selected this photo, sent it to the printer then rolled his chair back from the bank of screens and stood up slowly.

His knees cracked as they straightened and he leaned back to stretch the tension from his spine and walked stiffly over to where the printer was steadily spooling out the picture on a full sheet of paper. He opened one of the drawers in the unit beneath it, selected one of the cell phones inside then switched it on and peered through the slats in the blinds at the dry, rocky world outside.

His compound stood on a steep hill in the Sierra Madre Mountains, fifty miles from the US border, impossible to approach without being spotted and therefore easy to defend. It was also blowy as hell, the grit-filled wind howling in the roof timbers and making it sound like the whole place was haunted. It had been Tío's home for the last eight years, ever since he had got sloppy and ended up in a jail cell he'd had to expensively bribe his way out of. He'd gone into hiding after that and this had become his bolthole; a kind of freedom but one that looked and felt exactly like captivity.

He took in the dim, double-garage sized space that had become his world, the screens his eyes and ears on the world beyond. He lit upon the one showing the news channel. It was still broadcasting live from the desert, rain pouring down and steam floating up. Happy, soot-streaked faces waving at the camera as it flew overhead. His son had died and these people were happy. It made him want to go there and stab them all in the face.

The printer went silent and he picked up the photo and stared into the empty eye sockets of the skull. He remembered the hate he had seen in those eyes the last time he had been with Ramon. It had been a while back, a few months, after some trouble he could not now remember. He tried to recall the last thing he had said to his son; something angry, no doubt. He couldn't remember. It hadn't always been that way. They had been close until Ramon turned seventeen and was beaten up so badly he ended up with the plate in his head and an addiction to strong painkillers that eventually progressed to heroin. Ramon blamed him for that, and he was right to. If Ramon had not been Tío's son, none of it would have happened. And now he was dead, just like his sisters. All his children dead.

He checked the battery and signal on the phone, took one last look at the room he had spent most of the last eight years inside and flicked the master switch on the wall. The seven screens blinked to black and the happy faces of the fire survivors vanished. It was as easy as that – flick a switch and they all disappeared. He could do that for real, had done it many times, sitting here, staring at these screens, but he didn't want to do that now. Not this time. This time he wanted to do more than send out orders and wait for results. This time his family had been hurt, so it was down to him to avenge them personally.

He took down a battered Western Express cattleman hat from a hook on the wall and an old pair of sunglasses from his shirt pocket with rainbow lenses like oil spilled on water and slipped them over his eyes, opened the door and stepped outside.

The sunlight was nuclear after so long in the gloom. The heat was brutal too, as if the whole world was warming up and getting ready to burn. He smiled at this thought and walked out into the sunlight. Two men sprang from the shadows and hurried over, making a big show of scanning the surrounding hills for movement, their hands resting on the stocks of their M60 machine pistols.

'Get the car and load some full gas cans in the back,' he said.

The guards looked at each other, puzzled, then one scurried off towards an outbuilding while the other stayed close and checked for intruders who couldn't possibly be there, given the small army of guards patrolling the wider perimeter, and the minefields and Claymores lining the roads leading up to the compound.

He had tried for years to have more kids. God knows he had fucked enough *putas* to seed a whole dynasty, but that, in the end, had been his problem. The life he had led when he was younger and the women who inhabited it were from the street, same as he was, their bodies and youth just another form of currency that, like all coin, quickly got dirty from too much handling. He had caught about everything going and been proud of the fact, like it was evidence of what a man he was. He had three kids too, further proof of his virility, and had thought that was plenty. He had a son to hand his empire on to when the time came, that was all he needed.

It was only later in life, after his relations with Ramon had soured, that he spotted a pretty girl on a TV singing contest, bought his way into her heart with record contracts and diamonds, and discovered the cycle of infection and cure, infection and cure, had burned away any ability he had to father more children. And now the three he'd had were all dead. His bloodline had ended and his name would die with him.

'Wait here,' Tío said, then pushed through the sun-gnarled door of a barn with a tortured shriek of old hinges.

The inside was dark and stifling and smelled of oil and trapped heat and dust. The windows were covered with boards that leaked sunlight through thin cracks that slashed through the darkness and threw light on two figures slumped on their knees in the centre of the space. They were tied by their wrists with climbing rope hanging from the central roof beam, their arms raised above their drooping heads as though they were silently pleading with God for a forgiveness they had little chance of getting. Their clothes were ripped, their jeans and shirts wet with dark blood. The faces of two young women looked down at them like angels in the dark, blown-up photographs that accentuated the family resemblance to their father.

Tío pulled off his shades and blinked away the darkness as

he walked around the edge of the floor, keeping close to the walls and avoiding the middle where the men were. The tin roof ticked above him and threw down so much heat it felt like someone had lit a fire on it.

'Man it's hot in here,' Tío said to the darkness, and took a five-gallon container down from the shelf. 'But I'll tell you something,' he unscrewed the cap and walked over to the far wall, 'hell will be hotter.' He placed the container on the ground and pushed it over with his foot.

Fuel spread across the hard dirt floor, fouling the air with its fumes, and a moan rose up from the centre of the room, followed by panicked breathing. It sounded wet and wheezy, the man's broken nose and the tape over his mouth making it hard for him to catch his breath.

'You smell that?' Tío said, taking down another can and unscrewing the cap.

The rapid breathing intensified. One of the men had lifted his head a little and was staring over at Tío out of one eye. The other was swollen shut. The second guy still hadn't moved. Maybe he was dead. Lucky for him if he was.

Tío took a step forward and splashed fuel over the conscious man, who flinched then yelped as the jagged edge of a broken rib sawed at swollen flesh inside him. Tío threw more fuel over him, splashing the other man too, who still didn't move. The conscious man was hyperventilating now, his eye wide and staring as he pulled at his bindings, ignoring the pain that came from it.

Tío emptied the can and threw it at them. It struck the unconscious man on the head and he grunted but didn't rouse. Tío smiled. He wasn't dead after all. The conscious man continued to freak and Tío watched, enjoying his frantic attempts to pull free, knowing each move must be agony with all the damage he'd already done to him. It didn't take long for him to wear himself out. He looked up at Tío, blood and snot blowing in and out of his ruined nose, knowing what was coming.

'You're Raoul, right?' Tío asked. The man nodded. 'You know what happened to Ramon after you dropped him off at the airfield, Raoul? You know what happened after you packed him away on that old plane and called whichever fucking scumbag had promised you money or pussy or whatever fucking thing you thought you wanted more than the painful and horrible death you're going to get?'

The man shook his head fiercely, his open eye wide and pleading. A sound squeezed out from behind the tape on his mouth.

'What's that? You didn't sell him out, that what you telling me?'

The breathing faster. The head nodding.

'You sure about that?' He reached into his pocket, pulled out a box of matches and shook them.

Raoul reacted as if an electric current had passed through him. He yanked hard on his bindings again, rubbing flesh from his wrists and shaking dust from the roof. Tío took the phone from his pocket, tapped an icon of a fly and selected a number from a list. Raoul was crying now, a wheezing, mewling noise that sounded like a whimpering dog. Tío stepped forward and ripped the tape from his mouth. 'Anything you want to say, Raoul? Anything you want to tell me?' He threw the bloodied tape aside and dialled the number he had selected.

Raoul gulped air and shook his head. 'Idindoit,' he said, his swollen mouth turning the words into one sound. 'Idindonothin.'

Tío put the phone on speaker. 'You swear that, Raoul?'

The phone rang, the sound of it echoing in the dark space. 'You swear it on your mother's life?'

'*¿Bueno?*' a woman answered.

Raoul howled when he heard his mother's voice. '*¡Mamá!*' he called out, but Tío cut her off before she could hear.

Raoul slumped down, sobbing, his body wracked with pain, his spirit broken. Tío put the phone away and took a single match from the box.

'You believe in heaven, Raoul?' He struck the match and it flared in the dusty dark. Raoul stared up at the tiny flame burning above him. Nodded slowly.

'That's good,' Tío said, turning the match in his fingers and watching the flame grow. 'But if you believe in heaven, you also got to believe in hell, no?'

He flicked the match and it arced through the air. Raoul screwed his eyes shut, anticipating the whoosh of fire. He didn't see the match land in the spreading puddle of fuel and snuff out with a barely audible small hiss.

'Well, would you look at that,' Tío said, his head cocked to one side and staring down at the blackened twist of match floating in the fuel. 'A miracle. God must have spared you for a higher purpose.'

Raoul gulped air, his mouth hanging open, blood drooling thickly down from it. Tío laughed, a great hoot that rang inside the confines of the cabin. 'It's diesel ya moron, you can't set light to diesel with a match. You need to heat it up or pressurize it first, get some fumes going, then it burns real good.' He turned back to the shelves and started hunting through the boxes of supplies, looking for something. 'The other thing that works is a wick.' The sound of ripping plastic cut through the gloom and Tío turned round holding up a large roll of kitchen towel. 'This'll work.'

He unwound a few sheets then stuffed them into the central tube so the whole thing resembled a huge candle. 'Diesel got a real nice steady burn, not like gasoline, that'll blow up in your face and burn itself out quick. Diesel will burn long and slow and hot and leave nothing behind but ash.'

He crouched down and dipped the wick into the diesel, turning it slowly to let the fuel soak in. 'If you want to get rid of anything and leave no trace, diesel is what you use. Aviation fuel is a lot like diesel, did you know that?'

Raoul was hyperventilating again and a strange noise came out of him. 'Idindonothin,' he said again between panicked breaths. 'Idindonuthin.'

Tío placed the diesel-soaked roll of towel upright in the puddle of fuel and struck a fresh match. 'You know what?' he said and touched it to the wick. 'I believe you. That's why I won't pay Mama a visit.'

He stood back, watching the yellow flame creep down the paper and start spreading over the main roll. He moved over to where the photographs of his daughters were hanging from nails in the wall, took them down and grabbed a couple more gas cans. Then he put his shades back on and stepped out through the door with another tortured shriek of metal.

Outside, the two guards were waiting by a white Explorer with its engine running. One was behind the wheel, the other standing by the open passenger door, still holding his M60 and checking the empty hills like a moron.

A shrill scream pealed out from the building and the guard's eyes flicked towards it. Smoke was starting to seep through the cracks in the door, but Tío didn't see it. He was taking his last look at the group of shacks that were the centre of his vast empire that turned over more money each year than most countries. It had taken him a lifetime to build and it was all for nothing. He was still living in a house not much bigger than the one he had been born in. He thought of all the smiling faces he had just seen on the TV screen, people who genuinely did have nothing – nothing except their lives and their freedom.

'Where to, boss?' the driver called out.

'America,' Tío replied and got into the back of the Jeep. 'Land of the free. Land of Redemption.'

42

The swampy odour of the interview room hit Holly the moment Donny McGee opened the door for her. He pointed at one of the chairs, the one reserved for suspects, and metal legs screeched against concrete as she pulled it out and sat down. Another chair faced her across a table that was bolted to the floor.

'You want anything, Mrs Coronado?'

'I want to give you my statement and then go home again.'

'I mean like a coffee, water, something like that.'

'No.'

'All right then. Sit tight, someone will be along soon to talk with you.' He closed the door behind him and she noticed there was no handle on the inside.

She turned to face the table and placed her hands flat against the scarred surface. It felt cool. She could hear sounds beyond the door, footsteps and conversations, but they all remained distant. None came her way.

She sat perfectly still, staring at the grey painted walls, the daylight leaking in through the bars of a small window, and the camera fixed high in the corner.

She waited.

* * *

Morgan and Mayor Cassidy were waiting too.

They were in Morgan's office, Morgan behind his desk in his antique chair, Cassidy pacing. Morgan was feeling calm and in control. His hands were stinging beneath his dressings and he glanced at his computer screen showing the feed from the camera in the interview room. Holly Coronado looked small in the picture. Small and isolated. He liked that.

'What if this doesn't work?' Cassidy asked.

He was driving Morgan nuts with his pacing. 'Then we switch to plan B.'

'Which is?'

'Why don't we wait and see if plan A works first.' Morgan glanced down at the cell phone lying on his desk. 'As soon as it's done, we'll know – and so will Tío. Then we'll see how things sit.'

'But what if it turns out this Solomon Creed or whoever he is hasn't got anything to do with anything?'

'I told you, Tío won't care. He was there, that's good enough for him, and he's connected to James Coronado.' He nodded at the camera feed. 'He's also been talking to the not-so-merry widow, so whichever way you look at it, it's going to be better for us when he's gone. One less problem. It's like the fire; that was our most immediate problem and we dealt with it. This guy is a problem too, so we're dealing with him. Maybe that helps us with Tío, maybe it doesn't. We deal with each thing as it comes.'

The desk phone rang and Cassidy jumped.

'Try and get a grip on yourself,' Morgan said, snatching the phone from its cradle. He nodded, then pushed a button. 'Hi, Pete, I got Ernie here too. You're on speaker.'

'Well there ain't nothing for either of you to hear.' The

voice was dry as sand. 'Didn't find a damn thing. If Jim had the files, they wasn't at his house.'

Morgan and Cassidy exchanged glances. More loose ends. 'Where are you now?'

'I headed back to the ranch soon as the wildfire was out.'

'Everything OK there?'

'A few horses spooked is all, the storm drain kept the fire back. Ellie was spooked too.'

'Did you hear about Bobby Gallagher?'

'I did. Terrible thing. Can't pretend I'm sad that he won't be bothering Ellie no more, but he was harmless enough. Hell of a thing to get himself burned up in a fire like that. I wouldn't wish that on no one. What about this stranger Ernie was telling me about – you got it in hand?'

Morgan rubbed at the spot between his eyes. It was typical that somehow all of this was his responsibility. Morgan looked up at Nathaniel Priddy staring out from the wall of sheriffs. He'd always wondered exactly how much he'd done to help build this town; more than he'd been given credit for, he guessed. They'd named this building after him but there were twenty others with 'Cassidy' written on the side. Just the way things were. Poor people did the dirty work while the rich people kept their hands clean and took all the glory. Least that's how it ran until someone staged a revolution.

'I got it in hand,' he said, and ended the call. He knew Tucker would be pissed at being cut off like that, which is exactly why he'd done it.

Cassidy huffed and turned away. Started pacing again.

Morgan sat back in his seat. The truth was he didn't need a backup plan because his original one was working just fine. Solomon had been an unexpected variable, but he would be out of the way soon. Holly Coronado was angry, but he didn't think she was dangerous, even though she had shot him. Tío was the only major thing to worry about. Mayor Cassidy and Old Man Tucker were shitting in their pants at the thought of him coming, but not Morgan. Morgan wanted him to come. He was counting on it.

The cell phone vibrated against the desktop and Cassidy stopped pacing and stared down at it. Morgan picked it up. Opened the message. Frowned.

'What?' Cassidy asked.

'He's gone,' Morgan said.

Cassidy nodded. 'Well that's that then.'

'No,' Morgan said. 'I mean he's gone. He wasn't in the house. Solomon Creed has disappeared.'

43

Solomon walked through the humid desert, glad of the boots on the flinty, spiky ground. The rain had carved tracks in the dust, wavy lines that followed the contours, as if hundreds of snakes had slithered through here. The day was starting to brighten again, the clouds thinning to let the afternoon sun and heat back in. His shirt was sticking to his back, but he didn't remove his jacket or ease his pace.

He headed northwest towards the spill piles of the mine. He wanted to head north, out across the burned desert to the Tucker ranch, but it was too far to walk. He could see the airfield stretching away in the same direction, the parked squadrons of aircraft forming patterns across the land. He would have to detour round that too, which would make the journey even longer.

He took the almost squeezed-out tube of sunblock from his pocket and rubbed more on the back of his neck and over his ears and face. It felt slimy and awful but he put it on anyway. He thought about the ugly hat he'd left in Morgan's car and wished he'd kept hold of it. He put the tube back in his pocket and pulled out a pair of sunglasses he had found in the house. They must have belonged to James Coronado too and he thought as he slipped them on that he was now walking in another man's shoes and seeing the world through his eyes too.

He continued onward, keeping away from the houses and out of sight as long as he could until he reached the road and the fence surrounding the mine. There was no sign of industry beyond it, only more abandoned buildings. He spotted the mine entrance through a gap in the spill piles and lifted the sunglasses to get a better view. Some barrels were stacked outside, next to a trailer with coils of clear tubing piled on the back. The wheels of the trailer were slightly soft and the barrels had rust around the bases showing they hadn't moved for some time. It seemed more like set dressing than actual equipment for a working mine. The low hum of an engine was coming from somewhere, steady and rhythmic, a pump most likely. It sounded as if it was underground but not far, not as far as it should be if it was flushing ore out of a mine that had already been depleted by years of heavy working.

The only modern thing about the whole place was the fence and the cameras on poles. The rest looked abandoned and felt deserted. He could see why the trusts were so important to the town. The mine couldn't be producing enough revenue to pay for the church lighting bill. Solomon continued down the road until the fence ran out and he saw what he had come here for.

The livery yard was set back from the road, the horses moving around in their corrals now the rain had stopped. They seemed skittish, restless, like a wolf was nearby. They were swirling around the corral like a slow tornado, pawing the wet ground, snorting and tossing their heads. A horse was the only way he could get to the Tucker ranch on his own. He didn't have a car and he hated being in them anyway. He wasn't even sure whether he could drive. Truth was, he wasn't sure he could ride a horse either. There was only one way to find out.

He left the road and walked beneath a high wooden arch with 'Sam's Livery Yard' spelled out on it in roughly nailed saguaro ribs. There were a couple of barns surrounding the corrals, an old-fashioned covered wagon and a stagecoach parked over by one of them. The wagon had the name of the livery yard stencilled on the canvas, along with a website URL that spoiled any sense of authenticity they may have been going for. There was a parking lot to his right with a beat-up old pick-up truck in it, suggesting someone was here. Solomon surveyed the yard, trying to spot them, and saw the girl instead.

She wasn't much bigger than an infant but her clothes and her stillness made her seem older, like a grown woman rendered in miniature. She was standing further up the track by a gate leading out to the desert, staring straight at him, her hands folded in front like she was in chapel. Her skin and hair were as white as his. She held Solomon's gaze, her face shaded and fringed by an old-fashioned bonnet, then turned and walked away, heading towards the gate and the desert beyond, her eyes scanning the ground as she went like she was searching for something. The horses nickered and moved away from her as she passed but she didn't seem to notice. Solomon watched until she disappeared round the edge of a barn then turned and saw a man staring right at him.

'You can see her, cain't ya?' He was leaning against the fence on the far side of a corral, his stockman's hat pushed far back on his head and gloved hands gripping a coiled lariat. Solomon turned back to the barn, searching for the girl, but he couldn't see her. 'What has she lost?' he asked.

'I ain't never got close enough to ask her. Most of the tourists don't see her at all, though their kids do sometimes – dogs too. All the folks that work here see her, but I guess we're used to her, or she's used to us. The horses sure know she's there. Don't usually see her at this time of day though. Usually it's evening, when the light is softer. She's burning like a light bulb today. We call her Molly.'

'Her name was Eldridge,' Solomon said.

The ranch-hand nodded. 'I've heard that said before.' He dropped his head to one side and squinted. 'Say, you're the fella they say brung the rain, ain't ya?'

Solomon smiled. 'Is that what they're saying?'

'That's what I heard.' The man continued to nod as if the world was suddenly making sense to him. 'Help you with somethin'?'

'I need a horse.'

'Well then, I believe you come to the right place. Anything in particular?'

Solomon studied the herd of animals moving between them, a mixture of Quarter Horses, Arabians and Palominos, his mind providing their names as easily as if they had labels stuck to them. He approached the fence and held his hand out flat. A tan Palomino sniffed at it, snorted and moved away.

'They can probably smell the smoke on you,' the ranch-hand said. 'They got real spooked by the fire. All I could do to stop them kicking down the fences and running wild.'

Solomon moved round the edge of the corral and the horses all edged away before he got near. A flash of white in the corner of his eye made him turn round, expecting to see the girl. Instead he saw a horse standing alone in its own corral, tossing its mane and looking straight at him. It was an American Saddlebred, a pure white stallion, easily seventeen hands high. Magnificent.

'You don't want that one,' the ranch-hand said. 'That one's mean and it ain't for hire.'

'What's his name?' Solomon asked, moving towards it.

'Sirius, though most of the guys here call him "Serious", cos he sure is one handful. That there's the mayor's horse, though he don't ride him much no more. I ride him when he'll let me to keep him exercised, but I don't like doing it and I guess he's none too fond of the arrangement neither. He's thrown me more than once, and I got the bruises and scars to prove it.'

Solomon reached the fence and held out his hand. 'Sirius,' he whispered, and the black nostrils flared then it dropped its head and started to walk towards him.

'Well I'll be damned,' the ranch-hand muttered. 'I ain't never seen him come to a stranger before.'

The stallion drew closer and Solomon watched the roped sinews of its muscles ripple between the white velvet of its skin. He could sense the power in it, like lightning made solid, and his mind began to riff on its name:

Sirius. Brightest star in the night sky. Worshipped as a god in ancient Persia. Sometimes depicted as a white stallion named Tishtrya – the rain maker.

The horse stopped in front of him and lowered its muzzle to Solomon's palm.

Maybe it was you who brought the rain and not me.

Solomon moved his palm up from beneath its chin and over the muzzle to stroke its cheek. The stallion stepped closer, its head moving over the top bar of the fence and dipping down to rub against the side of Solomon's head.

'Well look at that.' The ranch-hand shook his head and pushed his hat back about as far as it would go without falling off his head. 'You two are just about the exact same colour. You can't tell where one of you ends and the other begins.'

Solomon turned and studied the man. He was sinewy and lithe like the lariat he was holding, his skin burned leathery by living outdoors, making him appear older than he was. 'What's your name?'

'Name's Marty.'

'How about I borrow this horse, Marty? He looks like he could do with the exercise, and it'll save you a job.'

Marty smiled and shook his head. 'Like I said, this is the mayor's horse and he ain't for hire.' He pointed back at the main corral. 'I can fix you up with a grey Palomino, if it's the colour you're partial to.'

'I don't want to hire him, I only want to borrow him. Why don't you call up the mayor and ask him for me?'

The smile melted away. 'You want me to call Mayor Cassidy?'

'Tell him Solomon Creed respectfully requests the use of his horse for a few hours.'

Marty ran his hand across his forehead as though he was wiping sweat away and rearranged his hat on his head. 'I got his contact details back in the office, I could call him from the phone in there I guess.'

'The mayor and I have an understanding,' Solomon lied. He knew he needed a horse and he knew he had no money to hire one.

Marty looked at the horse then back at Solomon. 'All right then. But don't be surprised if the answer is "no".'

He turned and Solomon watched him walk away across the livery yard towards a wooden building decorated with posters advertising genuine cowboy experiences.

The stallion snorted and took a step back from the fence, tossing its head and shaking Solomon's hand free. Solomon looked up at the huge animal, all muscle and mass. 'OK,' he said. 'Let's you and me find out if I can ride.'

* * *

247

Marty pulled his glove off and pecked Mayor Cassidy's name into the office laptop one letter at a time to get his details then dialled the number on record. He straightened up and looked back out into the yard. Molly had appeared again. She was standing by the water trough, staring at the spot where he had left Solomon. It was the first time he had ever seen her do anything other than stare at the ground. The phone connected and the mayor answered, sounding anxious. 'Yes?'

'Mayor Cassidy. This is Marty over at Sam's Livery.'

'Oh, hi, Marty.' Now he sounded relieved.

'I'm awful sorry to bother you, sir, but I got a fella here name of Solomon Creed says he wants to borrow your horse.'

'He's … is he there now?'

'Yes.'

'Can you keep him there?'

'Sure. I need to saddle him up so I can easily stretch it out as long as – Jesus …'

A flash of white streaked across his view, snatching the words from his mouth.

'What? What happened?'

'It's him.' Marty craned forward and the brim of his hat hit the window and knocked it off his head. 'He's taken Sirius.' He watched horse and rider thread their way past the corrals and on to the track leading out to the desert.

'I thought you said he wasn't saddled?'

'He's not.' Marty stared at the slim figure of Solomon Creed hunched low on the horse's back and gripping its mane with his hands. 'He's riding bareback.'

44

Cassidy hung up and looked over at Morgan. 'He stole my horse.'

'Who?'

'Creed.'

'Why?'

'How would I know?'

'But … where's he gonna go?'

'I don't know. Away from here.'

Cassidy stared out of the window. Morgan's office faced the square, so he couldn't see much beyond the church opposite and the mountains rising in the distance. 'What are we going to say to Tío? He was supposed to be—' He turned round and lowered his voice. 'He was supposed to be our … offering.'

Morgan's face softened into a smirk. 'Well, you changed your tune. An hour ago you were wringing your hands about whether to give him up or not, now you're pissed he got away.'

Cassidy had never liked Morgan. Even as a kid he'd had a slightly sneering, superior manner and it had been made much worse by the addition of a uniform and some authority. Right now he hated him. He blamed him entirely for the mess they were in. He was the one who had suggested taking occasional shipments to boost the town's flagging finances. He was the one who had made the initial introductions to the cartels. And he was the one who'd said 'yes' to smuggling Tío's son into the country without consulting either him or Tucker. It was all his fault and now *he* was smirking at *him*.

'So what do we do?' Cassidy asked.

'I guess we try and find him.' Morgan leaned forward in his chair and picked up his desk phone. 'He won't get too far on horseback.' He punched in a number and waited for someone to answer. 'Rollins, it's Morgan. Put out a BOLO on one Solomon Creed, last seen at Sam's Livery, probably heading out of town on a stolen white horse.' He gave him a description then hung up. 'Might as well call the field too, see if we can't put something in the air and spot where he might be heading. We can still salvage this, don't worry.'

Cassidy shook his head. 'So much for keeping him off the record.'

Morgan shrugged. 'Times like this you gotta be flexible.' He began to tap in a number from memory, stopped when the phone began buzzing on the table. He glanced up at Cassidy, put the desk phone down carefully and picked up the cell. The caller's number was withheld.

'Yes?' He took a breath then nodded. 'OK.' He hung up. 'That was Tío,' he said.

'What did he say?'

'He said he was on his way.'

Cassidy felt the room get colder. 'Here?'

'Where else?'

'Why?'

'Why do you think?'

'But he never goes anywhere. Why would he come here? Why would he need to?'

The phone buzzed again, a message this time. Morgan opened it, read it, then turned it round so Cassidy could see.

'That's why he's coming,' Morgan said. 'Because debts like this he collects in person.'

Cassidy pulled his reading glasses out of his pocket and squinted down at the two word message on the screen.

El Rey

The town where Tío had been born.

The town that had betrayed him and paid the ultimate price.

The town that was no longer there.

45

Tío watched his message go then gazed out at the flat, dry land passing by. His old self, the man who had stayed in his hilltop hideaway for eight years, would not have sent the message. That man was cautious, careful, risk-averse, always with an eye on the future and doing what he could to safeguard it. He looked down at the seat next to him where the framed photographs of his daughters lay next to the printout of the burned skull. He had no future now. 'Pull over,' he said and the Jeep crunched to a halt on the side of the road. 'Get out.'

The driver glanced at the guard in the passenger seat, then they both got out.

Tío closed the messaging app and opened another, which looked like nothing more than a big red button. He tapped in his password – carlosmariasofia – the middle names of his three dead children, then got out of the car.

The taller of the two guards stepped forward, finger on the trigger of his M60, his eyes alert. He was called Miguel, had a father in the cemetery and a mother called Maria-Louise he sent money to regularly and who lived in a nice bungalow on the Baja coast. The other guard was Enrique but everyone called him Cerdo because he ate like a pig and looked a little like one too.

'Look back down the road,' Tío told them, and they obeyed, neither of them quite sure what they were supposed to be seeing.

Tío could just make out the buildings of the compound perched on a hilltop about three or four miles back. It appeared tiny at this distance. Insignificant. It was supposed to. Anything big or grand would have attracted attention. The only thing drawing attention to it now was the smoke coming from one of the outbuildings. Tío lifted the phone, took one last look and tapped the red button on the screen.

There was a rumbling like thunder that shook the ground then the whole vista erupted in dust and fire as all the defences tripped at once.

Miguel and Cerdo raised their guns and instinctively moved towards Tío as a second series of explosions shook the ground and the whole hilltop disappeared in a cloud of dust and debris. Tío watched until it settled enough that he could see everything was gone. His whole world for the past eight years, swept away at the push of something that wasn't even a button. So much for his legacy.

'Let's go,' he said and got back in the car.

They drove away, following the signs to Highway 15 that would take them north to the Arizona border.

Tío never once looked back.

46

Holly Coronado walked out of the Priddy building and into the bright afternoon sun feeling like she wanted to punch someone. No, not someone – Morgan.

They had kept her in the interview room for almost an hour before some timid man in a uniform stuck his head round the door and told her no charges were being pressed and she was free to go. Morgan hadn't even shown his face.

She hurried down the street, her anger driving her on. She had avoided going out since Jim had died, not wanting to face the public and their looks of sympathy. Now she didn't care. She was also aware that it probably suited Morgan and his cronies if she kept out of the way and her mouth shut. And that's why she was going to do the exact opposite.

The hospital had a strange holiday feel about it when she stepped into its antiseptic interior. There was a buzz about the place, a kind of euphoria that had been carried back by all the staff who had returned victorious from facing down the fire. She saw it shining in the face of the receptionist, only to vanish a moment later when she turned to Holly and recognized her.

'How do I go about requesting a copy of a coroner's

report?' Holly asked, and a look of pity passed over the receptionist's face.

She picked up a phone and pressed a button. 'Just a moment,' she said, in a way that made it sound like she was actually saying *I'm sorry for your loss.*

Holly turned away while the woman spoke to someone. She hated the fact that the tragic details of her life were so public. She hadn't even given her name but the woman had known exactly whose report she was asking about.

Two orderlies burst through a door into the reception area, their laughter heralding their arrival. It was strange for her to think of a hospital as a happy place, they held too many bad associations for her. The last time she had been in this building was when she miscarried, and the smell of these places always took her back to the dark days of her mother's final months. She had moved back to St Louis and spent days breathing in this hospital smell while watching the cancer gnaw her mom away to nothing. She was only sixty-seven.

Her parents had already been fairly old when they'd had her, a last snatched chance at a family after chasing down careers. They had always been the oldest parents at the school gate, the oldest at her graduation – the first to die. Her father was seventy-six when his heart had called it quits after a lifetime as a workaholic trial lawyer fuelled by coffee and cigarettes.

'Mrs Coronado ...' She turned and saw a man in a white coat holding out a manila envelope. 'It's a copy of the coroner's report on your husband,' he said. 'I thought you might come for it, so I got it ready.'

She glanced at the doctor's badge. 'Thank you, Dr Palmer.' She frowned as her brain caught up with what had just happened. 'How did you know I'd ask for it?'

'I treated a patient earlier – Solomon Creed? He was asking after it. He was asking about you as well. I figured once he caught up with you, you'd come for it. And here you are.'

'Yes.' She took the envelope and slid her finger beneath the flap. 'Here I am.'

'I had a read,' he said. 'I hope you don't mind.' Holly pulled out the folded sheets. 'The toxicology tests were all negative, and the BACS readings were negligible – that's his blood alcohol concentrations. He hadn't been drinking. He must have fallen asleep at the wheel or swerved to avoid something. His skull trauma is consistent with a car wreck. There were no other broken bones and no major organ damage. He was very unlucky. I'm sorry, Mrs Coronado. I hope this is of some help.'

She folded the papers and slipped them back in the envelope. 'Thank you, Dr Palmer,' she said, 'you must have to deal with a lot of death in your line of work and I appreciate your time.'

'Grieving is a hard process and it's often difficult to make sense of it. Knowing the details can be a big part of coming to terms with what has happened. It never gets easy, but it does get better. I thought you might want this too.' He handed her another envelope with a PD sticker and a crime number printed on it. 'It's what was in your husband's pockets when they brought him in here. We don't need to hold on to it any more.'

Holly took the envelope and felt something heavy shift inside it. 'Thank you,' she said. 'That's very kind.'

She felt tears welling up from somewhere deep and she turned and walked away before the doctor could see them and feel moved to offer any more sympathy. This was exactly the sort of thing she had gone out of her way to avoid. She didn't want people's pity.

She pushed through the main door and escaped the cheery, disinfected atmosphere of the hospital. Outside the heat was building again and she walked across the parking lot to the shade of some mesquite trees. She broke the seal on the envelope and tipped the contents into her hand. The heavy thing she had felt was Jim's car keys. They had a door key on them too, the key to their home, a key he would never use again. There was also twenty dollars in notes and change and a small piece of brown paper with a number on it and a printed note that read: *Your document request has been approved and is now ready to collect.*

It was a requisition slip from the town archive. Jim's study had been littered with the things ever since he'd started work on his book. The tear-off stub at the bottom was still in place. It meant he had never picked it up.

Holly checked the time then looked down the street to the museum building that housed the Cassidy archive. It should still be open, just about. She stepped out of the shade and into the heat. She didn't want to go home yet anyway. She wasn't sure she would ever want to go back there again. It was tainted now. They had trespassed there and torn it apart – along with everything else.

47

The moment Solomon's weight had settled upon the stallion he had known he could ride him. He could feel him, like an extension of himself, and only had to look out at the desert and the horse had taken him there. He couldn't imagine fixing a saddle to the horse's back and putting a barrier between them, it would be like placing a board between two people dancing the tango. That was what it felt like, like they were dancing, dancing at full speed across the flame-scorched desert, the thrum of the hooves like a heartbeat across the ground.

They had taken a wide course round the airfield because he knew people would be searching for him now. The rain had dampened the ground so he rode fast with no fear of kicking up dust. There were no cacti left standing in the fire zone, only blackened stumps and the pulpy remains of exploded flesh where the heat had boiled them from within then baked them into black puddles. He could smell their remains, the smoky notes of roasted organic matter with sweet hints of putrefaction already starting to blossom. The flies had smelt it too and were already feeding on the dead cacti and what-ever animals had been caught by the fire, teeming in black clouds like animated embers buzzing in delight at the feast.

Solomon reached the edge of the blackened ground and looked down into a wide gorge worn over centuries by a river. A wide stream snaked its way along the middle of the riverbed, rain running off from the mountains. On the opposite bank were lines of tracks in the drying mud where animals had come down to drink, drawn by an instinct that told them water flowed here when the rains came. There were no tracks on his side; everything his side was dead. He scanned the land beyond the river. To the northeast he could just see the fan of a windmill rising above the desert and turning gently in the breeze.

The Tucker ranch.

A turkey vulture flew overhead, the broad black cross of its wings moving leisurely across the sky, its primary feathers splayed like fingers. It turned slowly, its head cocked sideways to check him out, then banked away and drifted off to the northeast, the same direction he was heading.

Solomon moved down the bank to the stream, slid from the horse and crouched to cup water from the river. It tasted of ozone and earth and felt warm as blood as it slipped down his throat. The horse drank too, nudging him gently with its foreleg to check he was still there.

When the horse stopped drinking Solomon leaped on to its back and waded across the stream, then rose up the bank and broke into a steady trot, heading straight towards the distant windmill. Ranch buildings took form as they drew closer, lines of fences sketched on the land and curling round to form corrals. The horses inside them didn't move, adding to the stillness of the place. The only movement came from the windmill and the turkey vulture turning slowly in the air above it.

The ranch felt deserted and Solomon wondered if the

owner and all the hands had gone to fight the fire along the edge of their land or were inspecting damage and repairing it. Or maybe they were watching him through the crosshairs of a hunting rifle.

The horse moved on towards the still and silent buildings. He could hear the squeak of the windmill and was catching the smells of the place on the breeze: baked wood, animal dung and something fresh and sharp and metallic. The horse snorted and tossed its head as he smelled it too and Solomon understood why the turkey vulture had flown here rather than back to the burned wasteland where roasted treats lay thick on the ground. It was because there was something more enticing here, something that called to the primitive brain of the carrion bird. The smell of freshly spilled blood.

48

The Jeep bounced Tío from his daydream as it left the road and started travelling over rougher ground towards the western horizon. He had been remembering his father and the whitewashed, red-tin-roofed shack he had grown up in and how they used to sit in the shade of the front wall, resting after a day spent in the opium fields hidden high in the mountains. His father had been a *gomero*, an opium farmer, like all his uncles and everyone else he knew, tending the fields, irrigating the crops, then slicing the seed heads with razor blades and carefully collecting the thick white sap until they had enough to sell to the middlemen who drove around the area and screwed everyone on price: everyone except his father. He had never given in on a deal and had taught his sons that every dollar you gave away was a dollar you were putting in another man's pocket. He always said you had to have pride in yourself, in your work, and, most of all, your family.

Tío gazed out of the window and watched the distant poles moving past; slender sentries that did nothing to stop the flow of people and goods heading north. The track they were driving along ran parallel with the US border, the most crossed national border in the world – three hundred and fifty million each year, and that was only the legal ones.

When George W. Bush had been in office he had pledged to erect a fence along the entire length of the border, almost two thousand miles, at a cost to the American tax payer of almost three million dollars a mile. They had managed to cover about six hundred miles before the project ran out of money and the Obama administration shut it down. The gaps that remained were plugged with these tall poles fitted with security cameras and infra-red sensors to alert National Guard units or SWAT teams if there was any attempt to cross the border, any time of day or night. They created what they called a 'virtual wall' and Tío had an army of paid informants feeding him up-to-date information about which parts were being repaired, or were out of service. This was another lesson he had learned from his father – the value of information.

Once, when they had been waiting for the middleman to come and buy their sticky black loaves of opium tar, he had told him, 'The man who has the most information always has the upper hand.'

And it was true. The reason his father had always driven such a hard bargain was because he took the time to talk to the other farmers, check their yields and how much they were charging. It was a constantly fluctuating market and he would hold out for more money when the others, who never worked as hard as he did or tended their fields as well, fell short on their crop. He would use this informa-tion to sell at a premium, standing steady in the face of the middlemen who protested that he was robbing them blind with the prices he was charging. They always paid though. Expensive product was still better than no product at all and the extra cost would get kicked up the supply chain, so no one lost out. That's what his father had figured. But there was a flaw in his reasoning and ultimately Tío had learned from his father's mistake. And of all the lessons his father had taught him, this had been the most important, and the most painful.

'You want me to stop by the house, boss?' Miguel asked from the driver's seat.

Two small barns and a tin-roofed shack had appeared on the track ahead: a cattle station and pump house.

'Take it round to the far side and park up by the windmill.'

The front door of the homestead opened as the car drew closer and a man burned almost black by a lifetime spent in the sun stepped out.

'Flash the lights,' Tío said, 'twice fast then once slow.'

Miguel obeyed and the man on the porch turned around and went back inside, closing the door behind him. Tío remembered how hot it got inside a tin-roofed house like this, the hot metal pouring the day's stored heat down until you could hardly breathe. He and his brothers always had to stay inside whenever the middlemen came round. 'This is men's business,' his father had told them, 'but you need to learn it. You'll be men soon enough. So listen but don't talk and don't make a sound.'

Not one of Tío's brothers had made it past their fifteenth birthday. Two died of fever and Ramon, the eldest, the one he had named his own son after, was shot alongside their father. Tío had learned a valuable lesson from that too.

'Right here,' he said, and the Jeep pulled to a halt in the shadow of the small pump house built at the foot of the windmill tower.

Cerdo got out first from the passenger seat, pulling his M60 from the footwell and doing his secret service shit again. Tío got out next, not bothering to wait for Miguel.

He walked to the door of the pump house and threw it open, letting sunlight stream into the cramped, dusty interior.

'Take the stuff out of the trunk and give me the keys,' Tío said, stepping into the pump room and sliding a large polystyrene foam crate to one side to reveal a manhole cover beneath. Miguel held the keys out as Tío walked past and he took them and carried on over to the shack.

The rancher opened the door when he was still a few feet away. He stared out from the boiling darkness like a man peering out from hell. Tío could smell the sweat burned into the air and the fabric of the building.

'*¿Me sabes, eh?*' Tío asked.

The man nodded, a single downward jerk of his chin, his doleful eyes never leaving Tío's, the watchful fear in them showing that, yes, he knew exactly who the man standing in front of him was.

'*Tomas las llaves y vayansa.*' Tío held out the keys. '*Nunca te vuelves. ¡Nunca! ¿Entiende?*'

The man nodded again. He took the car keys and disappeared inside for a moment, leaving the door open. There was almost nothing in the house, a table and two chairs, a single cot pushed up against a wall with blankets piled on one end, a stove with an old-fashioned coffee pot on top and a five-gallon oil drum with its top cut off and a pile of scavenged mesquite twigs sticking up from inside.

The man reappeared clutching a battered canvas satchel he was stuffing an iPad into, the only thing that hinted at the greater income and lifestyle he enjoyed as a tunnel master. He walked past Tío without a word and headed straight for the parked car.

Miguel and Cerdo glanced up as he approached, gas cans dangling from their hands. Miguel looked at Tío, uncertain what to do. Tío shook his head and watched the dusty figure of the man close the trunk, walk up to the driver's side, get in and start it up.

The Jeep backed away from the pump house then drove off in a wide circle back towards the same track they had come in on. The tunnel master might have been living in this place for years, but he had driven away after one word from Tío and never even looked back. There was something powerful about that. Something liberating.

Tío stepped into the house and felt the heat close around him like a fist. He tore a strip from one of the blankets then went outside, winding it round his hand as he walked back to the pump house, thinking about what he had said to the rancher:

Nunca te vuelves. ¡Nunca!
Never come back. Never!

He stepped into the pump house, opened the hatch in the floor and lights blinked on automatically, illuminating the painted concrete sides of a wide shaft below. There was a hydraulic platform wide enough to carry almost a ton of product and Miguel dropped down on to it while Cerdo started passing everything down from the car.

Tío took in the landscape, this land he had owned and run far more effectively and comprehensibly than any government. This had been his kingdom and he had been its king, though he had never felt more free than he did now. He remembered the line from some song that had been a hit when he was a kid, something about freedom being just another word for nothing left to lose. That was how he felt now. Losing his son had set him free because he had nothing left to lose either. He turned and took one long last look at the country he would never see again.

Never come back.

Damn right.

Then he stepped down through the manhole and into the tunnel that would take him to America.

49

Solomon slipped down from the back of the horse and listened to the tick and creak of the ranch buildings cooling in the afternoon air. There were three long barns and a large wooden homestead arranged around a loose quadrant. The house seemed still, the tied-back curtains in all the windows revealing dark rooms framed by white-painted boards worn back to the wood in some places by the weather.

The flutter of soft feathers broke the silence as the turkey vulture settled on the roof of the pump house in the corner of the quad. The wind ruffled its feathers and rotated the blades of the windmill above it with a slow squeak. Other than that, everything was still, everything was silent. The vulture folded its wings and cocked its head to one side, looking straight at the barn facing the main house.

'I smell it too,' Solomon murmured, heading towards the two large barn doors hanging suspended from steel runners. There was a gap in the centre through which the smell of blood was leaking out. His horse moved away, over to a corral where other horses twitched and flicked their heads nervously, the smell of fresh hay and water drawing him as surely as the scent of blood drew Solomon and the vulture to the barn.

The afternoon sun was dipping towards orange now

and throwing a reddish light over the side of the barn, as if the blood inside had begun to soak into the building. He stopped short of it and studied the darkness framed by the outline of the doors. Inside, thin shafts of light cut through the dusty gloom from skylights set into the roof, sketching out the edges of horse stalls with feed baskets at head height, and a faded blue pick-up truck parked over to the left that smelled strongly of motor oil and hay. It was the same smell that had lingered in James Coronado's study. Whoever had ransacked the house had come from here. Tucker, he presumed, one of the inner circle.

The vulture's wings flapped softly behind him as it moved from the pump shack to a closer perch, drawn by the smell of blood. The bird did not seem at all wary of him, as if he saw him as a kindred creature.

Is this what I am? Solomon wondered. *A carrion beast drawn to the smell of death?*

He took another step and passed through the gap in the doors, out of the light and into the darkness.

The smell of blood was like a physical presence inside the barn, as solid as the shadows. It was coming from his right where no skylights leaked light and the blackness was total. He stared into it, listening for the soft breath of someone lying in watchful wait or the thrum of a heart charged with adrenaline, pushing blood into muscles that were coiled and ready to spring. He heard nothing.

He reached out, gripped the edge of the door and started walking forward, dragging it open in a steady rumble and spilling daylight into the darker interior of the barn. The body was lying against the far wall, the hands tied together by a rope that had been thrown over the ceiling beam. He was stripped to the waist, his grey skin streaked with blood.

'Old Man Tucker, I presume,' Solomon whispered.

The door banged to a halt against the end of the runner and Solomon gazed upon the study in death before him, examining his own reaction to it as much as the details of the murder. He knew this was a shocking thing he was looking at and yet he was not shocked by it, and it was this that disturbed him more than the slaughter. What kind of a man must he have been to feel nothing at the sight of this?

Behind him the turkey vulture hopped closer and he imagined it cocking its head to one side so it could feast its eager eye on the delights Solomon had revealed inside the barn. He envied the bird its pure, uncomplicated existence, refined over thousands of years until it was the perfect embodiment of its purpose. It did not need to analyse its responses or try to work out what they meant. Blood meant food. Blood meant survival. For Solomon, blood complicated things. It slammed a door in his face and meant he could not now question the man who had most probably broken into Holly Coronado's house and ask him what he had been looking for. No doubt whoever had killed him had asked, most likely got answers too. He had been tortured before he died. There were four raw patches on his exposed upper body where the flesh had been neatly sliced off in strips, two either side of his spine and one on each side of his neck, the precision of the cuts hinting at considerable skill with a knife and a familiarity with the torturer's craft.

The flesh is thinner in these places, Solomon's mind whispered to him. *The nerve endings are closer to the surface, making the cuts more painful.*

There was one final wound in the centre of the old man's chest above his heart and the dirt all around him was painted with arcs of arterial blood that had come from this deathblow.

The blood was still wet and fresh and Solomon wondered if the killer was still here. At the same moment, he sensed movement out in the yard. He turned. Saw the girl walking towards him. And saw the shotgun in her hand.

50

The elevator platform bumped to a halt against soft rubber buffers and lights flickered on in the first section of the tunnel. The tunnel extended north for almost a mile and had cost two million dollars to build, cheaper than the border fence designed to keep them out. Tío had built ninety tunnels like this along the western side of the border ranging from Baja California to Texas, every single one paid for with the profits from the very first consignment each had carried. Tío stepped off the loading platform and on to one of the railway carts. Miguel and Cerdo shifted a bag of weapons and the cans of gasoline off the loading platform and on to the carts, then Tío pushed a button to engage the electric motors.

The carts moved smoothly forward and Miguel and Cerdo crouched down as they left the loading area and the ceiling got lower. Tío sat down and settled in for the ride. It would take ten minutes to cover the mile of track and he closed his eyes and let the gentle movement of the cart rock him into a state of calm, thinking again of the day his father and brother died.

He and his brother Ramon had been hiding in the heat of the house, sent there by his father because the middleman was coming to buy their crop. They had heard him drive up in his car, greet his father, then the boom of a gunshot had shaken the walls. His brother had reacted immediately, pulling his work knife from his belt and running out the door. A second shot had boomed. Then there was nothing.

Tío had never forgotten that silence, how total it seemed, like it would swallow him up. He remembered hearing the click of the shotgun being broken and reloaded and realizing that it was just him now, him and the man with the shotgun. His father never liked his mother being around when the deals were being done, so always sent her down to the market in El Rey.

He remembered hot tears running down his cheeks, tears of fear and anger. He had bitten his fist to stop himself from sobbing, because he knew the man would be listening, trying to figure out where he was, and the thin wooden walls of the shack would offer no protection against a shotgun blast. For the first time in his life he'd realized there was no one there to protect him, no one but himself. Tío on his own. Tío when he was still Hector Rodriguez Alvarado. Tío when he was only two weeks north of his eighth birthday.

He remembered his hand closing around the handle of the knife he had been given as a gift on his birthday to use in the fields, because he was becoming a man now and a man needed his own knife. He didn't feel like a man right then, tasting the blood from biting his fist and the salt of his tears. The crunch of footsteps drew closer and he wondered if he could be quicker than Ramon, dart outside and stick the knife in the man's neck before he could shoot. His anger and fear almost drove him to do it, but then something made him stop. He knew he was fast but not faster than a bullet and the man would be aiming right at the door, waiting, because it was the only way in and out of the shack. It was his survival instinct that had made him stop; stronger than fear, stronger than anger even. He heard another soft crunch outside and realized that if he did nothing, if he stayed where he was, the man would come into the shack and shoot him where he stood. He couldn't leave witnesses and he couldn't afford to wait it out either. There were two dead bodies lying out there for everyone to see and the sound of the gunshots would have echoed down the valley. Soon, people would come to see what had happened and the man needed to be gone. Another crunch. Closer now.

Tío moved away from the wall and slowly across the room so as not to make any sound. He had pushed the blankets together on the cot he shared with Ramon, moving them into a pile so it might look like he was hiding there, then stole back to the door, still wide open after Ramon had run through it, and pressed himself flat to the wall.

The barrel of the shotgun appeared first, sliding into view through the crack between door and wall. The middleman followed, squinting into the dark cabin with his sun-drenched eyes. Tío saw his face and recognized him. He was called Tuco, a sour man his father had a particularly low opinion of.

'He's nothing but a thug with family connections to the bosses,' he had told them once after one of his visits. 'He has no brains and he knows I know it. I can always make him pay more than he wants to because he's too stupid to outsmart me.'

Tuco stepped through the door and moved towards the bed. Tuco the thug with the family connections. Tuco with the shotgun and the blood of his father and brother on his hands. He levelled the shotgun at the bed. And Tío ran.

He slipped from his hiding place and burst through the door, nearly tripping over the body of his brother as he headed across the ground towards the jagged rocks that marked the start of the mountain path.

There was a bang behind him as Tuco turned and caught the barrel of the gun on the edge of the door. Tío darted right then left, zigzagging across the ground like a rabbit with a dog after it. He reached the entrance to the mountain track just as a boom echoed down the valley and rock exploded around him. He felt a sharp sting on his leg but he kept on running, keeping below the level of the uneven ground as he ran up the path and into the mountains. Another crack of gunfire sent shards of rock flying through the air but nothing hit him and Tío was gone before Tuco could reload.

He'd spent three nights in the poppy fields, drinking water from the irrigation tanks and listening to the farmers who came up to work the fields. He learned that Tuco was telling everyone he had found his father and brother already dead and that someone must have robbed them and taken the youngest boy with them. To Tío's amazement, the farmers didn't question the story at all. They were only interested in who might have done it and whether they might be in danger themselves.

He cried that first night, furious at the injustice of the world and frightened and hungry and alone. He felt such anger; anger for his mother, grieving for a dead husband and son, and worrying about her missing child. He wanted to go to her, show her that he was OK, only he knew things could never be OK, not now. He was frightened of going back too. If he told everyone what had happened they would most probably despise him for running away instead of trying to fight like Ramon had done.

He had lain there for two days working out what he should do, hiding in the fields of poppies with the petals falling round him like snow. He was feverish and hungry and his leg was starting to swell around the spot where the buckshot had caught him. The opiates in the pollen numbed the pain in his leg a little, though not the one in his heart, and they gave him strange dreams where he imagined he was talking to a shining man trapped inside a mirror who told him how he could get his revenge.

He thought about all the advice his father had given him and how, in the end, none of it had been any use. He was dead and the man who had killed him was alive. He realized then that it was not enough to have the most information, or the upper hand in a negotiation, or the best product to sell at market, you also had to be the one with the power. And he would never have any power if he ran away. So he went back down, limping all the way on his bruised and swollen leg.

His mother had wailed when he walked back in the door, crying in relief and horror at the sight of the dirt- and blood-streaked, half-starved little boy she thought she had lost. She cleaned him up, gave him food and summoned his uncles so he could tell them what had really happened. He'd felt a great relief as he spoke, like he was shifting a huge weight off his back and handing it to them. They were the grown-ups, his father's brothers, Ramon's uncles too, they would get justice for them both.

He remembered lying on his cot, his alone now Ramon was dead, while his uncles talked on the far side of the room, a rumble of low voices, the sound of serious things being discussed. Finally Uncle Herrard had walked over, sat down on the bed and told him he was never to repeat what he had told them because Tuco was Don Gallardo's cousin and no one would believe the word of an eight-year-old son of a dead *gomero* over his. He'd said he needed to move away, for his own safety, and that they would arrange for him to go to Tijuana where a cousin had a fishing boat. Tío had been dumbstruck. He didn't want to move away from his mama and he didn't want to become a fisherman. What he wanted was for one of his uncles to go down into the town, find Tuco and put a knife in his heart for what he had done. But they were going to do nothing. Only he could avenge them.

The next day he waited for his mother to go and fetch the water, then he slipped out of the house and walked down the road and into El Rey. There was a café in the market square where all the important people ate their meals and he headed straight to it. He saw Tuco sitting at a crowded breakfast table drinking fresh orange juice and shovelling eggs into his fat mouth. He had wanted to run over right then and stick the fork in his neck, but he knew he had to be patient if he wanted to stay here. Tuco was sitting two seats down from Don Gallardo, head of the family who ran everything. He watched him, stuffing his face and laughing at the boss man's jokes. He knew he would have to be smart if he wanted to one day sit at that table in the centre of the town, and have people laugh at his jokes and make sure no one would dare try to hurt his family again.

He'd waited until they'd almost finished eating then slipped out of the shadows and walked towards them. Tuco saw him first and went pale. It had made Tío feel good, like he had a little power already. The table fell quiet as he got closer, even Don Gallardo stopped talking and turned to look at the little boy walking over to his table.

Tío came to a halt, bowed, then spoke. 'Señor Tuco, I want to thank you,' he said in a voice that surprised him with its steadiness. 'If you had not arrived when you did the banditos would have surely killed me too. Please take this as a symbol of my family's thanks.' He held out his hand and placed his father's ring on the white linen tablecloth. He had found it by his mother's bed. She must have taken it off his father's hand before they buried him, worried about the future and no money coming in.

Tuco looked at the ring but didn't touch it.

'The boy is offering you a gift,' a voice said. 'Be polite and take it.'

Tuco did as he was told, his soft hand reaching forward and scooping the ring away.

Tío stared into the face of the man who had spoken.

'What's your name, boy?' Don Gallardo asked him.

'Hector,' Tío had replied. 'Hector Rodriguez Alvarado.'

Don Gallardo nodded. 'You're a smart boy, Hector. A boy with manners and respect. I like that. Nobody wants trouble here.' He shot a look at Tuco. 'Trouble is bad for business.'

That was when Tío realized they all knew. Every man at that table knew that Tuco had killed his father and brother, but all they cared about was business. His father, his uncles, all the mountain farmers who worked the poppy fields were no better than animals in their eyes, mules to do the heavy work so they could reap the harvest.

'You come here tomorrow, same time,' Don Gallardo said. 'I got a job for you.'

And that was how he had got out of the fields and into the organization.

Tío opened his eyes as the carts began to slow and caught Miguel looking at the thin silver chain he was gripping in his hand. 'This was my mother's,' he said, flicking a small silver locket with an image of Nuestra Señora de Guadalupe engraved on to it. 'And this was my father's –' He held up the thin gold wedding ring, the same one he had placed on

277

the white linen tablecloth as a tribute to Tuco. 'You've got to keep your family close, am I right? Nothing more important than family.'

The tunnel started to open up a little and the ceiling became higher, then the carts slowed to a smooth stop by a loading platform identical to the one they had left behind on the Mexican side.

'Welcome to America,' Tío said, rising from his cart and stretching the kinks out of his back. 'Land of the free.'

51

The girl was about nineteen, her white-blonde hair falling loosely over her shoulders and down the front of a white cotton dress that made her seem ghostly. Her eyes were pale like Solomon's and seemed to stare right through him.

Blind, his mind told him. *Ellie Tucker is blind.*

The pump-action shotgun she held in her hands swung back and forth along with her slow swinging gait and Solomon could feel her scrutiny even though she could not see him.

'I know you're there,' she said. 'I crawled out the window, you son of a bitch, and I can hear to shoot better than most can see to, so don't try nothing. I called the cops too. They're on their way right now, so you better not've hurt my daddy none.'

Solomon felt the skin tighten on his neck. If the cops were coming he needed to be gone from here. He looked at the shotgun.

Winchester 12 – 'The Perfect Repeater' – 20 gauge – accurate up to 50 feet – six rounds fully loaded, which he had to assume it was.

He glanced at the corral. His horse was drinking from a water trough about twenty feet away, a lot of distance to cover while trying not to make a sound, and still well within range when he got there. His horse would make a noise for sure. Maybe if he was running away she might let him go, leave him for the cops to chase. He studied the way she was holding the gun, tight to her body as if it was part of her. She could shoot, he was sure of that. But would she? She stopped, her head tilted over to one side, listening to the tick of the buildings and sniffing the air. Her face hardened.

'What did you do?' Her voice was raw, angry. 'I smell blood, what did you do?'

The turkey vulture hopped away, disturbed by her voice. She turned towards the faint flap of wings and fired without hesitation.

The bird exploded in a boom of blood and feathers and cartwheeled away across the dirt. She racked another round in the chamber with a smooth, well-practised grace and listened again through the dying echo of the gunshot, her head tilted towards the spot where the carcass of the bird now lay bloody and tattered.

Solomon heard the wail of a siren, in the distance but getting closer. Ellie heard it too and tilted her head back towards the barn, the gun swinging round until it was point-ing at a spot marginally to the right of where Solomon was standing. He couldn't tell if she wanted to keep him here until the cops arrived or shoot him before they did. Either way, it was a bad deal for him. He looked over at the parked pick-up truck to his right, the only thing close enough to give him any cover but still too far away. He breathed slowly, hyper aware of every sound. The siren grew louder. The gun barrel moved back and forth in a small arc that passed through the spot where Solomon was standing. Then his horse snorted on the far side of the yard and the barrel jerked towards it.

'Ellie,' Solomon shouted, snatching her attention back to him. The barrel swung back and he leapt to his right just as a shot boomed inside the confines of the barn, shaking dust from the roof beams and chewing up the horse stall he had been standing in front of.

He hit the dirt and rolled forward using the momentum to flip back on to feet that were already running. He heard the snick-snack of the pump action and pictured her, following the sound of his footfalls, the gun following as if radar-controlled. He wished he was barefoot again so he could feel the ground and cushion his steps better. She would know he was heading for the truck and, if she was as good a shot as she claimed, she would aim ahead and fire at where he was going to be, not where he was. He stopped dead at the thought, straightening his legs and skidding to a stop just as another boom shook the barn and chewed the wall in front of him to splinters.

Solomon threw himself forward again, sprinting then diving for the truck, hitting the ground as a fourth boom rang out that ripped the licence plate off the rear fender and sent pain singing through his trailing foot. He landed heavily and rolled over, putting the engine block between himself and Ellie. There were pockmarks in the leather of his boot where the buckshot had hit. The skin beneath stung, but the leather had held. He could still run on it – if he got the chance.

He dropped his head down and peered through the dark oily gap under the truck. Ellie's bare feet were planted in the dirt in a solid sideways stance showing she was still aiming at the truck. The siren was louder now. He had minutes to get away and she still had two shells in the shotgun. If he tried to run, she would shoot him, no question, probably hit him this time. But if he waited for the cops to arrive they would hand him over to whoever he had seen prowling through Holly's house with the silenced pistol. He had to get away in the next minute or he might not get away at all.

He looked around for something he might throw to cause a distraction but the floor was clean. He thought about slipping his boots off and using them, but they had already saved him from injury.

The siren howled. Ellie didn't move. But he had to. He reached up and grabbed the handle and the door creaked open.

'Steal my daddy's truck and I'll kill ya,' Ellie called from the yard.

Not much of a dis-incentive. She was going to shoot him anyway.

He looked inside, saw keys hanging down from the steering column, and thanked God for trusting country ways. He leapt forward through the door, arm outstretched, and felt springs dig into him from the worn seat. The keys jingled as he grabbed them and twisted them round. The engine coughed. Didn't catch. Then the whole world exploded in jewels of glass as the side window blew inwards. Ellie had fired level, assuming he was sitting in the driver's seat. He twisted the key again and the engine coughed. He had maybe a second before she realized her mistake and repositioned. The old engine turned again then caught, the big V8 shaking pebbles of glass down on top of him.

Solomon threw himself forward and out of the cab just as buckshot tore up the bench seat he had been lying on. He scrambled to his feet and started running, out of the shadow and into the sunlight towards his horse. Behind him he heard the slide rack again and a dry click as the hammer fell on an empty chamber.

His horse flicked its head and backed away as he drew closer, forcing him to slow down or risk it bolting. The siren was loud now, bringing men with more guns, all of them fully loaded. He grabbed the horse's mane and hauled himself on to its back, found his balance and made to turn. Then he stopped.

When the cops arrived they wouldn't be able to follow him by car but they could on horseback. He edged the stallion towards the gate, kicked the top loop clear and pulled the gate open.

The horses inside nickered and snorted and backed away, favouring the familiarity of the corral to the freedom he was offering. He gave his horse some heel to drive it forward, forcing the herd round. They moved reluctantly, their eyes rolling to white in confusion then one of them panicked and broke away and the rest followed, the ground shaking with hammering hooves as the herd poured out of the gate and scattered across the desert and away from the ranch.

Solomon kicked his horse and followed them. From the corner of his eye he saw the police car, a dust cloud behind it as it barrelled into the yard. Ellie was standing with her head to one side, lost in the noise. Solomon wished he could have told her what Bobby Gallagher had said before he died, that her name was the last thing he had spoken. Maybe he would get the chance later, but right now he had to get away.

He caught up with the rear horses and kept low on the stallion's back, making it harder for anyone to see which horse he was riding. He rode hard, keeping up with the herd until the desert swallowed him up, and the ranch was lost from sight.

VII

'The fewer our wants the
more we resemble the Gods.'

Socrates

RICHES AND REDEMPTION
THE MAKING OF A TOWN

⸎

The published memoir
of the Reverend Jack 'King' Cassidy

T HE MEN HAD BEEN DEAD for some long while. There were two of them, their ragged clothes binding a loose collection of bones and hide together in something approximating the shapes of men. Smaller bones gleamed white on the ground, fingers and foot joints scattered around and picked white by whatever animals had been drawn by the scent of a meal. There were flies here too and it struck me that this was why there had been so many, and so quickly, up at the wagon.

Tools lay on the ground among the bones: a rock hammer, a drilling spike, a chisel – mining tools that had been brought for gold but used to dig for something far more valuable to two men dying of thirst in the desert. The gully was pockmarked with holes, about twenty or so all told, some waist deep, others barely more than scrapes in the ground. The dead men's hats lay on the ground next to their skulls, the jaws pulled open in silent screams by skin dried almost black by the heat. The tops of their skulls shone white through the hide and I realized why. They had been scalped.

I froze where I stood, as if the savages who had done it might be waiting in the trees still. But as my staring eyes took in the scene my rational mind reasserted itself and calmed my pounding heart. I reasoned that whatever had occurred here must have done so a long time since and therefore whoever had done it was similarly long gone. There was no evidence of further violence or butchery, which made me think the scalps had been taken when the men were already dead, their hair making easy trophies for a passing band of savages who must have taken their provisions and horses also.

I moved further into the gully, picking my way carefully between the scattered bones, checking each hole and praying I might find some sign of the water these men had sought and that I now so desperately needed. Each hole was as dry as the first and my fear began to rise again. I knew that without water I would likely end my days here too, and that right soon. But it was as I was conducting this bleak and fruitless inspection that I spotted a scrap of yellowed paper snagged on the long thorns of a mesquite sapling. I pulled it clear and opened it carefully, mindful that time and the elements had rendered it fragile. It was incomplete but there was enough of it remaining to send a cold chill through me despite the heat choked air. I stumbled backwards when I recognized the marks upon it, my mind screaming with what it meant, then scrambled back up the bank.

Eldridge was where I had left him, my untouched canteen lying on the ground by his side, his ruined hand curled into a fist on his chest. Flies buzzed around it, feasting on the blood that oozed from his torn flesh and stained the folded square of paper it held. I worked it from his grip, carefully folded it open and laid it down on the ground next to the scrap I had found by the scalped prospectors. I took my own map from my own pocket and laid that down too.

They were all three the same.

I had wondered what evil I might encounter out here in the burning wastes, little realizing that I had already faced it. Sergeant Lyons had taken my last dollar in exchange for this worthless map, but he had taken much more from poor Eldridge and his family and the two prospectors lying mouldering in the far gully.

I resolved then, as I stared down at these maps that might as well have been death warrants, that I would not allow my life to be forfeit to this snake of a man who had betrayed us, and who knew how many other poor trusting travellers besides, for nothing more than a handful of silver.

I re-saddled my mule as the sun slipped lower, discarding everything not essential to survival. I kept a little food, two blankets for warmth in the night and shelter in the day, and a third of my empty canteens in hope that I might happen across some water, or another traveller who might spare me some, or that God might lead me to a fresh source. I arranged the pale Christ and the Bible under the shade of a mesquite tree in a rough approximation of the church I still hoped to build here then opened the Bible and prayed to God to give me strength enough to make it back to the fort and bring Sergeant Lyons to justice for what he had done. And as I prayed, the wind found its way under the trees and the pages riffled then settled at one of the few passages where the priest had marked some scripture:

And the LORD went before them
by day in a pillar of cloud, to lead
them the way; and by night in a pillar
of fire, to give them light;

I read the passage over and over, waiting for the heat of the day to fade a little and praying all the while that God would indeed guide me. And when the day faded I led my mule out of the shadows and into the softening sunlight. I paused on the rise of an ancient bank and gazed out at the vast rolling expanse of broken wilderness ahead of me, the dipping sun throwing deep shadows across it. I felt exhausted just looking at it and thinking of all the distance I had already travelled when I still had hope in my heart and water aplenty in my pack and how I now had to traverse it again with neither. I don't know what caused me to turn at that moment, for I had no reason to other than a strange sensation of being watched. Whatever the reason, turn I did, towards the stand of trees I had so recently quit. And that was when I saw the thing that would change my future.

It burned to the south and east of my position, a light so bright and steady it seemed as if a star had fallen from the heavens and burned still where it lay in the sand. It shone in a place where the range rose to form a horse-shoe of red mountains. A hot breeze blew steadily from the same direction. It smelled of creosote bush and sweet desert blooms and my heart lifted when I nosed it – the smell of rain in the desert. My mule turned and tossed his head for he smelled it too and the passage the priest had outlined shone now with fresh meaning. The light was in the opposite direction to the fort but I tugged the reins of my mule without hesitation and headed towards this peculiar pillar of fire shining brightly in the gathering night.

I followed that light for several hours until the night was full dark and the light was like sunlight within it. And when I reached the origin of it I discovered a hole like a doorway cut into the night through which the light poured. It shone upon the ground, lighting up a boulder that had been split clean in two. Spring water bubbled up from the ground between the two halves and I fell into it, drinking and crying and laughing.

I stayed there until dawn and when the sun came up the pillar of light faded away. It was then that I saw what else was in the water: bright flakes of gold and deep green crystals. And I wept again for I realized that here were the riches the priest had promised, fortune enough to build a church and a town besides.

And that is my tale, or as much of it as I will tell here.

There are other things that happened to me out in that desert that I will not speak of, for they will serve no purpose other than to muddy the clearer waters of my better intentions. And though I have done things I regret, the heaviest burden I carry is something I do not, in fact, regret at all. For I made my choices with a free will, a sacrifice for the benefit of others.

I have become famous in my lifetime for finding a great fortune out in the desert, but in truth there is another treasure, far greater than the first, that I discovered late in my life after a great amount of study. I found the way to it hidden in the pages of the priest's Bible. I had always suspected the book contained a clue that would lead me to riches, but by the time I found it and understood its meaning it was too late for me and so I resolve to take the secret of it to my grave. Maybe someone else will find it. Or perhaps it is meant to be forever lost. It is not for me to decide.

We serve God and we serve each other in different ways. And God knows what I have done. I hope He understands why I did it. I do not expect Him to forgive me.

Poor Eldridge died before I could fetch the water back to him, but I made sure Sergeant Lyons danced at the end of a rope for what he had done. So it is to Eldridge and his poor tragic family that I now dedicate this memoir. To him, to his, and to that great lost treasure still out there, waiting to be claimed.

In Our Father's holy name.

Amen.

JC

52

Mulcahy drove off the highway and on to the dirt track, following the directions the GPS was giving him. He kept his speed down so he didn't throw up too much dirt or shred a tyre. The message Tío had sent him had given him map coordinates and a time he had to be there. He glanced at the time-to-destination display on the GPS. It was going to be close.

Through the tall grass he could see a barn up ahead, the only building for miles. He checked the coordinates. This had to be it: rough wooden boards fixed vertically to make the walls, a steep tin roof painted with red oxide to keep the weather out – same as the barn he had just come from. He had been having an internal conversation about what he'd had to do there on the drive over, beating himself up about it and at the same time trying to justify it.

The man had been old, he was probably close to death anyway.

Your father's old too. Would you want him to die like that?

No, but at least I made it quick.

Well, I'm sure he died grateful.

I could have killed the girl, but I didn't.

I'm sure she's grateful too.

What choice did I have?

You could have walked away.

Then Pop would have been cut into tiny pieces. And I would have spent my life on the run.

And this is better?

Yes. If it works out, this is better.

Keep telling yourself that.

I will. Now shut up.

He slowed as he drew closer then drove a slow circle round the barn, looking for any parked vehicles or signs of life. He pulled up in back so anyone coming up the track would not see the Jeep, then he opened his window and cut the engine. Listened. The tall dry grass shushed all around him and the first sounds of evening were already starting to creep in – chirping grasshoppers, the buzz of green toads by an unseen pond, cactus wrens marking their territories with loud char-ing calls that sounded like electronic alarm clocks. High above him a jet was scratching a white line across the sky. Nothing else moved.

He got out of the Jeep and added the crunch of his boots to the sounds of the coming night. He held his Beretta in one hand and his phone in the other. He checked his messages in case Tío had sent him further instructions. He hadn't.

He moved away from the car, studying the surrounding

land. The nearest high ground was an escarpment about three miles to the west, too far for a sniper if that's what this was about. If someone was planning an ambush here they would be out in the grass somewhere. Except the animals were too lively so he was fairly sure he was alone.

He turned his attention to the barn and approached it from the back, checking the weathered sides for any splits or knotholes that might have eyes peering through or gun barrels poking out. Despite its weathered appearance, it was actually pretty solid: no gaps, no holes.

He made his way round to the front and inspected the heavy lock holding the door closed. It was a thick, six-number rotary dial combination made from carbon steel. The hasps were toughened-steel too, the only indicator that there might be something more valuable than cattle feed stored inside. He pressed his ear to the warm planks of the door and listened to the silence inside for a while then stood back and moved round until he was standing on the shady side of the barn.

He waited.

Checked his phone. Checked his signal. Checked his messages in case he'd missed anything. He thought about calling his old man again, but he had nothing new to tell him. Not yet. If he still smoked, now would be the perfect time to spark one up, but he didn't even have that any more. What did he have exactly?

A faint whirring noise started up, like the whine of an electric mosquito, and he pressed his ear back to the warm boards of the barn. It was coming from inside. His phone buzzed. New message. Six numbers, too short to be a phone number. He realized what it was and he moved back to the front of the barn, his shadow falling over the heavy lock. He dialled the numbers into it, copying them from the message. It clicked open and he unthreaded it from the hasps then opened the door.

The barn was about three-quarters full of hay bales stacked one on top of another to form walls with gaps between them wide enough to drive a forklift down. The forklift itself was parked to the left of the door, a thin skein of cobwebs drifting between the forks and the driver's cab showing it hadn't been used for a while. The whirring sound was coming from deeper inside the barn, somewhere beyond the hay wall. Mulcahy flicked off the slide-mounted safety of the Beretta and pulled the slide back to work the oil in a little then moved inside.

It was hotter inside the barn than outside, the air thick with hay dust and pollen. He moved down the main corridor of stacked bales towards the whirring sound, the sweat already beading on his skin and tickling down his spine beneath his shirt. He reached the end of the corridor, peered round the edge and saw a large area framed by four high walls of stacked bales. The space was empty, a mat of loose straw covering the floor. He stepped into the open, scanning the tops of the four walls from behind his gun. Then the whirring sound stopped.

Mulcahy tensed in the silence, waiting for the crackle of gunfire or the whoosh of an explosion. He spun round at a noise and a section of floor started to lift, spilling straw on the ground. Tío's face appeared in the gap and he smiled when he saw the gun pointing at him. Mulcahy flicked on the safety and made sure Tío saw him do it.

'Take this and help me out,' Tío said, handing Mulcahy the framed photographs of his daughters. Mulcahy laid them on a hay bale along with his gun, then hauled Tío out of the hole.

'Hand the stuff up,' Tío called down to two men stand-ing in the elevator shaft and gasoline sloshed inside cans as Mulcahy hauled them up out of the manhole and laid them on the straw-littered floor.

'Heads or tails?' Tío said from behind him.

'What?'

'Just call it.'

'Tails,' he said, hauling another gas can out of the elevator shaft.

He heard the soft ting of a nail flicking a coin then a slap like someone swatting a mosquito. 'Tails it is,' Tío said.

One of the guys handed up a bag and Mulcahy could tell by the solid weight and the way the contents shifted inside that it contained guns.

He turned to place it on the ground next to the gas cans and saw the barrel of his own gun appear and point down into the pit. It twitched twice, the suppressor and subsonic rounds making the shots sound like sneezes. The fatter of the two guys fell backwards, his head banging against the steel and sending a deep bonging sound echoing down the shaft.

The taller man made a move to reach inside his jacket. 'Don't,' Tío said.

He didn't.

'Take it out slow with your finger and thumb and hand it to him.'

He obeyed and handed the gun to Mulcahy.

Tío nodded down at the body of the fat guy. 'If the coin had been heads then it would be you lying dead in a hole. What do you think of that?'

The taller guy looked down at the dead man, lying on his back and staring up. There were two small holes in his face,

297

one in his left cheek and one above his right eye, which was red with burst blood vessels. Blood spread from the back of his head like a dark halo. The tall guy stepped away to stop it getting on his shoes.

'God must have saved you for a special reason,' Tío said. 'He must like you, Miguel. Let's see how much. Pick up the last gas can.'

Miguel didn't move and Mulcahy felt the air thicken.

'You're going to pick the can up,' Tío said. 'You know you will, so you might as well get on and do it.'

Miguel's eyes flicked between the gun and Tío.

'How's the weather down in La Paz?' Tío said. 'Those salty Pacific breezes must be good for aching old joints, no?'

Something flared inside Miguel and Mulcahy thought he might leap up out of the pit and go for Tío's throat. Instead he blinked then stooped down slowly and picked up the gas can.

'Good boy. You think your mother knows what a good son she has? I bet she does. Apple of her eye. She knows who you work for and what pays for her nice little retirement home, all safe and quiet, away from the border towns and all those bad people? You think she knows her good son is bad people too?

'You don't have to answer. It's not for us to decide who is good and who is bad. That's God's business. And God saved you from a bullet so he must think you're some kind of hot shit. Let's say we up the ante a little and see if he does it again. Here's what's going to happen. You're going to take that can of gas and pour half of it over your dead friend there and the other half over yourself, OK?'

Miguel didn't move, a rabbit frozen in headlights, staring death in the eye and unable to get out of its way.

298

Mulcahy glanced over at Tío. He had a weird look about him, like he was on some drug that had made his skin go slack and his eyes glassy. Shark's eyes.

'You don't think God will save you this time?' Tío shook his head. 'Man, if I was God, that sure would piss me off. Where's your faith, Miguel? OK, let's see if we can't find something else you believe in more.' He held his phone out so Miguel could see the screen. It was showing an address in La Paz, Baja California, and a moan escaped from Miguel's throat when he read it.

'You know that address?' Tío asked, moving his thumb over the screen of the phone. 'Sounds fancy. Let me see if I got someone nearby I can send round and take some pictures so I can see for myself. Maybe I'll get them to swing past a gas station on their way over.'

Gas sloshed in the can as Miguel unscrewed the cap, his breathing getting heavier as he measured what was left of his life with each half-twist. The cap came away and he turned to the body and started splashing gas over it.

'Save some for yourself,' Tío said, and Miguel looked up at him, his eyes dark and defeated and full of hate. Tío held the phone out again so he could read his mother's address on it. Miguel stood up straight, slowly tipped the rest of the gas over himself then threw the can on the floor, sending another clanging sound echoing down the elevator shaft. He closed his eyes and started to pray.

'So you're talking to God again now,' Tío said. 'You should make your mind up.'

Mulcahy still wasn't sure where this was going or how it was going to end. Now would be the time to start asking questions if that's what this was about, but he didn't think it was. He didn't know what this was.

'Get out of here,' Tío said, and Mulcahy and Miguel both looked at him in surprise. Tío pointed at the big red button on the lifting platform. 'Hit the button and get lost. Go run to your momma in La Paz.'

Miguel blinked then reached out slowly, still half-expecting a bullet or some fresh brand of cruelty. He pushed the button and the mosquito whirr of the engines started again as the platform began to sink down.

'Would you do something like that to save your father?' Tío asked, squatting down and unscrewing the cap from one of the other gas cans.

'I am doing something like that,' Mulcahy replied.

'No. Hurting other people ain't the same as hurting yourself. Ain't the same thing as laying down your life to save someone else's.' He grabbed a handful of straw, twisted it into the open neck of the can then fished a lighter from his pocket. 'You ready?' he said.

Mulcahy eyed the Molotov cocktail. 'Ready for what?'

'The end,' Tío said. He sparked a flame and held it to the straw wick, tilting the can until the flame was roaring around the neck, then he took a step forward and dropped the burning can straight down the shaft.

It took a second for Mulcahy to register what had happened. The roar of the burning fuel filled the pause, getting quieter as the can fell down the elevator shaft, then there was a thud, and then there was screaming.

Mulcahy stepped over to the edge of the shaft and an updraught of heat pushed him back. He could see Miguel way below, a bright ball of fire in the shape of a man, beating at himself and bouncing off the walls. He raised the gun he'd taken off him, sighted centre mass and fired. The shot was thunderous in the elevator shaft and the burning man fell forward. Mulcahy fired four more times until the figure stopped moving.

'Ramon would never have poured gas over himself in order to save me,' Tío said, peering into the shaft.

Mulcahy felt the weight of the gun in his hand. It was an FN Five-seven, a *mata policia*. He had fired five shots, which meant there should be five still in the magazine. He could shoot Tío now and do the world a favour – do Tío a favour too, most likely. But then his father would be killed and dumped somewhere and he would have to live with that forever, and the people he had already hurt would have been for nothing.

'The car's parked in back,' he said, holding out the gun with the grip towards Tío. Tío took it and nodded, like Mulcahy had passed some test. 'We should get out of here,' he said, walking towards the daylight and away from the smell of burning flesh.

Not long now – Mulcahy reminded himself.

Just a few more hours and all this would be over.

53

Solomon rode with the herd until they hit the river then dropped down into the gully and crossed back to the fire-scorched bank. He slipped to the ground and let his horse drink while he took handfuls of black ash and mixed it into a paste with dirt and water then smeared it on the horse's flanks and back. They would be looking for him in earnest now. He had fled the scene of a murder. He couldn't ride into town the way he had come out: too close to the airfield, too visible. But he couldn't ride across the fire-blackened desert either, not on a pure white horse. He continued to camouflage the horse using methods the native tribes had employed for millennia then did the same to himself, darkening his white skin and hair with grey ash from the ground.

Discovering Old Man Tucker's body had changed everything. His death didn't fit the narrative he had been constructing in his head, with Holly and James Coronado on one side of the coin and the town elders on the other. But Holly couldn't possibly have killed him. The body had been fresh when he found it and she was in custody. Also a woman was unlikely to have been strong enough to have delivered the death blow through the sternum. He pictured the body in his mind again, the neat slit above the heart. There was something not right about it:

the flayed skin, the way he had been … displayed. That's what it was like, a display – it spoke of violence and of someone using pain to extract information, but the stab to the heart suggested a degree of humanity as well as skill and control. He thought of the man with the silenced weapon standing calmly in James Coronado's study. A man used to dealing in death. A man who had already been in Holly's house. He wondered if maybe he was looking for the same thing Tucker had been after, the same thing he was now sure that James Coronado had died for. And what had Tucker told him, he wondered, before the killer had delivered the coup de grâce? Judging by the abruptly abandoned mess in Holly's house, Tucker hadn't found anything. Which meant the killer would probably circle back there. Wait for the lady of the house to return. Maybe sharpen the knife he'd used on the old man while he waited for Holly. So he could ask her questions.

Solomon stepped on a boulder and remounted the horse, the smeared mud already almost dry in the warm air.

He thought of her, tied up with strips of skin removed from her back like Tucker, and kicked the horse forward. They rose up the bank and set off at a gallop across the charred earth, the stallion's hooves kicking up puffs of drying black ash as they thundered along. Maybe he couldn't save her husband, but he could save her. He needed to warn her, tell her what had happened. He remembered her slipping her phone into her pocket before she left the house. He needed to get that number. But he also needed to get a phone.

He could see the town drawing nearer now and activity around the crash site – more uniforms to avoid. He was far enough away that they wouldn't see him, but he didn't want to take any chances. He steered the horse in a wide arc around them and drew closer to the town. There were still a few people clustered round a fire truck, some of them still in their funeral clothes, which set a thought running.

When he had told him that James Coronado was dead, Morgan had looked up; an unconscious gesture that Solomon had picked up on. He followed the remembered line of Morgan's gaze now to where the evening sun was throwing long shadows across the red face of the mountains. He saw it about a third of the way up the lower slopes – a cross, made of plain board and painted white so the sun would catch it. The cemetery where James Coronado was buried.

Solomon dug his heels into the horse's flank to urge it forward. They kept records of burial plots at cemeteries – who was buried, special maintenance requirements – and contact details of living relatives.

54

Cassidy was sitting in the family pew at the front of the church when his phone rang.

He had set it to silent, but the church was so quiet it might as well have been playing the Sousa March. There was no one else around so he let it ring, the insectile buzz shimmering through the quiet until, finally, it gave up. He had come here for peace and to pray and to think. He did not wish to hear whatever news the phone was bringing. He doubted it would be good.

It rang again almost immediately and he opened his eyes and stared at the twisted altar cross ahead of him. 'God give me the strength to see out this day,' he whispered and pulled the phone from his pocket. 'Cassidy,' he said, his whispering voice loud in the quiet of the church.

'It's Morgan. Tucker's dead.'

He sat bolt upright. 'What?'

'We got a call from Ellie that there was an intruder at the ranch and by the time we got there, Pete was dead. And guess who was riding away on your horse.'

Cassidy struggled to take it all in. 'Pete's dead?'

'Yes.' Morgan's voice dropped lower. 'And he was tortured first.'

Cassidy felt sick. 'Why would they torture him?'

'Why do you think? To get information. Which means they'll most likely be coming for us next.'

Cassidy turned and looked back towards the door, checking there was no one there, though he had locked it from the inside so knew there couldn't be.

'Where are you?' Morgan said.

'Church.'

'Good. That's good. You should stay there. You'll be safe. Throw up a few prayers while you're at it.' Cassidy bristled at that but said nothing. 'Listen, I've stepped up the manhunt for Solomon Creed. We're hunting a murderer now, not a horse thief, but I've kept it local – only my men, no outside agencies, nothing on the wires.'

'Why?'

'Because we don't want him captured, we want him dead. If we get outsiders in, they'll ask him all kinds of questions. We can't afford for that to happen.'

Cassidy stood and started walking past the cross to the dark fresco beyond. 'What's the point?'

'What do you mean?'

Cassidy stopped in front of the mirror and stared at his dim reflection, the painted devil on one side, the angel on the other. 'Say Solomon Creed is responsible for the plane crash and we give him to Tío, you think that will be enough? Remember that last message we got from him?'

'El Rey.'

'Exactly. It means the whole town is at stake now.' He shook his head and stared hard at his reflection, forcing himself to gaze upon the man he had become. 'We can't let the people suffer because of what we did. This town is what's important, and the town is the people. We need to protect them, not ourselves. The people are what's important. I deserve whatever's coming to me.'

The painted devil stared out at him, the painted angel too.

'Call everyone,' Cassidy said. 'The DEA, the FBI – anyone who wants Papa Tío's head on a plate. Tell them you've discovered a conspiracy here to import drug shipments using the airfield, and that you believe Tucker and I are behind it. I'll back that story up if I make it that far, there's no need for you to go down too. The town will need someone to look after it. Tell them about the crash, tell them who was on it and tell them you think Papa Tío is on his way here to personally wreak his revenge. Tío may be able to muster an army, but so can we. We need to save the town – that's all that matters. I'll take my chances, either way.'

55

Solomon saw the track cutting up the scree-sided lower slopes of the Chinchuca Mountains and steered his horse towards it. A sign pointed up, a simple board cut in the shape of an arrow, a cross burned on it with a hot iron to show day trekkers they were on the right track. He doubted there would be any tourists plodding their steady way up to the cemetery today, not after the fire. It would be some time before it was business as usual in this town.

He hit the track at a trot and kept it up as they rose, pushing the horse hard enough to make good time, but not so hard as to exhaust it. He would need the horse for more than this journey. The sun was dropping lower now and bathing everything with the warm blood glow of dusk. He could see the town below him, long shadows stretching from the taller buildings, the church glowing white in the centre of everything, white like the cross marking the cemetery above him, white like he was.

He reached the top of the track where it forked left and continued up the mountains and right to where the tall cross stood by a stone hut. A wall stretched away from it on both sides, high railings sticking up with spikes on the top. The hut had a deep verandah and a tie rail and trough for horses.

There were water bowls for dogs and a map of the local area on a board with hiking routes and points of interest marked on it and a sign saying 'No guns please – graveyard is full'. Another sign in the window of the door said 'Closed' though the big iron gate was wide open.

Solomon walked the horse over to the trough and slid to the ground. There were noises coming from beyond the hut, the faint scrapes of a shovel across ground. Solomon breathed in, instinctively trying to catch the scent of whoever was there, but the wind was in the wrong direction.

He stepped on to the porch, carefully cushioning his footfalls so they made no sound, and peered through the window into the darkened office. He saw shelves filled with graveyard memorabilia and the same things he had seen in the stores down in the town. Jack Cassidy's memoir was stacked up by the cash register. He tried the door, hoping that whoever was working in the graveyard had unlocked it and forgotten to flip the sign round, but it was locked tight.

The scraping sounds continued and he heard some soft clangs as the blade of a shovel patted the ground.

Gravedigger. Probably tidying up James Coronado's plot after the funeral. He might have information about the funeral. Holly's contact number. A key to the ticket office. Something.

Solomon moved softly across the boards and peered round the edge of the wall.

The cemetery was small and densely planted with bodies. Simple boards bristled up from the ground, white flaking paint with names carved on them picked out in black. Most graves were over a hundred years old. The only stone tomb was in the centre, close to where a large cottonwood offered some shade, its roots nourished by the graves. A pick-up truck was parked under it, barrels of tools lashed to the back. A man in green overalls was working on a patch of ground a little way beyond it, shovelling stones on to a fresh mound of earth and patting it flat. Solomon watched him work, his back to him, his eyes fixed on the ground. It was the same man Mayor Cassidy had pointed out when the fire was still raging, the man who had given him the cap he had left in Morgan's car and the sunscreen he'd been using. Useful man to know.

Billy Walker.

Solomon glanced back at the pick-up. If there was an information sheet relating to the cemetery, it would be in there. Probably be a phone in there too. All of which was academic because what was also in there was a very large dog. It sat behind the wheel, its huge head pointing at its owner, its tongue lolling from its mouth, the half-open window next to it smeared with drool.

American bulldog, his mind told him. *Powerful, loyal, known to form extremely strong bonds with their owners.*

He glanced back at the office door. He could break the glass, but the man might hear. The bulldog would for sure. He leaned close to the door; it was fitted with security glass, a grid of wire running all the way through it. It was bound to be alarmed too, a building like this, isolated and out of the way. Hard-wired to the local police. Smash the glass and a cruiser would show up. No good.

He studied the locks. There were two, both heavy-duty. He pictured the tumblers and barrels within, the deadbolt, the levers, the detainers.

Could he pick them?

Perhaps, if he had the tools. But he didn't and the door would be alarmed too. He would need a key or a code to disarm that, and he had neither. He looked back round the edge of the building.

Billy Walker was finishing up now, scraping the last loose rocks into a pile on James Coronado's grave. A triangle of sweat had soaked through the back of his overalls and the band of his cap. He must have been here for some time, tidying up, clearing away. Long enough that he might not have heard what had happened at the Tucker ranch. Either way, it was a risk he had to take.

Solomon moved silently back to the trough where the horse was drinking, cupped his hands into the water and rubbed at his face and hair to wash the ash from it. Then he grabbed one of the dog bowls and filled it.

The dog turned its head towards the sound of Solomon's boots crunching across the gravel. Its ears pricked forward and it barked, a single deep cough that stopped Billy Walker working and made him turn round. He squinted at Solomon from beneath the shade of his cap and leaned on the handle of his shovel.

'Hello again,' Solomon said, waving a greeting and holding up the dog bowl. 'Thought your dog might want a drink.'

Billy shrugged. 'I guess so.'

Solomon drew closer to the truck and looked in at the solid knot of muscle and teeth. 'What's his name?'

'Otis.'

'Is he friendly?'

'He's friendly enough if you're giving him food or sumpn' a drink.'

Solomon placed the bowl down in the shade and opened the door to let Otis out. The truck rocked on its springs when he jumped down. Otis ignored Solomon and headed straight to the bowl, sniffed it, then started slurping the water down.

'Tough to be wearing a fur coat in this weather,' Solomon

said, stepping out of the shade and walking over to Billy. 'Is that James Coronado's grave?'

Billy turned and looked at the neat mound of stones as if he had only just noticed it. 'You knew him?'

'Long time ago. I heard about what happened and was in the area, so I thought I'd come by. Then the fire happened and …' He let the sentence trail off. 'Thanks for the hat, by the way. I left it with Chief Morgan to give it back to you. Didn't figure on bumping into you again. He took me over to Holly's house so I could pay my respects, only she wasn't there.' He stared down at the grave. 'Reckoned I'd come here instead.'

'You missed the funeral,' Billy said, dropping the shovel on to a tarp along with a rake and a pair of work gloves.

'I guess I did.'

Billy rolled his tools in the tarp and walked up the slope to his truck. The dog glanced up from his bowl then carried on drinking.

'You wouldn't have any idea how I might contact the widow, would you?' Solomon said. 'Be a shame to be in town and not get a chance to say hello and offer my sympathies.'

Billy dumped the tarp in the back of the truck and turned to him. 'You don't got her number?'

'I lost my phone. Must have dropped it out by the fire line. Lost all my numbers too. Pain in the ass.'

Billy nodded then moved round to the driver's seat and reached inside. Solomon tensed. If he knew what had happened at the Tucker ranch, now would be the moment he would pull out a shotgun.

'I saw what you did there at the fire line,' Billy said, pulling a phone out of a dashboard charger. 'Taking charge and shifting the line like that. That was a ballsy move. I guess this

312

town owes you something for that. You can use my phone to call Mrs Coronado if you like.' He handed him the phone and pulled a folder out of the door pocket with a map of the cemetery pasted to the cover. 'I got her number in here someplace.'

something ...

56

Holly Coronado descended into the cool, polished gloom
of the town museum, a worn, stone block of a building that
faced the church and filled one whole side of the town square.
It had originally been the Copper Exchange, built to house
all the offices and personnel who ran the mine and traded
copper when the town was booming. Now it was part town
hall, part museum, with the museum on the first two floors
and the archive in the basement.

She caught Janice Wickens coming out of a pebbled-glass
door with 'Archive Office' painted on it and noted the look
of sympathy that passed across her face.

'Mrs Coronado,' she said. 'I'm so very sorry for your loss.'

'Thanks.' Holly forced a smile. 'I was wondering if I could
check something.'

Janice already had the key in the lock. 'Well, I was fixing to
close up for the day.'

'It will only take a moment, please.' She held up the
requisition. 'Jim had this in his personal things. I wanted to
pick it up for him.'

Janice Wickens was a metronome of a woman who lived
in a house wrapped in plastic to keep everything clean and
in perfect order. Precision was important to her, more

important than friends even, and Holly could feel the turmoil her request had roiled up inside her. 'Please,' she said. 'For Jim.'

Even the plastic-wrapped heart of Janice Wickens couldn't hold out against the wish of a widow invoking her dead husband's name. 'One moment then,' she said, turning the key and opening the door again.

Holly followed her into a room with oak panels and wide floorboards and a counter at waist height that made it feel like an old mutual savings office or the clerk's desk in an old hotel. Janice took the requisition slip, checked the number on it against a handwritten ledger, then disappeared through a door leading to the main archive.

Holly paced and waited. Checked the time on her phone and frowned when it started ringing. She didn't recognize the number. She let it ring a few times, debating whether to let it go to voicemail. Then she answered. 'Hello?'

'It's me. It's Solomon.'

'Hi,' she stepped away from the counter.

'Where are you?'

'I'm in the Cassidy archive.'

'Where's that?'

'In town. Opposite the church.'

'What happened at the police station?'

'Nothing. They left me alone in a room for a while then let me go.'

'OK, you need to get out of there now.'

'Why?'

'Because Pete Tucker's dead.'

'What! How?'

'It doesn't matter. Listen, don't go home. Don't talk to the police. Don't talk to anyone. I think you're in danger. You need to get out of town as fast as possible. Don't let anyone know where you're going.'

Holly felt like the ceiling had started to lower and the walls were closing in. 'Where are you?'

'Up at the cemetery.'

'I want to meet up.'

'Not here.' There was a pause and Holly turned to the door. She could hear Janice returning on the other side. 'The place your husband died, is it easy to find?'

She knew exactly where he had died but hadn't wanted to go there. Not now. Perhaps not ever. 'Yes. All right yes. It's about three miles east of town on the Chinchuca road, the road that winds up through the mountains. There's a stone near the road with a wagon-trail marker on it like an eagle.'

Janice Wickens walked back in holding an envelope. Holly smiled and Janice handed it to her then turned the ledger round so she could sign for it.

'OK,' Solomon said. 'I'll get there as soon as I can. Be careful.'

She signed her name, feeling as if she was watching everything through the wrong end of a telescope. 'I will.'

The phone clicked and she looked up. Janice was regarding her with concern. 'You OK, dear?'

'Yes, I'm fine.' She placed the pen down on the ledger and started backing away, trying to remember what she'd said and how much Janice might have heard. *Don't talk to anyone*, Solomon had said. She felt panicked. 'Thanks for this,' she said, holding the envelope up. 'I appreciate your time.' Then she turned and left the room, her boots sounding far too loud as she hurried away across the polished stone floor.

57

Solomon ended the call and studied the stone tomb in front of him.

He had drifted away from Billy Walker during the conversation to stop him overhearing and found himself beside the largest grave in the cemetery. Like the mansion in the centre of town it was bigger and grander than anything around it and had been constructed for the same man. He read the carved inscription on the stone:

REV. JACK CASSIDY
PIONEER. VISIONARY. PHILANTHROPIST
FOUNDER AND FIRST CITIZEN OF THE CITY OF REDEMPTION
DEC 25TH, 1841, TO DEC 24TH, 1927

The stone was white, like the church. Imported. There were marks along the top and sides, jagged lightning bolts where the stone had cracked open and been repaired with cement that didn't quite match the stone.

'What happened here?' he asked, running his hand over the cracks and feeling the edges of the broken stone.

Billy didn't reply and Solomon felt a shift in the air. He

turned to find himself staring down the barrel of a shotgun for the third time that day.

'Hands where I can see 'em,' Billy said.

He was holding a second phone in the same hand he was cradling the stock of the gun and Solomon guessed what had happened.

'I didn't kill Pete Tucker,' he said, raising his hands and taking a step forward.

'Stay right where you are.'

'You're not going to shoot me.'

'You want to find out? Keep on walking.'

'You ever killed a man, Billy?' Solomon took another step. 'Ever stared into his face and watched the life leave him? You don't want that on your conscience. Thanks for the phone, by the way.' Solomon lobbed it towards him and Billy followed it with his eyes, instinct telling him to catch it and stop it falling to the floor and breaking.

Solomon used the distraction, sprang forward and grabbed the barrel of the shotgun. He knocked it aside and pulled hard, yanking gun and man forward. A boom crashed the silence as Billy's finger triggered a shot and buckshot tore through the broad, heart-shaped leaves of the cottonwood. Solomon continued his spin, driving his elbow backwards, aiming for the forehead and not the nose. A hard blow to the nose could drive bone shard back into the brain and kill a man.

How did he know all this? How did his body know the moves to disarm a man pointing a shotgun at him? How did he know what would kill and what would not?

His elbow connected with Billy's head, snapping it back. Solomon yanked the barrel again, pulling it free from his hands.

'Otis!' Billy hollered. 'Otis – kill!'

Solomon continued to spin, using his momentum to pull him round. He felt the heat of his rage again, like an unstoppable urge. He drove his other elbow hard into the side of Billy's head, relishing the feel of the impact. Billy crumpled to the floor, eyes rolling up into his skull, and Solomon dropped down with him, his hand grabbing a stone from the ground, his anger like a physical thing now trying to burst out of him. He could feel the pressure of it in his chest and his hand squeezed the solid rock as he raised it over his head.

Bring it down, a voice inside him said. *Bring it down hard on this man's head. Break his brain out. That will ease the pressure. That will show you who you are.*

He could picture it – the rock, the skull, the blood – the images so vivid he thought he must have done it. The stone came down, hard and fast, and struck the ground by Billy Walker's head. Solomon wasn't sure what had nudged his hand away from its murderous path. It might have been him or something else. Whatever it was, it had spared a life and Solomon let go of the rock and pushed himself away before something else made him pick it up again.

He was sweating and breathing hard but not from the effort of the fight. It was his rage boiling inside him.

There was a grunt over to his right and he looked over at the bulldog, lying by the bowl, his great head resting on his front paws. He twitched, like he was trying hard to move, then grunted again, as much of a bark as he could manage before finally he gave up, closed his eyes and went to sleep.

Solomon took a deep breath. Let it out slowly then went to work.

He moved over to the truck and found a knife, some rope and a pack of black plastic cable ties in a box in the back. He used the ties to bind Billy's wrists and feet, then dragged him over to the trunk of the cottonwood and wrapped most of the rope round him, fastening him tight to the tree. He tied it off, cut a twelve-foot length from the end, then tucked the knife in his belt and found a crate of bottled water in the truck. He pulled two bottles free, drank one straight down before unscrewing the cap from the second and carefully pouring a quarter of the remaining Ambien into it. He had taken it from Holly's bedroom and used about a quarter of it in the dog's water bowl – enough to knock him out, not enough to kill him, he hoped. The dog was snoring loudly now so he must have guessed the dose right. He shook the bottle to dissolve the powder and left it next to Billy's slumped form so he would reach for it when he roused and send himself straight back to sleep again. Then he emptied the shells from the shotgun and flung it deep into the cemetery where it couldn't easily be seen.

The stallion raised its head from the trough when Solomon stepped on to the wooden porch, then lowered it again and carried on drinking. Solomon glanced down the road and the pony track, checking no one was heading his way, then moved over to the map by the door.

He found the cemetery marked on it and traced his finger along the lines of roads until he came to the one leading east into the Chinchuca Mountains. It curled and looped like the coils of a long, thin snake, following the contours of the land.

Solomon looked out across the town to the mountains beyond, his hands working the rope now, knotting and tying it quickly and expertly while his eyes studied the line of the road, calculating how he could get there without riding through town. The track he had arrived on continued in the right direction, but only for a way; after that he would be cross-country, which was why he needed the rope.

He tugged a final knot tight and walked over to the horse.

'Come, Sirius,' he said, slipping the rope halter over his head. 'We're going for an evening ride.'

He secured the rope halter behind the stallion's ears then jumped on his back, settled then moved in circles around the car park for a minute, testing it. It was good, it allowed him to sit up straighter and made it possible to steer him by the head. He would need that over the loose terrain he was about to cross. He wouldn't be any use to anyone lying in a gully with a broken arm. He wouldn't be any use to Holly.

Was that why he was here? Was he here for her and not her husband? He did feel responsibility to her. That was why he had taken the Ambien. He didn't want her to die. He knew if he let that happen he would have failed somehow, though he couldn't say why.

He moved away from the building and towards the track, glancing out at the burned desert stretching away to the northwest. The sun was sinking lower in the sky now, a burning disc of shining copper. He thought about the ranch beyond and the bloodied body in the barn. He thought about the man with the gun in Holly's house. He thought about who might have sent him and what else might be coming their way. Then he turned on to the track and eased the horse into a trot to make time over the easier terrain, his shadow leading the way, long and dark across the broken land.

58

Mulcahy stared at the dirt track unspooling ahead of him.

He was driving, the smell of gasoline clinging to his clothes and skin, the smoking barn getting smaller in his rear-view mirror. The little execution-and-burn situation had disturbed him. He had always had Tío down as a fundamentally reasonable man, ruthless but reasonable. What he had just seen had no reason in it. And if you took reason away all you had left was ruthlessness and that didn't fill him with confidence, given his father's current situation.

'What did they do?' he asked.

'Who?'

'Those human candles we left back in the barn.'

'I didn't trust them. They annoyed the shit out of me too. I can trust you though, right?'

'Of course you can,' Mulcahy said. 'What else am I going to say?'

Tío laughed and slapped his leg. 'I like that about you. No bullshit. You should be crawling up my ass, the situation I got you in, but you're still calling it like it is. I need to get me some more people like you instead of all these kiss-asses.'

The wheels bumped across the verge as they rejoined

the road and the shadow of their vehicle stretched out on the road ahead of them as they started heading east.

'Tell me something,' Tío said, like he was asking for a bit of advice. 'How come you're so loyal to your pop?'

'He's family.'

Tío shook his head slowly. 'No, he's not. He's no more your father than I am.'

Mulcahy's hands tightened on the wheel. He had never told anyone about his childhood – partly from shame, partly from loyalty – though he'd figured someone with Tío's resources could dig it up if he wanted to. He obviously had.

'So your mom,' Tío continued, all his attention on Mulcahy, like he was feeding on his discomfort, 'what was she – a dancer, a whore?'

'You probably know better than me,' he said, forcing his voice to stay steady. 'I never really knew her.'

'No. I guess not. How old were you when she took off – seven?'

'Six.'

'Six years old and she ups and leaves you with some loser she's only been banging for a coupla months. What kind of a bitch does that?'

Anyone else, anyone in the world, and Mulcahy would have taken his Beretta out right there and shot them straight through the head.

'You ever find out what happened to her?' Tío continued, probing, enjoying it.

Mulcahy shook his head. He'd had plenty of opportunity to find out during his time as a cop. He had a name, a physical description, a last-known whereabouts and access to all the missing persons databases. But when it came down to it, he didn't want to know, not the details at least. He knew enough to figure that it wouldn't be a happy ending, so what was the point in knowing exactly how unhappy or what specific form of sadness it had taken.

'Why don't you take a guess,' Tío said, like he was suggesting a game of I-Spy to pass the time.

Mulcahy focused on his breathing like a sniper preparing to take a shot. He could feel his heart hammering in his chest and sweat starting to prickle at his scalp. Tío knew, he could hear it in his voice; he knew what had happened to his mother and he was about to tell him.

'What you think?' Tío persisted. 'Overdose? You think she was beaten to death by some fucked-up john? Or she cut her wrists in some rat-hole motel when she couldn't face another day of her shitty life? You must have wondered about it.'

'Can't say I ever did.'

'Bullshit. You must have thought about it all the time when you was a kid, wondered what had happened to your mom, why she'd never come back for you.'

'No,' Mulcahy said, trying to shut the conversation down. 'I didn't.'

'Well, that's cold. I thought you was a good kid, the way you stick your neck out for your old man and all, even though he ain't really your old man. Now I find out you don't even care what happened to your real mother. That's stone cold. That's ice. I'm disappointed in you.'

Mulcahy shrugged. He hoped Tío would drop it, but knew he wouldn't. He was enjoying it too much and information was his thing, knowing something that you didn't know, telling you things you didn't want to hear.

'Tell you what I'll do,' Tío said, taking his phone from his pocket, 'you take a guess at what happened to her and if you're close I'll call my guys and get them to cut your pop loose right now. What do ya say?'

'What if I don't want to play?'

'Then I'll get them to break something instead – a finger, an arm maybe – and I'll stick it on speakerphone so we can both hear him screaming. How's that sound?'

Mulcahy didn't say anything. He was trembling and trying hard not to show it.

'Come on, we got to pass the time somehow. These long desert roads bore the fuck out of me. You see that rock up ahead?' Tío pointed at a large red boulder by the side of the road. 'When we pass that, you got to give me your answer. I got to put a time limit on this thing, and don't you be slowing down to stretch it out neither. If you cheat, I'll get them to cut an ear off and you'll still have to give me an answer.'

Mulcahy glanced down at his speed. He was doing a steady fifty. The rock was a mile or so away, rising up above the desert like a tombstone. They would reach it in a minute. Maybe two. No more.

He hadn't thought about his mother much in years, blocking her out like a traumatic experience he wanted to forget. When he'd been little and she was freshly gone, his pop had talked about her a lot, like she was away somewhere, visiting a relative or something, and she'd be coming back any day. Whenever they did something fun he'd always say, 'We gotta remember to tell your mom about this.' So for a long while she remained present in his life even though she wasn't there. And because of this he genuinely thought she would come back one day and that they'd carry on as a family, all together, like his pop clearly wanted to – like *he* wanted to.

Then, when he was eight or nine, his pop took him to a diner one day and there was a woman there, sitting in a booth, a woman who wasn't his mother. His pop had sat next to her and held her hand and said, 'This is Kathleen, she'd like to live with us and be a family, what do you think about that?'

Well, he hadn't thought much, but they bought him a cheeseburger and a chocolate shake and an ice cream and his pop laughed real hard at her jokes, so he thought, if it made Pop happy, maybe it would be OK.

Kathleen had been nice enough but it hadn't worked out. Pop stopped laughing at her jokes pretty quick and she got mad that he was always on the road and spent too much time at the track or in back-room poker games. And because Pop was away so much he had ended up home alone with Kathleen and, though she was never mean to him, he could tell by the way she looked at him that she didn't like him much. 'He sure must have loved her to keep you around like he does,' Kathleen had said to him one day, about a week or so before she moved out for good. 'He sure don't love me nearly so much.'

There were a few Kathleens over the years, well-meaning women who thought they could turn his father into a home-bird instead of a night owl. All of them went the same way as the first. But with the Kathleens around, Pop didn't talk about his mom any more and it was his aunt who finally told him, 'You know your momma ain't never coming back for you.'

She had said it one evening when his pop was on the road and he was at the kitchen table in his school clothes eating a Kraft dinner. 'Woman like that don't got time for no children. Bad for business is what it is. She stuck around long enough to get her hooks into your daddy, then she took off leaving you behind like a pair of shoes she got tired of wearing. She picked a good man to dump her child on, I'll give her that much, but I won't give her nothing more. You should forget about her. She's forgotten you by now, if'n she ain't dead in a ditch somewheres.'

'Here comes that rock,' Tío said. 'You got an answer for me?'

Women like that …

He had found a picture of her once in his father's room, hidden behind a framed school photograph of him that Pop kept on his bedside bureau. It was a flyer for some revue bar featuring a reed-thin, red-haired woman dressed for the tango, all long hair and legs. 'Hot Salsa starring Blaze' it said. Her face was in profile but he recognized enough of himself in it. The picture was creased, like it had been stuffed in a jacket pocket. The next time he looked for it, it wasn't there. He wondered if one of the Kathleens had found it and made Pop get rid of it. Maybe his old man got rid of it himself.

Mulcahy had hung on to that image of her, young and beautiful, even after he became a cop and saw how fast the street wore down women like she had been, all those crumbling beauties with caricatures of their younger selves painted on to sagging skin, walking the streets and working the bordellos, winding up dead in alleys, or in dumpsters or abandoned cars, beaten and bloated and tossed aside like sacks of garbage.

Working Vice, he had also seen the lives the kids of these women led: dead-eyed and feral, lousy with fleas and stinking of piss, parked in front of cartoon channels while their mommas went to work in the bedroom or sometimes behind a thin blanket tacked to the ceiling to make a divider. That was the life his father had spared him and that was why he owed him so much.

The rock grew big and red by the side of the road and they cruised past, the sound of the car's engine reflecting back off its side.

'She's dead,' Mulcahy said.

Tío shook his head. 'Not good enough. You got to do better than that if you want to win a prize. How'd you reckon she died?'

'Overdose.'

'Final answer?'

'Yes.'

'Died of an overdose. Eeeeergh. Wrong.' Tío swiped the screen of his phone and started reading. 'Madeleine Mary Kelly, born April 3rd, 1952, also known as Blaze, Scarlet, Red Riding Hood, Mary Kennedy …'

He swiped the phone again and held it out. Mulcahy wanted to knock it from his hand. He wanted to scream and cover his ears so he didn't have to hear whatever Tío was about to tell him.

'… is now known as Mary Schwartz and living in Southlake, Texas with her husband Garry Schwartz and their two lovely teenage sons.'

Mulcahy felt like someone had reached into his chest, torn his lungs out then stomped on them. He couldn't breathe. His ears were singing. He looked at the phone, his eyes struggling to focus on the photo. It showed two boys, awkward and a touch overweight, standing either side of a country club couple, a balding man with a paunch that strained against the middle of his pink polo shirt, his cookie-cutter corporate wife beside him. She was slightly taller than he was, her red hair straightened and salon shiny, her face collagened and Botoxed and filled with expensive dental work that gleamed from her full smile.

'Eyes on the road,' Tío said, and Mulcahy snatched at the wheel, breathing fast, pulling the Jeep back on to hard black-top from where it had almost drifted on to the soft verge.

'How that make you feel?' Tío asked, still holding the phone out, taunting him with the photo. 'She upped and left you with a stranger, then traded up. Looks like she made a smart choice though, huh? Dumping her unwanted kid on some travelling salesman so she could hook up with Mr Country Club here. What you think he drives – Lexus? Lincoln Town Car with the full package? She's probably got a Mercedes too, little two-seater in a garage bigger than your old man's apartment.' He let that thought sink in before carrying on. 'Mr Mom here works for some big travel company, something in accounts. Sounds boring as shit to me, but I guess it's nice and safe. How much was it your old man was into me by the time you stepped in and settled his debts?'

Mulcahy swallowed. His mouth had gone dry. 'Just north of three hundred.'

Tío nodded. 'Three hundred g's. I bet this guy earns that in a year – probably more with bonuses and all his health and dental crap. Yep, I reckon your mom made a smart move, dumping you and that loser you call your pop. She saw a chance and she took it. You got to admire someone for doing that.'

Mulcahy nodded. 'I guess you do.'

He could see buildings on the road ahead, a motel or something, and he fixed his eyes on them to stop from sliding off the road again. Everything he knew about himself had been turned on its head in the space of a few minutes. He had always thought his mom was living some tragic life and that was what had stopped her from coming back or looking for the son she had abandoned. Either that or she was dead. It had never occurred to him that it might be shame that had kept her away: not shame of what she had become but shame of what she had left behind.

The buildings started taking shape, a Texaco sign fixed to a large concrete awning stretching across a six-car forecourt.

'OK if we stop for a minute?' he said. 'I need a bathroom break.'

'Why not,' Tío replied, squinting through the windshield at the old-fashioned gas station with its modern pumps. 'We can get us some more gas too. And more cans to put it in.'

59

Morgan was pacing now.

The coroner was in the Tucker barn with Donny McGee and a couple of forensic techs borrowed from the King Community Hospital who were processing the crime scene. They didn't get many murders so the medics wore two hats and drew extra pay they rarely had to do anything to earn. They sure were earning it today. Morgan had moved away to the open gate of the corral so no one could overhear his conversation.

'You heard about the explosion in the Sierra Madre Mountains?'

He had a phone pressed to one ear and another in his hand. 'That tells me he's coming, and right now.'

He held the other phone up, angled his head back and squinted at the screen. 'I also got a report from border patrol …' His eyes were getting worse the older he got, but he refused to wear glasses. 'They found a barn on fire with a tunnel underneath it and some bodies inside. Right on the border, about an hour and a half away from here.' He listened to the voice on the other end of the phone. 'OK, good. I got one of our SWAT teams heading here right now and some other armed units.'

The other phone started ringing, a bell that made it sound like an old phone. He squinted at the number. Recognized it.

'I'll be ready,' Morgan said. 'Don't you worry about me. We're all set here.'

He hung up and switched phones, the frown melting from his forehead. 'Hey, sweetheart,' he checked his watch, 'you finishing up for the day?'

He glanced over at the barn again to make sure no one could hear. Flashes lit up the inside as somebody took pictures. It was nigh on impossible to keep anything of a romantic nature private in a town like Redemption but he and Janice Wickens had managed it for almost three months now.

'*Just locked up*,' she said.

It had started off as a necessity, getting her onside so she would keep an eye on what James Coronado was pulling from the archives. Then it became something else. She was so different from him but it seemed to work. He couldn't imagine life now without the home-cooked meals and the warm body to hold at night. Life was good, was about to get a whole lot better. All he had to do was get through tonight.

'Listen, honey,' he said, 'I'm not going to be able to get away. I can't tell you exactly what's going on, but you should head on home. Have yourself an early one. And lock your door.'

'*Lock my door! You've never said that before.*'

'Well there's some stuff going down. I got it, don't worry.'

'*I'm not worried.*' He could hear the smile in her voice. '*Is it anything to do with James Coronado?*'

Morgan turned away from the barn. 'Why do you say that?'

'*Because I just had Holly in the office. She had a requisition chit for something Jim had asked for but never collected. She was ... I don't know, a bit distracted. She got a call while she was here and that made her worse.'*

'Did you catch the name of who she was speaking to?'

'No.'

Morgan glanced over at the barn. The medics were wheeling the body out now and heading to the ambulance. Over at the house Ellie was sitting on a rocker with someone next to her, holding her hand and talking to her, though she didn't seem to notice. She just rocked back and forward, the shotgun resting across her knee while her blind eyes stared out at the reddening sky.

'I think she was going to meet someone,' Janice said, drawing his attention back. *'I can't imagine who. She seemed agitated though.'*

Morgan stepped aside to let one of the ranch-hands ride past. He was pulling a couple of loose horses behind him, dragging them back into the corral. Morgan had a good idea who she was going to meet. *'I was worried about her,'* Janice said. *'Considering what she's been through.'*

'Don't worry,' Morgan said, heading back to his cruiser, parked over by the ambulance. 'I'll take care of it. You go home now. And don't forget to lock that door.'

60

Holly walked the long way back to her house, avoiding the main road and as many residential streets as she could. She didn't want to be seen, not after what Solomon had told her.

The news of Pete Tucker's death had shaken her deeply. She had thought of him as her enemy, partly blamed him for her husband's death, but when she heard he had been killed her reaction had surprised her. It hadn't made her feel happy or avenged. She just felt sad and empty, like death was becoming commonplace and meaningless here. A few hours previously she wouldn't have cared. She had buried her husband and walked home through the rain with no thought in her mind but to switch it all off and turn her back on everything. Now she was keeping to the shadows, fearful of losing the life she had so casually wanted to end.

It was Solomon who had changed that. Solomon with all his contradictions: a man who seemed to know so much about things yet nothing about himself, and who still maintained he was here to save her husband, as if the usual parameters of life and death were no barrier to him. He had shamed her with his determination and commitment to finding the truth. He had reignited some spark of life in her that she thought had sputtered out.

She reached the junction to her road and carefully peered around the corner into it, expecting to see some big black vehicle parked outside her house. There was nothing. The back road she had arrived by joined hers about halfway up. She had come this way figuring that anyone watching for her would expect her to come up the hill from the main road, not down it.

She began walking towards her house, keeping to the shady side, alert for any sign that there might be someone there. Solomon had told her not to go back but she needed a car and figured that stealing one would attract far more attention than simply getting her own. She had no idea how to steal a car anyway and didn't know who she might trust enough to call up and ask to borrow their. This had seemed the best option, or it had at the time. Now she was here she wasn't so sure.

She crossed the road about forty yards back from her house and cut up the driveway of a property she knew to be empty. She slipped down a passage between the house and the garage and entered the rear garden. It was like hers, cultivated but wild and open at the back to the desert beyond. She moved through the garden and stepped over the low fence marking the boundary. She could see the backs of the houses and made her way to her own using the trees and plants as cover. She had the key to the car in her pocket. All she had to do was get in it and drive away.

It felt strange, creeping up to her own house through grasses and flower beds that she had planted and had always associated with relaxation. Now it was a place of trepidation and fear. She crouched behind the same clump of deer grass Solomon had hidden behind and studied the house. It seemed still, empty – but that didn't mean it was.

She watched for a while then moved across the ground, keeping low, heading for a gate that connected the garage to the house. Her car was beyond it. It had been sitting there for a week and the battery was old and sometimes needed boosting. Maybe this hadn't been such a good idea after all. Too late now. She pulled the keys from her pocket and held them tightly in her hand, the jagged edge of the key out in front like a tiny knife.

The hinges on the gate squeaked as she opened it. On any other day she wouldn't have noticed but today it sounded like the loudest noise in the world. Her Toyota was right in front of her, the red paintwork and windows streaked from the earlier rain. She moved to the driver's side, eyes wide and fixed on the house. The doors *thunked* as she unlocked it. She opened the driver's door and slid behind the wheel. The key rattled against the ignition slot, her hands shaking, and she had to lean forward to see what she was doing before it slid into place.

Please start – she whispered and pulled the stick into neutral. The car was old and so was the handbrake, so she always left it in gear to stop it rolling down the hill. *Please start* – she said again.

She twisted the key. The engine turned, sounded sluggish. Didn't start.

A hand banged on her window and Holly's heart leaped into her chest. She turned to face whoever was standing there.

'Margaret,' she said, more a sigh of relief than a word. She wound her window down and glanced back at the house.

'You OK, Holly?' her neighbour said. 'Only I saw you drive away in the police car earlier.'

'I'm fine, Margaret, thank you.'

Margaret leaned in and lowered her voice. 'Heard someone took a shot at Chief Morgan.'

'Imagine that,' Holly said, and twisted the key in the ignition again. The engine turned and laboured then coughed into life. It was a piece of junk but at least it was a reliable one.

Margaret stepped back. 'Well, so long as you're OK,' she said. 'Anything you need, just holler. Anything at all.'

Holly smiled and revved the engine a little to warm it up. 'Thank you, Margaret,' she said, checking the street behind her for cars. 'That's very kind.'

61

Mulcahy stood by a grey sink that had once been white and splashed water on his face. The faucet said 'cold' but the water dribbling out of it was blood-warm from sitting in the pipes all day. He had let it run a while but it hadn't made any difference.

He looked up at his reflection. The washroom was a piss-stinking sweat box with a bulky air-conditioner that filled the room with a death-rattle sound and moved hot air around. The mirror on the wall was small and rectangular and framed in blue plastic with a starburst crack on one corner where it had been dropped on the concrete floor. The glass was cracked too, probably from the same incident, a single jagged line running diagonally across the middle in a way that made the upper part of his face appear slightly out of line with the lower. The mirror hung from a length of greasy string hooked over a nail that had gouged a crater in the plaster resembling a bullet hole.

Mulcahy ran his hands through his hair and studied the split image of his face. He could see his mother in it. Same eyes, almond-shaped and slightly turned down at the outsides in a way that made her look sultry and him sad. Same colouring too: pale freckled skin and auburn hair that suited the Irish name his father had given him. He wondered if his father saw her in him too and that was why he often seemed mad at him. Maybe it wasn't him he was mad at and never had been. He pulled his phone from his pocket, checked the time then called his father's cell.

He opened the door a crack while it dialled. Tío was standing by the pump, the sky behind him glowing red like an ember. He was half bent over a five-gallon can, the price label still tied to the handle, one hand on the gas nozzle sticking out of the can, the other on his hip. He didn't notice Mulcahy spying on him. He was too busy studying the legs of the woman at the next pump who was leaning against a Harley while her boyfriend filled it up. To anyone else he would look like a small-time Mexican farmer getting gas for his generator. The phone connected and he let the door close.

'*Bueno.*'

'Could I speak to my father please?'

There was a sigh and some handling noise then his father came on the line. 'What the hell, Mikey!'

The sound of his father's voice made his throat feel tight. 'You OK, Pop?'

'I been better.' He sounded tired and old and frightened.

Mulcahy swallowed, cleared his throat. 'They treating you OK?'

'I guess. They ain't hurt me again, if that's what you're asking.'

'They ain't going to hurt you, Pop. You'll be out of there soon, you just got to hang in there a little longer is all.'

'How much longer?'

'Not long. They're going to get a call in a little while, then they'll let you go. When they do you take off. Don't go home, don't go anywhere anyone might know you. Check

339

into a motel someplace, eat takeout and watch TV for a few days until you hear from me, OK?'

'OK, but I don't got much cash on me.'

'I'll make sure you get some. Just do what I say, all right?'

'What the hell is this, Mikey? What did you do?'

Mulcahy closed his eyes. He wondered if his pop would have ended up where he was if he had never met his mother. Would he have carried such sadness around with him and gambled so hard? Who knew. It didn't matter really. He was in a fix and Mulcahy could get him out of it. That was what mattered. Everything else was just details.

'Listen, Pop …'

'What?'

'You know I appreciate all you ever did for me, you know that?'

'Sure. What are we talking about here?'

'I love you, Pop.'

'What?'

'Nothing.'

'What you saying that for?'

'In case.'

'… In case what?'

'In case I forget to say it later.' He cleared his throat again and wiped water from his cheek with the back of his hand. 'Put Gomez back on, would you. And remember what I said.'

'Sure, Mikey.' There was a pause, then his father spoke again, softly like he didn't want anyone else to hear. 'I love you too, son.' Then he was gone.

Mulcahy stared at his split image and wiped more water from his face that wasn't water any more.

'¿Si?' The voice sounded bored and Mulcahy wondered how many of these kinds of jobs he had done.

340

'Thank you for looking after my father,' he said. 'I appreciate it. You'll be getting a call soon. When you do, give my father some cash. A few hundred or so will do it. I will consider it a personal favour and will make sure you get paid back triple.'

'The fuck you say?'

'Just wait for the call,' Mulcahy said. 'You'll understand when you get it. And give him his cell back too. He won't give you any trouble. Wait for the call.'

He hung up before the man could say any more, this stranger who would kill his father without thinking twice. He studied his cracked image. His mother's eyes staring back but leaking tears for his father. He doubted hers ever had. He wondered if they had ever cried any for him.

He opened his messages, found one he had been sent a month earlier when he had first been contacted with the proposition he had ultimately taken, the one that meant he might finally be free. The message contained a phone number and he dialled it. The phone clicked in his ear as someone answered. 'We're an hour away,' he said, wiping away his tears with the back of his hand. 'You can track me on this number, I'll leave it switched on.'

'Good. We'll be waiting.'

'One more thing.'

'What?'

'My old man. Any chance you can let him go now? He's old and the stress of all this will kill him if he spends any more time with a gun to his head.'

'I'll make a call.'

'Thanks. I told the guys holding him to give him a few hundred bucks too – you think you could remind them of that?'

'You want me to get him a hooker and some takeout while I'm at it?'

'I'm giving you the keys to the kingdom here, a few hundred bucks is nothing.'

'All right, I'll tell them. Just make sure you're there in an hour.'

'We'll be there.'

There was a click and the phone went dead.

Mulcahy slipped the phone in his pocket and looked at himself again. He blotted his eyes on the sleeve of his shirt. He didn't want Tío to see he'd been crying. Tío fed on the discomfort of others and Mulcahy didn't want to give him any fuel.

An hour.

He took a deep breath of unpleasantly moist, piss-tainted air and blew it out again.

One more hour.

62

Morgan was parked on the main road behind a hotel sign that kept him hidden but gave him a view of the junction into Goater Way, the street Holly Coronado lived on, named after Susan Goater, muletrader, and one of the town's original citizens. He watched the red Toyota pull out on to the main road and head out of town. He hunkered down as it passed him by then rose again and watched in his mirrors until it was far enough down the road for him to pull a U-turn and start following.

He was driving the County Coroner's Plain Crown Victoria because it was about the most inconspicuous car ever manufactured and was a lot more discreet than his cruiser. Still, he kept at a steady distance. From what Janice had told him, Holly was jumpy and he didn't want her to spot that she was being followed: he wanted her to carry right on to where she was going and take him to Solomon Creed.

Solomon was the one loose end he still needed to tie up. He'd run some further searches on him, got a friend of his at the hospital to check the AMR to see if he was on the Medical Register, but he wasn't. If he'd got his medical training in the United States there was no record of it. He'd even tried to find out if there was a national register for albinos, but all he got was a Facebook page that looked more like a political action group. He had scanned through some of the pictures but Solomon didn't really resemble any of the people on it. They were generally more pink – pinkish skin, pink eyes, freaky – whereas he was pure white and his eyes were a pale grey. He was extraordinary-looking, he had to give him that. Probably had no bother at all with the ladies. Hell, plenty of women would be into him, thanks to all that vampire shit they had these days. Maybe that's what he was – a vampire.

He caught sight of the Toyota up ahead, the brake lights glowing red before turning off and heading up another road. Morgan slowed right down. He didn't need to follow close to know where she was going. The only place that road led to was the cemetery and this road was the only way in or out.

He turned on to the road then pulled over and left the engine running while he checked his phones. No messages on either. He unclipped the safety tab on his holster and removed his gun, checked it over, oiling the slide, removing the magazine and slotting it back in again. He had never once fired his gun anywhere but the range, not even to shoot cans out in the desert. That didn't mean to say he couldn't. But Solomon was a fugitive from justice now, which meant he was more likely to do something stupid and desperate. And if he did, he would put him down, no question. There was far too much at stake for some loose cannon to come along and mess it all up.

Morgan flexed his hands and felt the ache spread beneath the dressings then picked up his phone again and dialled dispatch.

'Hi, Chief.'

He never could get used to caller ID. 'Hey, Rollins, you ever off duty?'

'Never. What you need?'

He told him then sat back and waited, thinking about Janice Wickens and the easy life he might have with her if she didn't get too clingy and naggy like they usually did.

Four minutes after he'd put in the call, a cruiser drew up alongside him. He wound his window down and saw Donny McGee behind the wheel and Tommy Miller riding shotgun. 'Follow me, boys,' he said, and put his car in gear. 'Get your-selves ready for a resisting-arrest-type situation.'

He pulled away and threw the car into the turn on the mountain road. He crunched over the loose gravel and kept the speed up until he saw the red Toyota parked up ahead by the tourist office. He pulled up in front of the car and Donny slid in behind to stop it from getting away.

Tommy was out first, a dark vest tied tight over his shirt, his gun pointing at the ground as he ran. Donny was close behind. They ran past Morgan's Crown Vic and he followed.

He heard shouts ahead then a scream and he took out his gun and picked up his pace. He passed through the gate and saw a pick-up truck parked in the shade of the cottonwood and Billy Walker tied to a tree with his dog Otis asleep on the ground next to him.

Margaret Bender was standing between Donny and Tommy, hands raised, eyes wide as she pleaded with them. 'He was like this when I found him,' she shrieked. 'I was trying to untie him.'

Morgan stepped forward, starting to realize what had happened. 'Where's Holly Coronado?'

'I'm not in trouble, am I, Chief Morgan?' She looked terrified.

'No, you're not in any trouble. Just tell us why you're driving Holly Coronado's car.'

'She asked if she could borrow my station wagon because she wanted to get rid of a bunch of stuff – you know, Jim's stuff. She said after the funeral she wanted to clear out some things, take them to the church hall.'

'That doesn't explain why you're driving her car, Mrs Bender, or why you came up here.'

'She said she left her purse up here at the funeral and couldn't face coming up to get it, so of course I said I'd be happy to fetch it for her and she gave me the keys to her car, then asked if I wouldn't mind doing it while she was away borrowing mine.' She pointed at Billy Walker and his dog. 'They were like this when I got here. I didn't have a thing to do with it.'

Morgan looked over at them. Donny was on his knees, checking Billy over.

'He's alive,' he said. 'Dog's alive too.'

Morgan turned back to Margaret and caught her staring at the dressings on his hands. He clenched his fists and felt them sting.

Goddamn woman had played him for a fool again.

VIII

*'Nothing beside remains. Round the decay
Of that colossal wreck, boundless and bare
The lone and level sands stretch far away.'*

'Ozymandias'

Percy Bysshe Shelley

From the private journal of
the Reverend Jack 'King' Cassidy

I write these words on the twenty-third day of December in
the year of our Lord nineteen hundred and twenty-seven.
Two days from now it will be my birthday. I will be eighty-six
years old, or I would be if I were to make it that far. In truth
I do not intend to. I cannot face another gang of well-wishers
or panegyric sermon that will do nothing but make me shrivel
inside. I deserve none of it. I am weary of life and am sure it
feels the same about me. We are like a married couple who have
long since fallen out of love and run out of things to talk about.
There is only one thing left to say, but, as I have no one to say it
to without poisoning their life in the way it has poisoned mine,
I will take the coward's path and write it down instead. Before
I quit this life and face the consequences in the next, I need to
confess the great secret I have carried with me ever since I found
the fortune that has so shaped my life. But to do so requires that
I restore some omissions from that millstone of a memoir of
mine and complete the picture of what I did and who I truly am.

The account of my travels in my published memoir is true up
to where Eldridge lay dying of thirst in the mesquite stand with
me close behind. It is true also that I prayed to God then to
grant me safe passage back to Fort Huachuca so I might bring
Sergeant Lyons to justice. But I also prayed for other things,
which I omitted from my memoir out of shame. For the thing

I prayed for most was a selfish thing. I prayed for God to spare my miserable life. I begged Him not to let me die out there all alone save for the company of dead strangers. I pleaded for Him to show me what He required of me that He might spare my life. And when those prayers were met with silence I rejected Him. I took the Bible I had carried so far and threw it aside in anger, calling Him cruel and powerless and hateful to have led me on and brought me here only to abandon me to death and oblivion. And as I raved and howled in my self-pity the wind blew through the trees and riffled through the pages of the Bible, turning them not to Exodus, as I wrote in my memoir, but Genesis. The priest had marked a section here too and when I read it now I saw new meaning in it. I had prayed to God to spare my life, to show me a sign of what He wanted of me, and here was my answer:

> *And they came to the place which*
> *God had told him of; and Abraham*
> *built an altar there ...*
> *and bound Isaac his Son, and*
> *laid him on the altar upon the wood.*
> *And Abraham stretched forth his*
> *Hand, and took the knife to slay his*
> *Son.*

I stared at Eldridge, so close to death already that I knew I would kill him by not sharing my few remaining mouthfuls of water. What difference would it make if I used a swifter weapon?

Without a second thought I rose and walked back to the jumbled pile of my possessions and retrieved my large gold pan. Then I went over to where Eldridge lay in the shade, took him under the arms and dragged him to where the pale Christ on the cross was propped against a tree. I took my knife from my belt and, before I could dwell on it more, I cut his throat in front of that makeshift altar.

He was too weak to fight, or perhaps just ready and willing to die. He lay perfectly still as the life pumped out of him and into the gold pan I had laid beneath his neck. And when he was dead, and the pan full of his blood, I led my mule over and let him drink of it. So thirsty was the poor animal and so starved of nutrition that it drank without hesitation as if it was the purest spring water fresh from the ground.

And so did I, God help me, so did I.

There is no describing a true thirst to someone who has never known one. It is a demon that grips your body and soul until you can think of nothing else and would drink anything, anything at all to be rid of it. I have heard stories of castaways, sailors driven mad by drinking seawater because there was nothing else to drink and, though they knew it would drive them to madness, they drank anyway. Thus I gorged on the warm blood, praying to God and offering Him this blood sacrifice like the prophets of old, one man's life to save another, one man's life to save many, and I asked Him to grant strength to my animal so it might carry me safe and spare my miserable life. I thought of the Catholic sacrament and how worshippers of that Church drank the blood of Christ and I closed my eyes and imagined that I was drinking the blood of the Saviour as they did. And indeed it did prove to be my saviour, for I would surely have perished there had I not been quenched by the warm spring of that man's life.

Afterwards I sat across from Eldridge in the shade of my strange chapel, the pale Christ at one end, the open Bible beside me. And when I set out at dusk it is true I saw a light burning in the desert to the south and followed it to the spot where water and riches bubbled from the ground, but there is more to it than I recorded in my published memoir. Much more.

I followed the shining light as darkness fell around me, the beam from it casting stark shadows across the undulating landscape like a fixed lighthouse on a frozen sea. It was shining straight at me and no matter where I moved it always seemed to follow.

It was full night now and the light so bright within it that it outshone the stars. I could hardly look at it direct and had to tilt my head down so the brim of my hat shaded my eyes and follow instead the pathway of light laid out upon the ground. I glanced up from time to time to see if I was getting closer but it was impossible to tell. Then, three hours or so into my trek, when I was beginning to doubt my own sanity, my mule suddenly stopped and I looked up and finally saw where the light was coming from, or more precisely — what.

At first I thought it was a doorway cut into the fabric of night leading to some dazzling, sunlit world beyond. But as my eyes adjusted a little I saw it was not a door at all but a mirror, long and narrow and set on a floor-stand. There was something so out of place about finding such an object way out in the middle of this wild and savage country that for a moment this seemed more remarkable to me than the sunlight shining out of it. There was a small dark patch in the centre where my own reflection stood. I dropped the reins and took a step towards the mirror, moving to the side a little and watching the dark shape of my reflection move too and the bright, reflected land shift behind it. It appeared to be the same desert I was standing in, same rolling landscape and distant mountains, though the season seemed different there. There was more green and flashes of bright colour — reds, purples, and yellow — where green shrub and grass and cactus flowers bloomed. Nothing thrived in the desert I stood in, only death. The sky in the mirror was different too: storm clouds boiled grey and heavy with rain at the distant mountain peaks, explaining the strong smell of creosote bush that flowed from the mirror, mingling with the fresh smell of the flowers. Somewhere in the mirror land it was raining.

I continued walking in a slow circle around the mirror, like an amazed spectator at a conjuror's show invited on stage to prove there was nothing behind the magic cabinet. The mirror itself was plain, a simple wooden frame with no carving or other ornamentation.

I moved round to the front again and saw that the reflected view now showed a new part of the desert. The mountains were gone and in their place I could see the prairie running all the way to the horizon. The mirror land was so hot there were whole lakes of rippling heat-haze upon it and in the near foreground sat a large boulder. I had seen its twin as I had approached with my mule, but the boulder in the mirror was different. It had been split clean in two and where the two halves fell away from each other, spring water bubbled from the ground, sparkling in the sunlight and forming a crystal pool around the broken rocks.

The sight of it made me gasp and I took a step forward, forgetting that what I was seeing was only a reflection. I hit the mirror hard, banging my forehead against the cold glass and stumbling backwards and on to the ground. I looked back up and gasped again. For though I was sprawled on the floor my reflection was still standing and I realized with dread and amazement that the person in the mirror was not me.

63

Solomon picked his way carefully across land that shifted and crept and fell away beneath him. The lower slopes were made from centuries of gravel and earth that had been chipped off by the weather and washed down from the higher mountains. Plants and grasses had taken dominion here, their prodigious, drought-hardy roots spreading wide and binding the earth together, though a horse and a man riding over it still showed how fragile it was. There were no other hoof prints on the land he was crossing and anyone following him would have to do so carefully and steadily or risk losing their footing and tumbling a long way down to the lower slopes. Even so, he checked behind him regularly. He had promised Holly he would meet her at the spot where her husband had died and did not want carelessness to make a liar of him.

He made it to the road just as the sun dropped level with the top of the mountains and stayed parallel to it, walking the horse through gullies and rain-swelled streams. The land continued to rise and the ground became rockier with towering shards of stone pushing through in places to create forests of craggy boulders. After ten minutes' walking he saw another slab of rock up on the roadside, a white monolith with an eagle carved on the surface above the words 'Historic Wagon Route'.

He moved up to the road, stopping by the stone marker and checking the way ahead. A hundred yards further on the road curved away and disappeared behind a bluff of red rock. Beyond that was a broad view of the valley with a jagged range of mountains in the distance that seemed familiar. He made his way towards it, listening out for cars, and spotted oil patches on the bend, smeared across the surface.

He reached the curve, dropped down from his horse and led it off the road by the rope halter. He tied it to a mesquite shrub then turned and studied the road, dropping his head a little to put himself at roughly the same eyeline as the driver of a car.

The surface was in a good state, no potholes, no dents showing evidence of fallen rocks that might have caused a driver at night to swerve instinctively after catching the flash of it in their headlamps. There wasn't even a crash barrier in place where the outer curve of the road met the verge, nothing to suggest any danger here, and yet this had to be where James Coronado had left the road and died.

He stood up and looked back down the road. A car was approaching, the rattle of its engine chugging steadily up the hill. It was still some way off so he turned his attention back to the road. He stepped out into the centre, reading the story of what had happened here – the arcing brushstrokes of rubber following the gentle curve of the road, the broken edge of rock standing out against the smoother edges either side. Something heavy had gone over here, breaking off the lip as it fell. Small drifts of sharp-edged rocks and rubble showed where the same object had been hauled back up again and more oil had soaked into the dirt beside pressure marks showing where the lifting gear had parked to pull the car up out of the gully.

Solomon moved over to the edge and peered down, letting his eyes adjust to the deepening shadows. There was lots of growth at the bottom of the gully, creosote, spiked crowns of agave, tufts of hopseed spreading in thick patches across the ground, their roots clinging to the nutrient-enriched dirt that had collected in the dip. Some had been flattened, crushed by the weight of the car. A couple of saguaro grew here too, tall enough so that the ribbed domes of their tops were visible from the road. A third one lay on its side, smashed and broken, struck by the car on its way down.

The sound of the approaching car was louder now, the engine note deep and labouring. He turned and saw the station wagon struggle round the distant corner with Holly at the wheel. He held his hand up in greeting and her face lightened when she saw him. She rattled closer then pulled over on to the verge short of where he was standing, turned off the engine and got out.

The sounds of evening were creeping in now and the light was starting to soften. She joined him at the road's edge and looked down into the gully. Solomon saw everything through her eyes now: the smashed cactus, the flattened bushes, the gouged earth and scarred rocks where the car had been dragged back on to the road. It spoke of the violence that had happened here.

'It's strange,' she said. 'I avoided coming here because I thought it would be too painful. But now that I'm here, I don't feel anything at all.'

'Who first told you about the accident?'

'Mayor Cassidy.'

'Not Morgan?'

'No. I think the mayor heard about it and wanted to tell me himself. That's when he told me they would bury Jim in the old cemetery, like that meant anything. Who cares where someone is buried when they should still be walking around?'

'Did he tell you what happened here, specifically?'

'Only that Jim apparently lost control, left the road and died of a head injury.'

'He didn't elaborate on the nature of those injuries?'

'No, but you can see for yourself.' She pulled an envelope from her back pocket and handed it to him. 'You asked me earlier about the coroner's report, so I got a copy.'

Solomon smiled and took the envelope. 'Very smart,' he said, removing the report from inside. He devoured the contents, his mind flashing with information as it processed the dense, technical detail. 'Interesting,' he said, looking back down into the gully, matching up what he had just read with what he was seeing. He frowned and tilted his head to one side, studying the damage and picturing what had caused it.

'What?'

'This report says your husband died of a cerebral oedema caused by a major trauma to the right temporal bone. The temporal bone is here—' He pointed to a spot above and in front of his right ear. 'That's not where you generally get injured in a car crash. Usually the frontal bone hits the windshield or the steering wheel. He could have slid off the road sideways, of course, lost control then banged the side of his head as he hit the bottom of the gully, but then where are the tyre marks? A slide like that would leave rubber on the road, and he would need to have been travelling at a fair speed in order for the impact to break his skull as comprehensively as this report suggests, but when his car left the road he was only travelling at around ten to fifteen miles an hour.'

'How do you know that?'

Solomon pointed at the smashed cactus. 'Look at the saguaro. You see where the impact was? It's in the middle section; the top is relatively unscathed, only a few splits and dents from where it hit the ground. A car travelling at any speed would have taken the top off it and hit the bank over there somewhere.' He pointed to a clump of untouched sagebrush on the far side of the gully. 'And look at the roots.' His arm swung down to a large hemisphere of knotted ropes that had been partially lifted from the ground. 'It was growing only about six or seven feet away from the edge, so the fact that the car hit the midsection suggests it must have almost fallen off the road. I'm going down to take a closer look.'

He followed the faint tracks left by work boots along the verge then dropped down the slope and slipped his way to the bottom. There were deep gouges in the gully wall where the car had been dragged back up to the road, and splintered branches and twigs showing where the car had come to rest at the bottom. Solomon dug the toe of his boot into the ground. It was soft and loose, not compacted and baked hard like most of the desert. The bushes were soft too, and the saguaro would have slowed the car further as it fell.

Slow speed. Soft landing.

He scanned the quiet gully, half in shade, half in evening sunlight. 'Your husband did not die here,' he called up to Holly. 'Not from the car crash, at least. Everything here's so soft he might as well have landed on an airbag. I'm coming up.'

Holly was smouldering mad by the time he made it back to the road. She was staring down into the gully, her jaw set tight. 'I should have shot Morgan with buckshot instead of salt,' she said.

Solomon smiled. 'There are better ways to get even than with a blast from a shotgun.'

She shook her head. 'Not many.'

He moved over to his horse, untied him then led him back to the road. 'Ever wonder what your husband was doing here on the night he died?'

Holly looked around at the lonely stretch of road then out to the view of the darkening valley. 'Not really. He used to take off sometimes to clear his head. Some guys fish, others hunt, some go bowling. Jim liked to drive. I guess that night he just ended up here.'

Solomon followed her gaze out to the distant mountain range. 'I don't think so,' he said. 'I think he was here for a reason. What's further up this road?'

'There's a viewing platform a mile or so on where you can see down the whole valley, then more road and mountain passes until you hit Douglas.'

'What about a camp site?'

Holly frowned. 'Actually there is one. It's not permanent, there are no facilities or anything.'

'Is it easy to find?'

'Should be a sign on the road for it somewhere.'

Solomon hopped up on to the back of the horse and settled. 'Then that's what your husband was doing on this road.' He dug his heels into the stallion's flanks to get it moving. 'Come on,' he said. 'Light's fading. I'll meet you there.'

64

Mayor Cassidy was sitting in his office, staring out of the window at the evening light when the first armoured personnel carrier rumbled into the square.

Since hearing of Pete Tucker's murder he had been facing up to the very real chance that he might not make it through the coming night. As a result the world shone now with a different light. Everything he did carried extra meaning as he considered that it might be for the last time: the last time he would drink a cup of coffee; last time he would see a sunset, or watch the evening light darken on the slopes of the mountains, or catch the movement of it in the jacaranda leaves.

The truck pulled to a halt in front of the church and men emerged from the back wearing uniforms the same blue-black colour as the vehicle. They were carrying guns and wearing helmets and dark-visors. Some wore full-face combat masks which made them seem sinister and robotic. A tall man got out of the front passenger seat and looked over at the house.

'Thank God,' Cassidy whispered, rising from his chair and checking his phone for messages. Where the hell was Morgan?

He hurried down the front steps and across the grass towards the church as a second vehicle pulled up and more men got out. In the quiet of his study he had been imagining the night ahead like some old-style western, the town defended solely by a few lawmen and some plucky civilians with shotguns and rifles against hordes of professional killers. There had to be twenty or thirty men here, trained men with modern weapons. This was more like it.

'Ernie Cassidy,' he said, extending his hand over the top of the wall to the tall man who had the air of command about him. 'I'm the mayor here and boy are you ever a welcome sight.'

'Andrews,' the man said, crushing his hand in a reassuringly solid handshake. 'Any idea where I might find Chief Morgan?'

'I'm sure I can rustle him up for you. I presume he's appraised you of the situation here?'

'He has. Don't worry, sir. We got this.'

Cassidy glanced past his shoulder at one of the masked soldiers standing guard behind him. 'How are you going to … I mean, what's your plan here?'

'The fewer people know that, sir, the better our chance of success.'

'Of course, I understand. Only, there are a lot of civilians here. Shouldn't we warn them? Get them to stay indoors at least? Evacuate?'

'We do that, we risk scaring off the target. And if we don't get him now he'll only hit you again later. We can't guard the town forever. We took a risk coming in heavy-handed like this, but we understood the need to secure the town quickly. We took the decals off the trucks and the uniforms, so if anyone asks you can say we're here because of the plane crash.'

'I understand,' Cassidy nodded. 'Just make sure you get him.'

'Oh, we intend to, sir. Make no mistake about that.'

The County Coroner's car crunched to a halt beside them and Morgan got out.

'Captain Andrews?' he said, moving towards the commander and shaking his hand. 'Chief Morgan. Thanks for getting here so fast. What do you need from me?'

'We need to cover the three main roads into town,' Andrews said, walking towards the middle of the square and taking Morgan with him. The stone wall prevented Cassidy from following and he lost the conversation. Andrews started pointing out of town and up at the roofs of the higher buildings and Cassidy felt a pang of sadness at finding himself excluded from the business of defending his own town, like being a kid again and not being asked to play ball.

He looked around at the black-uniformed men with their automatic weapons and body armour. Maybe he would see another dawn after all. And when the smoke cleared and the questions were inevitably asked, he would tell the truth and take whatever was coming to him. Saving the town was all that mattered to him now.

65

Solomon trotted along the line of the rising road, keeping an eye on the distant escarpment and watching the subtle shift in the landmarks. After about a half a mile he came across a wooden sign planted in the ground next to a dirt track running up and away from the main road. The words painted on the sign were cracked and flaking but still legible – 'Spirit Mountain Camp Site'. A smaller sign hung beneath on metal loops: 'Closed for the summer – mid-April to mid-October'.

He could hear the rumble of Holly's borrowed car behind him and waited until she came into view before easing his horse forward and up the softer ground of the track.

The camp was hidden around the curve of the hill, far enough back from the road to give campers the impression of being way out in the middle of nowhere, but close enough to the road so they could drive back to town in twenty minutes if they needed to. It was little more than a collection of traditional ramada shelters with woven branch roofs supported by thick mesquite poles. A mountain creek burbled nearby, swelled by the recent rainwater, and Solomon rode over to it so his horse could drink, passing firepits ringed with white stones. He imagined faces gathered round them, eating food hot from the fire, listening to ghost stories while they stared into the flickering flames. James Coronado's face had been one of them once.

He slipped from the horse's back and let it walk over to the stream. He could see the whole valley from up here – the burned desert, the airfield, the town with its streetlights starting to wink on as the evening gloom deepened. The sun was sinking fast and casting long, deep shadows across the ground, as if night was leaking up from the earth to drown the day. The mountain range opposite was silhouetted against the sky, making the V-shaped niche stand out. Behind him he heard the rumble of the old engine struggle up the track. It cut out and there was the squeal of a door hinge then Holly walked over to where he was standing.

'This is where your husband came the night he died,' Solomon said.

Holly looked out at the view and around at the deserted camp site. There was nothing to indicate anyone had been here in months. 'What makes you think that?'

Solomon pointed at the 'V' in the distant mountain range. 'That is in the background of every group photo hanging in his study. He'd been camping here since he was a kid. This was a safe place with happy memories for him, a private place – especially at this time of year when it's out of season – the perfect place to retreat if he felt under threat.' He nodded down at the town nestling in the valley. 'He could literally gaze down on his problems and put them in perspective.'

The horse snorted and tossed its head, clearly bothered by something. It pawed the ground and moved along the stream and away from the camp.

'What is it?' Holly asked.

'Not sure.' Solomon sniffed the air and followed the horse's gaze. He took a step forward, reaching out with his predator's

364

senses for any sight, smell or sound from whatever had spooked the horse. The shadows were deepening as the light leaked away, making figures appear in the folds of the rock face that stretched up behind the camp. He took another step. Saw movement in the shade of the furthest ramada. Sniffed the air again and caught something that made the hairs prickle on the back of his neck and arms.

Blood. But not fresh.

He followed the scent deeper into the camp to one of the firepits. There was a pile of blackened ash in its centre whereas all the others were filled with mesquite straw and dry grass blown there by the summer winds. Someone had been here. They were still here. He could feel their eyes upon him. He looked up. Scanned the camp site, his body tensing. Night was falling fast and smothering what little light remained, turning the camp site into a place of darkness and deep shadows. He saw something, close and to his right. Movement. He turned to it and his eyes widened when he saw what had caused it.

Holly appeared next to him, following his gaze. 'What is it?'

'Your husband did come here,' Solomon whispered, staring deep into the shade of the ramada. 'He died here too.'

'How do you know?'

'Because he's still here. I'm looking at him right now.'

The ghost of James Coronado stood in the dark crease of the shadow, confusion clouding his face.

Holly followed Solomon's gaze. 'I can't see him,' she said, frustration and emotion fraying her words. 'I can feel him, but I can't see him.'

'He's by the post at the edge of the shadow,' Solomon said. 'He's staring right at you.'

A sob burst out of her. 'Tell me what he looks like.'

'Like he did in the photograph, though the colour has gone from him. He looks a little like … He looks like me.'

Holly wiped a tear from her cheek and took a step towards him.

'He's fading,' Solomon said. 'When you move closer he starts to melt away.'

Another sob. She walked faster.

'He's going,' Solomon said, but she didn't listen. She stepped into the shadow just as the ghost vanished entirely and hugged the air where he had been. She stood like that for long moments, rocking from side to side, whispering that she loved him, that she missed him, that she would give everything to see his face again.

Solomon moved over and put his hand on her shoulder. She turned to him and let her arms drop. She smiled a sad smile, then stepped forward and kissed Solomon full on the lips and held him tight as if she was holding somebody else.

'Thank you,' she said. 'He wasn't supposed to die. We were supposed to have a life together. I never got to say goodbye. This was closer than I thought I would get, so thank you for that.'

Solomon touched his lips and in the empty depths of his memory a truth floated up. He had not been kissed for a long time, not in the tender way she had kissed him, and the thought made him feel very alone. But there was something else in the kiss, something his mind identified and made him catch his breath at the significance of it.

'Do you think this is where he died?' she asked, looking down at the ground.

'No,' Solomon said, sniffing the air and following the scent of blood to the edge of the firepit. There was a stone missing from the ring that surrounded it. He surveyed the camp site but couldn't see it. It could be anywhere: in the stream, hurled away down the side of the escarpment, tossed out of the window of a moving car. He didn't need to find it to know what it had been used for. He crouched down and raked his fingers through the mixture of soft earth and dry straw by the missing stone. The ferrous smell of blood grew stronger.

'This is where he died,' he said. 'Right here. He was hit on the side of the head with that missing rock. That's why he had a fractured right temporal. He was most likely struck from behind by a right-handed man. Be hard to hear someone creeping up with the sound of the wind and the hiss of the mountain stream. It's dark here too.' He looked around at the place, rapidly sinking into shadow. 'Whoever did it must have followed him, killed him here then staged the crash back on the road.'

'Morgan.' Holly said it like she was cursing.

'Probably.'

Holly knelt beside him, ran her hand over the darker ground as if she was caressing it.

Solomon looked back at the place where the ghost had been then rose from the floor and walked over. Night had made the shadows inside the ramada solid now and he couldn't see well enough to search the area. 'Do you have a light?' he called over to Holly.

She moved over to him, pulling her phone from her pocket. She handed it to him and the bright screen cast a cold glow on the ground and the upright of the post. There were marks in the wood, cut with a knife and darkened with age. Solomon ran his finger along it, tracing the letters – JC.

'This is where your husband used to sleep on his boyhood camping trips,' he said, imagining him working his name into the wood after lights out, leaving his mark here for the future. Solomon studied the ground.

'The mesquite straw has been disturbed here,' he said, sweeping it aside with his hand. The ground beneath was not hard and compacted like the rest was.

'There's something buried here,' he said. He realized now why the ghost had drawn his attention to this spot.

66

Captain Andrews stood at the red painted line of the city limits, looking out at the blackened desert growing darker in the evening light.

Behind him his men were busy securing the area and taking up positions in the buildings by the road and in the old miners' shacks. They all knew who the target was and the job they were here to do and the mood was focused and sharp and combat-ready. They were setting up for an ambush, but they could stage a defence just as easily if that was required.

There were thirty-eight men in all, each armed with an AR-15 Tactical Carbine assault rifle with Trijicon 3-Dot Tritium Green night-sight. There were two SDMs – Squad Designated Marksmen teams: two shooters, two spotters – with long-barrelled M6A2s already in position, one by the side of the billboard, one in the gas station, both covering the road. No one was going to come down this highway without being lit up, and this was the road they would be coming in on. He knew that for a fact.

'You got a number for the crash investigators?' Andrews asked Morgan. 'No need for them to get caught up in this.'

Morgan found the number of the NTSB coordinator on

his phone and dialled it. When it started ringing he handed it to Andrews.

'This is Captain Andrews, 27th DEA tactical arms unit,' he said when someone answered. 'We have intel of a high-value target inbound to the town of Redemption, undoubtedly armed, possibly hostile. We have taken up defensive positions along the city-limit line and can see your work lights. For your own safety, I need you to pack up your team and ship out as fast as you can before they get here.'

A way out in the desert, Morgan saw the work lights blink off. A couple of minutes later a Jeep and a van started heading back to town over the heat-deformed road.

Andrews raised his field glasses and lensed the desert again.

'Anything?' Morgan said.

'Not yet. Should be good for another half hour, I'd say.'

Morgan glanced back at the town. 'In that case, I got a small problem maybe you could help me with.'

Andrews finished his sweep of the desert. 'What problem?'

'Nothing a small team of your men can't help me fix. I got a fugitive I need to bring in.'

'You know where he's at?'

'Yeah,' Morgan nodded. 'I got a pretty good idea.'

67

The tin box was buried about a foot below ground, right up against the mesquite pole. Solomon's fingers scraped across the smooth surface of it and he dug down the sides, trying to pull it up and out of the hole, but the earth had been baked hard again in the short time it must have been here.

'Could you find me a stone or a stick?' he asked, and the ramada went dark as Holly removed the glow from her phone and used it to search around outside. It was dark now with no moon yet to light up the night.

Solomon continued to dig, feeling around the tin with his fingers. Holly returned with the light and a stick she had found in one of the firepits. He used it to scrape the dirt from around the edges, loosening the earth until he could hook his fingers underneath and tug it free.

He laid it on the floor and brushed loose dirt from its surface. It had once contained shortbread but the rust-pitted surface suggested that it had been underground for a while, longer than a week. Solomon prised the lid off and they both leaned in to look inside.

It was filled with folded sheets of paper. Solomon took them out and saw other items below that were mottled with age and had likely been there as long as the tin had been buried. There was a small stack of baseball cards held together with a rubber band that had almost perished, a pocket knife that had rusted shut and a hand-drawn map showing a rough chart of the camp site, an X marking where the tin had been. 'Lost Cassidy Riches' was written across the top in childish handwriting.

'Seems your husband's interest in the Cassidy legend started young,' Solomon said.

He placed the tin on the ground and unfolded the pages that had been on top. There were two folded sets of documents and Solomon opened the larger one first then held them under the light of Holly's phone to read them.

'They're not financial,' Holly said.

Solomon shook his head. 'It's a chemical analysis of groundwater samples taken from around the town.' He flicked through all five pages of it. 'It recommends immediate discontinuation of all mine works and a major programme of remedial water treatment to remove certain harmful reagents from the groundwater.' He turned to the last page where the chemicals were listed. 'This report is dated almost a year ago, but Morgan said the mine was still producing.'

Holly shook her head. 'Whenever Jim talked about the town finances he never mentioned it as a source of income.'

Solomon nodded. 'I walked past earlier and the place seemed abandoned.'

'So if they shut down the mine like this report recommended, why pretend they didn't?'

'And why would your husband hide this document?'

Holly turned to him. 'You think this was what they were after when they trashed my house?'

'Maybe. Let's see what else is here.' He picked up the second piece of paper and unfolded it. It was a photocopy of an architect's drawing outlining the footprint of the church. He spread it flat, looked at what was on it and felt like the sun had come out from behind a cloud.

The elevation revealed shapes in the building's design that had not been apparent at ground level. It showed the traditional cross-shaped foundation, but that wasn't what had drawn Solomon's attention. The plinth the altar cross stood upon was outlined in the drawings too. It was an 'I', the exact same shape and size as the mark he had on his arm.

He held the plans to the light so he could read what was written on them. It seemed to be a combination of notes from the original document and some new ones that had been added in green ink. The older notes detailed how the altar plinth had to be positioned above something called a resting stone. The new notes, written in James's hand, posed two specific questions:

> *Is the resting stone where JC is buried?*
> *Is the 'I' the key to the lost Cassidy riches?*

Solomon frowned. 'Is Jack Cassidy not buried up in the cemetery?'

'Apparently not. Some treasure hunters broke into his tomb a few years back after reading that line in his memoir about taking the secret of the lost riches to his grave. They obviously took it literally. They posted pictures online. It was empty.'

Solomon remembered the repaired cracks he'd seen on Cassidy's tomb up at the cemetery. 'So where *is* he buried?'

'Who knows? The mayor maybe, but if he does he's not saying.'

Solomon studied the drawings again. The resting stone

placed directly beneath the altar, most sacred spot in the church. 'I think your husband had an idea,' he said, pointing at the 'I' shape in the centre of the plan of the church.

Holly looked at it. 'Oh my God,' she said. 'Take this,' she handed him her phone, then set off in the darkness. Solomon listened to her receding footsteps through the sounds of rushing water and thought he heard something else. His horse snorted over by the stream and the light came on in Holly's car. He tilted his head back and sniffed the air but a steady breeze up from the valley brought him nothing but dust and only the smells of the road and smoke. He turned his attention back to the documents, re-reading the list of chemicals and studying it again, letting his teeming mind furnish him with more information about each one. There was a small mark by one of the chemicals on the list, made in the same green ink he had seen on the plans: TCE – *trichloroethylene*.

Halocarbon, clear non-flammable liquid, no smell, initially used as an analgesic but now discontinued due to health worries, commonly used as an industrial solvent.

He focused harder, digging deeper into what it was. And in the torrent of information he saw something that explained exactly why James Coronado had taken this particular document and hidden it, and why they'd had to kill him to keep him quiet.

'Look at this –' Holly reappeared from the dark with an envelope in her hand. 'It was the last thing Jim requisitioned from the archive before he died.'

Solomon took it and pulled the drawing from inside. It was a design for the altar itself showing detailed drawings of both the copper cross and the plinth it sat upon. Solomon studied the diagrams, the side elevations, the shapes they made and he understood. 'This is it,' he said. 'This is my connection to your husband. I'm here to finish what he started.' He undid a button on his shirt and reached inside. 'When I arrived here, the only possessions I had were the copy of Jack Cassidy's memoir and this,' he held up the cross he wore around his neck.

'The altar cross?'

'That's what I thought, designed by Jack Cassidy, just like he designed all of this, the church, the decor, even the plinth the cross rests on. "Not bad for a man who started life as a locksmith",' he said, quoting what the mayor had said to him in the church.

He held the cross up and saw it now for what it was. Not a cross but a key.

He looked back down at the document Holly had brought. 'Your husband had almost discovered the lost Cassidy riches,' he said. 'He was so close.'

He studied the drawing of the altar cross and the detailed elevation of the stone plinth it was to rest on. There was an inscription on the upper face of it that would be hidden by the base of the cross. It was the first commandment:

I
_____

**THOU SHALT HAVE
NO OTHER GODS BEFORE ME**

Solomon studied the 'I', carefully drawn so that it was positioned low down and central to the plinth. Then he held up the cross round his neck and turned it end on so he could see the shape of the base. It was the same. The base of the key formed an 'I'. And he had just found the lock it fitted.

_____

375

He stared out into the solid darkness, thinking about how they might get into the church, breathing in the smells of night – the still damp earth giving up its scents, creosote and sage and something else. Something that shouldn't be there. He breathed deeper, trying to fix on where the odour of gun oil and sweat was coming from and realized too late that it was coming from everywhere.

'Stay calm,' he said to Holly, and caught the confusion on her face. 'We're about to meet the man who killed your husband.'

Bright lights flashed out of the dark, blinding them in an instant. 'Nobody move,' Morgan called out. 'Hands where I can see them.'

More lights flicked on and black figures surged towards them. Someone grabbed Solomon's arms, yanked them behind him and cable-tied him.

'How did you find us?' Solomon asked.

'Billy Walker,' Morgan replied. 'Woke up and told us what he'd heard of your conversation. Said he thought you might be heading to the crash site, so I figured you'd wind up here, smart pair of people like yourselves.'

Holly lunged for him and strong hands had to hold her back. 'And how did *you* know to come here?' she screamed. 'You knew because you killed him.' She spat at him and it caught him on the chest.

Morgan looked down. 'That's the second shirt you've spoiled today.' He stepped forward and backhand-slapped her across the face. 'I've been waiting to do that all day,' he said. He shoved her aside and picked up the documents from the floor. 'Sorry we messed up your house searching for these,' he said, pulling a lighter from his pocket. 'If your husband had been smart, none of this would have happened.'

He sparked a flame and held it to the edge of the pages of the groundwater contamination documents until they caught. He dropped them in the firepit, watched them burn, then turned back to them with a smile. 'That's one loose end tied up. Just you two to square away now. Come with me,' he said, walking away across the deserted camp. Someone shoved Solomon from behind to make him follow. 'There's someone I want you to meet.'

68

Mulcahy rumbled over the rippled road, picking his way carefully across the heat-damaged surface. It was hard to tell in the dark where the blacktop ended and the scorched desert began, and he didn't want to end up in a ditch or with a shredded tyre.

Tío was humming something to himself in the passenger seat. He had hardly said a word since he had taken such delight in filling Mulcahy in on his family history. He had spent most of his time fiddling with his phone or staring out of the window, occasionally pointing his finger at a bird or a passing car and making the sound of a gunshot like a bored five-year-old on a long trip.

Mulcahy had already seen Tío's influence though, stretching ahead of them like an invisible tentacle. There had been no patrolmen at the barriers blocking off the heat-damaged road and there was no one up ahead at the crash site either.

'Pull over,' Tío said, pointing at the twisted nest of black metal ahead of them.

Mulcahy eased the car to a stop and Tío got out and walked over to what was left of the plane. He crouched down and peered through the twisted spars and ribs of metal. Mulcahy knew what he was looking for, but doubted it would still be there. He hoped it wasn't.

It occurred to him that he had travelled hundreds of miles to end up right back at this same spot. Maybe he should have stayed put and saved everyone a whole heap of bother. Some people would still be breathing and walking round if he had, though his father would not be one of them. He switched off the engine, got out of the car and joined Tío on the road.

'He was there,' he said, pointing into the heart of the wreckage. 'Looks like they cut him free and took him away. The morgue in town is my guess. They might have shipped him out, but I doubt it. Better to take whatever samples they need in a clinical environment than out here with the dust blowing everywhere. If you want your son's body, it'll be in town.'

Tío nodded then leaned back to stretch the kinks out of his spine. 'Let's go find him then,' he said and started to amble across to the car.

Mulcahy stayed where he was. 'What's the move here, Tío?' Tío stopped walking and turned to face him. 'You pulled me off what I was doing to come play chauffeur and now we're standing out here in the middle of the desert, staring at a town I know you want to burn to the ground, but there's only two of us. Now I want to do what I can to get my old man off the hook here, really I do, but I can't see the move. Are we waiting for some people? Is that what we're doing? I'm flattered if you think I'm all you need to wreak vengeance on a whole town, but, truthfully, I think we may need some help.'

Tío smiled. 'Don't worry about it,' he said, and got into the car.

Mulcahy shook his head, got in the car and turned the engine on. 'So this is the move, we just drive into town?'

'Anything wrong with that?'

'Well, I'm guessing after what I did to that rancher on your behalf they might be on their guard somewhat.'

Tío's smile grew wider. 'I'm counting on it. Now if you want your loser dad to see another dawn you shut your mouth and take us into town.'

'They're back in the car, sir.'

Suarez was one of the two SDMs on the detail. He was lying prone in the bed of a pick-up truck to give him some elevation and watching what was happening a couple of miles out of town through the sight of his long-barrelled M6.

'On the move. Inbound.'

They were too far out for a shot but he could see the two figures well enough and they were getting clearer the closer they got.

'Let me know when you got a positive ID,' Andrews said through the comms.

'Roger that, sir. Should be in a couple of minutes or so. They can't drive too fast over this road.'

He kept the crosshairs on the passenger, following the movement of the car, his finger on the trigger guard.

69

Morgan drove fast.

He was in his cruiser, barrelling down the mountain road towards the twinkling lights of Redemption. Holly and Solomon were in the back, their arms still cable-tied behind them, forcing them forward in their seats.

'So where is the money coming from?' Solomon asked, pushing himself back into his seat as they rounded another tight bend. 'Not the mine, clearly.'

'What do you care?'

'Just trying to put the pieces together.'

'It's drugs,' Holly answered for him. 'It's always drugs.'

Morgan shrugged. 'Everyone gets so moral about drugs, but they happily smoke their cigarettes and drink their liquor. People want drugs too, so who are we to tell them they can't have them? It's prohibition all over again – and look how that turned out.'

'They're illegal,' Holly said, 'they ruin people's lives and bring misery and death, and you're supposed to uphold the law.'

Morgan threw them round another bend and Holly banged her head on the window. 'Sorry,' Morgan said. 'Let me ask you something. You ever fought in a war? 'Cause I have. They call this a war on drugs, but it ain't no war far as I can tell. Wars can be won and this one can't, least not by some small-town cop like me with a badge and a pump action in his truck. I know what war looks like and it ain't this. This is capitalism, supply and demand. It's the biggest industry around here, that's for sure. Bigger than mining ever was, only it don't pay a single cent in taxes. You only have to drive across the border to see how that works out: roads full of holes, poverty, crumbling infrastructure. You got to invest in people if you want to build a community folks want to live in. You got to put something back. The cartels don't put anything back and they don't put a whole lot of store in people neither. People are disposable to them. So, yes, Mrs Coronado, we took their money. When the mine stopped producing we went into a new business and a lot of the money went straight into the public purse so we could fix the roads and pay people's salaries. The sheriffs hoped they could walk your husband through the reasons we had done what we did and make him see the sense in it. But he wouldn't come down off of his moral high horse. He had all these ideas for getting the town back on its feet, weaning it off its dependence on the trusts. Even said he thought he knew how to find the lost Cassidy fortune – you believe that? Like some old legend could save this town.

'He started going through everything, looking for a legitimate way out of our problems. That's how he found out about the groundwater contamination. We'd buried it because we couldn't risk shutting the mine down. We needed people to think the mine was still producing to account for all the money coming in. When Jim found it, he went nuts. Said he was going to blow the lid on everything. So … we had to make a decision.'

'And that decision was that you needed to kill him to keep him quiet,' Solomon said, a statement not a question.

Morgan's eyes flicked up in the rear-view mirror. 'People die in wars,' he said. 'One man's sacrifice for the greater good. Just the way it is.'

Solomon could feel Holly shaking beside him. If her hands hadn't been bound and there wasn't a Perspex divider between her and Morgan she would have killed him for sure, he could feel her desire to do it coming off her like heat.

'What about the cleanup?' Solomon said.

'There was no cleanup. The levels we found were low so we made a decision. If we started cleaning up the ground-water, people would ask why and we couldn't risk losing the mine. We stopped using the chemicals though, cut the workforce right down and started running water through the mine instead.'

'Do you know what TCE is?' Solomon asked.

'No, should I?'

'It was one of the chemicals that showed up on your report.' He glanced over at Holly. 'It's been connected to birth defects and neo-natal abnormalities. It's also known to cause miscarriage in the early stages of the second trimester.' Holly stared back at him, her face a mask of shock. 'Now you know why your husband acted like he did,' Solomon said, quiet enough so that Morgan wouldn't hear. 'His loyalty to the town evaporated the moment he realized it may have caused your son's death.'

Holly's eyes misted and she looked away and out of the window.

They were arriving at the airfield, the hulking, jagged shapes of parked aircraft stretching away beyond the security fence, lit yellow by sodium lights. The main part of the airfield was to the left of the road, squadrons of military and civilian aircraft all lined up in neat rows.

To the right was the museum, stocked with a hand-picked assortment of vintage aircraft, restored and maintained on site. The lights were off in the main building and the entrance gates closed. They drove on and pulled over by an extra-wide double gate, big enough to bring even the largest aircraft into the museum from the airstrip on the other side of the road. Someone had left the gate open wide enough for a vehicle to pass through. They drove in and under the wings of a bomber, then headed towards a large hangar on the far side of the field.

'We flying somewhere?' Solomon asked.

'No,' Morgan replied. 'I very much doubt it.'

70

'Got him,' Suarez said.

He could see the passenger clearly now in his night-sight. He recognized the face from the earlier briefing and also from the poster that had been pinned at the number one most wanted spot on the canteen wall for the last eight years.

'Who's the driver?' Andrews' voice murmured in his earpiece.

Suarez shifted the scope and phosphorescent green smeared his vision. 'Don't know him. Not a known associate.' He shifted back, following the movement of the car, anticipating it so he could keep Tío's head in the crosshairs.

He was about five hundred yards away now, inside his trained range. A shot had a seventy per cent chance of a kill, and that percentage was getting better with every yard. 'What's the order?' he murmured.

'Hold on.'

Suarez continued to follow them, switching between Tío and the driver.

He had been trained to clear his mind at times like this but for once his training was failing him. Instead he was thinking about what would happen if he did take the shot. He would be famous, the guy who took out public enemy number one, like Charles Winstead, the guy who shot Dillinger. Except now he could write a book and get a movie deal out of it. All his training and he would be famous because of one shot. But none of that was going to happen because he wasn't going to take the shot. Not at Papa Tío at least.

He let the sights drift back to the driver, his finger tightening on the trigger. If he got the order to shoot, it was this guy who would be the target. He dialled back the magnification a little as the car drew nearer. He could see them both now. A bright green smear drew his attention.

'The passenger is reaching down for something,' he said.

More bright green phosphorescence smeared and flared in his vision as Tío's hand rose up again. 'He's waving something,' Suarez said. 'Something white, like a sheet of paper or a napkin.'

His finger relaxed and returned to the safe position alongside the trigger guard. 'He's surrendering,' he said. Then he looked up from his scope and saw that he was right. Papa Tío was turning himself in.

IX

'… all things are cleansed with blood, without bloodshed there is no forgiveness.'

Hebrews 9:22

IX

From the private journal of the
Reverend Jack 'King' Cassidy

I have tried over the years to recall what the man looked like, if indeed he was a man, but in truth I do not think I ever saw his face. The light, which lit the land around him and shone into mine, seemed to come from inside him, so bright I could not look directly at him. I recalled another of the priest's highlighted passages that had made no sense to me until now:

... and his face did shine as the sun,
and his raiment was white as the light.

I threw myself forward in fear and awe and began to pray, begging forgiveness for all my sins, for I believed my judgement had come and this angel had come to deliver it. And when none came I held up my hands and asked the shining man what he commanded of me and his voice came back like a whisper inside my head.

'What do you most desire?' he said.

I replied with the answer I had given to all who had questioned me on my long journey. 'I wish to build a church of stone,' I said, 'where God's words of peace and love might be spoken aloud until they have driven all savagery from these lands.'

The angel spoke again, its words intimate and soft in my head:

'But what do *you* most desire?'

And I knew then that he had seen through my half-made

answer. I do not think I had admitted the truth even to myself before that moment, but his light shone so bright it lit up the darkest corners of my soul and I realized I could not hide anything from this angel and that, though he had asked me a question, he knew my answer already.

'I want to be somebody,' I replied. And when he said nothing further I spoke on, my words drawn out like yarn by his silence. 'I want to be a man of substance. I want people to remember me when I'm dead and say, "That was a man that did great things, that was a man who found a fortune and used it to build something in the desert, something that will live forever." I do not want to die as a nobody. I do not wish to be forgotten.'

And there it was. The truth. My truth.

The angel's silence continued but I said no more, for I had nothing more to say. I had confessed fully and I knew even his bright searching light could illuminate nothing more in me.

At long last he spoke and his words were soft and kindly. 'You are an honest man,' he said, 'and honesty like yours is rare and holds great value to me. So in exchange for that, and if you are willing, I shall give you what you desire.'

I wept into the dirt, hardly daring to believe I had reached this dreamed-of moment when only a few hours earlier I had abandoned the Bible along with my resolve to continue my pilgrimage. Only the light had changed my mind and drawn me on. And now here I was, making bargains with angels, or with Christ the Saviour, or maybe even with the Lord God Almighty Himself.

'I am yours to command, Lord,' I said to the shining man, for whatever he was — man, vision, angel — I knew he was lord over me. 'Whatever you would have me do, I will do it, and gladly.'

There was a mighty crash like a mountain splitting in two and a flash so bright I saw it clear as day though my eyes were tight shut and my face pressed hard to the dirt. The ground shook violently beneath me like a dynamite blast through bedrock, then all went dark and silent.

I don't know if I was knocked senseless for a spell but I lay there for a long time and when I eventually looked up I saw nothing but darkness. The mirror was gone. My ears sang from the loud noise still and made me feel disconnected, as if I was floating in the vast night sky. Then the singing faded and a new sound crept in, the sound of running water.

I scrambled across the dirt towards it like an animal, drawn by my raging thirst. The darkness was solid to my light-ruined eyes and I made my way by sound alone, feeling my way over the ground and cutting my hands on the sharp edges of rocks and the spines of cacti in my haste to reach the water.

Something huge loomed out of the darkness and I cried out and pulled away in terror. The stink of sweat and death sloughed off it and I wondered if I had died out in the desert, that the light I had seen had been the dying dream of a man driven mad by thirst and exhaustion and I was now in some terrible limbo populated by death creatures, cursed for eternity to crawl through the spiky darkness, tormented by the sound of water that I would never find. The thing ambled past then snorted and I realized what it was — not some diabolical beast sent to torment me but my mule, drawn to the same promise of water as I.

I stood and grabbed the hair of its hide, and let it lead me on, trusting its animal senses more than my own. And when it stopped and the smell of wet earth and the sound of bubbling water filled the air around me I fell to the ground and into the cool shallows of a pool.

And I drank.

*It was the sweetest thing I ever did taste and I drank long
and deep of it, sinking my face beneath the surface and feeling
the soothing cold water against my sunburnt skin. I wanted
to fall into it entire and cleanse myself like a sinner at a river
revival, but the pool was scarce more than a hand's width deep
and though it bubbled up readily from some fresh crack in the
earth, it soaked away fast, the land being every bit as parched
as I was. I took one last, long draught then unhitched every
canteen from my saddle and tossed them into the pool. I threw
my gold pan in too, scouring it with wet dirt and swilling
away all trace of its most recent use before chasing my floating
canteens through the water, pushing each one under until every
flask had been filled and stoppered.*

*I sat back from the edge of the widening pool, taking steady
mouthfuls of the sweet water from one of the newly filled flasks
and wondering at the miracle of it all. I must have fallen asleep
like that, for I seemed to blink and it was morning and the pool
now lapping at my feet.*

*I gazed for the first time upon the water that had appeared
so miraculously in the night. It was now about the same size
as a large corral, the spring still bubbling vigorously at its
approximate centre and sending ripples out to the irregular edges.
Two halves of a large boulder lay split clean in two like the shell
of a nut, exactly like the reflected image I had seen in the night.
I turned to where the mirror had stood and saw a small bundle
lying on the ground. A cold shiver ran through me as I recalled
the dead child I had discovered on the track only the previous day.*

This could not be her.

It couldn't be.

*I stood slowly, my body cold as death, and walked stiffly
over to the bundle. It was not the body of the poor starved child,*

it was only my Bible, wrapped in sacking, its pages open and fluttering in the cold morning breeze. It must have slipped from the saddle in the night and I saw that its spine had cracked in the fall and the pages were loose in the cover.

I stooped to pick up the book and felt a sharp pain arrow through my palm, which made me drop it again. I turned my hand over and saw a fragment of silvered glass embedded in the soft heel of my hand, a remnant of the broken mirror. I gripped it with my teeth and drew it out then held it up, somewhat fearful as to what I might see reflected in it. But all I saw was myself, and the ordinary land stretching out behind me stained red by the blood that clung to the surface of the glass.

I tucked the shard into my shirt pocket, took up the Bible again and pushed the pages back together, checking the book from cover to cover to make sure it was all there.

But it wasn't.

A single page was missing. It was from the book of Exodus, verse twenty, where Moses comes down from the mountain carrying God's ten holy commandments. I felt sick at this discovery and felt it augured badly that, through lack of care, I had allowed God's holy laws of all things to be lost in this wilderness. I rose up and searched the land all around for any sign of the missing page but found nothing and vowed to make amends for my carelessness however I might.

I carried the Bible back to the waterhole and placed it under a heavy rock to keep the thieving wind from its pages. Sunlight flashed on the surface of the water now, the canteens floating and bobbing like strange fish. I crouched by my gold pan to bathe my wounded hand in the water collected there and saw sunlight glinting at the bottom of this too – and something else. I stirred the sediment into murky clouds, my wound now forgotten, then lifted the pan and started moving it in small circles, tilting it forward a little each time to let the water and lighter particles of mud and rock slop out. When there was no more than an inch of water left at the bottom I let it settle.

Bright flakes of gold shone warm and yellow, along with crystals of lighter green. It was malachite, lots of it: the rock here was rich with copper.

I untied the kerchief from round my neck and tipped the contents of the pan on to it. The total haul was tiny, about the size of a robin's egg, but when I held it in my hand it felt good and heavy. I spent the rest of the day working the waterhole, taking samples from the pool and the surrounding land, but it didn't seem to matter where I stuck my shovel in the ground, it always yielded mineral-rich earth. The copper was everywhere.

When there was about an hour of daylight left I lit a fire and set a pan of beans atop it with some chunks of dried beef stirred in. Then I sat and drank coffee while it cooked.

The fruits of my labours covered the most part of a blanket now, a pile of ore rising almost up to the eye of my mule. The sight of it made me anxious. There was too much to carry and I would have to return with wagons to cart it away. But I needed to make it back to the fort first and get the legal papers signed before someone else happened along, drawn by the water, someone who might have a wagon or a faster horse and who might steal it all away from me yet.

How quickly the world turned. On my outward journey I had nothing to lose, now I had the world within my grasp and was filled with watchful fears because of it. I saw dust rising far to the north — maybe a dust devil, or maybe horses — and kicked the fire out, smothering the embers with dirt so no smoke from it could give a clue to my location. Then I sat, wrapped in blankets, and ate my cold banquet of beef and soaked beans, watching the land go dark around me.

I had come to this spot by a circuitous route but figured if I took a direct line back to the fort I could get there in four days. When darkness had swallowed the land I packed enough provisions for a week and gathered all the water bottles from the waterhole. What little remaining space there was in my saddlebags I crammed with rock samples and a couple of small dust bags filled with the finer material I had collected. Then I slung the pale Christ across my back and balanced the Bible on top of it all and lit out of there, leading the mule north by the light of the stars, little knowing what horrors still awaited me.

71

Mulcahy looked across at Tío.

'This your plan?'

Tío stared ahead with the same weird look Mulcahy had seen before, his eyes flat and defocused like he was on something, saying nothing.

They had been zip-tied and bundled in the back of a DEA paddy wagon without so much as a word and were now being driven through town at speed. They both had guards either side of them in full combat gear and tactical masks that hid their faces. It all seemed a little anti-climactic. There had to be an angle in this. Tío had bought his way out of jail before, maybe he planned on doing it again. But where would that leave him?

Mulcahy stared out of the narrow window at the town rushing past, streets he had driven down freely only a few short hours ago. He tried to think his way back and see if there was anything he could have done differently, but he couldn't see it. All roads led here. He had always been bound to do whatever Tío wanted him to do.

'Did you ever plan to let my pop go?' he asked.

Tío looked at him and smiled. 'You haven't fulfilled your half of the bargain yet.'

They passed the church and the building where the police station was housed. The van didn't slow, which made his heartbeat quicken.

Where were they taking them?

He watched the mine slip past then the chain-link fence and the rows of aircraft beyond. He was back where he had started that morning, waiting for the plane that would never show. The van slowed and slipped through a gateway then under the vast expanse of an aircraft wing.

'Look at these things,' Tío said, 'powerful enough to fly to the edge of space, enough firepower to destroy a town, now rotting away in the desert. How many people you think are dead because of this one plane?'

Mulcahy shook his head. It was déjà vu. Not only was he back where he started, he was having to listen to the exact same shit. Perhaps he'd died and this was his own tailor-made form of purgatory.

The van slowed then stopped in front of a large hangar. The rear doors were pulled open with a gust of cool evening air and the guards hustled them outside.

Morgan appeared from inside the hangar, walked over to someone who seemed to be in charge and spoke to him for a few seconds. The man in command nodded then looked around, checking there was no one else there. He walked back over to him and Tío. A knife appeared in his hand and for one moment Mulcahy thought he might kill Tío right there. Instead he slipped it between Tío's wrists and snicked it upwards, cutting the zip-tie free.

Tío rubbed his wrists and turned to Mulcahy. 'This is my move,' he said. 'If you know there's going to be DEA waiting for you, make sure they're bought and paid for.' He turned to the commander and took the knife from him. 'Go back to the church and get to work,' he said. 'I want you to tear the beating heart out of this community. Just leave me a gun and a couple of your men.'

The commander pulled an FN Five-seven from his holster and handed it to Tío. 'I'll stay,' he said. 'You're paying me to protect you, so I'd feel better if I was close enough to do it.' He beckoned another guard over, one of the soldiers in full combat gear, his face hidden behind combat mask and visor. 'The rest of you head back to town.' He turned to Morgan. 'You too. You don't need to be here for this.'

Morgan looked at Tío then the commander, then nodded and left.

Tío stepped forward and snicked Mulcahy's ties free then handed him the knife. Mulcahy studied it. It was seven inches long with a sturdy quillon, sharp enough for paring skin from muscle and solid enough not to bend. He didn't need to ask what it was for.

'You still want to save your father?' Tío said. He turned to the commander, who handed him the framed photographs of his dead daughters and the printout of the blackened skull. 'Get me the name of the bastard who ordered my son's death.' Then he turned and walked into the hangar.

72

Solomon heard the van approach, then voices outside and footsteps approaching.

He was hanging by the arms from a steel beam that spanned the width of the hangar. The rope bound his wrists and was pulled so tight he practically had to stand on tiptoe to relieve the pain in his shoulders. Morgan had ordered him to take his jacket and shirt off before stringing him up. The gun pointing at Holly had ensured he had obeyed. Holly was tied up next to him and hanging from the same beam. He had not made her strip down, which suggested to Solomon that whatever was coming was coming to him.

The footsteps grew louder then a man stepped into view, short and squat and with thinning black hair and bad skin. He walked past Solomon and made his way over to a workbench lined with neat racks of tools. He took three photographs and carefully arranged them along it, taking his time, getting it right according to some design he carried in his head. Two were framed and were of young women, smiling at the camera with some reserve and some intelligence in their eyes. The third showed a skull, blackened by fire, a rectangle of metal bolted on to it. It wasn't framed and the man had to rest this one against an oilcan and hold it in place with a wrench.

'*¿Quien te envió?*' the man asked, when the pictures were in place.

Solomon studied the photographs, the girls clearly related, sisters probably, the blackened skull still unfathomable but a portent of nothing good.

'Who sent you?' he repeated, in English this time, and turned to face him. He resembled the young women in the photographs, or they looked like him, which was unfortunate for them. Solomon guessed the skull might have resembled him too before the fire burned everything away.

'My family,' the man said, following his stare. 'My flesh. My blood. My bone. All rotting now. All gone. These people called me Papa. Everyone else calls me Papa Tío. You heard of me?' Solomon shook his head. 'Yes you have. Now tell me who sent you.'

'I haven't heard of you,' Solomon said. 'And nobody sent me.'

Tío nodded at someone unseen and Solomon felt the rope bite into his wrists as it was pulled tighter.

The knife felt cold when it first touched his skin then flared into white heat as it started to cut. He could feel the burn of it as it sliced through his flesh – just below the skin, above the muscle – severing capillaries and nerve endings in a sensation so intense and so far beyond pain that it almost flipped over into pleasure. Solomon gasped and shuddered and tried not to howl while the waves of whatever he was feeling washed over him then gradually ebbed away. Hot blood spread down his back and dripped on to the oil-dappled concrete. It felt like someone was pouring hot water down his back.

He opened his eyes and looked over at Holly. She was staring at him wide-eyed, her shock rising to new levels with each atrocity she was forced to witness. Solomon winked at her to reassure her, or maybe himself because he had no idea how this was going to pan out. He looked back at the photographs on the workbench. 'Who's the skull?'

Tío stared at him with his dead eyes. 'You know. You know who I am and you know who he was too.'

'No. I don't.'

'Then let me tell you. He was the reason I did everything, the reason I breathed in and out and got out of bed in the morning. I heard someone say that having kids gives you a reason to live the second half of your life. That's true. Only someone took away my reasons, piece by piece, and I think you know who it was. So if I have to cut it out of you piece by piece to find out what you know, I will. I got nothing left but time.'

He nodded at the knifeman standing behind Solomon, the man who had sliced him and was about to slice him again, in all the same places the old man had been cut.

'Wait!' Solomon said, realizing something. He turned as much as he could and spoke to whoever was behind him. 'What's your name?'

'What does it matter?' a voice replied.

'Kind of intimate, don't you think? You sliding a knife into me, slicing bits of me away. The least you can do is give me your name.'

'Michael,' said the voice. 'Michael Mulcahy.'

'Are you two gonna start fucking or are we going to get on with this?' Tío said.

Solomon ignored him, chasing something down now, making sure his next question was loud enough for Tío to hear. 'Tell me, Michael, why did you stage the torture of Old Man Tucker?'

Tío's eyes shot over to Mulcahy. 'What's that?'

'The cuts in the skin were all made post-mortem. I wondered at the time why Ellie Tucker hadn't been alerted by the screams of her dying father – she didn't know he was dead when she came out to find me. And how come you didn't lock her up more securely, kill her even – a blind girl taken by surprise should have been no trouble for someone like you. Then it occurred to me that she might not have heard any screams because there hadn't been any. You killed him quickly, mercifully even, a quick stab to the heart that made him bleed out fast and would have killed him in seconds. Then you made it appear like he'd been tortured. Why do that?'

Tío pulled his gun from his waistband and pointed it at Mulcahy. The commander and the guard pointed their weapons too. 'That's a good question,' Tío said. 'Why *would* you do that?'

Mulcahy walked forward so Solomon could see him. He was holding a bloodied knife in his hand and studying it like he had never seen it before. 'It was the blood, wasn't it?' he said, seemingly untroubled by the fact that three loaded guns were pointed directly at him. 'The cuts were too clean because the old man had already bled out.'

Tío shook his head and pulled a phone from his pocket. 'You know the only reason I haven't put a bullet in your head is because I want to see your face when you listen to your piece-of-shit father die in agony.' He pressed a button to speed-dial a number and put it on speakerphone. The sound of ringing echoed in the hangar. Nobody picked up. Tío checked his phone and dialled the number again.

'They're not going to answer,' Mulcahy said, looking up from the knife. 'My father has been safe for about an hour now. The guys who were holding him don't work for you any more, Tío. None of us do. Things change. People change. You're not in charge any more.'

The commander and the guard shifted position so their guns were now pointing at Tío. Tío looked at them then back at Mulcahy like he had just sprouted horns. 'Are you serious? Who is in charge then? You?' He laughed and pointed at Holly with the barrel of his gun. 'Her?'

'Me,' the other guard said, his voice muffled behind his full-face mask. Tío whirled round and pointed his gun at him. 'You don't want to shoot me,' the guard said, and Tío's gun dipped as he recognized something in the voice.

The guard crouched slowly and laid his automatic rifle on the ground. Then he rose back up and unclipped the side fastening of the mask. He slipped it off along with his visor and helmet revealing a six-inch scar on the side of his head. 'Hello, Papa,' Ramon said. 'You miss me?'

Tío stared at his dead son. Mouth open.

'Put the gun down, Papa?' Ramon said. 'I think we need to talk.'

73

Cassidy watched the truck pull up by the church and the soldiers get out.

He was standing by his study window, the lights switched off, the shutter open enough for him to see outside but not enough for people to see in. He didn't want anyone to know he was there. He told himself this was sensible, given the situation, but in some deep-down part of himself where he buried the things he didn't like to look at he knew the real truth. And the truth was he was scared.

He had thought, with the arrival of the DEA task force, he would have felt secure, that this would have drawn a line under his fears for the town. Morgan certainly seemed happier. He could see him out of his window now, talking to one of the soldiers and pointing at the church. More soldiers appeared next to him and began unloading things from the back of the van, big black boxes that took two men to lift. They carried them down the path, shuffling towards the church with straight backs and bent knees, and started stacking them by the door.

Cassidy considered heading out and offering to help, partly because he wanted to be more instrumental in the defence of his town but also so he could find out what was in the crates.

Morgan glanced over in his direction and Cassidy froze. He didn't want to give away the fact that he was there with a movement. He didn't know why he felt this but he indulged it. Morgan studied the house for a few minutes then looked away again.

Cassidy let out a breath and realized he had been holding it. He watched Morgan walk away, following the shuffling pairs of black-clad soldiers as they carried the heavy crates towards the church. Morgan reached the door and opened it for them using a key only a few people in town had in their possession. Pete Tucker had been one. Jim Coronado too, briefly. It suddenly struck Cassidy that he was the only one of the three sheriffs left. Again, it put him in mind of the old-time westerns where some lone marshal played by Gary Cooper or John Wayne stood up to the outlaws for the sake of his town, though he didn't feel much like either of them at the moment. He felt more like the coward who hid in the barn until the shooting was over.

He watched the soldiers carry the crates into the church and glanced over at the panelled door by the fireplace that led down to the tunnel connecting the house to the church. It had been built by Jack Cassidy in his later years when his fame had become a burden to him. The tunnel meant he could leave the sanctity of the residence library, appear like an apparition among the townsfolk to preach his weekly sermon, then be gone again before the prayers had ended.

Cassidy looked up at the portrait hanging above the fireplace. It had been painted in Jack's later years when success and money had softened the edges of him a little. His eyes had never softened though and they seemed to be staring straight at him now, challenging him to stand up and be brave.

Cassidy took a deep breath then walked over to the panelled door and felt inside the edge for the hidden catch. The door sprung open and he listened for a moment, trying to hear any sound that might have been communicated down the tunnel from the church. He heard nothing, not even distant voices.

He started down the stone steps, careful not to make a sound, and headed down into the earth and onwards to the church.

74

Tío kept his gun pointing at his son, his naturally suspicious mind convinced that this must be a trick. It couldn't be Ramon, it couldn't. He studied the lines of his face for something out of place but found nothing, stole a glance at the photograph of the fire-blackened skull, the metal plate exactly where it should be.

'I staged that,' Ramon said. 'Paid some motorbike freak of a meth head who'd had his head all smashed up in a crash to take a short plane flight and deliver a package. It was a bomb, but he didn't know that.' He nodded at Mulcahy. 'Nobody knew, not even the people I trusted.' He looked at the photograph, rubbing at the spot on his head where his scar was. 'I guess we all look the same under the skin. You know, it was real nice watching you just then, seeing how cut up you were about me being dead and hearing all those nice things you were saying about me. You never said anything like that when I was still alive.'

Tío opened his mouth to speak but Ramon held his hand up to stop him. 'It's OK, Papa, I guess I deserved some of it, the things I did, the trouble I caused.' He continued rubbing at the scar on his head as if it was hurting now. 'I knew you were never going to bring me in on the business.'

'That's not true.'

'Shhhh. Let's be honest now. No lies. I figured I had to work out some way of showing you that I was up to the job. You'd have to hand it all over to someone eventually. No one lives forever. Only I don't think you ever figured that person would be me. Nobody else did either, but people hate uncertainty, so I offered them continuity. So what do you think, you proud of me now? You think I'm enough of your son to be a worthy successor?'

Tío shook his head, still trying to process the fact that his son was still alive. 'I always wanted you to take over,' he said. 'I never figured you were ready.'

Ramon opened his arms wide and smiled. 'Put the gun down, Papa.'

Tío lowered his gun, opened his arms and embraced his son. He closed his eyes and felt as if his heart had just started beating again, like he had broken surface after a long swim in the dark.

His son was alive. His son was alive.

He held him tight, like he hadn't done since he was small, and felt the warmth of his own flesh hugging him back.

'You never gave me any credit, Papa,' Ramon whispered softly. 'How was I ever supposed to become king with you sitting on the throne and never ever leaving your mountain-top fortress? I had to figure a way round that too.' He hugged him tighter. 'And here you are.'

The pain was sudden and intense.

Tío gasped and stumbled back, reaching behind him for whatever had caused it. Wet warmth pulsed over his hands and down his back and he could feel a coldness creeping into his core. Wetness pattered on the floor behind him and when he turned Mulcahy stepped away from the spray. He had a knife in his hand, different from the one he had held before, thin as a needle and wet with blood – his blood. Tío tried to raise his gun but it felt too heavy.

'I'm sorry, Tío,' Mulcahy said as Tío's knees buckled and he fell forward on to the ground. 'You didn't give me any choice.'

Tío was kneeling on the ground now, his head drooping forward, his eyes staring down at the concrete floor where his blood was pooling around him. He felt cold, so cold, a deep cold he had not felt since childhood when he had hidden in the poppy fields and the fever from his buckshot wounds had started coming on.

He turned his head, searching for Ramon and saw him looking down on him with the light of triumph in his eyes. 'I'm proud of you,' Tío said, clutching at his chest where his heart felt like it was splitting in two. 'I never knew you had it in you.'

Then the coldness squeezed the last warmth from him and he slumped forward on to a floor wet with his blood and as red as the poppies from his childhood.

75

Holly gasped when Tío's face hit the concrete and Solomon turned to her.

Her eyes were staring down at the body and she had gone almost as white as Solomon was. He realized she had probably never seen someone killed right in front of her before and she was likely going into shock, her mind shutting down rather than trying to deal with what it was witnessing. None of it had bothered him at all. Seeing a man stabbed through the heart and bleeding to death did not seem exotic to his strange mind.

'The king is dead,' he said, loud enough so everyone would hear. 'Long live the king – but for how long, I wonder?'

Ramon turned to him. 'What's that you say?'

Solomon stared into flat, bottomless eyes. 'King killers rarely last long. Perhaps it's because their reigns always begin with such a clear demonstration of how easy it is to end it again.'

Ramon stepped up to him, so close he could feel his breath on his face. 'You know you're still tied up so the smart move would be to show me some respect here? Lucky for you, you did me a favour, turning up when you did and drawing so much attention. You were like a fat little maggot wriggling on the hook I'd set for my papa.' He looked down at the body on the floor, blood spreading out from it in a steadily widening pool. 'But now I landed the fish, I guess I don't need the maggot any more.'

He turned to Mulcahy and pointed at Holly. 'Cut her down and put her in the car. You're both coming with me.' He pointed at Andrews. 'You – burn this place down and everything in it.' He looked back at Solomon. 'And I mean *everything*. He dies as hard as it gets, understand. I don't want to be hearing no gunfire while I'm driving away neither, no mercy shots. Meet us back at the church when you're done.' He glanced down at his father's body. 'Least a son can do is respect the last wishes of his father.'

Then he turned and walked away, heading into the black square of night framed by the hangar door.

76

Cassidy felt his way along the tunnel. He didn't want to turn a light on and alert anyone in the church that someone was coming and he'd walked it enough times in the light to be able to do it in the dark. He could hear voices now, echoing down from the church but he couldn't hear what they were saying.

He reached the stone steps leading up to the vestry and walked up them steadily, taking one at a time and placing both feet on each step before proceeding to the next so he could better maintain his balance and avoid making any sound.

He made it to the top of the stairs and pressed his ear to the door, trying to work out how close they were. From the scuffing of shoes and dragging of furniture it sounded like they were right in the heart of the church over by the altar.

Very carefully he opened the door and peered into the church. The vestry area was curtained so he couldn't see much. He listened for a few moments, only moving forward when he was sure no one was close. He pressed his head flat against the partition wall and peered through the narrow gap where the curtain didn't quite meet it.

Four black crates were lined up along the central aisle with one of the soldiers crouching in the middle of them, doing something on the floor that Cassidy couldn't see from where he was. The soldier stayed hunkered down for a moment then stood and walked away, his footsteps echoing until the bang of the closing door silenced them entirely. Cassidy heard the key twist in the lock. Waited a minute in case anyone came back, then broke cover and moved across the flagstones to the aisle.

He lifted the lid on the first crate and saw four five-gallon cans lined up inside. He unscrewed the cap from one, glancing nervously at the door, still terrified someone might come back. The cap came loose and he smelled the chemical fumes. It was gasoline. Eighty gallons of it lined up inside his church.

He moved to the centre of the aisle where the soldier had been crouching and saw a smaller box with a keypad, a display screen and a slot for a key. The screen was blank, which suggested it wasn't live yet. Cassidy wasn't exactly sure what it was but the thought of what it might be made him go cold.

He looked back at the door and fished his phone from his pocket, thinking about who he could call. Everyone he might once have called was now dead – Stella, Pete Tucker, Jim Coronado. Morgan was the only one left, but he had helped transport this giant Molotov cocktail into the church. Hell, he'd even used his key to let them in. He racked his brain for someone else he could trust and started going through the contacts menu on his phone. Who would stand up against a bunch of armed soldiers? Then it struck him. The soldiers, or whatever they were, must all be fake too. Morgan had never called up the DEA and told them what was happening here. Which meant Cassidy still could.

He moved quickly to the window where the signal would be better and dialled the number of someone he knew in the sheriff's department over at Globe – someone he trusted.

If he could tell them what was happening here they could send over some real agents, or get a helicopter airborne to offer air support and chase these people away from his town before they had a chance to arm this bomb and do some real and terrible damage.

The beeps of the dialling phone sounded much too loud in the quiet of the church and Cassidy pressed his cell phone against his jacket to muffle it, raising it to his ear only when it had stopped. He glanced back at the door, waiting for the ringtone to sound. Instead it beeped twice and a 'call failed' message flashed up on his screen.

He checked the signal. Saw he had no service. Moved back to the vestry where he usually had a stronger reception and found he had no service there either.

He hurried back over to the vestry and down the steps, heading through the dark to his office and the phone on his desk. He listened at the door again before opening it, paranoid that someone might be there, waiting for him. He heard nothing and burst into his study, grabbing the phone from its cradle and raising it to his ear.

It was dead.

They'd cut the landlines and his cell still had no signal. They must be jamming it somehow.

He was on his own.

77

Solomon watched Andrews pour the contents of a gas can over Tío's body, making sure it was nice and soaked. The liquid was straw-coloured – aviation fuel. He poured the rest on the ground around where Solomon was standing. His mind was humming, sucking in every detail, measuring distances, fixing on the details of how he could get out of here. He could see his shirt and jacket, folded on a bench by the exit. He pictured himself putting them back on and walking out of the door. He willed it to happen.

Andrews splashed more fuel up the walls and over the workbench opposite. He watched it drip down the faces of Papa Tío's dead daughters and soak into the picture of the skull, the skull that wasn't Ramon. Solomon thought of Ramon now with Holly. His interest in her was the only thing keeping her alive, but it wouldn't last. He needed to get free and find them before Ramon tired of her. But first he had to stay alive.

'You don't have to do this,' he said.

Andrews ignored him. He unscrewed the cap from another can and kicked it over, the fuel spilling over the floor towards Solomon's feet, the fumes choking the air.

'How much are they paying you?'

Andrews found some oily work rags and dipped them in the fuel on the floor, stepping back to keep his boots dry. He picked the rags up and let them drip a little then pulled a lighter from his pocket and struck a flame.

'It's not so much the money,' he said, staring at the flame not at Solomon. 'It's more what they will do to my family if I don't work with them.' He turned the soaked rags, teasing the flame around it until it was almost curling up to his hand. 'It's nothing personal. I'm sorry.'

Then he dropped the burning rag in the puddle of fuel, turned and walked away.

78

The sound of the lock opening echoed in the empty church then Ramon pushed the door open and walked in, sniffing the air like it smelled bad. 'Fuckin' hate churches,' he said. 'Give me the creeps.' He studied the exhibits by the door, the mannequin standing by the covered wagon, the Long Tom sluice box still working away, refining nothing out of nothing. 'What is all this shit?'

Morgan appeared behind him, an M-6 assault rifle slung across his shoulder. He hadn't held a weapon like this since Iraq and he liked the feel of it, like he was doing proper work. 'It's for the tourists,' he said, 'to get them to come over here and visit the church.'

Ramon nodded. 'Guess you gotta try something. So where's the mayor?'

'We haven't found him yet,' Morgan said. 'We've searched his residence, but it's empty. There's a tunnel over there leading to it. Thought he might be hiding in there.'

Ramon turned and stared at Holly, standing in the doorway, handcuffed between two guards.

'They got bedrooms in this *residence*?'

'Yes – it has bedrooms.'

Ramon smiled. 'Then let's go check out this tunnel.'

He moved down the aisle, past the crates of gasoline and the detonator box, heading to where Morgan had pointed. Morgan went in front and led him over to the vestry. The guards followed with Holly.

Morgan pulled the curtain aside and stopped. He'd been wondering when the best time to broach this subject might be and figured now was as good a time as any. 'The church …' he said, turning back to face Ramon.

'What about it?'

'Do we have to burn it?'

Ramon looked puzzled, as though Morgan had just suggested the sun might like to rise in the west for a change.

'I mean, I know why your father wanted to burn it down, as some sort of symbolic gesture of revenge because he thought the town had betrayed you and caused your death. Only we didn't betray you. We helped you. And you're not dead. So, I was thinking maybe we didn't need to torch the church now either.'

Ramon smiled. 'You like this church?'

Morgan nodded.

'Then find me the mayor and we'll talk about it. Can't have any loose ends here, not if you want to keep doing business.' He stepped past him and stopped by a wooden door set into the wall. 'This where you think he might be hiding out?'

'Possibly.'

'Then you go first,' Ramon said, stepping aside. 'You're the one holding the fuckin' M-6.'

79

The moment Andrews turned away Solomon grabbed the rope with his hands and flipped his legs up, turning himself upside down. Pain lanced through his shoulder where the skin had been peeled away, but he used it to help him focus. Feeling pain meant he was alive so he welcomed it.

He wrapped the rope round one ankle and trapped it with his other foot, holding himself upside down for a moment while he prepared. He would only have one chance at this. The flames were sweeping quickly towards him like a miniature version of the wildfire he had fought earlier in the day. If they caught him, he would be dead. He would get no second chance.

He pushed hard with his foot to keep the rope trapped, then bent at the middle and reached up with his bound hands. The rope was thin and hard for his foot to keep trapped so his weight pulled him down a little, down towards the flames directly burning on the spot where he had been standing. He grabbed at the section of rope above his knees and held it as tightly as he could, then loosened his feet and slid them further up the rope, feeding it round his leg while all of his weight was supported by his hands.

The heat was rising fast, sucking the oxygen from the air and making everything harder. He trapped the rope with his feet again, reached up with his hands and grabbed a little higher, moving up the rope a few painful feet at a time until the steel beam was only a foot or so above him. The heat was building now and the effort of supporting his weight was draining his strength but he resisted the urge to lunge for the beam. The next move would be risky. He had to release his leg from the rope and hook it over the beam while his weakened hands held him. One mistake, one slip, and he would fall head first to the burning concrete twenty feet below.

He was having trouble breathing now, smoke filling the air as it began to consume the contents of the warehouse. He gripped the thin rope as tightly as he could, released the brake of his ankle and felt the rope start to slip between his fingers. His strength was gone, he was falling. A feeling fluttered at the back of his mind that he should be stronger than this, that he *used* to be stronger. He shoved it aside and threw his leg up and over the steel beam and hooked it over just as his hands let go. The hard edge of the steel dug into the back of his knee and he gripped the rope again to steady him, hooked his other leg over, hanging there for a moment, batlike in the smoke and the heat.

The whole section of hangar beneath him was burning now. The fire had consumed the workbench and the body on the floor and was spreading fast to the rest of the building. If he waited any longer he would be trapped here and the fire would choke him.

He levered himself up, careful to keep his balance, then stood and walked steadily along the beam, as fast as he dared, heading for the part of the hangar the flames had not yet reached. Ahead of him another beam jutted out with a block and tackle set resting on steel runners to help move heavy engines and aircraft parts around. Chains dripped down to the concrete floor below it, offering him a way back to the ground. He was so focused on it he didn't notice the rope tightening around his wrists until it snapped tight and almost tugged him off balance. He stared down at the roiling inferno beneath him and managed to steady himself by taking a step back. The rope around his wrists was still secured to a stanchion that had somehow remained untouched by the fire. He was trapped with the fire spreading and the air getting hotter and smokier all the time.

He forced himself to walk back into the heart of the heat though every instinct was screaming at him to run. The rope slackened and he flicked the loose loop of it into the heart of the blaze where it caught light immediately and started to burn. Solomon hunkered down, bearing the heat for as long as he could while keeping a nervous eye on the spread of the fire. It had almost reached the chains now. He recited the words written on the church wall to help focus his mind and help him endure the heat:

Only those who face the fire yet still uphold God's holy laws
Only those who would save others above themselves
Only these can hope to escape the inferno and be lifted unto heaven

He thought of Holly and the kiss she had given him. The psycho with the scar had said they were heading back to the church, something about honouring the last wish of his dead father. He needed to get there, but first he needed to get away from here.

He stood and moved towards the spreading edge of the fire, glancing back at the burning rope as it tightened. He reached the spot where he had been stopped before, widened his stance a little and tugged at the rope.

It held.

The entire length of the rope was burning now but the

core remained firm. He tugged again, as hard as he dared, wary of it breaking suddenly and upsetting his balance.

Still it held.

He glanced over at the chains, his escape route. The fire already there and moving past them towards the exit where his folded shirt and jacket lay waiting. He had to get there. He had *willed* it to happen.

He squatted down, lowering his centre of gravity and yanked harder, then again, harder still, desperate now, risking his balance. It gave suddenly with a dull twanging sound that rocked him on his haunches. He grabbed the steel beam to steady himself then rose up and practically ran to the block and tackle. His hands were still bound but there was no time to free them. He reached down for the dangling chains and felt the heat in them from the fire below. He grabbed them as tightly as he could then rolled forward and off the beam.

The chains rattled as they took his weight and Solomon swung beneath them, feeling the links digging into his hands. His forward motion sent the tackle block moving along its runners and he swung his body to keep it going. Below him everything was burning and smoke made it hard to breathe and see. He closed his eyes and kept on swinging until the block hit the end of the runners, then he let go of one half of the chain and rode the other half down to the ground in a noisy rattle. He landed on the detached tailpiece of a plane and slid to the floor.

The fire was all round him, the heat radiating off it unbearable. He covered his head with his hands and flashed to a memory of Bobby Gallagher, bones sticking out from charred flesh. He saw the door ahead, the exit bar at waist height and ran at it. He grabbed his shirt and jacket from the chair and burst out into the night, flames chasing him through the door. He hit the ground and rolled, gulping the cool sweet air. He kept on rolling, using the cooling ground to squeeze the heat out of his skin and put out any flames that may have stuck to him, ignoring the pain coming from his back where grit stuck to the wet flesh of his peeled skin.

He came to a stop, looking up at the stars. He could hear the trapped fire rumbling in the building close by and the sound of a car driving away and heading back to town. The church was over a mile away, possibly two. It would take him maybe fifteen minutes to run there fully fit, longer in his current state. The mine was on the way though, and so was the corral.

He staggered to his feet and walked over to the nearest plane. It was a P-51 Mustang, polished to the same shine as the Beechcraft that had crashed. He crouched by the wheel and started rubbing the rope binding his wrists against the sharp edge of the landing gear housing. He glanced up and saw himself reflected on the underside of the wing, his white skin and hair darkened with ash and dirt. He looked like a creature of soot and smoke.

The rope frayed and fell apart and he stood and rubbed blood back into his wrists. The fire was pouring out of the hangar door now, a tongue of flame curling out to lick at the night. He grabbed his shirt and jacket from the ground and tied them round his waist by the sleeves. Then he started to run as fast as his exhausted body would allow, through the gate, on to the road, and back towards the town.

80

Mulcahy sat in the passenger seat of the transporter, staring down the pathway to the church door. The radio was turned low and filling the cab with the burble and crackle of local emergency traffic. Andrews had tasked him with listening out for any incoming units that might cause them problems, which was fine with him. It got him away from Ramon and gave him time to think.

He'd expected to feel relieved once his father was out of danger but instead he felt empty. Killing Tío hadn't brought him peace either. He had quite liked him, oddly enough, despite the hold he'd had on him and his asshole behaviour on the journey over.

He thought about their conversation in the car and the picture he'd shown him of the mother Mulcahy had thought was long dead. He wondered if his pop knew about her and felt a strong desire to call him up, but he couldn't. They were running a cell-phone jammer to stop all calls and the land-lines had been cut too. He'd have to talk to him about it when he caught up with him. Maybe. He didn't want to break the old guy's heart again, not after all he'd been through. At least he was a free man now, no more ties to the cartel. That was the deal he had done with Ramon, the price of his betrayal.

He wondered whether his pop might also regard it as a betrayal if he told him he wanted to look up his mother. Perhaps he'd go anyway and not tell him, visit her and her country club husband, stir a little trouble into the neatly tucked away life she'd made for herself, walk up to her front door and say, 'Hi, Mom, remember me? I'm the kid you had when you were a stripper, the one you dumped with a travelling salesman so you could start your life all over again.' The thought of it was appealing, but he knew he wouldn't do it. No point. What would she do, cry? Slam the door in his face? It would probably only make him feel even more empty, worse than he did now.

The radio chatter punctured his thoughts and he listened to a state trooper out on the highway, killing time with the dispatcher from another town. Simple little lives, all squared away in their own little worlds, the way his used to be. He wondered about Ramon. He couldn't imagine that working for him would be the same as working for Tío. He'd already seen enough evidence of the chaos in him, the lack of control, and it worried him. There would be a bloodbath somewhere down the line with Ramon in charge and he didn't want to be anywhere near him when it happened. He needed to get out, break the cycle. That's what they told you in therapy when you were trying to kick the booze or the drugs. You needed to break the cycle. That was what he had been thinking about ever since Ramon had first approached him. Because a window of opportunity had opened up here and he had planned all along to escape through it.

He checked around, making sure none of the others were close by, and unhooked the hand transmitter on the radio. When he was still in the force he'd had to learn a whole bunch of emergency frequencies and their various uses for fieldwork. He punched one into the radio and raised the mic to his mouth. 'Emergency, this is an emergency, over.' He spoke low, his restless eyes scanning the night.

Nothing.

He switched to another channel and repeated the call.

Still nothing.

He was about to switch again when a voice buzzed back. 'State your situation, over.'

'This is retired Captain Michael Mulcahy,' he said, and he gave them his old badge number so they could check him out. Then he told them exactly what his situation was.

81

Morgan led the way through the Cassidy residence, feeling a kind of thrill about it. He had only ever been in the entrance hall and the library before, never anywhere else. He'd never even used the john, and Lord knows there were enough of them to choose from.

They hadn't found Mayor Cassidy lurking in the tunnel or in his office, and the guards had already searched the rest of the house, but Ramon seemed in no hurry to leave.

'This is some nice place,' he said, walking up the grand staircase and taking it all in, the wood panelling, the crystal chandeliers, the oil paintings of desert landscapes. 'My old man lived in a shitty shack on the top of a dusty mountain. All that money he had and he still lived like a *gomero*.'

He stopped by a huge canvas showing a nightscape. A solitary figure stood with his back to the viewer, facing a bright shaft of light coming through what looked like a doorway cut into the dark. 'What's the story with this?'

'Jack Cassidy painted it,' Morgan said, 'same man as built this house – church too,' he added, hoping to steer Ramon back to the subject of not destroying it.

'What's the story though?' Ramon said, studying the painting. 'Who's the guy?'

'I don't know. Maybe it was Jack. I think the shining doorway is supposed to be a mirror, though. He built one into another painting he did – in the church.'

Ramon ignored the hint and continued walking along the upper hallway, opening doors and checking the rooms like a man thinking of moving in. He reached the end of the hallway and opened a final door into a large bedroom with an old, solid bed sitting in the middle and a fireplace with two chairs arranged around it. A door was set into the far wall through which an old-fashioned, roll-top bath could be seen.

'Now that's what I call a bedroom,' Ramon said, walking right in and looking around. 'Bit old-farty for my tastes, but I guess you could rip it all out and pimp it up a little – hot tub back there in the bathroom, some mirrors on the ceiling. What do you think?' He looked directly at Holly.

Holly said nothing.

Ramon smiled and turned to the guards. 'Make yourselves useful. See if you can't find this mayor. Me and the lady, we're going to hang here a while. Test drive some of these soft furnishings.'

82

Holly heard the bedroom door close behind her then a soft click as the door was locked.

She stared down at the floor, the floorboards polished and scuffed by a hundred years of Cassidy feet. She tensed, waiting for Ramon to grab her. Her hands were still tied in front so she couldn't do much about it if he did. She could kick him maybe. Stamp on his feet. She could feel him, standing between her and the door. The locked door.

A floorboard creaked as his weight shifted and she stiffened but he moved past without touching her. The mattress springs creaked as he sat on the edge of the bed and she could feel his eyes, crawling over her.

'Look at me,' he said. And she did, through hair that fell over her face like a dark veil.

He studied her, like she was a horse or a dog he was considering buying, then reached out and patted the bed beside him.

Holly looked at his hand, then back to his eyes. She didn't move.

Ramon cocked his head to one side, reached behind him, pulled something from out of his waistband then held it up.

Holly stared at the knife, the blade catching the light as he turned it slowly in his hand. 'So how do you think this little situation is going to shake out?' he said.

Holly felt herself starting to tremble and she clenched her whole body against it. She didn't want him to see and think she was afraid of him. She wasn't afraid. She was angry. 'You don't care what I think,' she said.

'Oh, I do,' he said. 'You know I could just have you if I wanted to, right? You know it. I know it. Tie you to the bed, hold a knife to your throat, cut you if you tried anything. We can play it that way if you want, but what's the point? Why take the hard road when there's a much easier path leading to exactly the same place?'

He laid the knife down on the bed and pulled out his phone. 'Let me show you something.' He rose from the bed and unlocked his phone as he walked over, his attention on it rather than her. Holly glanced at the knife. Too far to reach. Even if she made it, her tied hands would make it hard to do anything with it. And Morgan was standing outside the door with a loaded gun.

Ramon stopped in front of her and held up his phone. 'See this?' Holly glanced at the screen and gasped.

A pair of eyes stared out from a smiling ruin of a face, the exposed teeth white against the red. Holly wondered how the girl could possibly smile after whatever atrocity had been visited on her. Then she realized the truth. Her lips had been cut off.

'Rosalita,' Ramon said. 'I gave her the same choice I'm giving you – easy way or hard way. Guess which one she took. Brave girl. Beautiful girl. Shame.' He swiped the screen and another savage image appeared, different eyes staring out of the same appalling redness. 'Carmelita. She said *No* too.' He swiped again and Holly looked away, nausea rising inside her.

'Look at the screen,' Ramon said.

She shook her head, took a step backwards and banged against the locked door.

'Look at the screen,' Ramon repeated, his voice cold and calm.

Holly took deep breaths, fighting her revulsion.

'Look at the screen,' his voice softer now. 'It's not what you think.'

She looked.

No red this time. No staring eyes. This girl's eyes were closed. She was maybe twenty years old, her black hair spreading over the pillow, looking glossy under the camera light.

'Maria,' Ramon said. 'She gave me what we both knew I was going to get anyway. She *gave* herself to me. You understand? Same destination, different journey. So,' he said and lowered the phone. 'Which is it to be?'

He was standing so close she could feel his breath on her face. She looked past him to the bed. The knife lying upon it. Probably the same one that had cut away the beauty of those ruined girls.

She took a deep breath to steady herself then stepped forward, past Ramon and towards the bed. Every instinct screaming 'run'. She focused on the simple act of making her legs move, one step after another.

She reached the bed and turned, her legs buckling as she sat down on the edge of it, making a point of ignoring the knife lying next to her. Ramon regarded her for a moment then nodded and started walking over, unfastening the belt on his jeans as he came.

He stopped in front of her, his waist level with her head and only inches away. 'You do what I want, understand? You give it to me.'

Holly thought about that morning, standing by her

husband's grave, burying her old life then walking through the rain intending to finish the job. Only she hadn't. And now, in this utterly wretched situation, she realized how much she wanted to live. She would do anything to preserve her life now. Anything.

She reached up and started to undo the buttons on the front of Ramon's jeans. Her hands were tied tight, palms facing each other, making it hard for her to grip anything. She could feel Ramon watching her. He reached down for the knife and Holly froze, images from his phone flashing through her head.

'Don't make me take it.'

Holly nodded, her eyes on the blade. He turned the knife round until it was level with her face, held it there for a second, then slid the blade between her palms, the metal cold and hard. He sawed through the rope and it fell to the floor. Holly rubbed at the raw marks on her wrists, her fingers tingling as the blood returned.

She looked back at the buttons of Ramon's jeans and a single tear ran down her cheek as she remembered the last time she had done something like this and for whom. She blinked it away, not wanting him to see it. Not wanting to give him that much.

She worked as slowly as she dared but the zip came undone quickly now she could grip the buttons. His breathing grew heavier as she reached her hands round his waistband. He still had the knife in his hand, barely a blade-length away from her eye. It moved away a little as she eased his jeans down over his hips.

And she yanked down hard. Hard as she could. Dragging his jeans down below his knees. She pushed herself up at the same time, shoving him backwards.

He roared in anger and the knife scythed through the air as his arms windmilled, trying to keep his balance, but his bunched-up jeans were like shackles and he fell hard, catching his head on the edge of a table.

'Fucking bitch,' he roared, lunging at her with the knife, jerking himself forward across the floor and stabbing at her fleeing heels.

Holly darted into the bathroom and slammed the door behind her.

The blade thunked heavily into the wood on the other side and she heard splintering as Ramon twisted it free again. There was a key in the lock and she fumbled at it, her hand shaking so hard she had to use both hands to turn it. A deadbolt slid into place just as the door jumped from a heavy impact on the other side.

'Stupid bitch,' Ramon yelled through the door. 'Now I'm going to have to take it.'

Holly turned, heart hammering, eyes wide, looking around for a weapon, or a way out – anything.

83

Solomon ran.

He ran through the cooling night, the raw patch of skin throbbing on his back and stinging from the sweat running into it. The brand on his arm hurt too, aching and pulsing in time with his pounding heart and his feet across the ground.

The road sloped away towards the town, which helped a little, but it was still a long way to run after already burning up so much energy getting out of the hangar.

He could see the church ahead of him, lit by low spotlights, its size making it seem closer than he knew it was. It was still there at least, though he felt anxious about that. He could feel the cross banging on his chest as he ran and he used thoughts of what it might unlock to drive him forward:

Have to get to the altar …

Have to find Holly …

Have to save James Coronado …

The mine rose up out of the night, ugly piles of dirt, and forbidding fences. He ran past the gate, the warning signs fixed upon them, then beyond the fence to where the track left the road and led to the corral.

He slowed as he approached it, trying to silence his loud and hungry breathing. He was about to try to steal a horse from a place he had already stolen from, so stealth was very much in order.

He reached out with his senses, listening through his breathing for signs of anyone there. The corrals were empty and the lights in the office were off and he wondered if the horses were no longer here. He listened for any sound of them and caught the snort of an animal coming from the furthest barn.

He moved towards it, skirting round the edge of the open spaces, keeping to the corral fences.

He was halfway to the barn when a security light tripped on. He froze in place, half expecting more lights to flood the yard and voices to sound as people with guns came to investigate. Nothing happened. After a minute the light switched off again and he continued on his way, crouching lower and using the fence to hide his movement from the motion detectors.

He could smell the horses in the barn, earthy and warm, and he reached the door and laid his hand upon it. There was a heavy padlock, threaded through a solid hasp holding the door shut. He looked around for something to try to force it or break the lock free. That was when he noticed the figure standing by a rainwater butt only a few feet away from him.

The suddenness of the ghost girl's appearance made Solomon's racing heart flutter a little faster. She was staring right at him, her old-fashioned clothes too large for her tiny frame. She looked down at the ground then melted away as quickly as she had appeared.

Solomon stepped over to the spot where she had stood and studied the ground. Some flat rocks had been wedged beneath the rain barrel to level it. One of them had a small indentation next to it the same shape as the rock, showing that it had been recently moved. He crouched down and pulled it out, saw the key in the dirt beneath it and smiled.

'Thank you,' he whispered, taking the key and fitting it in the lock.

He picked out a black Palomino, the colour chosen to blend in better with the night, and rode it out of the barn, his legs still trembling from his recent run. He pointed it at the road and galloped across the yard, setting off all the security lights at once.

He didn't see the girl, standing in the shadows, watching until the lights blinked off again before turning her head back down to the ground to continue her endless search for whatever it was she had lost.

84

Morgan had been pacing in the hall, fretting about the situation with the church when he heard the shouting behind the bedroom door.

He rushed over and found it was locked. He thought about shooting the lock out but didn't want to hit anyone with a stray round so he stepped back to kick it open just as the door opened.

'She's in the bathroom,' Ramon said, pulling his jeans up and fixing his belt. 'Shoot the lock out and drag her out here.'

Morgan hurried through the bedroom to the bathroom door. He tried the handle first then shouldered the rifle and aimed at the lock. The shot boomed and the wood around the lock splintered. Ramon stepped forward and kicked the door open.

The room was empty.

'She's outside,' Morgan said, pointing at the small square window hanging open in the corner.

Ramon smiled. 'Well all right then. The only thing I like better than fucking is hunting. So let's go catch us a deer.'

He grabbed the M-6 from Morgan and hurried out of the room.

* * *

Holly slipped her way across the copper-clad roof, feeling the trapped heat of the day radiating up into her bare feet. She had taken her boots off to give her better grip and was slipping her way to the far corner of the house, the side furthest away from the church and all the activity and people.

She reached the corner and peered over the edge. It seemed much higher looking down than it ever had gazing up and she gripped the edge of the roof to steady herself. A drainpipe ran down the side of the house, but she hesitated to reach for it.

She heard a loud bang and splintering wood behind her, muffled by the half-closed window but still loud enough to carry. She took a breath, dropped her boots down to the ground below and almost faltered again when she heard how long it took for them to hit.

'Move,' she told herself, and she did.

She lay flat on the roof and swung her legs over the side, feeling her way down with her feet until they found one of the brackets fixing the pipe to the wall. She gripped it with her toes then reached down with a hand to grab hold of the pipe and began slowly shimmying down, taking it as fast as she dared and willing the ground to appear beneath her.

85

Ramon burst out of the front door of the Cassidy residence and jumped down the wooden steps on to the gravel drive.

Over by the church a couple of the soldiers were looking over, alerted by the gunshot, their hands resting on the stocks of their weapons.

'I got this,' Ramon called over, and they turned away again.

Ramon walked backwards from the house, looking up at the roof. He couldn't see anything up there, though she could be hiding on the other side. He loved this feeling he got when he was hunting, the clarity of thought, the singularity of purpose. He turned and scanned the garden, studying the avenues of trees between the house and the church. She could be hiding behind one of the broad trunks, but he doubted it. The guards had been surprised by his sudden appearance, which suggested that nothing else had come this way recently.

Morgan appeared at the door, his police-issue firearm in his hand. 'What's back there?' Ramon asked, nodding at the far side of the house.

'More garden and an orchard.'

Ramon set the M-6 to single shot, raised it to his shoulder and moved forward, rounding the edge of the house and staring into the dark garden beyond. The lights that lit the square and the church did not reach this part of the garden and the jacarandas threw deep shadows over everything.

Ramon listened out, heard a rustling about a hundred or so yards away and raised the gun to a firing position. He flicked on the night-sight and a circle of garden lit up in front of him, phosphorescent green in the scope.

He saw her almost immediately, a bright smear of movement. She was holding her boots in one hand and running fast, keeping to the shadows and weaving through the trees, her other hand held in front of her to ward off the low branches she couldn't see in the dark.

Ramon could see perfectly. He followed her progress, anticipating her movements and steadying his breathing. She was running almost directly away from him, making her a much simpler target to follow. 'Too easy,' Ramon murmured, sounding disappointed.

He pulled the trigger and watched the figure drop in his sights. It did not get up again.

'Stay here,' he told Morgan and started moving into the shadows. 'Won't be long.'

86

Andrews looked up when he heard the shot.

He was standing on the road that ran alongside the church, staring back towards the airfield and the distant glow of the burning hangar.

'What was that?' the man in the truck beside him said. 'Sounded like a shot to me.'

'Nothing to worry about, sir,' Andrews said, not believing his own words. 'But you should go home and stay there until further notice.'

The man had driven up a minute ago, all wide eyes and questions. He lived back up the road close to the airfield, said he'd seen smoke rising from one of the hangars and people moving around. 'You know the phones are out too?' he persisted.

'Please, sir,' Andrews repeated, 'go home. Everything is under control here.'

The man shook his head, put his truck in drive then pulled away, making a slow, wide circle in the road before heading back in the direction he had come from.

Andrews watched him drive off then angled his head down to talk into his lapel mic. 'This is Andrews. What's the report on those gunshots?'

'It was Ramon,' a voice came back. 'He shot someone out back of the house, I think.'

'The mayor?'

'Negative. The mayor is still at large, whereabouts unknown.'

Andrews shook his head and started walking back to the church.

Things were becoming too risky here and the longer they stayed, the worse it got. If he could see the burning hangar from his position then plenty of others would see it too. That plus the gunfire meant it was time to leave as far as he was concerned, loose ends or no loose ends. He reached the church door, unlocked it with Morgan's key and stepped inside.

A figure loomed out of the dark and his scalp tightened before he remembered what it was. He didn't like old churches at the best of times, let alone ones someone had put a spooky-assed dummy inside. He continued walking up the aisle towards the line of crates. Be doing everyone a favour, levelling this old tomb of a place.

He crouched down by the detonator unit and slotted his key into the arming switch. The display lit up, a line of red zeroes.

Ten minutes ought to do it.

He punched it into the timer and twisted the key again to arm it. He watched the numbers start counting down then propped the detonator against one of the crates, pulled the key out and walked back towards the door. The detonator unit contained two kilograms of C-4 explosive, enough to crack the stone floor and blow out all the windows. The gasoline would do the rest. Tío had wanted to light up the sky. Pity he wouldn't be around to see it. Now it would be a useful diversion to occupy the town and let him and his men get away.

Ten minutes to clear out and be gone. Plenty of time.

He closed the door and locked it behind him, the sound of it echoing to nothing in the vast empty space of the church.

87

Holly dragged herself forward, pushing at the ground with her good leg and letting the other one drag behind.

She had been shot, she knew that, though it didn't hurt much, not as much as she thought it would. When the bullet hit it had felt like someone had punched her hard on the leg above the knee, and she had fallen down and then not been able to get up again. It was only when she felt the blood that she realized what must have happened. There was a lot of blood, she could feel it though it was too dark to see. She worried that the bullet had nicked an artery on the way through and she was bleeding out. She felt if she could just make it out of the shadows and back into the light, maybe she would be OK.

A light appeared and danced in front of her on the ground, as if her thought had summoned it. It moved up and shone in her face, then the toe of a boot slid under her hip and levered her on to her back.

'Not bad for a running shot in the dark,' Ramon said from behind the flashlight.

There was a pressure on her leg then intense pain as he pressed his boot down on the entry wound. She howled with the pain and grabbed at the boot with both hands, desperate to push it off her.

'Didn't even catch the bone, by the looks of things,' Ramon said.

He took his boot off her leg and turned the flashlight round so she could see the knife he was holding. 'Now where were we?' he said, and he started to unbuckle his belt with the hand holding the knife.

Holly felt around on the ground for something, anything. Her hand closed around a small piece of branch that had broken off a tree. She held it up in front of her.

Ramon laughed. 'The fuck is that?' He lashed out with his boot, kicking her hand hard and knocking the branch from it.

Tears of anger and pain burned in her eyes. She felt around on the floor again, desperate not to give in, found the stub of a stick and raised it up.

Ramon swung the rifle towards her. 'You think that's gonna save you?'

Holly stared up at him, refusing to close her eyes or look away. She waited for the gunshot that would end her pain and felt the earth start to tremble beneath her. Ramon glanced off to his right and she realized he must feel it too. She could hear it now, like a heartbeat drawing closer.

The rifle swung away towards whatever was bringing the thunder and Holly followed it and saw a dark shape surging through shadows like a piece of night made solid. Ramon took a step backwards, bringing him closer to where Holly was lying. He aimed at the shadow and Holly swung her arm round as hard as she could and jabbed the piece of branch into his leg.

Ramon flinched from the sudden pain and his finger squeezed a round off. He fired wide. He tried to readjust and ignore the pain in his leg, but he never got the chance. The shadow hit him and galloped straight through him as if he wasn't there.

88

Solomon wheeled the horse round and dropped down close to where Holly was lying. There was a flashlight on the ground and he grabbed it and checked around. Ramon was on his back, a deep dent in his head where the horse's hoof had caught him. It had peeled the skin away, broken the metal plate and pulled it back to expose a small square of his brain beneath. The rifle was lying next to him and Solomon picked it up and carried it over to Holly.

'How did you find me?' Holly asked when he knelt beside her.

'I heard the gunshot,' Solomon said, tearing at the sodden material of her jeans so he could examine her leg, 'then I heard you scream.'

There was blood, plenty of blood, but not enough to make him think she would bleed out. He undid her belt, pulled it through the loops of her jeans then wound it round her thigh and cinched it tight above the wound.

'Hold that,' he said, handing her the end of the belt. 'It'll control the bleeding until we can get an ambulance to you.'

'Am I going to die?' she asked.

'No,' Solomon replied. 'Not if I can help it.'

'Hands where I can see them,' a voice called from the shadows.

Solomon turned to see Morgan emerging from behind the trunk of a jacaranda tree, his gun pointing straight at him.

'Your hands,' Morgan repeated.

Solomon stood slowly, lifting his hands in front of him. He stepped away from Holly so that Morgan could see Ramon, lying dead on the ground behind him.

Morgan shook his head when he saw him. 'It's all one big damned mess is what it is. This was supposed to be a new beginning. New business partner, more shipments. Cassidy didn't want it, neither did Tucker, that's why they had to go. There would have been so much damn money coming through this town we'd all have been rich. Maybe that's why they didn't want it. And now look …' He stared at Ramon, lying on his back, eyes open and a fist-sized hole in his head. 'Who am I supposed to do business with now?' He turned to Solomon. 'Why did you have to come here? Everything was fine until you arrived.'

'Not according to James Coronado.'

'Oh Jesus, spare me all the "*I'm here to save him*" crap. You can't save him. Any more than you can save yourself.'

He raised his gun, aimed it at Solomon's head and a shot rang out.

Solomon gasped and watched Morgan fall to his knees, his gun dropping from his hand and on to the floor. He turned to where the shot had come from and saw Holly pointing Ramon's rifle up at the spot where Morgan had been.

'Not rock salt this time, you son of a bitch,' she said, her voice already slipping out of focus.

Then the rifle fell from her hand and her eyes rolled up into her head.

89

Andrews was heading back to the van, scanning the square for movement, when he heard the gunshot.

'That's it, we're moving out,' he said.

Mulcahy was hunched over the radio, riding the scanner. 'We should take the desert road,' he said. 'Not the one past the airfield or the one through the mountains.'

'Why?'

'I've been picking up some radio traffic from two tactical units. They must have been tipped off by someone, or could be they saw the fire. One is inbound from Douglas, the other's coming from Globe. I've heard nothing from the desert road. Guess they have it down as impassable, but it's not. I drove in on it.'

Andrews nodded and leaned his head towards his lapel mic. 'All units listen up. RV back at the transporters immediately and prepare to exfil. Repeat: RV at the vehicles and let's get out of here. Now!'

He checked his watch and glanced over at the church. 'We need to step on this, that thing's going up in less than seven minutes. Where's Ramon?'

'Over behind the church,' Mulcahy said. 'Don't worry about him, he can come with me.'

'You sure? He's going to be pissed I gave the order to pull out without checking with him first.'

'I'll cope,' Mulcahy said. 'I just spent two hours in a car with his old man. Can't be any worse than that.'

90

Cassidy lay in the quiet of the church, listening for any signs of movement. He had heard the door being locked but wanted to be sure before he showed himself. He knew they were looking for him, he'd overheard someone say it, and he didn't want to be found. He felt like something terrible was going to happen here and that perhaps he was the only one who could stop it.

He sat up and looked out at the silent church through the canvas arch of the covered wagon. He couldn't see anyone and the lack of lights suggested there wasn't anyone to see.

He moved as quietly as he could, aware of every creak as his weight shifted inside the old wagon. He stepped out on to the floor and listened again before moving towards the line of crates in the central aisle.

He saw the red LED numbers shining brightly in the darkness, the display showing 5:24.

Then 5:23.

5:22.

Cassidy fell to his knees, his hands fluttering over the surface of the thing, hoping for something so simple as an 'off' switch. The numbers continued to tumble and the 5 became a 4.

Outside he heard an engine start up. Everyone pulling out before the bomb went off. Why would anyone want to destroy something so beautiful and sacred as a church?

The numbers continued to tumble, faster than seconds it seemed. He thought about walking it right out of the front door, but there could still be people out there who might make him put it back again, or shoot him and put it back in here themselves. He didn't care about his own safety, he felt he had forfeited that with all the bad choices he had made. He had made them for good reasons though. It was all to save the town. Perhaps he had failed at that too. But he could still save the church, that much was in his power.

He could save the house his ancestor built.

91

Mulcahy moved towards the Cassidy residence, wary of the two gunshots he had heard coming from the other side of it. He knew Ramon was back there somewhere, Morgan too, and he thought the woman was in the mix as well. He pulled his Beretta from his holster and held it in front of him.

Behind him the armoured trucks started up, their heavy engines shattering the night with their roars as they moved away. By the time he reached the house they were gone and he listened out to the sounds of the night through their fading rumble. He cocked his head to one side and tightened his grip on the gun.

He could hear the sound of heavy footsteps shuffling across the dry grass and getting louder. He waited until he was sure they were in safe pistol range then stepped out and pointed his gun straight at the figure emerging from the shadows.

He frowned when he saw who it was. 'I thought you were dead,' he said.

'Apparently not,' Solomon replied and carried on walking. 'If you're going to shoot me, get it over with, otherwise give me a hand. She's been shot and she needs to get to the hospital.'

Mulcahy looked past him into the shadowed garden. 'Who else is back there?'

'The psychopath with the plate in his head.'

'Alive?'

'No.'

'What about Morgan?'

'He's there too.'

'Alive?'

'No.'

Mulcahy relaxed a little. 'Well, that saves me a job. Let me help you there.' He holstered his gun and took the girl from Solomon. Her leg was a bloody mess and he carried her over to the wide wooden porch and laid her down on one of the outdoor sofas.

'Can you call an ambulance,' Solomon said. 'She's lost a lot of blood.'

Mulcahy checked his phone. 'I can now they've switched the jammer off.'

Solomon nodded and looked over at the church. 'Make sure she's OK,' he said.

Mulcahy inspected Holly's leg as the ringing tone sounded in his ear. It was a clean in-and-out wound, no hollow points or anything else that might have blown a chunk of her leg off. It could've been a whole lot worse.

'State your emergency,' the voice sounded in his ear.

'Gunshot wound. Female in her late twenties. She's been shot in the leg and she needs an ambulance.'

'State your location, sir.'

'Cassidy residence. You might want to send some extra folks down while you're at it. There's been some gunfire here. Couple of people dead.'

He hung up before he could get drawn into a conversation he didn't want to have. They would send cops for a gunshot wound callout, though he wasn't sure what cops were left.

He looked up and realized that Solomon was gone. He stood and walked over to the edge of the porch and spotted him halfway down an avenue of trees. He was heading for the church.

'No!' Mulcahy called after him, remembering what Andrews had said. 'Get away from there.'

Solomon heard Mulcahy calling him, telling him to keep away from the church but all it did was make him start running towards it. He felt drawn to it like a drunk to a drink.

He felt so tired now, but he pushed himself on, one foot in front of the other. He wanted to know what was hidden beneath the altar. He *needed* to know.

He pulled the cross out from under his shirt and held it in his hand, not understanding how he had come by it or what it might mean, but knowing all those answers were close. The wall was in front of him now and the church just beyond. Somehow he had to get over that, get into the church and find what was hidden in the plinth. The lost Cassidy treasure. His to find. And maybe something of himself.

The explosion was like a thunderclap, so deep and loud he felt it in his chest. The ground beneath him erupted and he was thrown upwards into the lower branches of a tree. He reached out with his hands to try to protect his face but he hit his head hard on a branch and the world went blinding white for a second. Then he felt himself falling, and the sound of the explosion was gone, and the whiteness faded to black.

92

Andrews was driving past the burned billboard on the edge of town when he heard the explosion. He thought of the creepy mannequin by the old-fashioned wagon and smiled at the thought that it had been obliterated. The blast and the fire would keep everyone busy for hours, days even. It was the perfect diversion to help them slip away. It had been as neat as it could have been: no men lost, minimal gunfire and none of it from his men. Objective achieved. As far as missions went, they didn't get any better.

He fixed his eyes on the road ahead, plotting the best route through the potholes and ridges on the surface. They passed the tangled wreckage of the plane and headed away into the night, the blackened desert blending perfectly with the dark sky. It felt like they were flying instead of driving. He felt like he was free.

The light flicked on ahead of him when he was almost at the junction, so bright it flooded the cab and forced him to slow right down.

'Stop your vehicle,' a voice commanded through a loud-hailer.

More lights came on either side of them. The headlights of vehicles parked out in the desert.

'We have you covered on all sides,' the voice came again. 'Stop your vehicles, turn off your engines and step outside with your hands where we can see them. I repeat, we have you covered, do NOT attempt anything stupid.'

Andrews stood on the melted edge of the road with his hands on his head, the rest of his men lined up alongside him. He stared out at the black desert and felt oddly relieved that it was over. All the deception and anxiety about the next call and what he would be required to do to keep his family safe. He knew some of his men had turned for money, but not all of them, and he wondered if those others in the line were feeling as relieved as he was.

A captain stepped in front of him and regarded him coldly from behind his visor. 'Real shitstorm you've stirred up here. Not sure the department's going to get out from under this one any time soon.' He shook his head and looked along the line. 'Which one's Mulcahy?'

'He's bringing up the rear,' Andrews said, staring back down the road towards the town. He could see the glow of the fire over at the airfield, but that was all, no headlights coming up the road and no fire in the centre of town.

Then he realized what had happened.

X

---

*'How terrible is wisdom
when it brings no profit
to he that is wise.'*

Sophocles

X

From the private journal of
the Reverend Jack 'King' Cassidy

*I*t happened late morning on the third day of my journey.
     I had fallen into a kind of limbo, putting one foot in
front of the other over land so flat and unbroken and featureless
that it had lulled me into a wakeful sleep where my body kept
on walking while my mind drifted like a cloud in a clear sky.
So detached was I that the savages were almost upon me before
I knew they were even there.

     There were three of them, their brown skin shining with
animal fat, their heads covered with the skulls and horns of
mule deer, making them appear like demons on horseback.

     They had moved in on my blind side, my view of their
approach blocked by my mule and the large canvas sack on its
back. If I had spotted them sooner I could have slipped my rifle
from the saddle and warned them away with a few shots, but
if I reached for it now they would be on top of me before I
could fire.

     A recently slain Coues deer lay draped across the neck of
the lead horse with two fresh holes in its side and ribbons of red
streaming down the horse's flank and dripping on to decorative
tassels stitched along the bridle reins. I was a poor shot at best
and the tight group of arrow-holes in the dead deer showed that
these savages were not.

     The savages saw I had spotted them and broke into a gallop.
I was frozen where I stood. They would be on me in a moment

and there was nothing I could do. This was how it would end. I focused on the tassels jostling with the movement of the lead horse, catching the sunlight and shining mostly brown or black except for one much paler that made me realize what they were.

They were scalps.

The sight of them conjured the fear I had felt in the shadow of the burned mission and also in the gully with the long-dead prospectors. It came so fierce and fast that it pushed the fear I felt into something else entirely.

I have often thought that emotions are not linear but circular in shape and that opposites are closer together than we imagine. Thus happiness can switch to melancholy in an instant and laughter to tears. This was what happened to me then. The sight of the swinging scalps turned my fear to rage.

I let go the reins of my mule and started walking directly towards the savages, reaching behind me for what was slung on my back. Two of the savages raised their bows, long arrows already fitted to the strings ready to fire, but the sight of the pale Christ surprised them when I produced it and held it up, and I was glad to see such a common emotion weaken their stony countenances. I lifted the cross higher, holding it before me like a shield as I continued my advance.

The lead horseman halted at the sight of me and the other two fanned out around him, their bottomless black eyes all fixed upon me. The savage in the centre spoke to them, his eyes still on me and the two with bows turned and rode away, slinging their bows over their backs as they went.

The remaining savage watched me come closer, the scalps swinging beneath his horse's neck. I could smell him I was so close and he smelled of death and blood.

I stopped in front of him and planted the cross into the earth as though I was driving a fence-post into the ground to mark a boundary. The savage's pony flinched and reared back a little, forcing its rider to bring it under control. I could only guess at what savagery this beast had witnessed, this hell-mount with blood dripping red down its flank and human skin and hair decorating its bridle, and yet it had been spooked by the figure of Christ.

A shadow seemed to pass across the savage's face and he spat on the ground and uttered a word that sounded like 'Sin' or 'Shin', then he kicked the pony's flanks, wheeled around and took off after the others.

I watched until they melted away to nothing in the shimmering mirror of the heat-haze, my arms shaking from gripping the cross. I had faced down evil with only my faith as a weapon — and I had triumphed.

I made it back to Fort Huachuca a day earlier than planned because I no longer skulked my way along, hiding in gullies or keeping to the lower parts of the land. I had no fear of being seen now. Nothing could touch me.

I rode through the gates and straight to the surveyor's office, where I retraced my journey, walking my fingers over lines of terrain it had taken me days to traverse on foot. The place I had reached was not clearly marked on their maps and they had to send for an Indian scout to try and pin down the location of it.

It was strange, seeing a savage wearing the clothes of a civilized man after I had faced his wild, half-naked brethren so recently in the desert. I described my journey to him — the stand of mesquite on the dry river, the twin peaks on a range that curled into a horseshoe of red mountains, and when I mentioned these the same shadow I had seen pass across the face of the mounted savage crossed his and he pointed to a spot on the map where nothing was marked save for a thin pen-line of mountains that petered out to nothing.

'Chidn,' he said, making the same sound the mounted savage had uttered.

'Chidn Chuca,' then he stared at me with what could have been fear or suspicion.

I knew Chuca meant 'mountain' because Fort Hua-chuca was named after the Thunder Mountains that rose around it. I asked the scout what Chidn meant and his eyes flicked to mine then back down to the map on the table as if he did not want to hold my gaze.

'Chidn means spirit,' he said in that flat-toned way the savages have. 'Chidn Chuca means Spirit Mountain. My people do not go to this place. It is a place of the dead, not the living. It is a bad place.'

I thought about this the whole time they drew up the papers, about why the savage had called me 'Chidn' then ridden away in what seemed like fear.

My answer came a few days later when I rode back out with hired men and wagons loaded with equipment to work my claim properly. This was probably the last time I ever felt truly content. My claim was now filed and secure, Sergeant Lyons was in the stockade with charges of murder and treason hanging over him, and I had a church to build and the means with which to build it. My future was secured. My legacy too.

It was near day's end on the fourth day when the horseshoe of mountains had begun to rise ahead of us that I saw it. It was caught on the trunk of a large saguaro and lay directly on my trail, almost as if it had been put there for me to see, which, thinking about it all now, I suppose it had. I steered my mule towards it and my heart soared when I saw what it was. It was the missing page from the Bible, caught there by some miracle. I halted the mule and slid to the ground, my heart pounding with the joyful prospect of being

able to make the Bible whole again and carefully peeled the
page away from the spines.

The page had been battered some in its journey across
the wilderness, the surface scoured by sand and grit until the
printed words had been all but removed. I turned it in my hand
and my heart almost stopped beating in my chest. I wish it had.
I wish I had died before ever seeing what was written there. But
I did read it and when I did the light went out of my life, and
I truly understood all that I had lost.

93

Solomon woke to the smell of disinfectant and disease.

He was lying on starched sheets and staring up at the ceiling of a small private room in the hospital. It sounded busy outside in the corridors. He tried to sit up and his head felt like it was about to split in two.

'Take it easy.' Dr Palmer was standing at the end of his bed, writing some notes on a clipboard. 'You banged your head pretty bad.'

'The church,' Solomon said, his voice dry and croaky.

'The church is fine,' Palmer said, hooking the notes back on the foot of his bed and walking round to his side. 'The Cassidy residence however …' He clicked on a penlight and shone it into Solomon's eyes. 'Any double vision? Nausea?'

'No. What happened?'

'They're still trying to figure it out.' He switched the light to his other eye. 'Rumour is that the mayor and Chief Morgan were involved in some kind of cartel deal that went wrong. Morgan got himself killed and Cassidy was locked in the church with a bomb. They think he dragged it into the tunnel between the church and his house to deaden the blast. They haven't found him yet, so …'

The church was still there. Solomon looked down at his chest. The cross was still there too. And so was the altar.

He glanced over to the door and saw his jacket and shirt folded on a chair next to it.

'Forget it,' Palmer said. 'You're not going anywhere. You took a real knock to the skull and you lost a significant amount of blood from that wound on your back. How did you get that by the way? It looks surgical.'

'No idea,' Solomon said, unwilling to get into it. 'Where's Holly?'

'In the next room. What about those bruises and contusions on your wrists – any idea how you came by those?'

'No. Is she OK?'

'She's stable. She lost a lot of blood but she's been transfused. That tourniquet she arrived with probably saved her life. I'm guessing that was you?'

'You need to take extra care of her,' Solomon said.

'We always do.'

'No, I mean extra care. Run an HCG test on her, you'll see.'

Palmer raised an eyebrow. 'Really?' He wrote more notes on the clipboard. 'You should take care of yourself too.' He hooked the notes back on the end of the bed and headed to the door. 'And get some rest. I don't want to find you wandering around the corridors.'

'Don't worry,' Solomon said. 'You won't.'

94

Solomon stepped out into the morning light and breathed in the cool air.

He stiffly slipped his arms into his jacket and started to walk towards the church, the new dressing on his back feeling tight beneath his shirt. His hands and wrists hurt, and he flexed his fingers as he walked along, trying to work some of the stiffness out. His legs felt shaky too.

'You need to get yourself in shape,' he muttered to himself as he stepped into the shade of the boardwalk and headed along it to the church.

There were trucks and fire crews and out-of-town police vehicles crowded around what was left of the Cassidy residence. The side nearest the church had collapsed entirely with half-rooms exposed as if a giant had smashed his fist down on it. A couch was hanging over the splintered edge of an upper floor and wallpaper fluttered like streamers in the morning breeze.

The church appeared relatively untouched, but as he drew closer he saw that a large crack had spread up the stone wall by the door like a streak of black lightning, and bright pebbles of glass littered the floor where the stained-glass windows had shattered.

There was a strip of black-and-yellow tape across the door with DO NOT ENTER written across it. Solomon ignored it and went inside.

The church was deserted, everyone clearly focusing their efforts on the ruin of the Cassidy house, probably still looking for the mayor, hoping they might find him alive, though Solomon doubted they would. Death must have seemed like a preferable option, given what else the mayor would have faced had he lived. The trusts would pass to the church now and there was little to no money coming in from anywhere else as far as he could see. Cassidy might have saved the church, but the town would die anyway, along with his name.

He moved down the aisle past the mannequin that had toppled over and now lay in stiffness staring up at the ceiling. All of the windows on the right-hand side of the church, the side closest to the blast, were broken, the depictions of the various commandments rendered abstract by the pieces that were missing.

Four large black crates were lined up along the aisle but whatever had been inside them had been removed. Solomon sniffed the air as he walked past and smelled the lingering ether of gasoline.

The altar cross lay toppled and dented on its side. Solomon reached the plinth it had stood upon and saw the words revealed on the inlaid stone surface, the exact same design he had seen on the drawings Holly had produced at the camp site.

I

———

THOU SHALT HAVE
NO OTHER GODS BEFORE ME

———

He ran his finger over the words and probed the 'I' and the mark on his arm throbbed in concord, as if it was a living thing anticipating what was about to be revealed.

The recess of the 'I' was loose, compacted dust rather than solid stone. Solomon leaned forward and blew on it to clear it and the hole got deeper. He repeated this, working the dust loose with his little finger then blowing it away, until there was no more left to clear.

He took the key from round his neck and carefully fitted it into the slot.

It was a perfect fit.

He twisted it gently, aware that the lock had not been used for almost a hundred years.

It was solid.

He took the key out again and moved over to where a candle lay on the floor, knocked over by the blast. He rubbed the tines of the cross over the waxy surface to lubricate it a little then moved back to the plinth, spat in the hole and tried again.

This time it shifted a little, and he wiggled it in the lock, twisting it ever more until something gave and the whole of the inlaid square of stone moved and a line appeared where it met the lip. Solomon pulled it up, using the key as a handle and revealed what lay beneath.

The niche was filled with a twist of cloth that had yellowed with age and been knotted in several places in the approximation of arms and legs to make a doll. Solomon reached in and lifted it out to reveal a book beneath. It was as small as a paperback and thin as a cigarette, its plain black cover tied shut with a long black ribbon that wound round each edge and was secured by a bow in the centre like a solemn Christmas present. There was a folded page trapped near the back of the book, bulging the pages either side of it.

Solomon carried the book and the linen doll over to a pew, lay the doll down on the bench beside him and pulled the frayed end of the bow to open the book. Inside the pages were filled with neat copperplate handwriting that swirled and looped across the page. Solomon turned to the first page and started to read.

I write these words on the twenty-third day of December in the year of our Lord nineteen hundred and twenty-seven. Two days from now it will be my birthday. I will be eighty-six years old, or I would be if I were to make it that far ...

He read quickly, learning the true account of how Jack Cassidy had really survived in the cauldron of the Arizona desert, the sacrifice of Eldridge, the drinking of his blood and the light in the darkness. And when he reached the end, where Cassidy told of the miracle of finding the missing page of the Bible out in the vast desert, Solomon knew what the loose folded page in the back of the book must be.

He pulled it out and examined it. It was old and yellowed and carried the ghost of printed words upon it. It looked as though it had been roughly scoured with grit to remove the original text, but enough remained for Solomon to see that he was indeed holding the missing page. It had been folded in such a way as to form an envelope and Solomon could feel something inside it, something flat and irregular and solid.

He unfolded the page, being careful not to tear it along the fragile creases, and a sliver of glass fell into his hand, along with a second folded page. He held the glass up to the light, turning it in his hand, and saw that it was a fragment of mirror.

He held it up to his face and caught his breath when he saw, not himself reflected, but a desert at night, vast and empty save for a dark figure standing close by and staring straight at him.

'Hello, Jack,' Solomon whispered.

He turned the triangle of glass in his hand and the reflected landscape shifted, showing him what the land had been like before the town was here. He could see the mountains and the sky, unchanged and timeless, and the 'V' in the mountain range, there long before it had served as a background to James Coronado's childhood photographs. And when he turned the glass back to his face the dark figure of Jack Cassidy had gone and it was only himself reflected. Or was it? There was something different about his eyes. They were darker now, a deep brown instead of pale grey, and his eyebrows had some colour to them too. He rubbed his thumb across the surface of the glass to clear the dust and regarded himself again. It was him but not him. A slightly fuller version of his previous self. A blank page, but at least with some writing on it now.

He slipped the glass into his pocket and was about to unfold the second sheet when he noticed writing on the inside of the sheet he had already opened. He held it up to the light and saw the faded commandments still faintly visible beneath a declaration written in brown ink:

I, the man known as Jack Cassidy, hereby pledge to exchange that most treasured and immortal part of myself so that a great church of solid stone may rise from the desert and spread God's word and charity until all savagery is driven from this land and Christian people have taken dominion here.
   JC

And there it was. Jack Cassidy's shameful secret. He believed he had sold his soul in the desert in exchange for a fortune and a church and a town.

Solomon gazed around him at the broken church and listened beyond the walls to the sounds of voices and splintering wood as people continued to search the rubble for Cassidy's last remaining relative. Maybe he had. The town certainly seemed cursed rather than blessed.

He took the second folded page and carefully opened it. It was as old as the first page and of the same quality and size. There was writing on both sides, a note from Jack Cassidy on one side and a dedication in a hand he did not recognize on the other. He read it and felt everything click into place.

He rose from the pew and hurried back to the entrance, taking the linen doll and the notebook with him. The Perspex box that protected the old Bible had shifted in the explosion with cracks around the screws that held it to the wooden base. Solomon pounded on the side of it and it came away entirely, exposing the old Bible beneath.

It had lain open at Exodus for almost a hundred years but Solomon closed it now and opened it again to the first few pages, searching for a dedication page. He didn't find one. Instead he found a fine tear close to the binding, three pages in. He took the page he had just read and held it up. The serrations at the torn edge of the page matched perfectly. This second page had been torn from this Bible too.

He re-read the dedication on it and smiled. He no longer needed to save James Coronado. He already had done.

95

Holly woke gradually from a dream of Jim.

They had been riding in the desert on one of those cool evenings where the light was like liquid warmth, and she woke with a smile on her face, which melted away as soon as she realized where she was.

She was propped up against some pillows, her leg heavily bandaged and tubes coming out of her arm. She felt like she'd been run over by a truck, but then the memory of what had actually happened came to her and the truck seemed like a better option.

Her whole body was in pain, both inner and outer. She looked around for an alarm button to press so she could call someone and maybe get a sleeping pill to send her back to her happy dream. That's when she spotted the folded piece of paper on her nightstand with 'Holly' written on it.

She reached over, pressed the button then picked up the folded sheet of paper and settled back on her bed. The note was written on a scrap that had been torn from her medical notes.

'Your husband was right,' it said. 'The lost Cassidy riches were exactly where he thought they would be. This page was torn from the Cassidy Bible. You can verify that by matching the ripped edge. The rest is written on your study wall.'

There was no signature, but she knew who it was from.

A second sheet of paper was folded into the note, much older than the first, and she carefully unfolded it now and saw old-fashioned writing on both sides of the page. She read the longer note first:

I have sinned, God knows I have sinned, but I pray to He who is merciful and just not to visit my sins upon those who carry my name by setting down this confession.

Before I found riches and built a church and made a town and a new name for myself I was another man with another family and another name. In my vanity I thought it was my family who was holding me back from all I imagined I could be so I abandoned them in order to seek my fortune, only to realize too late that there are no greater riches than the name you are born with and those who will carry it on into the future. By the time I realized this it was too late, I was already trapped by my new name and the fame of it and realized if I confessed the truth I risked the ruin of everything good I had wrought.

I did confess this grave sin once, to the priest who gave me this Bible, but he died and took my secret to the grave, as I now take it to mine.

The foundation I set up for abandoned families and the orphanage attached was my way of trying to find the family I had abandoned without risking the ruination of the Cassidy name. It was my penance too. I only pray that my lost family managed to thrive without me and that some time, in a more civilized future, the two halves of my broken past might be

re-united and made whole again. For as the priest told me
when he took my confession:

'A good name is to be chosen rather than great riches.'
Proverbs 22:1
JC

Holly finished reading just as the door opened and Dr Palmer walked in.

'How are you feeling?'

'Like I've been shot.' She turned the page over to the dedication on the other side.

'Apart from that, how are you feeling?'

'Awesome I guess.'

The dedication was in two parts. The first recorded when the Bible had first been gifted to a Father Patrick O'Brien by the Bishop of Limerick in 1868. The second was written in a different hand, a spidery scrawl that hinted at age or infirmity. The date was May first, eighteen seventy-nine and the message said simply:

I hereby bequeath this Bible to James Coronado,
travelling under the name Jack Cassidy.
Signed – Fr. Patrick O'Brien. MA

She read the names again then realized exactly what Solomon's note had meant.

The rest is written on your study wall.

She pictured Jim's family tree, traced back all the way to his oldest relative, the man he had been named after.

James Coronado. Or Jack Cassidy. They were the same.

He had spent his life idolizing the Cassidys, not realizing he had been one all along.

She looked up, aware that Dr Palmer had been speaking to her. 'Did you hear anything I just said?'

'No,' she said. 'I was a little …'

'Inability to concentrate can be one of the side-effects of hormonal imbalance, along with nausea and a whole bunch of other delights.'

Holly shook her head, confused. 'What are you talking about? What's wrong with me?'

Palmer smiled. 'You really didn't hear a thing I said, did you? There's nothing wrong, Mrs Coronado, nothing at all. You're pregnant.'

96

Mulcahy felt a jolt of déjà vu as he eased off the road and onto the ramp of the Best Western. The layout was different from the one he'd been in the previous day, bigger accommodation blocks and fewer of them, but the feel of the place was identical: impersonal; functional; slightly depressing. He parked by the reception office and checked cars as he walked to the office. Old habits.

A collection of tattoos and piercings in the shape of a man handed him a site map then the key to the room he pointed at and was back to playing Soda Crush on his phone before Mulcahy was even out of the door.

The sunlight hurt when he stepped back outside. He ran his finger along the paintwork of the Jeep before getting back inside, leaving a long clear line in the dust. He'd been driving through the night, stopping only for gas and coffee and his eyes felt like they'd been peeled.

The room he had chosen was in the block farthest from the road. It was a family unit, slightly bigger than the one from the day before, but otherwise identical: same kitchenette at the back; same lumpy twin beds facing a TV the same vintage as the A/C unit that rattled when he turned it on.

He grabbed the remote, turned on the set and sat heavily

on the bed. Springs dug into him through the thin sheets and bed cover. All he had to do was lie back and he would be asleep before his head hit the mattress. But he couldn't sleep. Not yet.

Sound and picture faded up on the screen and he nudged the volume up and channel-surfed until he found a local news station. The events at Redemption were all they were talking about, fragments of the last twenty-four hours of his life flashing before his eyes like an hallucination.

He forced himself to his feet and moved over to the kitchenette, his eyes fixed on the screen, faces and voices smearing into each other. He pulled the fold-up cot away from the connecting door and fitted his key in the lock. There was a noise on the other side, like someone had been standing there, listening. Mulcahy pulled the door open and stared at his Pop. His hair was sticking out like he'd just got up and he had dark bags under his eyes. He looked Mulcahy up and down. 'You look like shit,' he said.

Mulcahy felt the weight of the last twenty-four hours settle on him and something tightened in his throat. 'Mom got married again,' he said, before he knew what he was saying.

Pop blinked. 'I know,' he said. 'Good luck to her.'

Then he stepped forward and hugged him tight, like he hadn't done since he was very, very small.

97

Solomon felt the stretch of his legs and the wind on his face as he walked out of Redemption. He was on the road that passed the mine and the airfield and the livery yard. The horses were back in the corrals when he reached it, flicking their tails as they munched the hay that had been laid out for them. A couple of Palominos looked his way when he walked up the track and laid something on the ground where it couldn't easily be seen. They returned their attention to their breakfast before he walked away again. After a few steps he heard snorting and sensed something behind him. He stopped and turned to look back up the track. The ghost girl had appeared, standing where he had just been. She stooped down and picked up the twisted cotton doll he had left for her, then looked up at him, smiled and faded away.

'Goodbye, Miss Eldridge,' Solomon whispered, then he turned and carried on walking.

When he reached the city limit he stopped and stared back at the town. It seemed peaceful at this distance, the spire rising high above everything. He pulled the folded Bible page from his pocket and re-read the handwritten contract. Had Jack Cassidy really done a deal with a demon in exchange for the church and the town he was looking at, or did he just think he had, this contract no more than the brain-fevered imaginings of a man driven mad by heat and thirst and religion?

There was a way to test it, his teeming mind had suggested it back in the church, and he reached into his pocket now for the book of matches he had taken from beside the candles. He took out a match, struck a flame and held it to the paper's edge. The flame curled around it then caught.

Solomon gasped as hot pain bloomed in his arm. He dropped the burning page to the floor and pulled off his jacket and shirt. Someone at the hospital had fixed a new dressing to his arm and he ripped this off too and stared at the skin beneath. A new mark was beginning to form and he bit down hard against the pain of its coming. It was another 'I', lining up exactly with the first and as it formed a new word rose in his mind.

Magellan.

He said it aloud, repeating it over and over until the burning sensation began to ease. He looked back down at the ground where the last piece of the burning page curled into ash. The contract had been real. It had been real and he had just broken it. And the James Coronado he had come here to save had not been Holly's husband after all, or even her unborn son, it had been the original James Coronado – Jack Cassidy.

He stared at the mark on his arm, a 'II' now where the 'I' had been. A new name in his mind too.

Magellan.

Solomon turned the word over and facts sparkled around it like raindrops.

Ferdinand Magellan. Sixteenth-century Portuguese explorer. Often cited as the first person to circumnavigate the globe. Except he died before he completed the journey.

Was this to be Solomon's fate too, to circle the Earth in search of something only to die before he achieved it? His mind continued to shimmer with information.

Magellan – the name of an unmanned spacecraft that had mapped the surface of Venus.

Magellan Straits – notoriously dangerous sea route between South America and Tierra del Fuego.

Perhaps Magellan was a place he had to travel to, or someone else he had to save – or maybe it was nothing at all.

Solomon did his shirt up and put the jacket back on, reading his name again, stitched in gold thread into the label:

Ce costume a été fait au trésor pour M. Solomon Creed – This suit was made to treasure for Mr Solomon Creed – *Fabriqué 13, Rue Obscure, Cordes-sur-Ciel, Tarn.*

Maybe France was where he should go, to find the rest of his suit and the man who had measured him for it, someone who might remember him.

He slipped his arms into the sleeves and turned the collar up to protect his neck from the strengthening sun, then turned and started walking away from Redemption and towards – who knew what? He didn't expect to find easy answers but he hoped the journey would be interesting and for now he savoured this brief moment of peace, with the sun on his back and the wind on his face.

Just the road.

And him walking along it.

EPILOGUE

The computer pinged gently, cutting through the hum of air-con and the gentle tap of fingers on keyboards.

Harris looked up, his heart pattering a little faster inside the long-sleeved shirt he wore despite the heat outside to hide the tattoos on his arms. In the quiet world of forensic biology the sound he had just heard was the equivalent of the stadium roar that followed a touchdown or a home run.

They had a match.

He opened the documents the search engine had returned. Studied them. Frowned.

He glanced over at his boss sitting in the corner of the room, her large glasses reflecting the screen she was glaring at, making her eyes appear as if they had turned into mini-monitors. He was only a month into his placement and the main thing he had learned so far was that Dr Gillian (hard 'G') did not like being disturbed. She liked her people to think for themselves. She liked people who took responsibility for their shit, and she did not like people who wasted her time getting her to check their homework and rubber-stamp things that should be beneath her radar and were definitely below her pay-grade.

'Why have a bunch of dogs and bark myself?' she said – a lot.

Dr Gillian was old school and borderline abusive, but Harris also knew that the only reason this position had come up at all was because of those things and entry-level criminalist positions did not come up that often.

He glanced back at his screen and checked everything again, comparing the smudgy columns of PCR data from one lab sheet against those of another. It was a match, no question, a spot-on, no-room-for-error, bang-on match.

Except it couldn't be.

He checked the dates on the two samples. The first was five years old, the second had been submitted two days ago. That in itself wasn't surprising. Sometimes matches came from samples that had been collected decades apart. Since the lab had moved to the new building on Miracle Mile it had started processing more cold cases, digging back through evidence gathered way before the technology existed to pin crimes to the people who had done them. Their systems were linked to a wide network of other databases – CODIS, the FBI's DNA database, Interpol's DNA Gateway and several international foundations who kept and studied DNA samples for academic purposes. The five-year-old sample had come from one of these, and this was what told him something was wrong.

He checked the PDF files that had come with the sample, trying to spot what might have gone wrong. They had a match, but it couldn't be. There was no way. He knew that what he was looking at must be wrong but he couldn't figure out how. It had to be a mistake, and, most importantly, it was not his mistake, it was somebody else's.

'Doctor Gillian …' He cleared his throat to try to make

it sound less whiny. 'Would you mind taking a look at this please?'

The other two criminalists in the room looked up from their terminals, exchanged a glance then got on with their work again.

Doctor Gillian's bright reflected eyes fixed on him for what seemed like an age. 'You want me to get out of my chair and come to you?'

'Well, er … I guess I could forward you the files, but I have them open here and lined up, so it'll be quicker if …'

She stood abruptly, sending her chair wheeling away behind her to a mark on the wall showing where chair and wall had met many times before.

'This better be worth the trip, Mr Harris,' she said, striding across the floor to his desk. 'You better have a positive ID for Jack the Ripper or something, because anything less and I'm going to be most displeased.'

She came to a halt behind his chair and he pictured her windshield glasses reflecting his screens now.

He studied his monitors, seeing it all again, suddenly less certain now of what he had and what it might mean. Perhaps it was his mistake after all and he was about to be made to look like a dick in front of the whole office.

The silence stretched.

A hand reached down, took control of the mouse and started scrolling through the documents, checking the same things Harris had checked. 'Well, that can't be right.' Harris breathed out. 'You sure these files haven't got mixed up?'

'I checked them both; they're genuine.'

'They can't be.' She clicked on the lab submission form for the older sample and Harris re-read it, knowing Dr Gillian was doing the same. It was different from the standardized police forensics forms with lots of extra narrative detail and photographs showing the site the sample had been taken from. It had been filled in by a Dr Brendan Furst, lead archaeologist on the excavation of a burial site in Turkey known locally as Melek Mezar. They had found some remains including hair from which the DNA sample had been extracted. Carbon 14 tests had dated the remains as belonging to a man who had lived around four thousand years earlier. The other sample suggested the same man had been walking around a town in Arizona two days earlier – a man called Solomon Creed.

Dr Gillian clicked on this now then pointed at the screen. 'There's your answer. Look at where this came from and who filed it.'

Harris did as he was told. It had been filed by a Garth Morgan, police chief of the town of Redemption. The town name rang a bell. 'Isn't that the guy who was in bed with the cartels?'

'Yep. Dirty cop,' Gillian said, as if she was cursing. 'Wound up dead and did us all a favour. What's the case number?'

Harris hovered the mouse arrow over the number and a pop-up window appeared with a few headlines written inside. 'It's related to that plane crash,' he said.

'Then it's a mistake,' Gillian said. 'I'm certainly not going to bother anyone with a match with a four-thousand-year-old corpse on a sample submitted by a dirty cop. Junk it. Good spot.'

She moved away and Harris stared back at the screen, relieved that he hadn't been reamed out in front of his colleagues for asking a dumb question. He closed all the files, unlinked the match alert then opened a new search window and typed 'Melek Mezar' into it.

The top hit was a Wikipedia entry showing a photograph

of a town that could have been lifted straight out of the Bible. The buildings seemed to rise from the ground in square blocks with small black windows cut into them, everything the same colour, like pale dust. Another photograph showed what appeared to be a cave, the flash of the camera throwing light into the darkness and picking out the outlines of bones half-buried in the ground.

The article mentioned Dr Furst, the archaeologist who had submitted the DNA sample taken from the body pic-tured in the photograph. He had spent years searching for the lost tomb, believed to be the final resting place of some powerful, Messianic prophet who had lived a full two thousand years before Christ. Harris skim-read the section detailing the legend of the prophet, a shining man who had walked out of a fire and possessed deep and sacred powers, including the power to heal and the gift of prophecy. Many at the time thought he was a god, but Dr Furst had discovered that he wasn't. The DNA proved that he was only a man, despite the name the prophet had given the town in death. Melek Mezar is Turkish for 'Tomb of the Angel'. Harris smiled when he read that and filed it away in his mind to tell his girlfriend later. She believed in all that shit – angels, demons, vampires. She'd love it if he told her he'd processed some angel DNA in the lab. He closed the Wikipedia page and went back to work.

ACKNOWLEDGEMENTS

It's become a bit of a tradition of mine to compare the writing and publication of each book to throwing a large party. This particular bash has been a particularly long time in the planning and there are, therefore, an army of people behind the scenes who have helped plan the playlist and the menu and all those other things that make a party go with a swing and become something that, hopefully, people will come to, enjoy, and leave feeling happy or at least satisfied - and maybe even a little tipsy.

As often seems to be the way with my books this one started with a lunch at The Cumberland Arms, around the corner from my agent's office, where the holy trinity of Alice Saunders, Mark Lucas and Peta Nightingale listened to my vague outlining of various potential stories including one about a pale man who appears shoeless on a desert road at which they unanimously said 'That sounds great. Write that one.' Alice deserves special mention here. She plucked my first book from the slush pile five years ago and has had to suffer my infuriatingly imprecise working process and constant blind optimism ever since. This book was particularly hard to write, for various reasons, and she never lost her patience or temper - at least not to my face - and managed to hold it together when I finally delivered a manuscript that was 60,000 words too long, three months late and needed another four months work - and a 60% re-write - to turn it into the thing you currently hold in your hands. I am very lucky to have her, though I'm pretty sure she would be much better off without me.

Equally patient and supportive, as usual, have been everyone at HarperCollins - both in the UK and the US. There are whole teams of very bright, very clever and very hard working people in both camps who design the covers, write the copy, supervise the edits and make sure each book is as good as it can possibly be. These people do not earn vast fortunes and could undoubtedly earn far more doing almost anything else but they work in publishing because they love books and love their jobs and we are all the richer because of it. Heading up these teams are the twin capos of Julia Wisdom in the UK and David Highfill in the US who have edited more books than I will ever write and bring all of that experience to the table each time we work together. I say 'work' but in truth it often feels more like fun, or it does to me at least.

I also owe a huge debt to everyone at ILA - my always enthusiastic and very hard-working international rights agents. It is they who invite the rest of the world to each new party and they also recently threw a really good one of their own on the event of their 50th anniversary - a real party, not a figurative one.

Other names I want to throw into my huge 'Thank You' hat - the various people who have helped, inspired or supported me in different ways through the course of writing this (and all the other books) - are Kate Stephenson, Lucy Dauman, Adam Humphrey, Kate Elton, Sarah Benton, Jaime

Frost, Hannah Gamon, Emad Akhtar, Tanya Brennand-Roper, Tavia Kowalchuk, Kaitlyn Kennedy, Danielle Emrich, Andrea St Amand, Mark Rubinstein, Mark Billingham, Peter James, Paul Christopher, Brad Meltzer, Steve Berry, Kate at Wet Dark and Wild, Jackie at RavenCrime reads, Miles at MiloRambles, Matt at ReaderDad, Robin at Parmenion Books, Cristina-Maria Mitrea, Tracy Fenton at THE Book Club, Cheryl Dalton of (Secret World) Book Club, Mike Stotter, Barry Forshaw, Chris Simmons, Jake Kerridge, Shannon and John Raab at Suspense Magazine, Pam Stack at Authors on the Air, and all the other reviewers, authors and bloggers who have said lovely things about my previous books and helped bring them to a wider audience. To all you readers and Amazon reviewers and Tweeters and Facebook posters I thank you too. Writing a novel is a lonely business and the daily lift of new followers or likes or kind messages or nice reviews are like chinks of sunlight in the steady gloom. If you ever wonder whether you should contact an author, any author, to tell them you enjoyed their book the answer is always 'Yes'. We all write for you and without the readers, the bridge of story falls down. So please say 'hi' - I always say 'hi' back.

A special thank you must go to Staff Sergeant Taron Maddux of the Bisbee PD who kindly walked me through local Arizona town law - though I eventually built my own town and wrote my own rulebook. In the light of that it must also be very clearly said that none of the police officers featured in this book are based on him or his colleagues and that the town of Redemption bears only a passing resemblance to Bisbee and is, in truth, based largely on other Arizona places and my own imagination. Also I want to thank Tania and Lou and all the staff at Cafe Marmalade in Brighton - where

I work most days – for not seeming to mind that I can make a single cup of coffee last for three hours.

Closer to home I owe a massive thanks to my sister Becky Toyne who did a first pass edit and had to constantly jiggle her schedule and ultimately work unsociable hours due to my chronic lateness (note to reader: she's a proper professional book editor, not just a relative with a red pen). Also a nod to my three children, Roxy, Stan and Betsy, who are just hilarious and brilliant and remind me that the stuff going on in my head is actually less important than the stuff going on around me. And finally, and always most importantly, to my wife Kathryn for making sure the children didn't die and the house didn't burn down while I disappeared into my head for long months. Only the partners of other authors know what a weird thing it is to live with someone who conjures fables for a living: I would often gladly get away from myself if I could and the fact that she actually can but chooses not to is nothing short of miraculous and I am, and forever shall be, lovingly grateful.

Simon Toyne
Brighton
8th April, 2015